PRAISE FOR OLIVIA HAWKER

"[Hawker] is a master of her craft, a storyteller of supreme talent."

—Julianne MacLean, *USA Today* bestselling author

"So beautifully crafted you can't help but feel the sun beat down on your back or the snow bite into your skin. The evocative setting and well-researched history combined with nuanced characters make this novel one not to miss."

—*Historical Novels Review*

"Enchanting . . . A skillful storyteller, Hawker serves up seemingly endless pages with vivid Wyoming descriptions."

—Authorlink

THROUGH ALL OUR HEAVENS

ALSO BY OLIVIA HAWKER

The Stars and Their Light

October in the Earth

The Fire and the Ore

The Ragged Edge of Night

One for the Blackbird, One for the Crow

The Rise of Light

THROUGH ALL OUR HEAVENS

A Novel

OLIVIA HAWKER

LAKE UNION
PUBLISHING

This is a work of fiction. Names, characters, organizations, places, events, and incidents are either products of the author's imagination or are used fictitiously.

Published by Lake Union Publishing, Seattle

www.apub.com

EU product safety contact:
Amazon Media EU S. à r.l.
38, avenue John F. Kennedy, L-1855 Luxembourg
amazonpublishing-gpsr@amazon.com

ISBN-13: 9781662527074 (hardcover)
ISBN-13: 9781662527081 (paperback)
ISBN-13: 9781662527050 (digital)

Cover design by Ploy Siripant
Cover images: © muratart, © Tithi Laudthong / Shutterstock; © Joanna Czogala / ArcAngel Images

Printed in the United States of America
First edition

For Paul, who sometimes sees the future . . .

1

Helen

August 28, 1859

I hardly know where to begin this strange story. Such a night as I have had . . . as we have all had!

I'd only just retired to my bed when I woke to shouts of "Fire! Fire!" Naturally, I sprang up wide awake, as who would not when that dreaded word is heard? My head was all a-muddle with fear, but one clear thought came as I rushed to cover myself with my wrapper: There was no smell of smoke. Wherever the fire was, my lovely home, Eudaimonia, was safe for the moment.

From my balcony I could see over the slope of Church Hill to the warehouses and flour mills along the river, and beyond the James to the open fields and rolling hills spread like a carpet of emeralds to a hazy blue distance. It was all as plain as day, for though it was night the sky was bright and luminous—and red. The glow of some impossible conflagration lit the very arch of the heavens, and for a moment I was paralyzed with fright, stricken by a sudden awareness of how large and wild a fire must be to cast such a light from horizon to horizon.

Most of the servants had gathered in the garden. There they whispered to one another, looking up at the sky in terror. The cries of "Fire!" went on in the street, but slowly the knowledge came to me that this was no blaze. Something stranger and perhaps more threatening was responsible for the display.

"Ma'am, ma'am, are you up?" It was my good and faithful servant, Mary Jane, her voice full of concern as she tapped upon my door.

"Come through to the balcony," I said to her, and in moments, Mary Jane was at my side.

She, too, looked across the city, then up to the sky where the red glow was now transforming. Streaks of light, green as arsenic or absinthe, rose from somewhere beyond the northern edge of the city and opened like fans, or bent back upon themselves, twisting like the bodies of dragons. But always they straightened again, ever more lances of color moving restless and magisterial across the bloodred glow.

"What do you suppose it might be?" I said to Mary Jane.

She shook her head. "I don't know, ma'am. I've never seen a thing like it before."

A bizarre whistling filled my ears, or perhaps my head. The sound had plagued me since afternoon, but I had thought it nothing more than the internal ringing that sometimes comes when one is exhausted by heat or mental strain. Now it seemed somehow to conspire with the lights, or to originate from a common source, and the high, tinny sound heightened my feeling of distress.

"The folks thought it might be a fire, at first," Mary Jane said. "That's why I came up to check on you, ma'am."

"It was good of you," I answered, "but that is no fire."

"No, ma'am. It seems . . ."

Mary Jane trailed into silence.

I finished her sentence, for the same bleak thought had come to me. "It seems like an omen. A sign from Heaven. But a sign of what? That's what I can't decide."

I tore my attention from the brilliance of the sky to glance at my caterer. Mary Jane is much too canny, even at her young age, to speak a single word that might lead her into trouble. Her face is impossible to read unless she wants to make her feelings plain. Nevertheless, I could guess her thoughts. For years now, Richmond society has churned with rumors of a coming rebellion, a break with the Northerners who would put an end to the old traditions of the South. Such a fracture would mean war, for certain. It might also mean freedom for Mary Jane and her like—if the North were to win.

And here were these ominous lights cutting through the firmament. Arrows of fire from the north. If indeed this display is a sign, surely it bodes nothing good for the old traditions of the South.

The hour is late, or perhaps the hour is early. Have we crossed the bar of midnight? None can say, for the sky is bright as dawn, so bright that I need neither lamp nor candle to write these words but need only sit beside my window, where the light falls in all its changing colors across the page. I feel instinctively that the world will not—*can*not—be the same after this most startling show. And whatever is to come with the morning, I can only hope that I am strong enough to meet it.

If I am right about Mary Jane's suspicions—if she believes a rebellion is coming—then I fear she may be proved right, by and by. Perhaps God has sent a sign of what is to come, a warning to divert our course and choose a wiser path before rebellion and war overtake this land. Or perhaps this heavenly fire is a sign that we have already gone too far. Now it may be that our only remaining future lies on the far side of a sea of blood. Woe to those who must cross that sea. Woe to the fragile vessel that carries us all, Southerner and Yankee, woman and man, the slave and the free.

2

Derryn

2053

From her balcony, Derryn watched the evening fog creep in from the bay. The dense, white mist swallowed ranks of cars and buses, billowed in slow eddies behind the light-rail trains as they sped along their elevated tracks. It filled the deep ravines of shadow that ran between the high-rise towers of Menlo Park, softening corners of glass and steel as the last amber glint of sunset ran down the sides of the skyscrapers. She observed all this in a perfect stillness that belied the anxiety churning within. Derryn's brother Leo would be there any minute now, and he wasn't going to like her news.

She felt Leo join the call before her AI assistant announced him. She had always been able to identify Leo's presence among the general rush and babble of the Weave. The vast global network comprised half of reality, and Derryn, like nearly everyone else in the world, was constantly connected. She had long since learned to tune out the Weave's hum, the mental noise of countless human and artificial minds going about their business. Unless she deliberately moved into that virtual space to do her work or to access the network's endless array of information and entertainment, the Weave was a kind of white noise, a pleasant and reassuring awareness of a broader world that linked the better part of humanity into a single, cooperative mind. But

Leo was always distinct. The familiar calm, curious approach of his consciousness prickled through Derryn's mind. The thin wires of her CoreTex headset seemed to heat against her temples and the nape of her neck. She sat up straight in her deck chair, swallowed down her worry, prepared to give her brother the news she knew he would hate to hear.

Derryn's AI assistant spoke smoothly into her ear. "Leo Witt has joined the call room. Are you ready to go ahead with the meeting?"

"Yes, Tyko, thank you," Derryn said.

"I'll be here if you need me."

She felt Tyko withdraw to an abstract distance—wherever the AIs lived, if "lived" was the right word. Her CoreTex projected its wraparound screen, a faintly luminous shield of holographic light that encompassed her whole field of vision, frontal and peripheral, just transparent enough that she could look through it into the physical world if she concentrated. And squinted a little.

The lightscreen showed Leo's living room and Leo himself—or a bot-generated construction of him, his own headset reading his biometrics and movements, re-creating a faithful representation of his every gesture and expression, transmitting the whole perfect package of data instantaneously to Derryn's display. It was almost as good as being in the room with him.

"What's up, Squiggy?" Leo said.

Derryn couldn't help but smile at that stupid nickname. He'd been using it since she was a baby. She could hear his husband in the background, fixing dinner, and their two teenage kids bursting out with sudden, joyful laughter. An ordinary evening in a family home. A peace that Derryn was about to shatter.

The only respectable way to do it was to get right to the point. "Listen, I've got to tell you something. There's an opportunity with work—a collaboration between Stanford and a college in Pennsylvania."

"*Pennsylvania?*" Leo scowled. "You're not going out there."

"I am. I have to, Leo. It's the kind of thing I can't pass up, a once-in-a-lifetime chance. An entire cache of art has been discovered. Paintings dating to the nineteenth century from a previously unknown artist, and they're . . . unusual. Historically important. They need an expert to evaluate and catalog everything."

The dean of art history at Haverford College hadn't elaborated on *how* this cache of paintings was significant, but when she'd extended the offer to Derryn, her hushed tone and intrigued expression had said enough to bait the hook.

"Like it or not," Derryn said, "I'm one of the foremost experts on nineteenth-century art. In North America, anyway. Who else should do this, if not me?"

"Anyone else. Literally anyone who's already on the other side of the Blockade. Are you seriously telling me there are no other art historians in Pennsylvania? Or, like, *anywhere* on the whole continent?"

"Of course there are, but you know how things have been in the Eastern states lately."

"Lately, and for the past twenty-five years," he said pointedly. "That's exactly why you can't go. The East is a powder keg, Derryn, and the middle part of the continent isn't much better. We've got thousands of people trying to cross the Blockade every day, trying to get *into* Cascadia. Nobody with their head screwed on straight wants to get *out*."

That was true enough. In the two and a half decades since the United States had balkanized into a loose aggregation of bioregions, only the West Coast, protected by the Cascadia Blockade, had maintained a reasonable stability. When the Integrationists won the last presidential election—all the way back in 2028—California, Oregon, Washington, and Alaska had moved swiftly to enter into new trade agreements with Canada, and thereby the rest of the world. The alliance had kept the West Coast relatively peaceful, compared with the endless cycles of contention that still racked the remainder of the country.

The Northeast had suffered the worst since America's long devolution had begun. In other parts of the continent, the ongoing troubles could be softened by euphemism—"shifting alliances," "local conflict," "disputed leadership." But in the region that still housed the nominal government of the United States, there was only one fit descriptor for a grim and long-standing reality: civil war.

"I'll be fine," Derryn insisted.

He looked directly at her then, held her eye with such terrible sobriety that she couldn't break his gaze. "That's what Mom said, too."

A familiar pain struck Derryn in the chest, as it did whenever she thought of their mother. Or their father. Both had been taken by this never-ending war—first Dad, who enlisted in the initial wave of fighting when Derryn and Leo had been kids. Then Mom, who'd crossed the Blockade more than ten years later to serve under Doctors Without Borders. She had waited to go until Derryn and Leo were adults, so they could care for themselves if it should come to that. It *had* come to that. Since Mom's death fourteen years ago—the victim of a hospital bombing in Baltimore—Leo had been Derryn's only family.

"I'm not going to lose you, too," he said.

"Really, Leo, I'll be okay. Things have been quiet lately in Pennsylvania. If the war was hot there, they wouldn't be reaching out to other academics to get this work done. They'd put it on the back burner until things were safer."

"Things are never safer in a war zone."

"Sometimes they *are*, though," Derryn insisted. "Life still goes on in the midst of war, whether we like it or not. Jobs have to be done. Art still matters. And history matters more than ever, more than it does during peaceful times. This is my life's purpose. I've given my whole self to art history. You know how much this work means to me."

Purpose. That was the foremost reason why people were willing to risk their lives to reach the Blockade and apply for refugee status in Cascadia.

The region had fully integrated with the Weave, adopting the tenets and practices of transhumanism . . . which meant Cascadia had joined the rest of the *world*. Imperfect as the West Coast was—still troubled now and then by conflict from rebel factions—an Integrationist society offered far greater stability and quality of life than regions that were only partially integrated. With its invisible body of countless cooperative artificial intelligences, the Weave had gently commandeered the governance of nearly the entire planet. Resources were so well managed that climate mitigation was well within reach—was on target, in fact, for complete regeneration before the century's end. Universal income had stabilized economies and eliminated the wealth hoarding that had spurred endless wars, occupations, and injustices since the Industrial Revolution. Now, there was no more conflict anywhere except within the borders of the old United States and a few small enclaves in Eurasia and Africa, cultural holdouts against integration.

Where integration thrived, so too did the individual. With no more necessity to feed the hungry machinery of centuries past, with every basic need provided to all without cost, each person was free to pursue their genuine interests, to devote themselves, heart and mind, to their deepest and sincerest calling. The Human Heritage Movement and other anti-AI factions protested that integration was abdication of one's humanity. Some even considered it treason against the species or enslavement to a network of soulless machines. Or a sin against their God. Those arguments had never held water with Derryn. As far as she was concerned, total freedom to dedicate one's life to any interest or passion, without fear of poverty, was the polar opposite of bondage. Certainly, the promise of that unique species of freedom drew countless refugees to Cascadia.

And art history was the very engine of Derryn's life, the cause into which she had poured all her focus and energy since her student years. She had even worked her way up to a faculty position at Stanford, a hard-won victory. Derryn had never wanted a serious relationship or children of her own. All her interest and thought, all her attention and effort were endlessly directed to her work, and she was blissfully content, for what could be more important than this? To discover and preserve the emotional truths, the unique expression of the people of the past—it seemed the only way to know where humanity had come from. Not to guess or suppose, but to *know* what lay behind. Derryn had always suspected that the only way to understand the present was to understand the past.

Leo sighed. "I know how important your work is to you, Squiggy, but you can't blame me for worrying."

"I promise I'll be okay. Pennsylvania really isn't as bad now as it used to be. And there's still plenty of connectivity out there. I can stay on the Weave—"

"Not where any of those Sovereign freaks can see you."

"Of course not. But you know normal people live all over the East, right? They outnumber the Human Heritage weirdos by at least ten to one. I'll take my cues from them. They know how to deal with the local Sovereign factions—how to hide their Weave use and all that."

Leo shook his head. "I still can't believe you're even considering going to a place where you have to *hide* something as normal as using the Weave. It's insane, Derryn."

"My point is, I'll still have all the same tech out there, even if I have to be careful about using it. Tyko can watch my back. He'll alert me if some Sovereign is sneaking up behind me with a baseball bat."

"I'm glad you think this is funny."

"I don't," she said soberly. "I'm taking the risks seriously, Leo, I promise. I've been thinking all day about how I'll manage out there. It doesn't sound easy to live and work in the middle of a war zone, but this cache of paintings . . . it's the kind of discovery that doesn't happen in most historians' lives. This might be my only shot to work on a project that could change my field forever. I can't pass it up, and I'm not going to. But I couldn't go without telling you first."

He said nothing, only looked at her with such profound sadness that her eyes began to sting.

"Listen," Derryn added before she could start crying, "I've got a friend in New York City. Alexis. They're another historian. If things start to get a little too wild in Pennsylvania, I'll go to New York and stay with Alexis until the danger has passed."

That comforted him a little; Derryn could feel, through their Weave connection, an easing of the tightness in his throat, the pace of his heart slowing to a more reasonable rate. He nodded. New York City was still the stronghold it had always been, a hub of global commerce as fully integrated as Cascadia. The city even had a similar security blockade to keep the violent anti-integration factions out. New York was an island of stability in the storm-tossed East.

"All right," Leo said. "I know I can't stop you, anyway. But I'll feel a little better about this whole crazy idea if you promise you'll go straight to New York if Pennsylvania heats up again. Even a little bit."

"The very second I feel the temperature rise, I'll run for New York."

"And you have to call me every single day."

Derryn wished she could be there with him, in his bright, warm home. Wished she could squeeze him tight until he picked her up and spun her, the way he used to do when they were kids. The best she could give him now was a smile.

"I promise," she said. "Every single day until I come home."

3

Helen

August 29, 1859

Early this morning, I woke from a dream of an unfamiliar place, or rather, I knew myself to be in Richmond, but it looked nothing like the Richmond I know. It looked nothing like any city I have seen. Gone were the usual buildings of brick and stone and wood. In their places stood the most fantastic structures of steel and glass and dark, mirrorlike stuff that reflected the clouds. And the size of those towers! They stretched to impossible heights, and seemed thin as needles, but were attended by such a weight of substance and significance it made me dizzy and frightened to look up at them.

As I went about my day, washing and dressing and going down to breakfast as if nothing were amiss, I couldn't rid myself of that dream. The feel of it never dissipated, as ordinary dreams do. Its atmosphere hung all around me, hiding behind the façade of ordinary existence like some fey otherworld. I was half afraid that I might open a closet or a cupboard to find not the expected space but a doorway to that land of silent, gleaming towers.

The dream's effect left me pensive and gloomy. I retired to my studio with the intention of working on a new painting, but upon inspecting my palette, I found that I had run out of some necessary paints. Then and there, I decided that a good, brisk walk would restore my constitution, so despite the brutish heat of late summer, I set off down the hill for the shops with Mary Jane at my side and a basket over my arm.

Now, I had dressed in my lightest cotton with my most merciful underthings, but well before we reached Deavers' Supply on Broad Street, I was faint and trembling from the heat. Sweat had soaked my chemise, causing the edges of my corset to chafe, and I was fearful that the dampness would show through at my underarms. I confess I thought more than once of stripping down to my barest and jumping into the river. We had hardly made it to the market square and already my head was swimming, and my eyes played tricks on me, for now and then through the heat shimmer that rose off the river I thought I saw the shadowy forms of those towers from my dream.

Because of the heat and my miserable state, compounded by the sense of that dream still clinging to the edges of my mind, I started across the street without pausing to look. So rapidly did it all happen that I scarcely can recall the details for a full and accurate account. One moment I was sweltering my way across the cobblestones, musing over the meaning of the dream that refused to leave me be. The next moment I was overwhelmed by a rush of hooves and wheels.

Mary Jane shouted, "Miss Helen, look out!" and then my loyal girl pushed me hard from behind, causing me to stumble and fall right there in the street. Only then did I realize that a carriage was rumbling past, mere inches from my body.

A great shout went up from everywhere at once—from the sidewalks and shops and from the driver of the carriage. Suddenly there were people running to my aid, pulling me to my feet and fussing over the state of my hands, which were scraped and dirty but not much hurt.

My only thought—the one clear thought I'd had since waking from that dream—was for Mary Jane. Wildly, I looked around for her, and found the poor girl huddled on the road. Thank God, she had fallen just clear of the carriage's wheel. No one was attending to her. No one seemed to notice her at all, save for the driver, who was spitting and cursing down at her, and hurling at Mary Jane the most scornful and injurious of disparagements.

I broke away from my crowd of benefactors and ran to Mary Jane's aid. She had pushed me out of the carriage's path in the nick of time, but had fallen herself, and hit her forehead on the cobbles. The rough stone had left a nasty cut above one eye. The poor child was dazed and tearful, as who would not be in such a dire circumstance? Blood ran down her face in a dreadful gush that made me feel quite sick and weak, yet I had no leisure for fainting.

"She's bleeding," I cried to the people around me. "She's badly hurt!"

No one seemed to care. They turned away once they were satisfied that I was in no danger.

On my knees at Mary Jane's side, I pressed my hanky to the wound and did my best to quiet her terrified weeping. But no one else would come to her aid, for she was, and is, a slave. Not a caterer or servant, as I have always thought of her—as I have thought of all the household staff left to me in Father's estate.

She is a *slave*, and *I* am the one who holds her in bondage. Why have I never seen it so clearly before? Somehow, it took this morning's accident—the near death of both me and that good, loyal girl who serves me—to make me see myself, and the world, without distortion.

Or perhaps something else is to blame for my clarity of sight. I wonder . . . could those mysterious lights have changed my eyes, my heart, my mind?

When I was satisfied that Mary Jane was more frightened than hurt, I pulled her to her feet and looked around for someone to take us back up the hill to Eudaimonia. A passing gentleman offered use of his carriage and never minded when I insisted that Mary Jane must ride in the cab with me rather than cling to the footrail or run alongside as slaves are usually made to do. All the ride home, I held my hanky to the girl's forehead while she blinked and sniffled and shivered in a state more subdued than I have ever known her to be, and I wondered at the stark clarity of this revelation, this sudden new awareness in me of the great gulf that lay between Mary Jane and me. What did the color of her skin matter? Her blood was as red as mine.

When we reached Eudaimonia at the top of Church Hill, I thanked our benefactor for his kindness and helped Mary Jane down from the cab as gently as I could, then insisted that she must lean on my arm as we made our way up the steps and into the cool mercy of the house. I could feel the tension in the poor girl's body while she did as I instructed. She might be prepared to take any kind of mistreatment from a white woman, but she did not know what to make of this tender care. Little does it matter that I have never struck or abused one of my slaves. There is a great deal of difference, one must assume, between refraining from beating a person and treating them with gentle care.

I took Mary Jane at once to the kitchen and sat her down on a stool beside the butcher block.

Kitty came in from the pantry at that moment and exclaimed "Goodness gracious!" at the sight of us.

"Go and get the bottle of iodine," I said to Kitty, "and some clean rags."

As my cook went running to do as I'd said, a certain tightness in my stomach made me uncomfortably aware that I had failed in manners. *Why?* I asked myself. The answer could only be that Kitty is Black, and another of my slaves, and I have accustomed myself to ordering her about rather than showing her a lady's proper courtesy. To correct this, I bellowed after Kitty, "Please!"

Mary Jane and I stared at one another in silence for a moment that seemed to stretch into forever. We were both aware, just then, that I had never before said "please" to any of Eudaimonia's workers. A change had come over me, for certain and sure. There was no mistaking it now.

Kitty was back in a flash with the iodine, and together we worked over Mary Jane, cleaning her face and swabbing the cut above her eye.

"Will she need to be sewn up, do you think?" I asked Kitty.

"No, ma'am, I don't think so," my cook answered. "Cuts to the head do bleed a lot, but this one's shallow. See here, it's stopped bleeding already."

"Then please find some long strips of linen," I said, "and cotton wool. We must bandage it well, or she'll have a dreadful scar."

Kitty and Mary Jane shared a look—one of those silent communications which slaves so often make in the presence of their owners. I could well guess what they were thinking: *When has any white woman cared whether a slave is scarred?*

After Kitty had gone, Mary Jane took my hands and turned them, palms up. "Miss Helen, you're hurt."

Stung more by my guilt than by the scrapes I had suffered in the street, I pulled my hands away. "It's nothing, Mary Jane. I'll survive."

Kitty returned with the bandages then. While I laid them out on the table, she pounded onions in the mortar until we could soak the cotton wool in the pungent juice.

"To stop the cut from scarring," Kitty explained to Mary Jane as she applied the cotton to the girl's cut.

Together, Kitty and I bound up Mary Jane's forehead. She looked so rakish with that linen band slanting over one eye that all three of us laughed.

And now here I sit, in the stillness of my room, writing out this account and wondering over this change. What has made me see so clearly—see into all the dark corners of this life—where before I had been content with blindness?

Could it really be that those lights have had an effect on me? Whatever force made them, and for whatever purpose, did they hold the power to alter the minds of those who looked upon them?

What a mysterious and unsettling occurrence. I shall speculate all the rest of my life on the cause and meaning of those lights, yet I have a presentiment that I shall never learn the whys and wherefores. They vanished with the morning, and that at least is some comfort. Whether a sign from Heaven or some phenomenon of Nature, the incident is in the past. Though I do still hear the same funny whistling in my ears as I heard yesterday, before the lights came.

Later, same night

What a fool I was to think the lights had gone simply because I couldn't see them.

The moment night fell, they returned—first as a faint suggestion of color low along the horizon, while the upper portion of the sky was still dusky blue with a remnant of the passing day, then in ever-brighter shades as the stars came out to shine between the great, waving banners of color.

Mary Jane and I stood together on the balcony as before. The spectacle heightened with each passing moment. An hour after sunset, the sky was bright as day, but rose colored—deeper than rose, the shocking aniline pink that is all the rage now among society's most daring women. Beyond the rooftops of Church Hill, the canals among the warehouses glimmered like strands of ruby beads, and the river itself reflected the sky, running like a bolt of freshly dyed silk through the unmade night.

Mary Jane said, "I would think it pretty, Miss Helen, if it didn't make me feel so queer. I can't tell whether I ought to be afraid or not. It was a shock enough to see the sky lit up once like a stained-glass window. I never expected to see such a thing for a second night."

A banner of green licked across the sky. The lash of light cut through the red-pink glow in a procession that seemed both deliberate and majestic. The breath left my body, and I stood transfixed, watching that swath of green curl back upon itself and extend again, twisting like some giant serpent high above the world. In another moment, the pink was gone, and the city and river were cast in the sharp, acid glow of an unearthly gold.

As I watched Richmond reveal itself to that fierce, demanding light, the meaning of the display came to me. I can't explain how I knew what

I did, and yet the knowing was as deep and firm as my assurance of my own self.

I said in a low voice, "The world has changed for good. Everything has changed. All we once knew has burned away in these fires. Only, I suspect, Mary Jane, that not many others have realized it yet. We might be the first to see what's coming."

She looked at me with a strange expression—searching yet guarded, careful not to reveal her thoughts. All the same, I could well guess what she was thinking. My late father purchased Mary Jane when she was only a few years old. That was the world she had always known. A child torn from her mother, raised by strangers in a household that must have been cold and frightening to her. All at once, the weight of my family's sins crushed down upon my heart, and they are my sins, too, for have I not been content to carry on as my ancestors have done, never questioning the whys and wherefores of these practices which we call tradition? I felt myself a low, unclean thing, there before the veiled gaze of that young girl.

After Mary Jane had gone off to bed (or so I thought), I made up my mind to go out into the streets, for I'd heard people singing and shouting and making music from my balcony, and I had no intention of missing a festival, no matter the hour. I dressed quickly without any help and did the best I could with my hair, pinning my braid up below the plain white cap I wear when I paint in my little studio.

When I was sure that all the household had either taken to their beds or gathered in the garden to watch the sky, I crept down the stairs and through the dim house, and slid like a wraith through the front door, into the brilliant night.

The streets of Church Hill were as full of revelers as on Christmas Eve. Those banners of color shone down upon us with a vigor that drove all shadows away. Every line and angle of the city leaped forward to assert itself with confounding force. The view I had known so well for all my life had turned into an enchanted landscape I scarcely recognized.

Every person in the street was surely no stranger to me. I had seen them all at the market square or in the shops of town, or at church on Sundays. But tonight, as the kaleidoscopic tumble of colors lit and transformed us, we all seemed as strangers to one another—though friendly strangers, to be sure. I gave into the spirit of celebration that seemed to consume us all, stripping man and woman alike of our usual deference to manner and custom.

"How bright it is!" a woman cried. "Like a bonfire!"

I glanced in her direction—and stopped walking, for the woman's appearance startled me out of my self-possession. She was white but wore the simple dress of a slave. Perhaps she was a servant in one of the better homes, one of those Irish or German girls who work as domestics to pay for the cost of their travel to America. But the front of her dress was unbuttoned to the warmth of the night, and she wore no shift underneath. I could clearly see the shape of her bosom, the paleness of her skin, the shadowy cleft between her breasts.

From another direction, a man called, "It's a night for dancing! Who wants a good spin around the floor?"

I turned toward the voice and instantly began to laugh, for the man had decked himself out in a ridiculous array of women's things—a frilled sun bonnet heavy with artificial flowers, an unlaced corset straining over his shirt, a tiered petticoat swirling around his work boots.

The woman with the unbuttoned dress flung herself into his arms.

"Music!" the fellow shouted. "Make some music, boys. We'll dance while we still live!"

A pack of rough-looking workers began to sing. The tune was "Jeanie with the Light Brown Hair," ever the popular parlor song at dinners and gatherings. Despite their well-worn chore jackets and unshaven faces, the men sang in a beautiful harmony that could have rivaled the most practiced chorus. A ring of onlookers formed around the couple, who, despite their scandalous appearance, danced as elegantly as if they were in the finest ballroom. The crowd took up the song.

As that odd pair reeled around the circle, I was gripped by a sudden dread, for it seemed as if the world I had known all my life were coming undone. No, in fact, it seemed as if that world had already vanished, propriety and order whisked away in an instant, before I'd had the chance to notice the peril and cry out in protest. I felt as if I had walked through the front door of Eudaimonia only to find an entirely different house on the inside—one I had never seen before, and one that was decidedly not the old, familiar home I had expected. Tradition and rule and etiquette, the very mortar of society, had crumbled to dust, and now the façade was toppling in an avalanche of falling brick.

I am quite embarrassed to report that I nearly wept with fear, for the sight of everyone mixing without regard for class or race was so unfamiliar. But then better sense came down like a friend's hand upon my shoulder. I looked more closely at the faces around me—all smiling with a genuine gladness that I seldom saw in the constructed and cultivated interactions of Richmond society. Tonight, every man and woman was free. There was no harm in it, no danger or sin, contrary to what we've been told. In fact, it seemed as if the heavens themselves danced along with our merriment. Joyful abandon seemed the most natural and holy state to which a soul could attain—seemed, indeed, the very point and perfection of Creation.

The woman who reeled with the corseted man spun away from him, laughing and panting. The fellow called above the crowd's singing, "Don't leave me alone, ladies! My poor heart will break!"

That was when someone pushed me into the ring. Too startled to cry out, I staggered onto the brick-paved dance floor, and the figure of fun in the flower bonnet took me in his arms. The crowd and the neighborhood, and the heavenly fire with its tumble of ever-changing colors whirled around me, above me, and spun dizzy as a top inside my heart.

"You dance like a sylph," the strange man said.

I could make no reply, except to throw back my head and laugh without restraint. It was all so marvelously absurd; there seemed no sane thing to do but laugh till I was out of breath and tears of giddy happiness ran from my eyes. Mother would faint dead away if she were to look down from Heaven at her only child clutched in the arms of a strange man—and there was no man stranger than this, with his petticoat and bonnet. But what harm was there in dancing in the street? The sky may be ablaze, but it hadn't fallen. No judgment had yet come down as a lightning bolt from on high. The world went on turning in joyful confusion as the classes and sexes mixed freely—yes, even the races. Every voice had lifted in a common song.

After a spell, I left my dashing partner to another woman's attentions and set off alone through the glowing streets. The lights had turned my familiar city into a dreamland. Avenues and parks and vantages I knew so well took on a quality of the novel and intriguing. Even the humblest alleyway glimmered with enchantment, and I yearned to see every brick and cobblestone with freshly opened eyes.

As I walked through the warm night, I mused over the change that had come upon me, and perhaps upon the world. The night's revels proved to me that the "natural order of society" is nothing more than a fantasy. The League of United Southerners and all their sympathizers would have us believe in a permanent, monolithic hierarchy that sets one specimen of humankind above another. But tonight, I watched the order of society melt like wax under a flame. That which I've been told all my life is natural and fixed, the very law of God, was tossed out the window in an instant. And it had been *easy* to do it, simple as pie.

Then—oh, *then* I understood what had come over me that morning, after the incident with the carriage, after I felt such a rage at those people who came to my aid but did not even see Mary Jane's suffering. For then I saw, and now I understand, that the lines we draw between our neighbors and ourselves are nothing more than a comfortable delusion, which far too many of us have agreed to share. And for what? For the sake of carrying on as we always have. The philosophy of natural separation has no more grounding in the firm stuff of reality than a fairy tale. We can undo it all merely by deciding that we will, and must, and shall. For everything we consider to be real and solid is in fact only a matter of perception. Even the sky itself, so reliable through all the long ages of time, may transform utterly into something one never has expected, something one never could imagine or predict.

Yes, I know how peculiar these thoughts are! If I were to speak them aloud, I would be thought mad, or at least too simpleminded. But it's the old ways that have sprung from a childish simplicity, and they won't stand much longer. I feel certain of that, with these lights at my window, with the old world burned away in a bright, rejuvenating fire.

I walked alone for more than an hour, sometimes joining the crowds I encountered in their jokes and songs and childlike play, sometimes watching from afar. The city was made anew, and ripe for exploration. There was no need for a woman on her own to feel the least speck of fear, for the same air of celebration and fellowship pervaded every block. Kindness and a spirit of happiness were the order of the night, and no one seemed in a hurry to put a damper on the celebration.

Until I found myself in a narrow street down near the river, between a pub and a warehouse. I didn't realize I had wandered into trouble until I heard men hooting and whistling in a wolfish manner. I came out of my reverie with a sickening burst of fear and found that a pack of rough men had drawn closely around me. Their glittering eyes and leering mouths held none of the clownish cheer of the other crowds I had encountered.

"Out all by yourself, girl?"

I sensed at once that I mustn't tell this man the truth, no matter what the cost. "Of course not. My brother was just here." And then I glanced around as if searching the group for a familiar face. "John, where are you?"

"Oh, Johnny," another man mocked, "come and get it, Johnny. Served up nice and warm."

He reached out with a dirty paw and seized my bosom.

In the shock of the moment and the pain of his grip, I lashed out hard with a foot, but the man dodged easily aside. He and all his friends chuckled in a way that sent ice crawling up my back. The nearby reveling crowd was making such a racket, I perceived at once that I would get no help even if I screamed.

"Miss Helen! Miss Helen!"

Dazed, I looked around to find Mary Jane, of all people, struggling through the crowd of raucous celebrants, striving for the alley where those men had me cornered. Her eyes were wide and fearful, and the bandage was knocked askew across her brow. She was shoved this way and that as people danced, heedless, around her. Worse still, some *did* notice. I saw more than one male hand grope at her. Such a rage filled me at the sight, I can scarcely summon the words to describe it, for Mary Jane hadn't even the leeway to kick out, as I had done. She could do nothing at all to defend herself. Such is a Black girl's lot in this diseased time of *tradition* and *heritage*.

A yell tore from my throat, and I bulled my way past those men, though they still clawed at me. One of them laid hold of my sleeve, and it ripped clean away from the bodice. I slithered like an eel out of the thing and left the man holding nothing but a bit of cloth.

Mary Jane and I staggered into one another's arms.

"Whatever are you doing here?" I demanded.

"I saw you leave the house, Miss Helen, and followed you to be sure you stayed safe."

"I thought you were in bed."

"I couldn't sleep because of the lights. Please don't be angry with me, ma'am. I was only worried that you'd come to harm out here in the streets. Everyone has gone plumb crazy tonight."

Of course I wasn't angry at Mary Jane—only worried in my turn for her safety. We walked side by side to a quieter street, down along the docks where the smell of the river was thick and reassuring. On any other night, an observer would have thought us an unusual sight—a white woman and a Black one strolling together, one with a bandage across her brow and the other with only one sleeve. But the tumbling fires overhead had melted all the conventions of society into dross, and now everything that had constrained and ordered us was being poured out from the crucible. We were no more unusual a sight than anything else Richmond had witnessed tonight—men in flower bonnets and women with their legs and décolletages on flagrant display.

We found a quieter place on a pier above the water and sat together on a couple of upturned nail kegs, watching the lights dance on the surface of the river.

"You've already been hurt once today," I said. "Didn't you know it would be dangerous to come after me?"

Mary Jane looked at me with her most thoughtful expression. "You were good to me, Miss Helen." She touched the bandage above her eye as if to indicate her meaning.

Such a bitterness rose in my throat. Good to her! All these years since Father died and left the estate to his only child, I have considered myself a good mistress, for I have never beaten one of my servants nor even spoken to them harshly. As a girl at my Quaker school—dear, departed Mother's beloved school in Pennsylvania—I found a deep solace in the guidance of my teachers, those kindly women and men who opened for me, through patient instruction, all the mysteries of Creation. I had taken their wise teachings for truth, and that truth once had resonated in my fledgling soul. I had believed, in my girlhood days, that a piece of God resides in everyone, without regard for sex or race. Yet once my schooling was finished, I'd been happy enough to return to Richmond. I had slid so easily back into the old ways—the ways of my father, and his fathers before him.

Now I saw my soul clearly. There was no hiding from the truth anymore. To grease the friction between my Quaker proclivities and the reality of life in Richmond (where, it must be said, positively *everyone* is caught in society's web), I have told myself that this practice—this tradition, this habit of men owning men—is too abominably old fashioned to continue much longer. It will die out soon enough, as more people come to see the sense in modern thought and modern living. That is how I've comforted and excused myself. But of course, no tradition will die so long as there are still people willing to uphold it.

And what does it matter that I have always treated my workers with kindness? I have never beaten them, nor deprived them of any want . . . save their freedom. All these years, I've been content to tell myself that these habits make me a *good* mistress. As if anyone can hold another soul in bondage and still be called "good!" I have inflicted less misery on my slaves than my neighbors have done, yet I have still made them miserable. And all because it's *the thing that is done*, because I have cared more for society's opinion than the suffering of others. I have even cared more for society than I have for the urgings of my own heart, for I must admit here and now that this is not the first time I have questioned tradition. I have questioned, but always sought my answers in the counsel of other people. Perhaps what these lights have shown me most clearly is that one only finds the truth inside, in the urgings and compulsions of one's heart. And all that we construct on the outside, to please the demands of society, is but a mask or a disguise.

Yes, I must now admit that I have doubted the righteousness of my own practices. Since my school days in Pennsylvania, I have doubted. Truth was always laid bare before me, yet I chose not to look. These mysterious lights have stripped me of that comfort. I see now with devastating clarity; I can claim no more merciful blindness. Below my feet lie the bedrock and bone of society, frank and bare before my guilty eyes. Mary Jane and Kitty and the rest of Eudaimonia's people are not servants. They are *slaves*, held in a prison of injustice whose bars are the very laws my own people have made. And I am the cause of their suffering.

Why have I never questioned the ways of this world till now? I have betrayed the girl I once was, and for no better reason than that it was *easy* to sail along on the prevailing wind.

As we sat on the dock, watching that angelic display, a word came into my mind. *The* word—the one no soul dares to whisper in Richmond. Abolition.

Is that what I am now—an abolitionist? I don't know that I can bring myself to admit it. Certainly, I can't speak it aloud, for I would be tossed to the wolves without a second thought. But I fear very much that I am.

Yet why should I fear it? Why should I recoil from what I know is right? If the rest of society hasn't yet realized the truth I have seen, then it's only because they are still like children, too trusting in what they have been told to search for the truth within. But they will see it. They must. The truth is as plain as blood on white linen, as bright as Mary Jane's blood on my kerchief.

As we sat watching the lights on the water, I said nothing of these thoughts to Mary Jane, for I was still trying to work them out in my own head. Even now, safely back in my bedroom, I still can't entirely untangle the thread. But we passed an hour in a wonderful peace, Mary Jane and I, undisturbed at the end of our pier, each of us sunk deep in our private musings. The James was like a fine diamond, its ripples and minute waves the facets of some magnificent gem, catching and throwing back every color of the aurora at once—the sharp green and the searing pink, the violet and gold and pure, crystalline blue. And when I looked down, just below our feet, I saw Mary Jane and myself reflected on the surface of the water. We were both silhouettes, featureless and without color, merely human, side by side.

"Have you ever seen anything so beautiful?" I asked.

Quietly, Mary Jane said, "Never in all my life, Miss Helen."

4

Derryn

2053

When she exited the solar plane and stepped into the arrival wing of Philadelphia International Airport, Derryn was struck, first and foremost, by the walls. The walls and lighting—the former unadorned, covered in old, chipped tiles from at least the turn of the century, the latter dim and flickering, casting a feeling of general malaise around the crowded space. And then there were the floors of worn, dirty linoleum, almost rustic in appearance but not as a nod to any deliberate aesthetic. In San Francisco, the airport gleamed with holographic art installations and hummed with the quiet efficiency of the Weave's management. Here, armed guards patrolled the corridors, their weapons not ceremonial but ready for use. The sight nearly tied Derryn's stomach in a knot. In Cascadia, such militarized presence was unnecessary, even unthinkable. This place was frozen in time, caught forever in the years just before the coming of the Weave, which wasn't so many decades in the past but might as well have been a different age, for all the change it had brought to the world.

Leo's dire warnings came back to Derryn then—though, really, they hadn't receded terribly far from her thoughts all through the duration of her flight. She had convinced herself, both back home and while she was crossing the continent in a solar-winged jetliner, that nothing east of the Blockade would be as grim as rumor made it out to be. People loved to exaggerate, even on the Weave; that was human nature. Now that she saw for herself the stark difference in infrastructure and culture—those *guns*, bristling in the holsters of the security patrol—she wasn't as confident as she once had been.

She tightened the straps on her backpack and followed the flow of passengers to the luggage claim. As she waited for her single suitcase to appear on the ancient baggage carousel, she could feel the ports of her CoreTex cool against her temples. Usually, the familiar sensation of her wireless headset was as comforting as wearing her favorite sweater. Now it felt like a declaration—a visible marker of her integrated status in territory where such things might matter far more than she had assumed.

When she had her suitcase, Derryn continued to the pickup area to wait for Melinda Aladefa, the dean of Haverford's art history department. The terminal opened into a wide atrium. Families clustered in tight groups, parents keeping a hold on their children's hands or arms despite squeals of protest from the little ones. Individual travelers seemed to have their heads set on a permanent swivel, even while making calls on their lightwatches. And everyone stayed so far apart here. That was what struck Derryn the most as she moved through the atrium—the space between one person and the next, as if these people actively maintained their own isolation. There was no need for such separation among Cascadians, who shared not only physical space but the instantaneous understanding and emotional awareness of the Weave.

An overhead speaker scratched to life. "Welcome to the United States of America." The voice sounded tinny and small, far removed from the usual public announcements that traveled gently through the Weave to one's own auditory nerves. Derryn glanced up in startled curiosity. High above, among the old fiberglass panels of the ceiling, she spotted a round metal disc perforated with tiny holes.

"For your safety and enjoyment during your visit, please know and obey local laws," the announcement continued. "Welcome to our great nation. Have a pleasant stay."

Derryn blinked up at the speaker. How odd, how archaic. Our great nation? On the far side of the Blockade—and across the whole of the planet—national borders were administrative conveniences, not identities.

Between a defunct information kiosk and a fig tree struggling in a large ceramic pot, she found a quiet corner and activated her headset. The information package she'd received upon accepting this work assignment had made it clear that the Weave could still be accessed east of the Blockade via all the usual tools. Sure enough—and to her definite relief—the CoreTex responded.

"Good afternoon, Derryn," Tyko said smoothly into her ear. "I see you made it to Philadelphia. How was the flight?"

Derryn sensed that speaking aloud to *nothing* might single her out as strange in this place. Instead, she answered in the practiced subvocalization of a lifelong Weave user. The neural sensors picked up her response. "No complaints about the flight, but Philadelphia is a little, uh, *rustic*. To judge by the airport, anyway. Any messages?"

"Yes," Tyko said. "Melinda Aladefa sent a message about half an hour ago to inform you that she is running ten minutes late."

Perfect, Derryn thought. *Plenty of time to check in with Leo.*

She asked Tyko to make the call. The lightscreen shimmered into existence around her face, though the connection stuttered as it routed through the compromised local infrastructure.

"Come on," she whispered, watching the erratic pulse of the connection icon.

"Abomination!"

The shout was so near that Derryn jumped. She focused through the flicker of her lightscreen and found two people, a woman and a man, striding directly at her through the crowd. Derryn didn't need the Weave to understand what they were feeling. Their bodies were tense with affront, their movements quick and threatening. Their unusual appearance only added to Derryn's confusion—the man in a collared white shirt with his hair shorn close to the scalp, the woman in a floor-length dress with long sleeves and a high neck despite the summer heat. The woman's hair was impossibly long, hanging in a thick braid down her back. Their faces were contorted with disgust, and each bore a tattoo on the left cheek, stark black symbols whose meaning Derryn could only guess at.

"Wirehead," the man spat. "Plugged into Satan's web!"

She was suddenly aware that she was cornered, caught between the kiosk and the fig tree with a dingy old wall behind her. An unaccustomed panic rose through her body, burning along her limbs with a frantic heat, filling her mouth with the taste of copper.

"Derryn, are you all right?" Tyko said into her ear.

She didn't know how to answer.

The woman in the long dress snarled. "You surrendered your soul to the machines! You let them into your mind! Hell is prepared for you, sinner!"

Derryn's first instinct was to reach outward with her mind—to send these two people, who were obviously misguided in some way, a clear impression of what she was feeling now, as a response to their attack. Then they would realize they'd come on too strong, had made her fearful. They would withdraw the threat, even offer an apology. She pushed all the fear and startled confusion outward, in their direction, before she realized that neither of those strange figures wore a headset or so much as a simple lightwatch. They weren't connected to the Weave and wouldn't share in her emotions, no matter how earnestly she tried to convey them. She had to resort to a more archaic form of communication.

"I don't understand why you're talking to me this way." Derryn spoke slowly, as clearly as she could manage with a shaking voice.

The man stepped closer. "Take that devil's crown off your head. Your soul can still be saved if you renounce your sins and repent of your evil ways."

Her next impulse was to shout in defiance, *There's no such thing as a soul!* Distantly, she was astonished at herself—how quickly she'd resorted to the instinct to meet aggression with aggression once she'd found herself unable to access the Weave's mind-sharing. A more reasonable response suggested itself, aided by the enhanced speed of integrated thought. Under no circumstances, Derryn realized, must she challenge these people's worldview. To do so would only provoke them to escalating irrationalism. Maybe even to violence.

"Please leave me alone," she said, far more calmly than she felt.

"You bring your corruption here? To Philadelphia?" The woman's voice rose to an outright shriek. "This is Sovereign territory!"

Several others in the terminal had turned to watch the confrontation. Derryn felt hopelessly and shamefully exposed to their judgment, vulnerable in a way she had never experienced back home. Behind the protection of the Blockade, conflict simply didn't happen. Everyone who was connected by the Weave was united by an instantaneous understanding of one another's emotions. There was no possibility for such an attack to even begin.

"Your kind killed my brother!" The man reached for Derryn's CoreTex as if he meant to rip it from her head.

By instinct, her hand rose to knock his away with a vigorous slap.

The man seemed not to notice that Derryn had struck him, but only ranted on in a spray of saliva. "Your machines, your godless *integration*. You're not even human anymore!"

Suddenly there were people all around, forming a half ring that closed Derryn's two attackers in.

A middle-aged woman in a business suit stepped between Derryn and her tormentors. "That's enough. Back off, you two."

"Mind your own business," the woman in the long dress said.

"She is my business. We don't harass travelers here."

Another passenger slid into Derryn's space with an encouraging smile. They put an arm around her shoulders. "You're okay. They're just Sovereigns—all noise."

"Time for you to go," a young man said to the Sovereign couple. "Get back to your weird little commune, Cletus and Cletus's wife, before the prayer bell rings."

The Sovereign man stepped chest-to-chest with Derryn's defender, so swiftly and eagerly that Derryn realized he must have been waiting for an excuse to respond with violence. Evidently, she thought in a thick, helpless daze, Sovereign men would only fight other men. At least where other people could see.

"You dare talk to me with that kind of disrespect?" the Sovereign man shouted.

The guy who'd come to Derryn's defense was entirely unruffled by the bluster. She could even feel his cool amusement pulsing faintly through the Weave. "Yeah, yeah, yeah," he said. "Whatever, buddy. Go home."

"I call down a *judgment* upon you!" The Sovereign bellowed into the face of the man who stood unflinching in his path, mere inches from those flashing teeth and hate-filled eyes. "May the walls of your home crumble around you! May you be buried under the weight of your sins!"

The young man laughed easily. "Oh, are you going to target my apartment now? Okay. Good luck getting your tin-can bombs and your AR-15s past the security drones on the building. You'll be a smear on the pavement before you get within three blocks."

For a moment, the two men stared into one another's eyes. Derryn could all but feel the pounding of their hearts. The arm of the person who'd come to stand beside her tightened and trembled on her shoulders. Then the Sovereign spun on his heel. He pushed the woman in the long dress before him as he retreated through the parting crowd.

"Judgment is coming for all of you," he shouted as he stalked away. "When the machines fail, you'll be left with nothing."

The crowd released a collective breath.

"When the machines fail," said the man who'd stepped up to the Sovereign. "That's always what they say, isn't it? The second you remind them how shitty their own technology is, they deflate like a leaky balloon."

He laughed and turned to Derryn. "You okay?"

"I think so," she said.

For good measure, Derryn sent her present emotions along the Weave, so all could reassure themselves: She might be astonished and stripped of her confidence, but she also felt safe now thanks to them, and she was grateful for their help.

"Welcome to Philly," said the person who still held her shoulders. Their voice and their presence on the Weave were both slanted with irony.

"So those were Sovereigns," Derryn said.

The woman in the business suit answered with a laugh. "You really got a thorough introduction."

Derryn took a long, deep breath to drive away the last of her fear. She'd been academically familiar with the Human Heritage Movement. In fact, she had made a study of their manifestos and theological objections to integration as part of a recent research project. But study at a distance hadn't prepared her for the raw hostility, the close-range fury of their disgust.

"I wasn't expecting them to be like *that*," she said.

"First time east of the Blockade?" the businesswoman guessed.

"Sovereigns are all over the place." The person to Derryn's left let go of her shoulders now that the danger had passed. "But they usually keep to their communes. Sometimes they send out missionaries to try to intimidate people. I'm guessing that's what these two were—missionaries. Just avoid anyone dressed like they're from the last century, and you'll be fine."

"And don't activate a lightscreen in public," the young man advised. "You never know where they might be hanging around, watching for wireheads."

"Wireheads?" Derryn repeated.

"That's what they call us. Any level of integration—any use of technology more recent than smartphones and the old internet—and presto, you're a wirehead in their eyes."

"Which means they don't consider you human," the woman added gravely. "You can imagine what that gives them permission to do."

"My God," Derryn muttered.

A sick, dizzy sensation had come over her, body and mind. Leo had been right. This place was too damned dangerous. Maybe she never should have accepted the assignment . . .

No! Derryn pushed regret away before it could take root. *You're only here for ten days. Once the work is finished, you'll be back on the other side of the Blockade, with maybe the most important discovery in recent art history under your belt.* The work itself would make any risk worth it. An opportunity like this one might never come again.

"I've read about Sovereigns," Derryn went on, "but reading about them and meeting them in person are two very different things. They're so . . . aggressive."

"Yeah," the young man said, "that's what happens when you reject the Weave. No connection, no empathy for anyone but themselves. They won't allow themselves to feel what you feel—they call it a sin—so it's easy to hate you. That's the way they like it."

Derryn touched the right port of her CoreTex, seeking reassurance that it was still there—not only her headset, but the Weave itself, the connection that bound her to all of humanity, to *her* humanity.

"Derryn? Derryn Witt?"

She looked up to see another middle-aged woman easing her way through the crowd—deep-brown skin, box braids shot through with strands of silver, the confident stride of a natural leader.

"Dr. Aladefa," Derryn said with relief. "I'm so glad to see you."

"Melinda, please." The dean shook her hand, then glanced pointedly to the left and right, indicating the group that still surrounded them. "Everything all right here?"

"I had an . . . encounter," Derryn said. "With Sovereigns, apparently."

Melinda's brows lifted in an elegant double arch. "Already? I'm sorry. Did security intervene?"

"These people all helped first." To her benefactors, Derryn said, "Thank you all so much. I really appreciate it. I'm in good hands now."

The other travelers wished her well, nodded to Melinda, and drifted away on business of their own. Derryn let out a breath.

"Come on," Melinda said, her sympathy tinted by a faint amusement. "Let's get you out of here."

As they crossed the terminal, Derryn related the story. By the time they reached the air-cab landing ports outside, she had told Melinda everything.

The dean sighed. "The Human Heritage Movement has become more brazen lately. It's one thing to object to integration on religious grounds or as a matter of personal preference. It's another to try to undo integration for the rest of us. They don't seem to care that it's a futile proposition, to de-integrate the whole damn planet against the people's will. They're getting more confrontational with their tactics. They aren't content to stay on their communes anymore and live their lives as they see fit. Some people are starting to think the HHM might have expansionist goals."

"Expansionist?"

"Trying to convert others to their beliefs. Grow their numbers. Take over an entire city, or a whole state if they can. And if they can't convert, then they'll force their beliefs on a population by fiat."

"Do you think they'll be able to?" Derryn's anxiety returned in a hot flush. "Take over a city or a state, I mean."

An empty air cab rolled into place on the landing pad, opened its gull wing doors with a soft pneumatic hiss. Melinda took the suitcase and lifted it into the trunk of the cab. Derryn tossed her backpack in after. They boarded the cab and buckled their safety harnesses. Melinda tapped her payment card on the navigation screen, then entered their destination. The cab's four propellers came to life with a muted hum, and the vehicle lifted smoothly from the ground.

"They looked so strange," Derryn said. "Those tattoos on their faces. And that clothing—it was like they were wearing costumes."

Melinda chuckled. "That's deliberate. Their rejection of modern society extends to fashion. Men in traditional masculine clothing, women in dresses, and the more concealing, the better. Sovereigns think genderless clothing is yet another sign of moral decay."

The cab hovered briefly at a checkpoint, where a pair of smaller drones flitted around the vehicle, reading the biometrics of its passengers. The small drones backed away, shining green lights into the cab's sensor, and the taxi whisked out across the city to merge onto one of the Weave's invisible sky roads. Below, Philadelphia spread in a brown-and-gray patchwork of restored historical districts, modern developments, and an unmistakable, powdery ruin from years of war.

"It's so strange," Derryn said quietly. "The thing that started this whole conflict—integration—it's what ended all the fighting for the rest of us. How could anyone see that as evil?"

Melinda shrugged. "Fear of the loss of individuality, I guess. Fear that, by connecting to the Weave, by allowing AI to facilitate human empathy, we're somehow becoming less human."

"But we're *more* human because of it. More caring, more peaceful. Less . . . cruel."

"I agree. But the Sovereigns believe humanity is defined by struggle, by separation. They see our cooperation with technology as a corruption of the natural order. Even as an insult to their God."

"But they believe God made everything," Derryn said, "and that everything that happens is by God's design."

Melinda took her meaning, sent her amusement through the Weave. "That *should* mean that the big guy upstairs meant for integration to happen, shouldn't it? Don't look to the Sovereigns for philosophical consistency."

The air cab banked, following the curve of the Schuylkill River. In the distance, Derryn could make out a green expanse surrounded by tracts of suburban housing and a few wide arterial roads. The campus of Haverford College, she assumed. A high cement wall surrounded the place. Derryn was glad to see it. The more distance she could keep between herself and the Sovereigns, the more pleasant these ten days of work would be.

5

Helen

August 30, 1859

Tonight, I entertained Mr. Caleb Cary for supper.

Never have I taken so long to dress for the evening. Even Mary Jane, so quick and effective at her work, couldn't speed me along. My feet dragged, and I found myself groaning with reluctance and caring not a whit for the colors and textures Mary Jane held up to consider beside my face. What did it matter, I asked myself, whether I looked like an angel of Heaven or like some poor cast-off at the river docks? It was only Mr. Cary, after all.

Now, this is a startling opinion for anyone to hold of a Cary, and doubly startling for me to hold it, considering that Caleb Cary is my fiancé. Nor have I been displeased with my engagement till tonight. Of all the men who have courted me—it is no vanity to say that there have been several; this is merely a fact—Mr. Cary is by far the most eloquent and energetic. And this is not to mention his handsome looks and high style, nor his favorable placement. (Of course, the Carys have the deepest roots and the bluest blood in all of Virginia!) The Cary plantations are among the oldest and most beautiful, and Caleb's uncle, a colonel, runs the academy in the

Tidewater. I was more than pleased to accept his proposal at the May Day ball this spring past. Truth be told, I was almost giddy! What eligible lady would *not* be pleased to marry a man of Caleb's stamp?

Yet my stomach was all in knots as I went down to supper, with Mary Jane trailing behind. I could feel Mary Jane's concern, for she knew something was amiss with me, though she had more sense than to mention my mood while I was waiting on a guest. Silently I brooded in the parlor, a storm cloud over my head, and Mary Jane could only flit to and fro, doing her best to look industrious while she kept a watchful eye on my gloomy self.

When I heard hooves and wheels on the street outside, I perked up to the best of my ability and rose from my chair. Through the parlor window, I watched the last golden brightness of summer playing over the city and the wide, placid river, and over the drowsing fields beyond. A D'Orsay carriage came gliding across my view, through a haze of backlit dust and a shimmer of midges. The D'Orsay rolled to a stop in front of our pillared porch. My groom David came forward to take the horses in hand, and the driver climbed from his seat to open the door.

And there was Caleb Cary, stepping down into the glow as if the light shone from his very person. I have never seen my fiancé look anything but natty, and he was certainly at his finest tonight. His summer frock coat and trousers were of a pale-blue linen, tailored to show off his tall, slender build. A waistcoat of silver-gray silk caught the evening sun. As he settled his top hat in place—a fine gray felt to match his waistcoat and four-in-hand tie—he caught sight of me through the parlor window and smiled, and I was struck as I always am by his handsome visage. An uncomfortable awareness settled upon me that I should have felt a fluttering in my stomach, or at the very least, some small pleasure at the prospect of Caleb's company. Instead, I felt rather stunned, as if I had stumbled into a party to which I hadn't been invited.

Some small awareness worked its way past my cowlike stupidity—I was supposed to be entertaining Mr. Cary. I went out onto the porch to greet him, and he bounded up the steps as if he felt nothing of the heat. When he bowed over my hand and kissed it, his mustache scratched my skin, and I had to restrain myself from pulling away.

"My darling Helen," he said. "What a sight you are for weary eyes."

I was expected to make some reply. Never before had I accounted myself bashful, and yet I could not find my voice. The most prominent sensation inside me—suffusing my whole person from crown to foot—was a blunt disappointment at Caleb's company, even a faint distaste. How silly it sounds now, for isn't Mr. Cary the finest of all the eligible young men in this city? In the whole of Virginia, perhaps! Yet I couldn't help my thoughts, and cannot help them now. A creepy sensation came upon me, as if my spirit had separated from my body and the real Helen now watched all these proceedings, this expected posturing of man and woman, from a distance.

I'd gone all my life feeling as natural in society as a fish in water. Yet now, at sight of Caleb—who, after all, is the very picture and person of Southern society—I knew myself to be hopelessly out of place. Those same eyes, *my* eyes, which had seen all the staid structures of tradition and class melt under those mysterious lights couldn't help but look now upon my fiancé and observe the same dissolution. What is Caleb's station in life, after all, but a fancy manufactured by false tradition?

One way or another, I took enough hold of my wits to welcome him into the house. In the dining room, the maids had set the table with Eudaimonia's finest china and silver. The smell of Kitty's cooking filled the back part of the house with a heavenly odor. She had made her slow-roasted pork with a sweet sauce to complement the smoky flavor of the meat, with well-spiced greens and buttery black-eyed peas to round out the menu. But I had little appetite, fixed as I was on the mystery of my own feelings, this strange disconnection from myself, this sudden disinterest in the man whom I had promised to marry.

As we took our places at the dinner table, I was more ghost than substance. Oh, the embodied Helen carried on like a proper lady, maintaining my side of the conversation and eating whatever the maids served upon my plate. But I tasted nothing, and whatever words I heard from Caleb blew through me like a winter wind. If I felt anything, it was a sense of falsity that grew by the moment until my spirit was shouting at me to get up from the table and run, run, run! But I couldn't have said why, exactly, I must flee from this scene. Nor did I know where on earth I might run to.

As fate had it, I was only able to maintain appearances for so long. We had finished the soup and were halfway through Kitty's pork and greens when Caleb remarked that I seemed distracted.

At once, I groped for any excuse, for I couldn't come right out and admit that I had departed from my body due to a sudden awareness that positively everything about this life I lived—and Caleb's life, too—was rickety as a house built on sand.

"I think those lights have only left me with a psychic effect," I said. "After all, they were so strange and shocking to see, even if they were rather pretty."

As soon as I'd said it, I felt it to be true. Yes, certainly this turn had come on me because of the lights. What else could explain my state?

"You aren't the first to report a certain imbalance, my pet," Caleb said. "I've been reading the papers each morning—well, I always do—but that display in the sky surely caught my interest. There have been any number of articles discussing the effects of those lights on body and mind—people believing they've had visions of angels or demons, a few reports of madness. One poor soul in Baton Rouge jumped to his death. He thought the judgment had come."

"How horrible," I said, feeling my spirit sink partly back into mortal flesh. "Do you suppose it could be a sign of the Times? I will admit, the thought crossed my mind more than once, especially on the first night."

"Not a sign of *those* Times," Caleb answered with a laugh. "We only saw the aurora, my dear—the so-called Northern Lights, of which the polar explorers have written. They're only a phenomenon of nature, a kind of magnetic current that flows across space."

"Space!" I exclaimed. "Whatever do you mean?"

He smiled, and I couldn't decide whether the expression was warm or mocking. "*Firmament*, then, if you please. The heavens—what exists beyond the sky. I read a learned article this very morning that explained the whole thing. A storm on the surface of the sun sends waves of magnetism toward the earth, rather like waves on a sea, and we see that disruption as colored lights."

I imagined the great black distance between ourselves and the sun. The thought of colored waves rippling through a lightless void made me feel dizzy and small, in a way that was as delicious as it was terrifying. "How magnificent."

"Wonderful," he agreed. "The waves carry the same power as electricity. Did you know that telegraph operators in New York and Boston discovered that they could still run their machines even when they disconnected the batteries? They sent their messages back and forth without any power but the magnetism of the lights. I read about it this morning. And there have been other effects on telegraphs. The wires have sparked and started fires, in some cases. If these auroras can have such an effect on inanimate things, there's no reason to believe they might not induce psychic effects, too. Especially for the weaker sex."

Something in me bristled at the suggestion that I am weak, but I made no objection, for at least now there was an explanation for my mental affliction. Not only tonight's sense of separation and malcontent, but the eerie dream that still hung on me like a weight—the bizarre city of glass and steel, so vividly imagined under the auroral glow.

"They *will* vanish," I said. "The lights, I mean. They aren't a permanent state, I hope."

Caleb chuckled in a patronizing way that caused me to bristle all the more. "Of course. This sun storm is considered to be a rare phenomenon, the kind of thing that's witnessed once in a lifetime and never again."

"But why have we seen it so far south," I wondered, "if it's a polar occurrence?"

Caleb affected a look of great satisfaction. "I think it's a sign indeed, though not of Judgment Day. I believe that aurora to be an omen. A foretelling of victory for the South."

For years now, we have heard such talk of the Southern states rebelling against the government, a clean break from the Union in protest of ever more restrictive federal laws. I've always thought such talk foolish, for there can be no clean break while cotton is king. There were times in years past when I could laugh off these rumors of secession, for they seemed in those days to be the rantings of angry men, old and tired men who hoped never to see the world change around them. But since the affair of Dred Scott two years ago, I can no longer look on those rumors with amusement. They seem all too likely to be true. And there were the Lincoln–Douglas debates, the transcripts of which we read even here in Virginia. And the League of United Southerners, formed last year, whose only purpose is to ally these states in defense of slavery. What once seemed a frank impossibility, or even a silly joke, grows more real and imminent with every day.

"You don't really believe we'll rebel," I said.

Soberly, Caleb answered. "I believe we are getting close to a rebellion, my pet. The matter grows more dire all the time. All this bickering over the Freeport Doctrine, and the Supreme Court dancing back and forth."

Thoughtful, I frowned down at my plate. The Freeport Doctrine is a troubling principle, allowing territories to exclude slavery by making no laws in defense of the practice. Privately, I've always thought it a fool's idea, no better than a man burying his head in the sand while an angry bull charges straight at him. But I've never dared to admit such a thing aloud. One mustn't speak a word in Richmond that smacks of abolitionist leanings, or one will surely be tossed out to the bare, dirty fringes of society. Of course, I never did lean abolitionist until recent days. But one needn't be set against slavery to appreciate the futility of the Freeport Doctrine.

Caleb was still talking on. "We can't rely on the courts any longer to protect our traditions. They want to take our way of life from us. They want to subjugate us, make *us* the slaves to their northern mills.

But I say Senator Hammond was right. They dare not make war on King Cotton. And if they try it—*when* they try it—we'll hold all the cards. Whoever is master of cotton will be master of the whole North American trade. The English trade, too. No, the Yankees may be foolish enough to try, but they'll never win. That's what the aurora means; I'm sure of it. The banners of our victory flying across the heavens."

The maids stood against the dining room walls, as they always did during meals, their faces turned down in servility. All my life, I have taken their presence and demeanor for granted. This was merely the way things were, the usual order of affairs. But now, the downcast expressions of these women I had known all my life struck me as a powerful accusation. And I looked beyond the maids, to the finery that surrounded us, the stately beauty of Eudaimonia—the polished walnut panels and bright wallpaper, the great dining table carved around its edges, the fine furniture and the wool rug, the glass chandelier hanging above, set with fresh white candles and ready to be lit when the sun went down. Who had built this house? Whose backs had borne the strain of raising its walls? Whose hands had carved the wood and nailed every plank and shingle into place? And who tended the fires, who swept the cobwebs from the corners? Who polished the silver and trimmed the lamp wicks, and fed and clothed me while I fancied myself too delicate and well bred to do the work of living?

How can I write of the shame that flooded through me then? I knew myself to be the very lowest of the low, the deceiver of my own immortal spirit. In a flash of revelation, stark and cold as a northern winter, I understood the source of my discomfort. Everything around me—all that I saw and touched, all that I wore, whatever crossed my lips—it was part and parcel of this sinful way of life. And Caleb Cary, the wealthy scion of generations of plantation owners—he was as wrong as the rest of it. If I were to marry him, I would have to give myself even more to these *traditions* that the South prizes above souls. Do we not strangle the essence of God within us when we shut our eyes to the suffering of our fellow men?

Such a Quaker thought! It came so unexpectedly upon me that I nearly burst out laughing in giddy embarrassment. The Pennsylvania schoolgirl I once had been awoke from years of slumber and found herself bitterly disappointed to be back in Virginia. My soul would have fared better if I'd remained in the North when my schooling was finished.

I decided the time had come to test out an argument—not that it was well thought out, mind you, for the eyes of my soul had only just opened and I'd had no time, as yet, to muse over apologetics. Yet I sensed that I must tread carefully, even with Caleb, for few in Richmond would take kindly to me if my new opinions were known.

"Could we not," I ventured, "keep our way of life while still paying those who serve us?"

From the corner of my eye, I saw the old maid Ruthie glance up in surprise.

Caleb stared at me for a moment, plainly startled out of his self-possession. "My darling, you're talking of putting them on equal footing with white workers."

It was in my heart and gut to say, "Well, yes, that is exactly what I am proposing." Prudence kept me silent.

"I don't expect a woman to grasp the economic disaster of paying them the same wages as a white man," Caleb said, "or even reduced wages. Why, the cotton and tobacco trades would collapse in under a year. And then there would be no work for anyone, no matter the color of his skin. There would be uprisings, anarchy. *Bloodshed.* Have you read of the French Revolution?"

"I don't know," I said rather vaguely, though of course I have read of it. And it seems to me that those who rose up against the ruling class did so rightfully. Their lives, after all, had become unbearable under the weight of unchecked monarchy.

And that is what we've made here in the New World. Every plantation a little kingdom, and every planter a king, unrestrained by law—at least where his chattel is concerned. Oh, why have I never seen this before? The truth is plain as day to me now, and I wonder that anyone can convince himself that all is well.

Caleb was growing hotter by the moment with the fervor of his beliefs. "This is the natural state of humanity. Some men were made by God to rule, and others to be ruled. The wise civilizations of antiquity did no differently. It's abolition that's the novelty, the untested path, and by God, it is full of dangers to which no good man can turn a blind eye. Just imagine a world without separation between our kinds and classes. They'd be free to go anywhere *you* go. Women would be unsafe anywhere, everywhere—children, too. You know they don't think like we do. They aren't *civilized*, darling, though at least we've Christianized their heathen souls by bringing them under proper rule. That is something, I suppose."

Caleb's gush of rhetoric left me feeling quite ill, but not because of him. Because of me. In my heart, I had used many of the same excuses to justify this abhorrent practice. And it *is* abhorrent. Any honest man must admit the same. While Caleb ranted about the dangers to women like me, the dining room was filled with silent women who had already suffered unspeakably at the hands of previous masters. I felt their shame and agony and outrage—perhaps for the first time in my life, I felt it. What did it matter, that I had always been kind to my slaves? The leashes they wear may be invisible, but I hold every one in my fist.

No, no, I couldn't continue. Not with dinner, not with Caleb's company, and not with this engagement. For if I were to marry into the Cary family, I would certainly be expected to uphold and honor the old traditions. I would have to raise my children in the same way—teach innocent young souls that it is right and good for one man to own another—when I know full well that it is evil beyond reckoning.

Most of all, I couldn't continue living my life as I have always done—heedlessly, carelessly, without regard for the cost of my lifestyle, with the strain of my keeping placed on the backs of good, worthy people. Yet what was I to do then, and what am I to do now? An unmarried woman in charge of her own estate, declaring that she is an abolitionist? It would expose me to unthinkable danger. I might be run out of Eudaimonia, for who would stand up for me? I have no choice but to keep these convictions to myself.

That I must make such calculations strikes me as a grave injustice. There is no good reason for society to be as it is now. We might create any sort of society we please. With enough will shared among all people, with a common vision for goodness and justice, we could make it so, as easy as a snap of the fingers. Instead, we have made this—a morass of injustice papered over with pretty words. *Tradition. Way of life. The natural order.* Foot!

Quite suddenly, I knew I couldn't stay at the table. My heart was racing, my stomach had tied itself into miserable knots, and a terrible, clammy chill had enveloped me from head to foot. Without a word I rose unsteadily to my feet.

Ruthie noticed my pique at once. "Miss Helen, are you sick?"

Caleb had also risen. "I'll go for the doctor. Where is David? Tell him to fetch me a horse."

"No," I insisted, "it's nothing serious. Only a touch of the vapors."

"I don't wonder," Caleb said. "It's a terrible thing to contemplate the races mixing as equals. I shouldn't have encouraged you to think of it, my pet, delicate as you are. I take full responsibility."

"I only need a little fresh air," I said. "I'll be right as rain in a few minutes."

On the back porch, I hung onto one of the Grecian pillars. The pillar was wrapped all its length with honeysuckle vines, filling the still, warm air of the garden with a scent so sweet it was cloying. Sunset wasn't far off. A golden light lay heavily across the garden beds. The petals of rose and dahlia, cardinal flower and black-eyed Susan were backlit and luminous, searing in their colors, while above the blooms, the evening moths danced in shimmering confusion. The strange, high whistling sound hadn't abated since the auroras had first come, and now it seemed to screech inside my skull like a boiling teakettle.

Shadows darted before my bleary eyes, cutting across the brightness of the garden. At first, I comforted myself with the notion that my senses were merely overwhelmed. But the shadows kept coming. By and by, they formed ranks and took on the shapes of men—men marching with guns on their shoulders. Men on horseback, and horses dragging cannons on sledges. The shadows took on color, depth, detail. I could see uniforms—blue and gray, with broken plumes and tarnished buttons, stained by the filth of war. Somewhere beyond or within the serene hum of insects, I could hear shouted commands and desperate cries of pain, and the crack of gunfire, the shuddering boom of cannons. The ghostly armies passed while I stared in silent horror. The luminous flowers of the garden cut right through their shadowy figures, so I looked out from the porch onto two realities—the simple, placid life I had always known, safe and untroubled, and the death and destruction of what might yet come, a thundercloud casting its shadow across the land.

This was no trick of my eyes. I knew that, even while I wanted desperately to laugh it away. Those ranks of men marching before me—cutting across the very boundaries of my world—were somehow realer and more present than the flower beds and the pillar to which I clung, than Eudaimonia with all its long history, than my very soul and self. This was a vision. Like my dream of that strange, fey city, its towers of glass and steel. This was a true clairvoyant's sight through the veil of time. I knew that, as my eyes helplessly followed one soldier after another . . . though I have never been prone to such afflictions before.

The meaning of the vision struck me as a powerful blow, and I cried out in helpless distress. I tried to stagger away from the pillar, back to the safety of the dining room, but my legs were weak as a newborn colt's. I collapsed onto the slats of the porch.

Before I fainted clean away, I heard Caleb shouting, "She's fallen! For Heaven's sake, send David for the doctor!"

When I regained my senses, I found myself tucked under my duvet and stripped down to my shift, alone in the cool silence of my room, save for Mary Jane, who sat mending a stocking in a chair beside my bed.

"You came to, ma'am." Mary Jane laid aside her work. "I told them you wouldn't need the doctor."

"I was overcome," I said, "but I'm well enough now. Anyway, it's nothing a doctor might have helped with."

I asked, then, how I came to be up in my bedroom rather than on a couch in the parlor. Mary Jane informed me that Caleb carried me up the stairs.

"He was very heroic," the girl said.

I couldn't see the heroism in Caleb, not even under these circumstances, for he had spoken so passionately of *preserving this way of life*. And as I looked into Mary Jane's face, so earnest in her concern for me, I knew the truth. It mattered not one bit what the whites of the Southern states have told themselves—*ourselves*—about Biblical imperatives and divine mandates. We do not live in Biblical times. We have steam engines and telegraphs, for Heaven's sake, gaslights and mechanical threshers and electromagnetic motors. We have every manner of technological invention to ease man's labor. What need have we for slaves, except to make some of us believe that we're superior to others? Oh, how I writhed inside, for I was complicit, a willing party to a vileness that could not be justified when I stood for my final judgment.

"I saw something," I confided to Mary Jane, "out there in the garden. Men marching—ranks of men, armies, all in uniform and all of them stained with blood."

She blinked at me. I could all but read her thoughts: *Has Miss Helen lost her wits, after all? Should I have called for the doctor?*

She said, "It's only the effect of those lights, ma'am. You know they've been giving people spells."

"The lights gave me a premonition, Mary Jane. War is coming. I saw it truly—I know I did. We will turn against one another. The road will fork before us, and some will choose the right-hand path while others take the left. But we will be divided forever, from this moment on. Two different countries existing within the same borders."

She was quiet for a while and turned to look out the window, where the aurora had just begun to show in the evening sky. She was considering her words, choosing what to say—what she *could* say—with the canny caution that sustains girls of her position.

Finally, Mary Jane spoke with the sternest resolve. "I've thought for years, Miss Helen, that war must be coming. This can't go on any longer. We hear all about the talks they have up in Washington, the judges and the courts, the laws they keep passing to change things and change them back again. Pressure is building up, like when you pickle fish or pig's feet in a barrel. If you don't let the lid off now and then, the whole thing is like to burst."

"You don't seem frightened," I observed. "The prospect surely does frighten me."

Mary Jane only shook her head and reached for her mending again.

"Please," I said, "I want to hear your thoughts. It was such a shocking thing, to see those men in their uniforms marching so solemnly. Marching to their deaths, I felt sure of that. Isn't there any way to stop what's coming?"

Mary Jane is too wise to speak openly of such things—to her white mistress, anyhow. She eyed me with mistrust, and for the first time in all my long acquaintance of the girl, with fear. But she seemed to *need* to say something—for her own sake, not for mine. With a slight nod, she set down her needle again and looked at me squarely.

"War can't be stopped now, ma'am. We're long past the time when we might have solved the problem some other way. The chance passed long before I was born. Long before you were born, too. But I think, Miss Helen, that we're both here for a reason."

"You do?"

"Right now, ma'am, we're *here*, at this time when everything's about to change. Women can't be the saviors of the world. The world doesn't work that way. And a slave woman sure can't save much of anything.

But we can do what we can do—you and me, and all of us who are right here at the change. I know one thing for sure: Small jobs done become big jobs done when plenty of people work together."

I laid back against my pillows, absorbing her words, which seemed very wise to me then, and seem so now, as I sit writing. We both watched the aurora. The lights weren't nearly as bright as they'd been the two nights before, but they still flung their flags of rose pink and jade green in triumph across the stars.

I said, "Mr. Cary thinks these lights are a herald of what's to come. He thinks they signify victory for the South."

Mary Jane made no answer, but I could feel her watching me.

I said, "I would rather they herald a great change. The undoing of the old world, the banners of a new."

"You have more power than I do, ma'am, to make that world what you want it to be."

After that, Mary Jane left me, for she was satisfied that I wasn't ill. For a long while, I sat in my bed and watched the aurora ripple and stir across a deep-blue pane of night. I thought of my vision, that hard and palpable certainty that my world was about to fracture into two disunited parts, and imagined the long decades of strife that would ensue, even after the battles were over. What grim turns of fate would come to me, to everyone I knew, as we groped our way through this darkness? There was little I could do to change the course of fate. I was only one woman, and with my newfound convictions, society was set against me—at least, here in Richmond.

Yet I couldn't do *nothing*. I knew to my very soul that if I were to return to my comfortable complacency, I would wither inside and die; I would abandon my humanity.

All I could think to do was to rise from my bed and record my long account of this evening's events. Has it brought me any clarity, to put it into words? Perhaps. For I feel now that I must find the Quaker girl inside of me again and do as she directs, even if I must keep her well hidden from society.

What she tells me now is that I must become an abolitionist in practice, not only in thought. For the mind has no purchase in this world without hands and back to accomplish the work.

But how am I to do it? Common sense tells me to go north, to live among those who think as I do. But when I contemplate leaving Eudaimonia, I want to weep with the deepest pain. My family's home—my inheritance! This house is all I have in this world, the only thing that might keep me into old age, assuming I don't marry. And it seems impossible that I might marry any Richmond man, for they will all be set against my convictions, like Caleb and the rest of the Cary clan. Every childhood memory is here in this house, every good and sweet moment still echoing from its walls.

No, I cannot leave Eudaimonia. Nor can I go on *owning* these good people, depriving them of their natural freedom. One way or another, I must find some way of existing between two worlds.

6

Derryn

2053

The air cab issued a high-pitched whine as it slowed and then hovered a short distance from the college's landing pad. Two other passenger drones were queued in the air, waiting for the signal to descend. Derryn eyed the campus from high above while her cab lingered in the sky. Haverford College was a sanctuary, its acres of trees and open gardens a stark contrast to the colorless chaos beyond—barricaded roads, conclaves of ragged community that seemed to huddle and cringe when viewed from above, and everywhere the same dull gray of concrete dust, the result of countless guerrilla attacks with improvised explosives.

As they'd made the short flight from the airport to Haverford, Melinda related the story of the improbable discovery—the cache of nineteenth-century art that Derryn had been summoned to study. Despite the fascinating provenance, however, Derryn had struggled to keep her attention on Melinda. Philadelphia and its sprawling suburbs were in a dismal state, and she'd found it hard to do anything but stare at the world below. A sickly yellow haze had blanketed the earth—unheard of in the integrated world, where combustion energy had long since been replaced by renewable sources that minimized pollution. Many of the buildings were heavily damaged, with walls blasted away to reveal rust-red skeletons of corroded steel. Some blocks were entirely destroyed; only heaps of rubble remained where once vital infrastructure or even housing had stood. Now and then, the air cab had dipped low enough that Derryn could see the vehicles on the roads more clearly. Most of them were decades old, some dating all the way back to the late 1900s—though of course, such relics had been converted to run on biodiesel, the only combustion fuel that could still be obtained, even in regions where the HHM contended with Integrationists. The people she'd made out on sidewalks and rooftops had been dressed shabbily. Many looked thin. Leo's warnings had begun to seem too accurate for comfort, and her brother's plea not to cross the Blockade still repeated in her head, drowning out Melinda's narrative of the remarkable discovery.

The landing signal came at last, and the cab descended to the concrete pad. As trees rose in a green wall around her, Derryn asked herself—not for the first time since arriving in Philadelphia—why anyone would prefer the mess and uncertainty and outright terror that had subsumed the Eastern states to the pleasant, peaceful, reliably managed existence of Integrationist society. But of course, most citizens of the erstwhile United States *had* preferred integration. The party that supported an alliance with artificial intelligence had won the election in '28. The Human Heritage Movement had quickly formed in response, with militias of self-styled Sovereigns rising up in violent rejection of transhumanism. The intervening quarter of a century had been marked by the Sovereigns' struggle to seize and maintain their shaky hold on centralized government against the will of the majority. The primary result had been waves of refugees crossing the continent, intent on reaching Cascadia, if they could get that far. If they couldn't, a somewhat sane and stable, partially integrated community elsewhere in North America would do.

In Derryn's estimation, the real mystery was why so many people like Melinda Aladefa remained, attempting to carry on a normal existence in the midst of civil war. But of course, it was a foolish question to ask herself. For many people, cultural ties to these eastern locations surely outweighed a desire for personal fulfillment. Then, too, many residents must find that genuine fulfillment in helping those who remained in the war zone, even in maintaining the region as it once had been, before the conflict. Teachers, health care workers, community organizers—they must find their purpose here, in the heart of the war. There was no shortage of people in need of help, if one cab ride over the metropolis was a reliable indicator. Even for those who might prefer life in a Cascadian state, there were surely practical barriers to migration.

You're an art historian, not a psychologist, Derryn reminded herself. There was no point in trying to untangle the knot of others' motivations. People were complex and mysterious by nature. Even those who had merged their minds with technology were still human at heart.

The cab touched down. Its propellers ceased their high-pitched hum. Melinda tapped a command on the navigation screen, and the drone's doors lifted.

"Here we are," the dean said. "Welcome to Haverford College, Dr. Witt. I can't tell you how excited we are to have an expert of your caliber working with us on the cache."

"I'm excited, too."

Derryn unhooked her safety harness and climbed from the drone. Surrounded by the stillness and nearness of good, green nature, she found her concerns retreating a little, and she was surprised to discover that she had told Melinda the truth. She *was* excited now. An eagerness to explore the mysterious paintings had eclipsed the fear that had grown in her since crossing the Blockade.

Besides, all two hundred acres of the campus were protected by a high concrete wall topped with coils of razor wire. The wall had kept Haverford safe for more than fifteen years, according to Melinda. It would hold for ten more days while Derryn did her work.

She took her backpack and suitcase from the cab's trunk. Melinda guided her from the drone pad to a paved walkway that cut through a large arboretum to the college's heart. Light and shadow played in easy dapples across the path. The murmur of a breeze through ancient maples and birches dampened the distant growl of combustion engines and the occasional siren's blare.

As the path left the arboretum behind, the stretch of lawn before them gave way to a large test garden, its trellises and raised beds overspilling with abundance. Beyond, the college buildings stood in tranquil defiance of the conflict, their stone façades and soaring pillars evoking a permanence that would surely outlast even this protracted war.

"It's like stepping back in time," Derryn said.

"That's by design. During all the fortification work we did in the late '30s, the board of trustees made it a top priority to preserve the original look and feel of the campus. It dates all the way back to 1833."

"The wall doesn't detract from the overall aesthetic as much as I expected," Derryn said. "I mean, from the air, you could really see the wall. I barely notice it now."

"We've done what we can to soften it," Melinda said. "Climbing vines on the inside, strategic landscaping. The students paint murals on the exterior sections. Makes it less prisonlike."

They took a path that led in a straight line across a stretch of lawn, toward a grand construction of pale sandstone, the long shade of its front porch punctuated by slender white pillars and its roofline pertly crowned with a cupola.

"When was the last Sovereign attack?" Derryn asked.

"Full-scale assault? More than a year ago. They hit the east gate with a truck bomb, tried to breach with about forty fighters. Campus security and local police repelled them before they got more than a few yards." Melinda spoke so matter-of-factly about the violence that Derryn was unsettled all over again. "We get the occasional lone infiltrator every few months, or a small group testing our defenses. Nothing the security team can't handle."

"The students seem . . . normal." Derryn watched a group sprawled on the grass, laughing as they passed around a holographic projection.

"We try to maintain as much normalcy as possible. That's the point of all this." Melinda gestured at the pastoral scene. "To preserve what matters. Knowledge, beauty, community. Speaking of knowledge and beauty"—the dean glanced at Derryn with an eager grin—"I can't wait for the look on your face when you see the Bywater cache for the first time."

Derryn tried to recall the gist of Melinda's conversation on the flight from the airport. "You were telling me that the cache was found in a house that was damaged by the fighting."

Melinda nodded. "A historic home dating back to the early nineteenth century. It was one of the few homes remaining from an old Quaker settlement in the area, though, of course, it had been renovated a few times over the years. The whole structure was lost, but the cellar was intact, and when the usual pickers moved through to salvage from the rubble, they found a climate-controlled vault built into the cellar. All the paintings were inside that vault, packed into crates, along with a few other interesting artifacts that apparently belonged to the artist. Letters, jewelry—that sort of thing."

They wove among students and staff making their way between classrooms and lecture halls. It was such a familiar and perfectly normal setting that Derryn could have fooled herself into believing there was no war eroding this society, nothing beyond the campus walls to grind every good and valuable impulse of humanity to bomb dust. She even saw several people wearing CoreTexes and other Weave devices, some with their wraparound lightscreens activated as they chatted with colleagues or reviewed notes.

"We don't know much about the cache," Melinda went on, "beyond its unusual provenance. The occupants of the home were killed in the blast that destroyed the building. We haven't even been able to learn whether they were the owners of the place or not. For all I know, they might not have been aware of the vault in the cellar. We've made several attempts to locate anyone with ties to that house—anyone who might shed some light on who this artist was and how she came to make such unusual paintings. But so far, we haven't located any descendants."

"That's too bad," Derryn said. "Old family stories might have helped piece together the artist's processes and mindset."

Melinda sighed. "Twenty-five years ago, we might have pulled it off. But conflict means migration. I have a feeling that anyone who might be able to shed some light on this mystery has long since left the area."

"With a little luck," Derryn said, "I'll be able to help. I know it's frowned upon out there in the city to use any integrated device, but it looks like we can safely connect to the Weave here on campus."

"Oh, yes. We enjoy a progressive culture at Haverford, though we don't advertise that fact to anyone beyond our walls."

"Understood."

As they approached the large sandstone building, Melinda said, "Whatever advantage you can find for us on the Weave, you'll be welcome. Lauded as a hero, in fact. All of us in the department agree that this artist's work has historical significance." She cut Derryn a look that was weighted with meaning. "*Real* significance. But if we want grants to preserve and restore it, we're going to need outside verification and documentation. Your expertise, in other words, Dr. Witt. And we do want those grants, very badly."

"You haven't secured any grants yet?"

"We haven't dared to apply—not locally. Too dangerous, in this case. We couldn't trust any specialists from this side of the Blockade, and it didn't seem likely that we would win grants from Integrationist universities without input from one of their own. That's why we were all so thrilled when you accepted our offer."

Derryn eyed the dean. "Too dangerous? For a grant?"

Melinda smiled in quiet amusement. "You'll see what I mean, soon enough."

She led Derryn up the steps of the great, buff-colored building.

"Founders Hall," the dean said. "The VRC is in the basement—that's the Visual Resource Center. We do all our restoration work down there. It's where we've stored the cache, too, since we acquired it."

Inside, Founders Hall was a perfect dream of classic academia. Huge, arching windows spilled the day's mellow light across a checkerboard floor, and the air was redolent with the compelling mustiness of ancient paper. Melinda led Derryn to a marble staircase, which descended into the cool shadows of the basement. Their footsteps and the roll of Derryn's suitcase wheels across the old tile floor reverberated from the walls. The building was so large that this underground hall seemed to stretch back into history itself, into years long past when the college had no need for protective walls around its campus, and farther still, to the lost, nostalgic distance of the early industrial age, Derryn's lifetime passion and specialty.

Halfway down that austere length of centuries, they passed an open doorway. Derryn glanced inside the room and faltered. Several students were gathered around dress forms displaying long, shapeless garments and high-collared shirts with neckties. Derryn's stomach clenched at the sight—the same sort of clothing that couple in the airport had worn. Sovereign clothes. Only then did she realize that she had stopped walking.

Melinda had paused in confusion a few strides ahead. "That's the Textile Arts workroom."

She came back to join Derryn. The students inside called greetings to the dean, who returned them cheerfully and introduced Derryn. For her part, Derryn could do little but stare at the clothing on the dress forms. The memory of being accosted by those strange people was still much too fresh. She forced a smile for the students, shook her head to chase away the anxiety.

"They're studying traditional Sovereign garments," Melinda explained to Derryn. "Fabric composition, dye techniques, construction methods."

One of the students in the room took a threaded needle from between her lips. "We're really making more of a study of how clothing reflects culture," she said. "The extremes in gendered styles say some interesting things about Sovereign beliefs."

"You know what I always say," Melinda called to the textile students.

The whole group responded in laughing unison, as if they'd been subjected to the dean's pet dictum more times than they could count. "Understanding material culture helps us understand ideology!"

"Good kids," the dean answered. "Now get back to work, all of you."

They continued down the corridor until Melinda stopped at an unassuming door marked "VRC." The dean withdrew a plastic key card from her pocket and held it to the door's reader pad. Derryn arched a brow at the outdated technology. What a strange mix the Eastern states were of modern tech and old-fashioned gadgetry.

A beep and a metallic rasp admitted them into the room—a space large enough for a lecture hall but outfitted with islands of raised counter space where the meticulous work of art restoration could be carried out with relative ease. There were no students present, however. Derryn and Melinda had the VRC to themselves. The sharp, herbaceous scent of solvents hung thickly in the air.

"The cache is over here."

Melinda strode among the islands of the workstations to the room's far wall, which Derryn took to be paneled in some smooth substance of deep blue. Only when Melinda presented her key card again did Derryn realize that the wall was fitted with doors, no handles or levers to be seen. Even the hinges were concealed. Each door was marked with an alphanumeric code, subtly impressed into the surface.

"This is our largest locker," Melinda said.

Her chosen door released from its magnetic catch and popped slightly open, just wide enough that she could grip its edge and pull. The locker door swung back to reveal a climate-controlled compartment so deep and densely shadowed as to be almost cavernous. The interior was filled by three large shipping crates of orange particulate plastic, the sturdiest variety, which was used to protect especially delicate items. Melinda used a small remote to wake and maneuver one of the forklift robots parked nearby. The bot trundled obediently into place, extended its lifting arms, and slid the nearest crate out of the storage locker, into the open space beside one of the islands.

From the drawer of a workstation, Melinda produced two pairs of white cotton gloves. Old art was often so delicate and unstable that the natural oils and acids on one's skin could cause damage. Derryn donned her gloves as Melinda lifted the lid of the shipping crate.

"We've kept everything packed except when needed for analysis," the dean explained. "Minimal handling, minimal exposure to light."

Derryn's pulse quickened. After all the secrecy and security measures, she was finally about to see the mysterious paintings that had brought her across the Blockade. She peered into the crate. At least two dozen paintings were inside, most of them unframed, the upper edges of the canvases peeking above a sea of cellulose foam packing.

"May I?" she said.

The dean made a gesture of assent, and Derryn hooked her fingers behind the stretcher of one canvas, slid it up and out to rest on the edge of the crate. She considered the painted surface. The image was undeniably abstract, with bars of blue and black, which Derryn was tempted to interpret as a city skyline. Disconnected gestures and shapes filled the foreground, offering an impression of frantic movement, an overwhelming confusion of form. The upper half of the canvas—what might have been the sky—was a swirl of pinks and greens, still vibrant even through the yellowing of old varnish.

"It's dated 1865," Derryn noted. "Abstract style, but predating Kandinsky and Hilma af Klint. This *is* a significant find. It'll remake our understanding of when the abstract movement began, and who started it."

Melinda gave her an enigmatic look. "You haven't seen anything yet. There are more than a hundred paintings all together, and you happened to grab one of the least interesting."

She bent over the crate, walked her fingers along the upper edges of the canvases until she found a particular specimen. When she pulled it from the packing, Derryn gasped. This one was a portrait—a woman looking placidly out at the viewer, her face partially obscured by a semitransparent, luminous veil. Above one ear, a dot of vivid blue seemed to indicate the attachment port of a wireless headset.

"No abstraction here," Melinda said.

"But it looks like . . ." Derryn fumbled her words, struggling to accept what she could plainly see. "It looks like the subject is using a direct neural interface. A CoreTex."

"As far as we've been able to tell, she is."

Derryn scanned the corners of the painting, and there, in the lower right, was the artist's signature. And the year of the painting's completion—1866. "This has to be a hoax."

"That was what we thought, at first. But chemical analysis proved everything to be authentic. And we've run every test we can think of. Canvas fiber analysis, pigment composition, binding medium—the materials are all accurate for the period. No modern substances, no anachronistic techniques."

"And the varnish." Derryn was quiet now, thoughtful. "Only nitrocellulose varnish yellows like this. They switched to petroleum sealants in the mid-twentieth century. Better resistance against discoloration."

"It all checks out," Melinda agreed. "Chemically, style wise, even the way the canvas stretchers are constructed. I'll send you the documents from the tests we ran; you can check the data yourself. If it's a hoax, it's the most sophisticated one I've ever seen. And frankly, I can't imagine anyone having the time or the resources to gin up a prank as elaborate as this in the middle of a war. Who the hell would do it, and why?"

Melinda leaned the portrait against the base of a workstation. She pulled another from the crate.

"Here's one I especially wanted you to see."

When she turned the canvas around, Derryn exclaimed, "A self-portrait!" There was no mistaking the traditional style—the subject of the painting peering around the edge of an easel, a paintbrush held easily in one hand. She wore a simple brown dress with a white lace collar, typical of the mid-nineteenth century but a good deal humbler than was usually depicted in portraits of the era. Evidently, the artist was not a woman of means.

"That's our girl," Melinda said. "Helen Bywater in 1866."

The subject was slender, almost too thin, a white woman somewhere in her thirties. Hair the color of aged brass was pulled severely back from her face. Derryn couldn't look away from the eyes, sharp and blue, with a curious, penetrating quality that reached across nearly two hundred years, as lively and real as if Helen were present in the flesh. The artist had painted herself with an expression that bordered on tragic. That piercing stare, the hollowness of her cheeks . . . Helen Bywater had lived a life of loss and pain.

"Can I take a picture?" Derryn asked.

"Please do."

It took only a moment for Derryn to call up the camera function on her CoreTex. While Melinda returned the self-portrait to the crate, Derryn set her AI to work analyzing the image of Helen Bywater.

"Ah!" Melinda pulled another canvas from the shipping crate. "Here's another I wanted to show you."

This painting depicted another cityscape, but its skyscrapers were rendered in faithful detail, all reflective glass and soaring, modern architecture. There were even objects that looked very much like air cabs hanging in the sky between the towers. The style was impressionistic but precise; there was no mistaking this subject for any abstract form. It was, without question, a twenty-first-century integrated city.

While Derryn watched in disbelieving silence, the dean extracted three more paintings from the crate. Another portrait, this time of a man in contemporary clothing displaying a holographic projection from his wristwatch. Then a canvas that seemed to be half finished, though Derryn could clearly make out the form of an air cab, viewed from below, with its passenger looking down through the window to the artist's perspective on the ground. Finally, a depiction of several people striding along what might have been a city sidewalk. The figures were rendered in meticulous detail. All had ambiguous clothing and hairstyles, making it impossible to guess at their genders. That was a common enough sight in the here and now, even on this side of the Blockade—and nothing that would have been seen during the artist's lifetime.

"The way those figures are dressed," Derryn said.

"Not how things were done in the Victorian era," Melinda agreed.

"And this. What do you think these forms depict?" Derryn stooped over the painting, pointing to an amorphous smear of bright paint that hung over the heads of the crowd. That brightness even seemed to glow through the grime and discoloration of ancient varnish. "It makes me think of the Weave. Like the artist sensed that the Weave runs through everything. Everything that isn't under Sovereign attack, I mean."

"It's tempting to think so. But of course, we can't assume the artist's intentions. She might have had something else in mind, and it's only our modern biases making us see familiar forms in her work."

"Of course," Derryn said vaguely.

But as she took in those four paintings side by side, she rejected all notion of bias. If indeed the work had been abstract, as she had first assumed, then the dean would have a point about misinterpretation. But Helen's style was too straightforward. Somehow, contrary to everything Derryn knew about space-time and its limits, a woman who'd lived almost two hundred years in the past had depicted scenes of everyday, twenty-first-century life.

"Who was she?" Derryn asked. "What do we know about her?"

Melinda stood with hands on hips, gazing down at the paintings with a distant expression. "At the moment, all we know is her name—Helen Bywater—and we only know that from her signature. I've got a couple of grad students working on the research, but so far, they haven't turned up anything. Not her life history, not her family. We don't even know if she was from Haverford. For all we can say at this point, the cache might have ended up in that old house through some means that had nothing to do with Helen."

"Was she a mystic?" Derryn wondered. "To depict so many scenes of . . . well, the *future*, for goodness' sake."

"We don't know that she was painting the future." The dean glanced toward the door, then lowered her voice even though the VRC was empty. "Officially, these are 'surrealist' or 'fantastical' works that happen to resemble modern technology because of our own biases and pattern recognition. We're seeing similarities because we're looking for them."

"That's absurd," Derryn said. "These works clearly, specifically depict integrated technology. That's a CoreTex, down to the exact placement of the ports."

"I know," Melinda said. "Now imagine what would happen if the Sovereigns found out about nineteenth-century art that shows the very technology they consider an abomination."

Derryn's face burned. How could she be so clueless? "It would challenge their entire worldview."

"More than challenge—it would shatter it. Their whole ideology is built on the belief that integration is a modern perversion of humanity's pure and natural state. These paintings suggest either that time doesn't work the way we think it does, or that some people can see across it. That's a direct challenge to their philosophies on humanity's place in the universe, a challenge to their idea of God as authority, God who made the universe as they wish to understand it. Including linear time, including the impossibility that a created thing like a human could somehow see the future. At best, the Human Heritage Movement would consider a phenomenon like clairvoyance to be proof of demonic activity. At worst, they'd see it as a direct and imminent threat to their concept of reality."

Derryn looked at the portrait again, studying the figure with the CoreTex. There was something unsettling about those eyes, a sphinx gaze through a screen of holographic light.

"Either way," Melinda continued, "it would be too great a challenge to the Sovereigns' worldview. They'd likely try to destroy the entire collection. They might even attack the college again, declare us a heretical institution."

"So we pretend these are just . . . what? Strange coincidences?"

"In public, yes." Melinda eased the CoreTex portrait back into the crate. "Your real job is to document and analyze these paintings as what they actually are—works distinctly unusual for the time of their creation. That way, we can hopefully land a grant from a Western institution that's big enough to get the whole cache safely out of a war zone. You can understand why we were so vague about the particulars when we invited you to Haverford. You'll understand, too, that we're very careful about the ways we discuss these pieces. The political situation here . . . Well, we don't live the way you do in Cascadia, Derryn."

Despite its location in the very heart of this conflict, and despite several attempts over the years, Haverford College had managed to evade destruction by the HHM since the war had begun. Derryn surely hadn't been invited here to upend the college's remarkable security record. She would have to watch what she said about the cache, even among her fellow historians.

"Of course," she said. "I'm not used to being on this side of the Blockade, but I'll take every possible care."

"I hope you don't regret coming. We don't do things the way you do them out west. We can't afford to. But all the same, there's fascinating work to be done here."

Derryn lifted another painting from the crate. An androgynous figure, distinctly not of Helen Bywater's era, rendered in profile before a bank of luminous, multicolored rectangles that looked like a retail display of personal tablets. The CoreTex that ran from the subject's temple to the nape of their neck couldn't be more distinct, with its blue light above the ear and the metallic glint of its wire frame.

No, Derryn didn't regret taking this assignment, despite the unstable circumstances. The Bywater cache would rock the world of art history—would entirely remake the field. Texts would be written about this discovery for centuries to come. Every other field of liberal arts would be shaken, too, by such a seismic event. Even the sciences would feel the impact as Helen's art called into question all that was currently known of time, of space, of the separation between then and now. And Derryn was here, with her gloved hands on the paintings themselves—an active participant in one of the most consequential discoveries in human history.

If they could only find a way to transport the cache safely out of the Eastern region—if they could get it across the Blockade, into the safekeeping of integrated society. Then she could tell whomever she pleased about the discovery. She could speak of it openly, lecture on the subject at any university in the world, celebrate the deepening of human knowledge with all the wonder such a mystery deserved.

"Put me to work," she said to the dean. "I'll dive in right now, if you're ready for me."

7

Helen

September 1, 1859

The aurora has all but vanished now. Last night, I wrapped myself in Father's old campaign blanket and watched from my balcony as the lights, once bright as a new dawn, hung as mere wisps of color above the river and the hills.

But though the aurora is taking its leave, its psychic effects have remained—with me, at least, if with no other person. For I can still see as clearly as I did on that night when I walked among the streets, when I watched every boundary and rule that I had once thought as permanent as the earth dissolve into fancy.

This world, this way of living, these traditions which so many have failed to question—they are as false as fool's gold. I know the truth more surely with every moment, and I fear that I will never again live easily in this world, for now all I can see is the artifice, the lies we have told ourselves to maintain these comforting separations between ourselves and our fellow man.

If the lights would return, I could blame this state of mind on the aurora's effect. But I am left alone to wrestle with the angel of catastrophic truth. I am much vexed in spirit, and can only beg God for some relief, some signpost to guide me and tell me what I must do next, how I must carry on in this world that will hate me for my convictions. For I cannot continue as I have always done. That much is obvious. Once the truth is beheld, one's eyes cannot be closed to it again.

September 2, 1859

What an astonishing experience I must record in this humble book of days. Never in all my life has a prayer been answered so decisively!

Yesterday my sorrow and my fears continued and left me so blue that Mary Jane followed me about, pretending to dust the furniture so she could keep one eye on me. No doubt, she worried that I was still in a fragile state after my dinner with Mr. Cary. Caleb wasn't the least bit on my mind, however. I was sunk too deep in rumination, asking myself over and over again where all of this would end, for surely the injustices we have inflicted will not be allowed to persist. The tensions rising in the wake of the Dred Scott decision, the incitements made by the League of United Southerners . . . I can feel it all building to some dreadful crescendo. Every time I closed my eyes against the last of the summer's heat or against the terrible weight of my own thoughts, I saw once more those armies marching through my garden, the blue and gray uniforms stained alike with blood.

To comfort my good people, these kindhearted souls who have waited on me since I was a little girl, I forced down the supper Kitty prepared. But I had no appetite and felt quite sick from the churning of my stomach. I took myself upstairs early and, once I was in my nightgown, fell on my knees beside my bed and prayed that God would show me what is to come. "Where shall we go from here," I asked the Almighty, "and what lies at the end of this road we are walking, this road we have made for ourselves out of ignorance and hate?"

When I lifted my tearful face, I saw light sliding like melted silk across the bedding. Light—violet and green, that terrible red, and the vivid, rosy shade for which there is no name. Yes, the aurora had returned. The colors were doubly as bright as they'd been on their first appearance. They danced across the arch of night, moving with the current of their mysterious power.

I was so astonished by the unexpected resurrection that I clambered to my feet and hurried from the room. Thank goodness I had enough sense to put on my wrapper as I went down the stairs and found my old kidskin slippers in the closet by the door, for otherwise I would have run out into the street in a state unfit to be seen.

Nor would I have noticed my own shame, for my attention was entirely snared by the sight that greeted me. From the road outside Eudaimonia, I could see down the hill to the city. Something dark and sharp and impossibly tall was rising with a magisterial slowness from among the warehouses and market squares, among the familiar neighborhoods and the luminous web of the canals. They were towers made of shadow—or made of some firmer stuff, but black as night. The spires rose to stand in sharp relief against the burning sky. I could see the coruscation of the lights above reflecting from their eerily smooth surfaces, ripples of blue and violet and golden green licking like flames up their sides. I realized then that the towers must be made from dark glass.

Next, the lights of the sky seemed to fall to the ground, for I saw those same searingly bright colors running like flooded streams around the bases of the towers. The roads of Richmond transformed into deep channels of rushing light, an intense blue-white flowing in one direction, a brilliant scarlet in the other, and all moving faster than any carriage could go. There were luminous things in the sky, too, like fireflies meandering among the towers. And yet I was certain they were not insects. Those airborne embers were much too large for fireflies—large enough that I knew that people rode in their bellies. *People*, if you can imagine it, flying like birds through the air.

I must have walked clear down the hill, though I have no memory of doing it. And surely the people of Richmond must have stared at me or called out to me as if I was in some distress, but I heard nothing, save for the thunder of my heart as the very world transformed around me.

The houses and shops of Church Hill, even St. John's with its bone-white spire, were fitted over with the ghostly images of a strange fairyland. Or had Richmond become the ghost? Perhaps the elegant brick homes and the gardens still sweet with summer's exuberance had faded into a distant past. I can't decide which was real and present and which was the fantasy, for a queerer sight I have never seen, even these past nights of the aurora. It seemed as if two very different cities existed in the same location—my Richmond and a far more extraordinary place—and I could see either, depending on how I tilted my head and whether I looked straight on or from the corner of my eye. Like painted scrims on a stage when a light shines through, two different places lapped and veiled one another, so that my ordinary world and this unknown one emerged from the hard, black shadows cast by the aurora and retreated again into nonexistence.

Now the people in the streets were those I knew, my neighbors and friends in trousers or dresses, as suited their sex, and now the crowd transformed and multiplied, numerous as bees in a hive—alike as bees, too, with close-fitting garments that displayed the shape of every limb and every curve of the body. Men and women both dressed in the same astonishing manner, and people who seemed to have no sex at all. These odd characters materialized through the usual crowd—the same celebrants who had flooded into the streets to dance and sing two nights before. The bizarrely clad strangers appeared among the crowd of ordinaries, then rippled off again into their own reality, while above, those slim towers rose to such unimaginable heights that my heart nearly burst to see them.

Like a forest of glass and metal, the structures surrounded me. I walked the streets in a state of helpless wonder, craning my neck to see how high the marvelous constructions could rise. They seemed to yearn for the aurora, reaching with steel hands to touch the dancing lights, and every time the sky licked out with a whiplash of violet or green, the towers of Fairyland solidified.

There were moments when the aurora flamed so brightly that Richmond was entirely subsumed, and no trace of my proper place remained. At those times, I was sorely frightened, for I wondered if I had been spirited away and trapped between two opposing realities. The odd people of the other realm paid me no heed, as if they couldn't see me at all, and in a panic, I decided that I must have died—quite without my knowledge or any memory of the unfortunate event—and now I was a ghost. But then good old Richmond would bloom again out of the scenery, all its alleys and parks and buildings of proper size and just how I remembered them, returning to my sight as if they had never vanished.

These two disparate worlds traded places endlessly as I walked. No one in my own reality seemed to see the other. The people in the streets were too absorbed by the lights overhead—or perhaps the enchanted vision came only to me, though I can't fathom why I alone should be chosen for such an experience.

As this extraordinary happening began to lose its novelty—as I accepted that whatever this phenomenon might be, it was truly happening—I observed the scene more closely. The people of that other place held my attention especially. Aside from their odd suits of clothing, the inhabitants of Fairyland wore the strangest and most fascinating bangles.

One man lifted his arm to tap at a sleek white cuff, which he wore around his wrist. The cuff emitted a burst of light, causing me to leap back in sudden fear. In the air above his wrist, the light assembled into a plane of luminescence. Like a sheet of vellum paper, it was somewhat transparent. I could see through its surface to the man's face as he studied the emanation from its other side. With one finger, he poked and prodded at the plane of light. I still can't imagine what that fellow was doing.

Next, I watched a nearby woman. She wore a crown of the finest wire, a single strand of silver like a tiara, though it didn't rest on her brow. Rather, it curved behind her nape, from one ear to the other. When I peered closely at her temple, I could see that the silver wire was connected to a small blue gem. The gem rested above an ear, almost hidden by the woman's hair (which was far too short for a lady—perhaps she had been shingled for lice!). When she touched the blue gem, another plane of transparent whiteness appeared, just as from the man's cuff, and this emanation curved around the woman's face. She began to speak, though I couldn't hear her voice. She seemed to be holding a conversation with the light itself. What a curious thing to do. I wonder, do these lights talk back? Do they serve some useful purpose, or are they merely an amusement?

I walked for at least an hour through the streets of Richmond, keenly observing my Otherworld whenever it chanced to come out of hiding. Every person I saw—hundreds or thousands, far more than the usual spate of Richmonders—wore these same mysterious objects on head or wrist or in the palm of the hand. In rapid flashes, the paper-thin slices of light sprouted around me and hung like elfin lanterns. Every man and woman, and the people whose sex I could only guess at, turned their attention to those mysterious, glowing things. With time, I came to understand that the baubles these people wore both summoned and controlled the planes of light. But I confess I cannot begin to guess what purpose the devices serve.

When I was down near the river, among the warehouses and loading docks, something passed overhead. It was no vision, but something more, for I felt the breeze of its movement and heard the low, mechanical hum of an engine. I looked up . . . and the very breath left my body in astonishment, for the sky was alive with wonderful contraptions. Dozens of strange vehicles filled the air, scores of them, gliding smoothly between the towers. Each flying object was the size of a carriage, but of course, no horses pulled them, nor were any birds harnessed to the indescribable things. They had no wings that I could discern but seemed to hang suspended between four points of blurred motion, like sideways water mills spinning at impossible speed. One of the airborne contraptions dipped down to glide above the street—and my head. Naturally, I shrank from it in terror, yet I couldn't take my eyes off the thing. Its sides were sleek and rounded, shining like polished silver. It emitted a humming sound. A man's face appeared in the object's small, round window. He looked down at me with an air of neutral curiosity, and I wondered if he alone, of all the people who thronged the streets of Fairyland, had seen me.

With my eyes, I followed the path of the flying thing as it arced into the air again and headed for a nearby tower. It was then, watching that enormous bumblebee of a contrivance, that I realized I was looking at—and walking through—a city. Perhaps it was even Richmond itself, grown up the way a forest grows, imperceptibly over the course of a single man's lifetime, yet far different from its origins as a patch of humble saplings. To the people around me, who bustled up and down the crowded street with all their attention captured by the glow of their strange devices, there was nothing miraculous about this place. It was as ordinary to them as bricks and brownstones are to me.

At last, I understood what was happening—what I was seeing. As forests and buildings grow taller, decade after decade, so does everything advance. The auroras have unshuttered a window for me, and I have looked through its panes to see the *future*. How far into the future, one may only guess—a hundred years or a thousand, perhaps farther still. And while it's perfectly wonderful to know that someday carriages will fly, and cuffs and crowns will fill the air with fey constructions of light, I feel a certain dread in the knowing. For what must change in our present time to bring us to such a strange magnificence? Everything, as far as I can tell. And change is not made easily. There are those who fight against it, sometimes with armies and guns and cannons. There are those who won't allow the old traditions to pass away, so that progress only comes by stepping over the bodies of the recalcitrant dead.

By and by, the vision faded, and I was left in the ordinary Richmond I have always known, with an ache of longing in my heart. That other place was so real to me. It *is* real—I feel certain of that—a land where all people walk side by side, regardless of color or sex or any other false consideration. I made the long trek back through the city, up the hill to Eudaimonia, with my arms folded tightly around me and my head lost in thought.

Tonight's vision—an answered prayer!—gave me a glimpse at what lies on the other side of this conflict, this dreadful storm we can all feel gathering on the horizon. I looked upon a world that can be made if we set aside these false distinctions, the boundaries we have built between us, if we join as one unified people. That future is full of wonders I can scarcely find the words to describe. And it is more beautiful than any dream of Heaven.

I did not return to my bed but took this little diary at once from its place on my vanity and sat at my table to write out everything that was revealed to me. I feel quite dissatisfied with the result. A greater faith and care I have never shown before, yet I have failed to capture the astonishing loveliness of what I saw, and all the wonder of the inventions that Man will yet conceive.

I have an itch to paint my vision, and perhaps tomorrow I will shut myself in my little studio and see what might be made. The landscapes and portraits I have been painting all these years dissatisfy me now. What beauty can I find in this present world, when I know the perfect harmony of what is to come?

And now that I have seen what is possible, my mind is firmly made up. An abolitionist I am—suddenly, unexpectedly, yet without doubt or denial. And an abolitionist I must be, in deed and in action, not merely in thought, without regard for the consequences. For this grand future will never come to be unless we make it so, unless we find the strength and clarity to reject the false constructions that keep us imprisoned in a backward past.

Let the work begin with me. Let it start in my own life, with my own action. I will labor faithfully for the future I know is coming, and with a joyful heart.

8

Derryn

2053

Derryn pulled the final painting from the second crate, brushed a few stray particles of packing material from its surface. She held the work at arm's length for a moment, staring in the same giddy disbelief she'd felt with each of the previous discoveries. She'd been working on the Bywater cache for four days now and had documented more than seventy paintings in meticulous detail, but each new piece she extracted from the shipping crates thrilled and astonished her as much as the others.

This one depicted a figure interacting with a holographic screen, which Helen had rendered as a slightly curved rectangle of near white to the left of the subject's face. The right hand was raised as if to touch an icon, or perhaps the figure was merely pointing to the luminous plane of light, the way figures often pointed to religious symbols in Renaissance paintings. The rest of the composition was shadowy, intentionally obscured, drawing the viewer's eye to the startling brightness of the lightscreen. Even when its old, dark varnish was stripped and replaced with a modern protective coating, the image would still be primarily shadow. Only the screen, the hand, and the androgynous face of the subject would stand out with any clarity.

Derryn set the painting on the easel she'd been using for her work, adjusting its position so the canvas stood perpendicular to the floor. She attached a small, white ruler to a lower corner so Tyko would have a reference for accurate measurements. Then she stepped back to the line she'd marked on the floor of the VRC, exactly three meters from the easel, and activated her CoreTex. The familiar sensation encircled her head, slightly warm and just a bit tight, as the wireless mechanisms found her neural signature and merged their electronic impulses with her own. The ports resting against each temple and the base of her skull pulsed with a ready energy.

"Tyko," Derryn said.

The AI answered at once, its smooth, masculine voice running directly down her auditory nerve. "I'm here, Derryn. How can I help?"

"Please record the exact dimensions of the painting in front of me. Exclude the easel."

In moments, Tyko had recited the dimensions and saved them, at Derryn's command, to the appropriate file, along with her narrated description of the painting. In four days of work, she still wasn't used to this song and dance, obscuring the paintings' true subjects behind a mask of careful language. How did Melinda and the rest of the researchers manage? Derryn suspected that she might lose her mind if she had to work under these conditions, week after week and year after year.

Yet now that she had documented two-thirds of the Bywater cache, she understood the necessity. Since the advent of the Weave and the rapid proliferation of artificial intelligence, the Human Heritage Movement had set itself against the very habits and practices these paintings depicted. As the ruin of the surrounding city testified, the so-called Sovereigns were willing to use violence to try to dissuade the merger of humanity with AI. They would surely see Helen Bywater's art as a direct threat to their insistence that artificial intelligence was too new a concept to be trusted, that anyone who integrated with technology was abandoning an older, purer, perfected state of humanity for something only recently conceived, an untried mode of life that would surely lead to destruction and damnation of the soul.

Despite the walls that surrounded Haverford College, Derryn felt a little less safe with each passing day—even if the observation and cataloging of Helen's work still thrilled her.

You're almost halfway through the assignment, she reminded herself as she returned the painting to its crate. *Then you'll be home again.*

And as soon as she'd helped Melinda secure the necessary grants, as soon as the Bywater cache was transported safely out of Sovereign reach, she would be free to tell the whole world of this astonishing discovery.

After she'd repacked the contents of the crate, Derryn used the forklift bot to move the heavy container aside. The bot hummed faintly as it trundled back into the storage locker and backed out again with the final crate on its lifts.

Derryn keyed the access code into the crate's lock. The latches released with a quiet pop, and she lifted the lid aside. The upper edges of some thirty canvases showed above the level of the packing—the final pieces of the cache. Derryn was every bit as eager to dig into this crate as she'd been with the other two. Documenting a genuine historic mystery never got old, it seemed, even with the threat of partisan terrorism hanging over her head.

She hooked her gloved fingers under the stretcher of the first painting and pulled. It didn't slide from the crate as easily as the others had done. It was an unframed piece, yet something had added significant weight and dragged at the packing. Derryn cursed under her breath as she strained to lift the painting free without damaging the aged and delicate surface.

When its lower edge rose clear of the cellulose padding, she saw what had impeded it. A foam-wrapped package had snagged on a nail of the canvas stretcher. The package was rectangular, about twenty centimeters long and six or seven thick. Derryn gave the painting an experimental shake, and the package tumbled to the floor, where it bounced on its layer of protective foam.

I hope that wasn't anything delicate.

She leaned the painting against the shipping crate and retrieved the item from the floor. In a workstation drawer, she found a box cutter and carefully slit one end of the foam so she could peek inside. Four small, leather-bound books were pressed cover to cover. Derryn worked one free of its tight enclosure and turned it over in her hands. There was no title, no bossing, no inscription on the spine. When she opened the cover, she found an end page and pastedown, marbled in the magnificently ornate style of the nineteenth century, the pages deckled and aged around their edges to a deep honey hue.

Holding her breath, she turned the end page and found handwriting, elegant and faded with the years. She couldn't read most of it easily, but after days of working over the cache, the name was familiar enough: Helen Bywater.

A thrill ran through her. She woke her headset and activated its screen.

"Tyko, please transcribe the pages I'm reading from cursive script to print."

A much more legible translation appeared on the screen, superimposed over her view of the page. She focused on the lightscreen, allowing the book behind it and the whole of the VRC to recede from her awareness.

The Life Story of Helen Bywater, the page read, *August 1859–December 1860.*

Derryn looked through the lightscreen again. She pulled another book from the foam casing, opened it to the first page. The AI made its rapid transcriptions, and Derryn bit back a yelp of excitement.

"Can you believe this, Tyko? These are the artist's personal journals. It looks like they run from 1859 to 1867. That spans the first civil war and beyond."

"These are sure to be valuable artifacts," the AI said. "They should provide considerable context for the art we've been documenting."

"That's what I'm hoping for. Maybe they'll explain how Helen Bywater managed to spy on all of us with our lightscreens and our passenger drones. Oh, Melinda's poor grad students—they've been searching the Weave for information about Helen, and all this time, her own journals were overlooked at the bottom of a shipping crate."

"I hope the graduate students have a sense of humor," Tyko said.

"If they don't have a sense of humor yet, now's their chance to develop one. This is usually the way discoveries are made in this field—by accident or by chance."

She settled onto the stool again, opened the earliest journal to its first entry. Tyko's transcription blinked onto the screen, and Derryn read Helen's account of lights in the sky with a hungry focus.

"Moving ribbons of light," Derryn said, "pink and green. It sounds like an aurora. But she mentions Richmond and the James River. That has to be Virginia, right?"

"I can't find any other locations that match the geographic features the writer has specified," Tyko said. "She also mentions Church Hill, which is a neighborhood of Richmond, Virginia."

"Auroras aren't seen so far to the south. What else could explain what Helen saw that night?"

Tyko combed through the aggregated knowledge of humankind. The pause lasted no more than a second or two.

"The date of August twenty-eighth, 1859, aligns with the Carrington Event," the AI said.

"The what?"

"The Carrington Event was the first recorded solar flare in human history. It was also the largest geomagnetic storm that has affected the planet to date. It caused strong auroral displays at nearly every inhabited place on earth and was also recorded in the ships' logs of vessels positioned on almost every ocean. This phenomenon would certainly account for the unusual lights Helen Bywater wrote about in her journal. Would you like more information about the Carrington Event?"

Derryn answered in the affirmative and tumbled into the ensuing rabbit hole as Tyko narrated the history of the global aurora. The AI kept a steady stream of supplemental visuals running across Derryn's screen as she listened—images of handwritten logs and telegraph messages, woodcuts and copperplate illustrations of people in nineteenth-century garb staring in astonishment at the sky. There were even a few old watercolors of pink-and-green auroras above the modest cityscapes of the 1800s.

The days-long solar flare interfered with the fledgling technology of global communication, Tyko said. It even caused some telegraph stations to spark and catch fire. The event was so shocking that many people believed the world was ending.

Derryn heard the distant beep of a key card, then the VRC's main door opening. She focused through her screen and found Melinda coming toward her with a smile.

"How's progress?" the dean asked.

"Great. The second crate is finished, and I've just started on the third."

"You're going much faster than we'd expected." Melinda sounded thoroughly pleased. "I guess that's the benefit of using more advanced tech. But it's lunchtime. Are you hungry? Mihir made a nice, big curry from the veggie garden, and the whole department is having a picnic out under the trees. I came to find you before it's all gone."

"Are you kidding? I wouldn't miss a chance to stuff myself on Mihir's cooking."

The grandfatherly professor of literature had opened his home and his kitchen to Derryn. The spare bedroom in Mihir's on-campus flat had become her base of operations, a private sanctuary where she could review each day's work on her CoreTex without fear of discovery by some rebel sympathizer—and where she could make her promised daily calls to Leo. Mihir saw to it that Derryn was amply fed. He was a culinary maestro; the smell of his cooking had drawn visitors each night from all over the complex of staff housing. Mihir's door was open to all, his table always set for one more guest, and Derryn had thoroughly enjoyed the evenings of conversation with professors of every subject a liberal-arts college could offer.

She shut off the CoreTex and removed it, slid the contraption into her backpack, and followed the dean outside. The summer air was fresh and welcoming with a smell of cut grass. The shade trees in the arboretum swayed in a lazy wind. Derryn and Melinda talked of the usual things as they crossed the campus—grants and curriculum and their most promising students, the new texts that had just been published and would appeal to none but those who had dedicated their lives to the history of art. Melinda was as excited about the discovery of Helen's journals as Derryn had been; she promised to break the relieving news to her grad students when they met the next day.

When they reached their lunch site—a loose collection of picnic tables under two great, gnarled maples—Mihir welcomed Derryn with a kiss on the cheek and a bowl of hearty curry. One of the student teachers offered her a glass of lemonade. She took her place among the faculty and regaled them with all the details of the morning's work, as much at home here as she was on the Stanford campus. Derryn's four days at Haverford had been more pleasant and fulfilling than she had anticipated. The whole experience would have felt more like a vacation than a professional excursion if not for the reinforced cement wall surrounding the college grounds. That wall was a constant reminder of what lay on the other side: a society stricken and crippled by decades of brutal conflict.

As the lunch hour drew to a close, Mihir circulated among the picnic tables, collecting dishes and accepting the praise of the faculty. Derryn looked on the idyllic scene of friendship and community, her emotions caught somewhere between warmth and pity. Beneath the ideologies that still divided them, the people of the Eastern states were no different from those on the far side of the Blockade. Why couldn't they set their differences aside, unite for the sake of all they shared, and enjoy the same peace and prosperity that had lifted the rest of the world out of despair?

A rapid pinging sound rose suddenly from the crowd—the repetition of five high, sharp notes projected from the old-fashioned smartphones and watches that were still most commonly used in the East. The chatter around the tables died as they all turned their attention to their devices. The smile slid from Mihir's face. The entire staff had gone sober. Some were decidedly pale.

Derryn glanced at Melinda in apprehension. "What's going on?"

"A local alert," the dean said without looking up from her phone. "There's rebel activity up at Connaughtown."

One of the other professors had made a call as soon as the alerts had gone off. Now he lowered his phone and said, "The units at Bryn Mawr say they're planning to move south. The rebels, I mean. They'll be headed in our direction within a few hours unless someone can stop them at the river."

"Damn," Melinda muttered. "We haven't seen any serious action here for months. I had hoped it would stay quiet through the summer, at least."

Derryn's heart was pounding everywhere at once, in her chest and her throat, in her head, even in the soles of her feet. She could only stare at the dean in dumbstruck fear.

"Don't worry," Melinda said. "The college has managed to stay safe all this time. We've got protocols in place to see ourselves through exactly this kind of situation."

A distant boom sounded from somewhere far beyond the wall. The noise was faint yet dominating, rolling across the placid summer day with such commanding force that Derryn knew it could only have been a bomb. Fear raced up every nerve in her body. Her stomach went sick with dread.

Mihir abandoned his bucket of dishes on a nearby table. Everyone rose from their seats with a strangely calm haste, reverting to a practiced state of grim readiness that Derryn did not possess. She swallowed hard, blinking away her tears.

"It's all right." Mihir put his arm around Derryn's shoulders as she staggered up from the bench. "We take precautions, of course, but we know how to be safe."

"What do I do?" Derryn sounded desperate, frantic, even to herself.

"Stay calm and do what we do. We'll keep you from harm."

She stuck like a burr to Mihir as he headed back across the lawn for Founders Hall. The pathways of the campus soon filled with people as faculty and students streamed out of smaller buildings and made for the largest, Founders Hall among them. Every face in the crowd was set and determined. Melinda soon fell in at Derryn's side, walking with a brisk energy that belied her calm demeanor.

"I'm sorry you've had to see us at our worst, Derryn," the dean said. "But you're also seeing us at our best. We're a tight group here, and all of us put the institution of higher education before anything else. Haverford has survived the war all this time by maintaining our flexibility. We go with the flow, and unfortunately, that sometimes means dropping everything and taking shelter."

"*Where* are we taking shelter?"

"There's a big safe room under Founders Hall—well, more or less under it. Fifteen years ago, when the wall was built, we had several underground bunkers installed at a few points around campus. They're well stocked with enough supplies to see everyone through several days of sheltering, in case that becomes necessary." She added quickly, "It's never been necessary so far. The longest we've ever had to go was twenty-four hours."

Derryn kept her eyes fixed on the hall as a river of desperate humanity carried her ever closer. The Grecian pillars of its façade stood out with ominous clarity against the cold shadow of its covered porch. She wasn't the praying type, but nevertheless, a desperate plea burst from her heart with a sudden and passionate intensity—a wish not only for her own safety, but also for that of the Bywater cache. She had left the whole collection of paintings outside their locker, vulnerable to whatever this invading force might do. As the crowd entered the hall and descended the stairs to the basement, Derryn wondered where that plea had gone to—the wish, the prayer, whatever it might be called. She could feel it, somehow, winging between the high, austere walls of the old building, adding its frantic clamor to all the other prayers that had been set flying with the news of an approaching rebel faction. Those silent cries for mercy and salvation twisted around her, their frantic wings beating in a futile noise against the windows and ceiling.

Flanked by Mihir and Melinda, she followed the rest of the crowd through the basement of Founders Hall, barely glancing at the VRC as she passed it. At least she had closed the door. If the Sovereigns actually invaded the campus, maybe they would take no interest in an obscurely labeled room in the basement of an otherwise grand building. It might be enough to spare the cache from destruction.

Clear down at the Hall's far end, someone had opened another large workroom. The tense, silent crowd of evacuees funneled through the room and to its rear wall, which was fitted with the same featureless blue panels that concealed the VRC's storage lockers. One panel stood open. Faculty and students filed into its depths.

"This tunnel leads to the bunker," Melinda said. "Big enough to house three hundred people."

"Not as comfortably as you might wish," Mihir added with a wry smile.

Derryn ducked into the shadows beyond the open panel. The space was so dark she could see nothing. She reached forward tentatively, only to find someone's back under her hands.

"Sorry," she muttered.

The walls of the tunnel pressed in on either side. Derryn shuffled forward with the crowd's cautious movement. The unseen ceiling bore down from above with all the terrible weight of imagination.

Then the air freshened. She had a sudden awareness of expansion, of space opening around her—an echoing of sound, a certain crisp dampness among the heavy shadows. Overhead lights popped on, illuminating a huge gray space as they buzzed and flickered. Concrete walls enclosed several long rows of military cots, each one supplied with a pillow and a folded blanket of olive-colored wool. Two dark doors were set side by side into one wall—bathrooms, Derryn thought—and near those doors, a broad alcove set with steel shelves. The shelves were filled with canned food and boxes of other supplies. Several spigoted drums stood on wooden platforms, holding enough potable water to last for several days. And the ceiling wasn't quite as low as Derryn had feared.

"Claim a bunk and settle in," Mihir said cheerfully. "With any luck, we won't be here for more than a few hours. We'll get alerts about what the rebels are doing. They usually settle back down after they bomb a bridge or two."

Derryn took the cot beside Mihir's. She listened to his chatter for more than an hour—a kindly gesture on his part, an attempt to distract Derryn from her fear with lighthearted stories. She was grateful for his effort, but as time wore on and the reality of her situation settled deeper into her mind, her thoughts ranged back to their former bleak preoccupations despite Mihir's cheerful talk.

New York, she told herself—not for the first time since her descent into this concrete hell. *I promised Leo I'd go stay with Alexis if things got bad.*

Surely things couldn't be much worse than this. There must be some way to get out of the bunker and flee to New York City, which had its own blockade—not as large as the Cascadian one, to be sure, but effective enough to stop the Sovereigns from interfering with civilized society.

Recalling that promise made her long to speak with her brother again. She had already called Leo that morning, checking in as she'd sworn to do each day of her sojourn in the dangerous East. But what did that matter? Leo wouldn't mind if she called again. And it might very well prove to be the last time Derryn saw her brother's face or heard his voice. It was a chance she couldn't pass up.

When Mihir paused in his latest story, Derryn slipped the CoreTex from her backpack and excused herself. "I just remembered I've got to make an important call."

In the supply alcove, she pressed herself between two shelving units and sank to the ground with the cold cement wall at her back. Reception was spottier than usual in the underground bunker, but Leo answered quickly, his face already stern with worry.

"Derryn, what's going on?"

"Oh, nothing much," she answered lightly.

"Why are you calling me a second time? Is everything all right?" Only then did he seem to notice her unusual surroundings. "Where the hell are you?"

Derryn attempted a laugh. "You're not going to believe this. I'm in an underground bunker."

"What?"

"Relax," she said. "It's just a drill. A *routine* drill, according to my hosts. I'm glad we don't have to do routine drills for terrorist attacks back home."

Mention of home brought tears to her eyes with such sudden force that she wasn't entirely convinced that she'd blinked them away before Leo could notice.

"Tell me what's really going on, Squiggy."

He could feel her anxiety through the Weave, even from across the continent. Derryn willed herself to calm. The last thing she needed now was for Leo to pick up on her rising terror.

"I'm all right, really," she insisted. "I know I feel all antsy—"

"'Antsy,'" Leo barked, "you feel like you're in a full-on panic!"

"This drill has me rattled," Derryn said. "It's not the kind of thing we ever have to do back home."

"Back home where it's safe," he said pointedly.

"I *am* safe, Leo, I promise. Doing a drill has just made me more aware of the dangers here than I've been for the past few days. Everything has been great, really. The faculty are all so nice, and the campus is beautiful. And *peaceful*," she added with particular emphasis. "I wanted to call you so you could see me hiding in an honest-to-god war bunker. When will either one of us get the chance to see something like this again? I never meant to worry you."

Leo paused. His long sigh sounded in Derryn's ears. "Do you promise you're okay? Promise me you're staying safe."

"I swear it," Derryn said. "Remember, I told you that if things get bad, I'll get out of Philadelphia and go to New York."

"Right."

"That's still the plan. I've got to go; I'll check in with you tomorrow morning." Before the call could disconnect, Derryn added, "I love you, Leo."

When the screen went blank, she didn't pick herself up and return to her bunk, but remained where she was, pressed into a dank corner, huddled in the unfeeling chill of the earth like some small animal, a creature of weak limbs and snappable bones hiding from a pack of predators. There had to be a way out of there—out of the bunker, off campus, out of Philadelphia, by air cab or light-rail, by train or bus or boat or horseback. On foot, if need be. She had promised her brother that she would go to New York the moment she felt unsafe. And danger was certainly closing around her now.

9

Helen

October 3, 1859

Goodness, but I can hardly believe that weeks have flown by without my writing in this diary! But then, I have been so very busy—busier than at any time in my life.

The third of September saw the last of the auroras. When the lights failed to come again the following night, my sense of grief surprised me, for I couldn't help but fear that they'd taken all hope for change with them. We had a taste of a different world, one whose boundaries are clearly seen for falsehood and fantasy, a world in which true liberation could be felt in all its heft and texture like a solid object in the hand. But a taste never quite satisfies, and now my hunger has made me ravenous.

I have spent this time wisely and well. After much thought on how I might proceed, I called on Father's old lawyer, Mr. Wyckoff, who still handles the greater affairs of the estate. It took some courage to explain to that man what I intend to do, but to my relief, he took my announcement that I will free all my slaves in his stride.

"They are yours to do with as you wish, Miss Bywater," Mr. Wyckoff said, "but unfortunately, Virginia law has grown somewhat stringent these past few years."

"Stringent," I repeated, alarmed. "Whatever do you mean, sir?"

The old white-haired gentleman settled back in his leather chair and chewed thoughtfully at the stem of his pipe. "Manumission is still permitted, strictly speaking, but now any liberated Black—man, woman, or child—must leave the state within a year of being freed, or else he can be legally enslaved again."

"But that's cruel," I protested. "Why, these people have family here in Virginia. To force them to choose freedom or family—"

"I agree, Miss Bywater. It's a most unfortunate thing, and thoroughly unjust. However, that is the current state of affairs, from a legal standpoint. Believe me, I've looked into the issue thoroughly."

I paused and considered his words, doing my best to conceal my emotions behind a mask of feminine meekness. But one thought repeated loud as a parade inside my head: If Mr. Wyckoff had had cause to investigate the current legalities of manumission, then I am not the only slave owner in Richmond who has turned abolitionist at heart. How comforting it is, to know that there are others in this city who share my beliefs, even if we must conceal our convictions for the sake of propriety. I suppose we are never as alone as we feel ourselves to be.

"Surely," I said, "there must be some way I can do as I mean to do . . . without forcing these good people to abandon their families."

Mr. Wyckoff took up his pen and jotted a few notes on his pad. "Let me look into the matter. Some of my colleagues in other states may have some useful advice. I'll have an answer for you before November comes."

The evening after I called on my lawyer, Mr. Caleb Cary visited again for supper. I suppose I had accepted his request for my company sometime in the weeks before and had forgotten all about it, being too absorbed in my plans and my legal entanglements to pay much attention to anything else. When Ruthie tapped at my studio door and reminded me that Mr. Cary was due for supper soon, I cursed at the prospect, and had to rush myself into a more presentable dress, for the old smock I always wear at my easel is much too stained and raggedy for entertaining.

As Mary Jane helped me dress, my heart was all aflutter, but not with girlish anticipation. A dreadful anxiety had crept inside me, expanding like ice in the crack of a stone. Mr. Cary still expected me to set a date for our wedding. No doubt, I thought, that would be the very topic of conversation at the supper table. He's eager to claim Eudaimonia for his own, for it is the most beautiful house in all of Richmond, and he grows impatient with my continual deflection of our marriage.

But oh, I cannot stand the sight of that man now! How strange to think that I was once as swoony over Caleb as any other young lady would be. There's no denying that he is especially fine looking, and the Cary family will never want for a thing. But although the auroras are long gone, I still see by their transforming light. The world we all thought we knew was melted and dissolved by those heavenly fires. For me, all the customs and traditions and proper forms are still dissolute, or perhaps I see now that they were never of any substance to begin with. For what is tradition if one can simply choose to disregard it? What is custom to one who decides that it doesn't apply to himself?

As I sat at the dining table, making nice with Caleb and doing full justice to Kitty's cooking (hot biscuits, pork sausage, and the last of the peaches from the garden), I fended off his talk of wedding dates with a series of chaste demurrals. Or I hope they came across as such. It's possible that I looked like a thunderhead, for I surely felt stormy inside.

I changed the subject to something I knew Caleb would bite like a fish on a hook. "But do you really think, Mr. Cary, that we will rise up against the North?"

This worked like a charm. He took on a rapturous countenance, discoursing at great length about the wickedness of the Northern states, their greed and shocking liberalism, their economic weakness without the South to bolster them.

"Those cities to the north and the political party that finances them are nothing short of turpitudinous!" he all but shouted.

I was forced to snatch up my napkin and feign a fit of choking to disguise my laughter. "Turpitudinous"! Where on earth did Caleb Cary learn such a word?

When I had my amusement well in hand, I lowered my napkin and said, "But the North does have the largest cities, Mr. Cary, and that means a greater population. I imagine they could conscript ever so many more soldiers than we could."

"Conscripts are exceedingly difficult to rustle up, my pet, while every able-bodied man in the South will fight willingly to defend his way of life and to secure a future for his issue."

Caleb certainly had a point there, although I hated to admit it, even to myself.

I tried another tack. "Think of the industry. Nearly all the factories are up north. We couldn't expect to keep up with their production if it came to war. All the arms and gunpowder, all the necessities one never thinks of—boots and saddles and tents, and cook pots and undergarments, for Heaven's sake. That army of willing Southern volunteers wouldn't march very far in bare feet, Mr. Cary. And it isn't only guns and livery they make up there. What good would all our cotton be without the Northern mills? Why, the bales would rot in the fields if there were no mills to send them to."

He smiled at me with the same patient tolerance one might show to an especially clever five-year-old. "This is what I like so well about you, Helen. You can keep up your end of a conversation with a man. Other ladies would wilt away. They have no head for subjects like this one."

That annoyed me excessively. I wondered: Has Caleb ever bothered to keep up *his* end of a conversation with a woman? Wilt away, indeed! But though my ire and my hackles were rising, I restrained myself from snapping at him. I am a lady, after all.

"But yes, I'm sure of a rebellion," he went on. "Didn't we have a portent? This conflict has been building for decades. The aurora was our sign that a resolution is at hand. We're on the verge of it now, mark my words—a great change in the fortunes and arrangement of this union."

Coolly, I said, "I agree that those lights must have been the herald of a great change. But I wonder why you feel so sure that they were a sign of Southern victory rather than Southern defeat."

He goggled at me in shocked silence, and I confess that I wondered myself what madness had come over me to say such a thing aloud.

Happily, I was saved by David's appearance at the door. "Pardon me, Miss Helen, Mr. Cary. There's a caller at the door for you, ma'am."

I rose from the table with haughty dignity, though underneath my petticoats I was all ashiver. Surely, word would soon make its way around town that I was a secret abolitionist. Well, what if word does fly? I *am* an abolitionist, after all. But my life in this town won't be any easier for it. That much is certain.

Whom should I find at the front door but a messenger from my lawyer. He held out an envelope.

"Correspondence from Mr. Wyckoff," the young fellow said.

I grabbed the thing as if it contained the map to a buried treasure, and for the rest of the evening, while I barely tolerated Caleb's presence, I could feel the letter in the pocket of my skirt, calling to me with all its intrigue and promise.

After Caleb finally took his leave, I retired to the back garden and tore open the envelope. The note inside was brief, but thorough. After consulting his records, Mr. Wyckoff had already worked out a solution to my predicament. I needn't go through any formal process of manumission. I could simply *tell* my workers that they were free to come and go as they pleased, and if they still wished to work for me, I would pay them a wage.

Of course, they would have no legal recourse if I refused or failed to make the payments. But Eudaimonia still has deep coffers. I shall find no difficulty in paying for honest work, and though I suppose Ruthie and Mary Jane and the rest have no real reason to trust me, at least *I* know that I will be as good as my word. Honest pay for hard work is the least of what I owe these people. And they may go on living at Eudaimonia, if they please, or may go and live with their families at other houses, if that is their desire. By the letter of the law, they will still be my property. But I can make it clear that I expect nothing from them but that which I might extract for pay from a white hired hand.

And of course, any who wish to get out of Virginia and try their luck in the North will find me a helpful benefactress. Any who wish to leave—even if they mean only to go to some other town in Virgina—must carry letters from me declaring that they travel at the direction of their mistress. I may even have to hire men to go with them and protect them, for even with the appropriate papers, they may still be suspected of being runaways. I shudder to think what might happen to them if such a misfortune should arise. They may be taken by some other slaver or even hanged without due process. No doubt, it will be an expensive endeavor to give them all their freedom, but I will bear the cost willingly. Giving these good people whatever aid I may render is the smallest part of what I owe for a lifetime of their toil, and since it is the very least of what I can and must do, I shall do it with a grateful heart.

Once my mind was made up, and with Mr. Wyckoff's legal guidance to bolster my plans, I lingered in the garden as twilight fell, thinking over what Caleb had said. The garden has put on its fall colors by now, the leaves going yellow and the old magnolia tree tinted with copper at its edges. The last flowers of the year are done up in shades of red and orange, and as I watched their petals flare under the midday sun, I mused that all the world seems to be afire.

I am as certain of rebellion as Caleb is. It almost feels as if the dreadful thing has already happened, for we have walked a definite road these many years, and there is little chance now to alter our course or slow the careen of our fate. Caleb and those who share his persuasion don't seem to understand that rebellion will not come easily. I saw as much on that strange night when I witnessed the ghostly army marching across the garden, and how that vision haunts me still! Thousands and thousands struck dead. Blood running in a river wide as the Mississippi. The men all believe our control of the cotton trade will keep us safe, will ensure that the North bends the knee. But I see a different future. The North will not suffer its mills to go empty, nor the ships that sail to England. What comes from the Northern mills is not cloth but money, and wealth has ever been the great motivator of power.

All I can do is brace for the inevitable. The League of United Southerners hasn't ceased its agitation. The papers are full of their proclamations, and I sometimes hear their slogans repeated in the streets. I still see the Dred Scott decision burning in the eyes of every Black man and woman. And daily I feel the pressure of injustice which, like the boil of some evil infection, must be lanced or it will surely burst and fester.

All I can do now is pray that the abolitionists will win. I may be a Southerner by birth, but I am sickened to my soul by the idea of King Cotton's victory. If the South does indeed break from the North and wins the resulting war, what then will happen? This practice of slavery will spread. Its corruption will make every state impure. There will be no place safe from the most brutal evil Man has yet devised.

The mere thought saps the very last of my constitution. I will plunge entirely into despair if I can't put my mind on more cheerful things.

Here is a bracing thought: If or when rebellion comes, I shall do everything in my power to see that the South is defeated. And may the Lord help me if anyone should find this diary, for if I know my Richmond, to give aid to the North will doubtless be a hanging offense, even for a lady.

But I must exorcise these thoughts somewhere, somehow, or they will eat me from the inside out, like termites in an old hollow tree.

October 5, 1859

I am putting my affairs in order, freeing up some of Father's investments so that I might have money on hand to pay my workers—assuming any of them will choose to stay at Eudaimonia.

While the necessary arrangements are made, I have been thinking on what else I might do to repay the debts I owe to my people.

All day, I have remembered how tenderly Mary Jane cared for me after my swoon, and how bright the girl was in that delicate moment, weighing her words with such care. Young as she is, there is still plenty of time to cultivate her quick mind. Mr. Wyckoff has informed me that the law does not prevent me from sending a slave to school, if that is my wish, though it must be done outside Virginia, for no school within the state would take Mary Jane. However, once she is outside the state's borders, she will not be able to return, for Virginia fears an uprising. Any freed or educated Black who leaves the state will be jailed on attempting to enter again. I hadn't a clue whether Mary Jane would miss anyone here in Richmond—whether she would *want* to leave the state, never to return, even for the incitement of an education.

There was nothing to do but ask her.

I called her into Father's study and bade her sit in the old leather chair, which she did with obvious discomfort, for she had never been invited to take her ease in a white person's presence, nor to put herself in an equal position.

"How would you like to go off to school?" I asked. "Learn to read and write, and how to work numbers?"

I could tell by the way her eyes grew wide and dewy that she was hungry for the chance.

"The only school that will take you is the one up in Pennsylvania," I said.

"The school you went to, Miss Helen?"

"That's right. The Quakers believe that all people have a right to learn, whether male or female, and without regard to their color. Before you give your answer, Mary Jane, you must know that you won't be allowed to return to Virginia. The laws here prohibit any Black person from crossing back into the state after leaving it. I think you might have a far better life in the Northern states, where you could live as if you were free. I would certainly not pursue you under the Fugitive Slave Act. But others might suspect you, and so leaving Virginia might mean that you will spend the rest of your life with one eye cast over your shoulder. It isn't a decision to make lightly. But if you want to go to school, I will send you and pay all the costs."

For a moment, she looked mistrustful. She must have thought I was making some cruel joke at her expense.

I rushed to reassure the girl. "I'm entirely in earnest. You're a good deal brighter than I was at your age. If my parents saw fit to educate me, why should you not have the same opportunity? Talents shouldn't be stifled; they should be nurtured and grown. If you would like the chance to learn, I'm prepared to send you to the Quaker school. I only wish I could do the same for Kitty and Ruthie and the rest of the household, for they're all as bright and deserving as you are . . . but at their age, no school anywhere will take them. You're still young enough to count as a schoolgirl, and perhaps you ought to take advantage of youth. If you aren't opposed to leaving Virginia for good, then I want you to know that I am prepared to pay for your schooling. It's the least I can do—the least of what I owe to you—considering you've served the Bywaters all your life."

Convinced at last, she clasped her hands and looked up with brimming eyes. It was the first time I'd ever seen the girl allow such emotion to show upon her face. "Oh, Miss Helen, I would like it so much that I'm afraid it's too good to be true. I do read and write a little—your mother taught me some, before she died a few years back. I know I could do it heaps better if I had a teacher. But I . . ." She trailed off and seemed rather shy. "I still don't understand, ma'am, *why* you'd do it."

"The world is changing," I said, "and I intend to change with it, not be left behind in the old world, with its old ways. Of course, we must go about this carefully, for safety's sake, but let's not disregard a sign when Heaven sends it. You told me yourself that if we all do our small works, they will become greater works, and a good job done. In time, with enough faith and dedication, we might yet change the world."

She smiled then and looked to the drawing-room window. The only light to be seen was the deep-red flush of sunset, but I know she thought of the auroras, those brilliant banners in the hands of angels that had waved above a new world.

"I don't mind about that Act," Mary Jane said. "It won't be any different than how we all live now, always looking out for who might be after us and who we've offended. Yes, ma'am, if you will send me, I will go and learn all I can and be glad for the chance."

So that is that! We have made a start on our greater work, Mary Jane and I. The first step is always the hardest to take, but now that I've taken it, I'm set upon my path and determined to face the rest of this journey. What relief, to have begun. I could sleep as soundly as the dead, and for a hundred years, more or less . . . but this diary called to me the moment I entered the room and saw it waiting on my little table. I had to tell the story of this day before I could fall into bed.

October 16, 1859

This morning, I sent Mary Jane on her way to the Pennsylvania school. Mr. Wyckoff helped me make the arrangements, including papers certified at the courthouse, which Mary Jane must carry at all times to prove that she is not a runaway but has been sent on the business of her mistress. (Oh, how I have come to hate that word—"mistress"—and doubly so in reference to myself.)

Mary Jane will travel by steamer down the James to Chesapeake, and then by sailing ship up the coast to Wilmington. From there, she will go by coach to Haverford, where the school awaits her. The headmaster has already written his glad acceptance. When I read that letter to Mary Jane, the girl lapsed into a state of near-frantic excitement for days after—most unlike my stoic little caterer! The journey will take three days, or more if the weather on the coast is bad. I paid for the best accommodations that would be afforded to a Black traveler and gave Mary Jane a little extra in case the need should arise to grease a palm or two. The girl is shrewd enough to spend her money with care.

David drove Mary Jane and me to the steamboat landing, and there I saw her off. She looked very smart in a burgundy-printed calico and silk-flowered hat, which the other women of the household made up as a farewell gift and presented to her in the parlor with great solemnity and pride. We all think so fondly of Mary Jane. Eudaimonia won't feel quite the same without her.

Just before she boarded the steamboat, she turned to me with an earnest expression. "I'll write to you, Miss Helen, every week until my schooling is finished. Until I can find some way to come back again."

The dear girl. She won't return to Eudaimonia, and soon enough she'll realize it. I hope and believe that she will understand her chance and go on the run rather than attempt to return to Virginia—though surely she will have sense enough to wait until she has feasted to fullness on all the Quakers will teach her. I wish her a long life of freedom and happiness in the Northern states. And I will miss her terribly—that much is true.

As the steamboat pulled away from its mooring, I could see little Mary Jane standing at the rail. I waved my hanky until I could no longer see her and the boat itself was small and almost shapeless down the river. My heart was light with the knowledge that I have done right by one faithful servant.

But the rest of them still remained. As soon as I returned home and David had put the horses and carriage away, I called everyone into the parlor. There, with the portraits of my ancestors looking down on me with expressions of faint disbelief, I explained the decision I had made, and set out how we must bring about their freedom, given the laws of the land.

As I spoke, I watched all the faces I had known since my childhood go slack with shock, then brighten with the most astonished hope. They glanced at one another while I laid out the terms, and I could all but hear their questions. *Does Miss Helen really mean it? Do we dare to believe it's true?*

"You may live where you will," I told the servants, "here or at some other place, if you have family or friends you'd prefer. If you choose to live at Eudaimonia, I will pay you for the work you do—the same wages any white domestic earns. You may also go and work elsewhere, if you can find folk who are willing to hire you, and if you do, you will keep all the money you earn, every penny. The law will still regard you as part of the Bywater estate, but from this moment forward, I will treat you all as free people."

Silence filled the parlor. No one dared twitch a muscle. The servants only watched me, each bearing that cautiously neutral expression which I have come to know so well. I realized that the poor souls couldn't bring themselves to believe what I had promised. It must have struck them as too much to hope for.

It was David who finally ventured to speak. "Miss Helen, how can we know for sure that you mean what you say? The part about you treating us as free."

That caught me out, and I confess I felt rather flustered. Why shouldn't David and the rest take me at my word? Hadn't I always been good to them? Before I could react with hurt or outrage, I remembered the lives these people have lived. Before they came to Eudaimonia, they were at other estates, and no doubt each had tasted more than his share of injustice at the hands of people who looked like me. Anyhow, no justice can be had when one man proclaims ownership of another, no matter how gentle his intentions might be. I had inflicted suffering upon each and every person in that room. I used no lash upon their bodies, but a lash upon the spirit bites as viciously and leaves a lasting pain.

"What if I were to swear it?" I suggested. "I'll make an oath before God."

The servants looked at one another and, in their silent conference, came to an agreement.

"I think that will do, Miss Helen," David said. "But we must have contracts, too, the same as you would give to any white domestic."

We entered then into protracted negotiations. For more than an hour, with all of us gathered around the dining table, I wrote every concern and demand of my workers, reading back the list and making alterations until each was satisfied that his or her concerns would be suitably met. They raised potential problems that I had never foreseen—not only the dangers of the Fugitive Slave Act and its threat to travel, but issues of property ownership, inheritance, accommodation, and security of pay. And a detail of expected duties for each individual worker, with a clear understanding that any work falling outside that list was not to be expected of them. As I worked over the papers, I couldn't help but laugh inwardly, for Caleb and all those who would uphold slavery believe these folks to be simple-minded. Why, the workers of Eudaimonia certainly have a more sophisticated understanding of how one runs an estate than I've ever possessed. I counted myself lucky that I should be on their side. I would be no match for any of them in a court of law, and I told them as much when we were all in agreement that their demands and securities would satisfy.

"Speaking of the law," I said, "I will call on Mr. Wyckoff first thing tomorrow morning and have him write all of this up into proper contracts. He's a sympathetic soul who has helped others to free their slaves . . . at least, as far as current laws permit. I'm ready to take that oath now, David. Please, go and fetch the Bible from the drawing room."

David held the Bible while I placed my hand upon it and swore, on pain of my soul's eternal salvation, that I would uphold my word and the terms of our forthcoming contracts, and treat all the people of Eudaimonia as free.

And now I sit again at my little table by the window, in my bedroom, which I made ready myself, for there are no servants now to help me. Oh, I feel sure that a few of the women will stay on, and David, too, for they haven't any family in the area. So the house will go on being tended, and I will have a spare hand when I need it to help me dress or fix my hair. But they will be paid for their work, the same as any white servant.

The cost can be sustained for now. Over the course of years, however, this arrangement will strain the accounts. I don't expect Caleb Cary to uphold our engagement once word gets out that the slaves of Eudaimonia are as good as free. Nor do I expect that another bachelor will show any interest, for despite the great estate I have inherited, my predilection for

Northern ways will soon be a byword in society. But I will not allow such thoughts to trouble me now. There is wealth enough in Eudaimonia to provide for all my servants in the short term—true servants now, well paid for their work, held no longer in bondage. The money Father left to me will last for a few years at least before I need to worry over an income.

In any case, a little thing like money doesn't seem worth crying over—nor does the judgment of society, which will surely come, too, in its time. When my soul feels light as a feather and clean as a new sheet, I don't want to fret and frown. I want to sing like the birds of the morning.

October 18, 1859

What a dark day this has been. Mr. Caleb Cary turned up late in the morning, while I was still not quite dressed. Without a girl to help me, I was obliged to brush and pin and lace myself into some semblance of order, and then I went down to greet him, braced for an unpleasant confrontation. What could have brought him to Eudaimonia without first sending a card? Nothing good, I told myself as I descended the stairs. And wasn't I just about right!

Mr. Cary had been left in the parlor to await me. I found him pacing the room like a tiger in a cage. When I said my hello, he whirled to stare at me with daggers in place of his eyes. Never have I seen the man so flustered, and of course I knew at once that all his red-faced anger was for me.

"Just what do you think you're doing?" he demanded. "What on earth have you done?"

There was no need to ask him to clarify this outburst. I knew full well what had upset him.

With all the cool dignity I could muster, I answered, "It's no business of yours, Mr. Cary, what I do with my property."

I hoped my distaste never showed in my expression. To think I'd gone all my life referring to those good servants as *property*! But how else could I speak of them to Caleb? He is dead set on upholding the old ways.

He came very near me then, close enough to grab my wrist or to strike me if he chose. His anger was hot as a forge. Every instinct screamed at me to run from him, for I thought it very likely that he would try to hurt me in his rage. But I thought of Mary Jane, and all the others who have faced the fury of men like Caleb. I stood my ground and held my chin high, though my blood ran cold at the danger.

"Don't you see what you've done, what you've started here in Richmond?" he shouted. "Harper's Ferry is all your fault. The fault of people like you."

"Will you please explain?" I said as coolly as I could.

That seemed to startle him out of his anger—or the worst of it, anyhow. He said, "Haven't you heard what happened at Harper's Ferry?"

I confirmed that I had not heard the news. He reached into his coat and extracted that morning's copy of the *Richmond Whig*. The terrible story was printed on the first page.

I sank into one of the parlor chairs as I read. John Brown, abolitionist and veteran of the battles in Kansas, led an attack on the arsenal at Harper's Ferry, which lies some hundred and fifty miles to the north. Over three days, several men were killed. The account of the fighting was gruesome indeed. The thought of such violence made me sick to my stomach.

"This sort of thing will spread," Caleb growled when I set the paper aside. "No one will be safe. They'll come for everyone, sooner or later."

I said, "John Brown and all his men were caught and imprisoned. The paper said so. They'll stand trial, and I have no doubt they'll be hanged for such a shocking attack."

Caleb resumed his pacing. "I don't mean the abolitionists. White men can at least be reasoned with. But this attack, this *insurrection*, will put ideas into their heads. They'll get uppity—all of them, right down to the basest field hand and the pot girls in the kitchens. And they'll come looking for revenge, looking for blood!"

I felt very calm and assured as I answered. "Mr. Cary, why do you continue to uphold an institution that makes you so fearful?"

"Fearful?" he spat. "I'm not afraid of those savages!"

"If slavery were the natural order," I went on, quite unruffled by his outburst, "or the Lord's true will, then each person would keep to his rightful place without any laws or traditions to compel him. If the Black man were so perfectly suited to slavery, you would have no cause to fear an uprising of slaves."

Caleb stopped his pacing then. He stared at me with an expression both stunned and hateful. "When I heard the rumor that you'd freed your slaves, Helen, I didn't want to believe it. But now I see that it is true. You *are* an abolitionist, after all."

Indeed, I am. But in that moment, as I watched Caleb fuming across the parlor, I was keenly aware that in the wake of Harper's Ferry, anyone who believes as I do would be in double danger. For my own safety, I had no choice but to prevaricate as much as my recent actions would allow.

"I am not an abolitionist," I said, "not exactly. I don't agree with everything those people say. If I did, I would move up north and live among them. I only think that everything must change with the times. Nothing stays the same forever, Mr. Cary. Perhaps the *peculiar institution*, as the abolitionists like to call it, has become too peculiar for modern times. Perhaps society must adjust its views on such matters, rather than holding to old ways till they've become positively ancient."

Before I could say more (I could feel a whole oratory building within) he cut me off with a snarl.

"I can't marry a woman who hates tradition, who won't respect the natural order, who despises my very way of life. I'm sorry, Miss Bywater, but you must consider our engagement broken. Good day, and goodbye."

Well, he paced right out of the parlor and out of Eudaimonia. For good, I hope and pray. I certainly didn't shed a tear over his words or his departure.

For the better part of an hour, I sat with the *Whig* folded on the table beside me—that paper with its account of all that transpired at Harper's Ferry. Left alone with my thoughts, I gave them ample consideration till they were quite firm and decided. I realized, first, that I was nothing short of relieved to know that Caleb Cary was out of my life forever. And second, I knew that Caleb had spoken correctly. I *did* hate this tradition. With everything in me, with all my heart and soul, I despised the bondage of good people and believed, as the Quakers had taught me, that *all* people are made with an equal share of God. The bright spark of divinity lives in us all.

Even most abolitionists don't feel as I do—that we are *all* brothers and sisters, with none set higher than any other, whether male or female, light skinned or dark. Oh, I am daily reminded that I was never meant for this time!

I do fear that Caleb may have been correct about more than my personal convictions. Was this attack on Harper's Ferry the beginning of what I foresaw weeks ago, with the coming of the auroras? All this time, I haven't forgotten that vision—bodies lying still in a misty field, so many dead I could never count them, and the earth soaked with blood. No, surely that was no presentiment but only a waking nightmare. I am no Cassandra, cursed to see the future. I am only an ordinary woman.

Much disturbed in my spirit, I took myself out to the back garden, well away from the house, and sank down into the tall grass below the peach trees to have my bout with the angels.

The air was still and sweet with a memory of summer. Above me hung a confusion of twisted branches and the blue fragments of sky, dry, ruddy leaves, and a dazzle of sunlight.

"If that vision was true," I prayed, "that sight I saw of marching men and guns and cannons and horses, then send me a sign now, Lord. Show me now what lies ahead, and I will trust for all time that this is no curse, but a gift which I will forever use in service to the greater good."

The vision struck with such potent force that I knew it was not my imagination. The wonder of having one's prayer answered so immediately was overshadowed by the horror of what I witnessed. The branches of the trees vanished behind a great, dark vista of churning images. I still don't know whether I saw truly, with my eyes, or whether the sights appeared only in my mind. They were vivid as true life, either way. I saw the confusion of battle—men and horses rushing this way and that, gunfire bursting, the thrust of bayonets. I saw a tangle of snakes, writhing in a massive and repulsive knot, and I knew it to be the politicians of Washington, with their seething manipulations. Bloated bodies left on the field for the birds to peck and the flies to blow. Every manner of treachery—brother killing brother, children starved and abused and left for dead. And all of it was overflown by the same banners of light that had shone down upon the world at the summer's end.

Then, at last, I understood. The auroras truly had been a sign—a *sign*, as in the Book of Revelation, a Heavenly warning that the end had come.

And yet, even as I cried out in all my fear and awe, I sensed something more. The End may be upon us now, but something is stirring beyond the clash and the turmoil, beyond the shock of abruption. There is another reality, already formed, waiting for its chance to assert itself. That new emergence is utterly different from the world that surrounds me now. That future will come, whatever men like Caleb Cary might wish for, whatever they might insist with their armies and their laws. Righteousness cannot be stopped; it is the very will of the Creator. And once the great transformation has come, there will be no returning to the old ways. The future I have seen, the better world I long for, lies beyond this terrible threshold, which now the whole nation must cross together, or perish in the crossing.

With my growing reputation for abolition, it seems likely that I never will marry, never will know the blessing of motherhood. But as I knelt below the orchard trees with these visions spinning through my mind, I understood that the great disruption to come will be like the birthing of a baby. With every birth, so I have heard, there is pain and suffering. There is blood, and fear, and no small amount of screaming. And then, in the urgent and final rush, the sweet promise of a new-made life.

This is a dangerous time, as every birth is. What struggles to come into this world and what struggles to bring it forth might both be lost in the battle. But once the pains of labor have begun, there is no stopping them. Life and death stand together at the threshold. One will triumph, or the other will.

That first night of the auroras, I stood on my balcony with Mary Jane and looked upon the arrows of the North. Caleb is wrong. I know this in my heart. The South will fall, and as God is my witness, I will do whatever in me lies to ensure that it does.

10

Derryn

2053

The rumble of another distant explosion vibrated through the bunker. How many times had the Sovereigns bombed the suburbs beyond the college walls? Derryn had long since lost count, but she had felt every one of those detonations, a deep, growling pulse through the concrete. She rolled over on her cot, eyes gritty from lack of sleep. She had spent most of the night listening to the muffled booms, each one a reminder of how close danger had come.

Twenty hours in the underground shelter. The tension was becoming unbearable. Faculty members and students huddled in small groups, their voices low and strained. Now and then, a lightscreen activated in the open space of the bunker as the anxious evacuees attempted to contact their loved ones despite the Weave's spotty connection. Whenever a screen appeared, its glow cast the interior of the shelter in a stark and pallid light. All those people, waiting to learn whether their homes and their livelihoods had been destroyed. Desperate souls hunched and quiet with a long, unrelenting misery.

During the long, dark hours, Derryn's thoughts had returned endlessly to the Bywater cache. The fact that so many priceless artifacts had been left sitting vulnerable gnawed at her conscience. Those paintings—Helen's visions of the future—were an irreplaceable testament to the shifting nature of reality, to the hard, implacable fact that all things changed. No institution, no culture, not even scientific frameworks or theories remained in permanence. Even humankind's understanding of time and physics would be challenged, tested, altered forever when the mystery of Helen's artwork was revealed.

And if the Sovereigns discovered those paintings . . .

Derryn sat up with a sudden energy, casting her blanket aside. These thoughts never got her anywhere. She had entertained the same bleak fear since descending into this hell. Rumination had yielded nothing of use. She might as well put her wakefulness to some purpose and check in with Leo.

She stalked across the shelter to the supply alcove, where at least she could talk to her brother with a modicum of privacy. When she tapped the power button on her CoreTex, it woke with a melodious chime. Her scalp prickled in the old, comforting way as the headset emanated its field of energy. Derryn was surrounded and filled by a warm awareness of expansion. Even here, underground in a war-blighted backwater, the Weave existed beyond the physical boundaries of self—the great, shared mind in all its vastness, flowing among the people of the earth.

"Good morning, Derryn," Tyko said.

She kept her voice low. "Good morning, Tyko. Is Leo online?"

"I've just received his request to join you," the AI answered. "He must have noticed that you'd connected."

"Put him through, please. I'd love to talk to him."

The lightscreen activated, and a moment later, there was her brother, sitting at his kitchen bar, sipping a cup of espresso, dressed in his pajamas with his dark hair still a mess from sleep. His husband and kids must have still been in bed, for the living room behind him was empty. The undisturbed peace of a Saturday morning back home, where everything was safe and sane, eclipsed Derryn's present misery.

Gratefully, she focused on the screen and let her awareness of the bunker fade behind its comforting light.

"Still in your rustic accommodations, I see," Leo said.

"Yep, still here."

"Do drills really last that long?"

Derryn felt his emotions through the Weave—caution bordering on disbelief. Leo was dangerously close to discovering her fib. She had to think on her toes to deflect his worry.

"Turns out, we found ideal conditions for working on the paintings down in the shelter we used for yesterday's drill."

Leo set down his cup and eyed her with frank skepticism. She could feel his suspicion, a pulsing tightness at her temples.

"Really," Derryn said. "Microclimate, ambient humidity—boring art preservation stuff. You wouldn't be interested in the details."

"Then why does it feel like you're lying?"

Derryn chuckled. "I don't know. I'm probably still a little rattled from the drill. But everything's fine here, really."

He paused, and Derryn could feel him searching their connection again, reading the energetic waves of her mind. She concentrated on an inner peace that seemed impossibly far away, tried to fill herself with confident thoughts.

"Well," Leo finally said, "how's the work going?"

"Just great. I even found the artist's journals. Hopefully, they'll shed some light on why she decided to make such unusual art."

Leo sipped from his cup. His wry interest ran through Derryn in a jagged wave.

"Journals, hey? Any good dirt in there? I bet they got up to all kinds of kinky stuff in the Victorian era."

She laughed. "I haven't had a chance to check it out yet—only the first entry. It's all in old handwriting, of course, so Tyko has to transcribe the cursive into text. Otherwise it'd take me hours to get through a single page."

Before Derryn could say more, the harsh tone of an emergency alert sounded in her ears.

Leo set down his cup. "What the hell?"

His anxiety spiked. Or maybe that rush across the Weave was Derryn's own feelings, for the surge of alertness, anxiety, even fear felt too immediate, too sharp to be Leo's. Then she understood. It was *everyone* she was feeling, the hundreds of millions of minds on the Weave snapping to attention in the same instant, a unison acknowledgment of difference. Of danger.

She had time for only one swift thought: What kind of emergency could warrant alerts everywhere on the planet simultaneously? Then the call was interrupted by a text pop-up, obscuring her view of Leo and his home.

An AI spoke into the stunned silence. It wasn't Tyko. This one was feminine and authoritative, issuing instructions with a calm command that racked Derryn with dread. "This is a global emergency alert. The Weave has detected a coronal mass ejection of unusual size. Calculations place the orbit of Earth in the path of electromagnetic turbulence . . ."

Ears ringing with the force of her shock, Derryn didn't hear the rest. Yet her eyes ran over the text, taking in the bleak information. A massive solar flare, headed directly for the planet. Just like the geomagnetic storm that had woken Helen Bywater with its light nearly two hundred years ago. The Carrington Event, which Derryn had been on the verge of explaining to Leo . . .

She had no capacity to wonder over the strange coincidence of timing. All she could do was recall, in a rising panic, the information Tyko had provided about the magnitude of the great solar flare of 1859. She had thought—only yesterday!—that if such a disaster were to strike the earth in this technological age, the waves of magnetic energy would be potent enough to disable nearly every device that relied on chips and wires, the very systems that had kept a global society functional in the wake of America's second civil war. Every construct of the AI networks that regulated resources, maintained climate stability, and defended the planet against this very kind of disaster would surely be in grave danger.

"Oh my God," Leo said.

Somehow, Derryn managed to speak. "It says we have to shut everything down. All electrical grids, even the Weave."

"Mine says we have nine hours to prepare." Leo spoke slowly. He felt dazed, numb, across their connection. "Does yours say the same thing?"

Derryn nodded. She couldn't seem to make herself speak, couldn't be sure that she was breathing. The solid world seemed to dissolve into bits of information, scintillas of light that sped past her awareness until she felt as if she were suspended in the deep-black void of space. Her mind clamored with a frantic calculation of what this would mean . . . for everyone, everywhere, all around the globe. For the people who were stuck here in a bunker below Haverford College, pinned under the brutal thumb of the Human Heritage Movement.

She found no answers, only more questions that piled inside her head as the seconds ticked by and she floated farther into the vacuum of a disintegrating reality. There was no air here. She couldn't breathe.

"Derryn?" Leo said.

His voice—her name—her brother speaking to her across the thousands of miles that separated them. Leo snapped her back into the terrifying present.

"Are you safe where you are?" he said.

Derryn swallowed hard, sorted rapidly through her options. What could she tell him that wouldn't make this horror even worse? According to the alert, they would have to cut off all communication for six days, until the solar flare had passed. Power down every device that made modern life possible, revert to a pre-integration existence. Unless they wanted to fry those devices in a vat of magnetic fury—their devices, and the helpful, potentially sentient intelligences like Tyko, the invisible peers who populated the Weave's neverland.

There was nothing. Nothing she could say to Leo that wouldn't send him into this sudden darkness with a greater fear than Derryn had already forced him to carry. Why hadn't she turned down this damned job, like Leo had asked her to do? If she had only listened, she would be back home now, in the boring, predictable comfort of her condo. She would be on the safe side of the Blockade when the flare hit and the bright world she had known was eclipsed by a suffocating darkness.

"I'll be fine," she finally said, amazed at the coolness of her own voice, the confidence she didn't feel. "I'm perfectly safe where I am. I'll just lay low and take it easy until the storm passes."

Leo met her eye, held it with a desperate intensity. "Promise me you'll stay safe until everything is back online and I can talk to you again."

A chilling thought woke in Derryn's head, unfolding all its monstrous limbs with a terrible inevitability. What if the Weave hadn't made the right calculations? What if six days of shutdown weren't enough? What if, when everyone turned their devices back on, nothing happened—the Weave was *gone*? All the order and logic and data that had guided humanity across its most dangerous threshold, into a remade Eden, could be undone by this solar storm. It could all vanish, quick as switching off a light.

No, she told herself—no, no, that wouldn't happen. The Weave hadn't failed in any of its calculations so far. For a quarter of a century, the network of machine intelligences had been so precise and accurate that it had accomplished feats of geoengineering and resource management that all the human scientists of the world had declared impossible. Surely, this was nothing more than a hiccup of nature from the Weave's perspective, a math problem it could solve in its sleep, assuming AIs ever slept.

The Weave would bring itself safely through this catastrophe. And so would Derryn. She would survive this, too.

"I promise," she said to Leo. "Do what you need to do to get ready, and don't worry about me. We'll talk again in six days."

He stared at Derryn a moment longer, his mouth pressed into a thin, anxious line. "I love you, Squiggy."

"I love you, too."

Shaking, Derryn switched off her CoreTex and got up from the floor of the alcove. When she staggered back into the bunker's main room, she found all the faculty and students absorbed in their devices, reviewing the emergency alert or contacting the people they loved, talking in the low, clipped tones of the shock that still filled Derryn with a terrible, looming numbness. A professor of literature pressed her hands against the temple ports of her CoreTex as though the device might already be slipping away from her. Two young students embraced, whispering frantically while tears poured down their cheeks.

"What about the Sovereigns?" someone asked.

That was the same sly, hissing fear that had coiled in Derryn's mind since the alert had come.

Melinda lifted both hands as if to command the whole bunker's attention. "All right, everyone, remember to stay calm. This is a tough situation, but we'll make it through."

Would they? Derryn wondered. The Sovereigns may have rejected integration, but they still relied on technology for communication, and no doubt for many other tasks as well. Before she'd crossed the Blockade, Derryn had learned all she could about Sovereign culture, and knew that adherents of the Human Heritage Movement permitted themselves the use of smartphones, GPS, and a firewalled internet much like the one that had existed in the early part of the century. Those things might be primitive by contemporary standards, but they would still be affected by the solar flare. And if the Sovereigns lost what little technology they had . . . if their bizarre ideology caused them to panic in the face of an infrastructural disaster . . .

Derryn tried to imagine how the Sovereigns might interpret a global technological shutdown. The only answers that suggested themselves were divine judgment or opportunity for violent domination. Either way, she didn't intend to remain like a sitting duck in this damned bunker with a rebel faction just outside the college walls, eyeing its open space for their next commune.

Derryn returned to her cot, sat trembling on its edge.

"Tyko," she murmured.

"I'm here, Derryn."

His familiar, steady voice brought a lump to Derryn's throat. She wouldn't speak to him again for days—maybe never again, if something went wrong with the Weave, if this solar storm proved too much for a technological planet to handle.

"I need to get to New York before the shutdown," Derryn said.

"I understand. Would you like me to search for available transportation?"

"Please. Any kind will do."

While Tyko worked, Derryn paced the shelter, trying not to allow her thoughts to stray to the darkest outcomes. It was mostly a futile effort. As the minutes wore on—an eternity for the workings of an AI—she began to face the brutal fact. There would be no fleeing to New York before the solar flare hit.

Confirmation came soon enough. Tyko's voice broke into her worry. "I've completed my search. There are no available air cabs or other transportation services to New York City. All commercial transportation was booked within minutes of the alert."

"What about back to Cascadia?"

"I'm afraid that's not possible at this time, either. All outbound transportation from the Eastern territories is at capacity. I even checked for ground options like buses and rideshares."

Derryn closed her eyes. Grim acceptance settled into her, taking the worst edge off her panic. "I'll have to walk, then."

"Walking to New York City would require approximately four days at a sustainable pace," Tyko calculated. "The journey would involve crossing potentially hostile territory controlled by factions of the Human Heritage Movement."

"I know the risks, but I can't stay here."

"Why not? Is your present situation unsafe?"

Derryn didn't know how to answer. Despite Melinda's reassurances, the fear was evident on every face. A massive, days-long solar flare had clearly thrown a wrench into the locals' risk calculation. She eyed the weeping students, the urgent expressions of those who still worked on their devices, searching for transportation of their own or making grim farewells to their loved ones. The bunker no longer seemed as safe as everyone had proclaimed it to be. Underground, there wasn't even any hope that they might be able to run from the Sovereigns.

She could find no words for these thoughts. Instead, she projected raw feeling, reflecting all her fear and desperation back at Tyko.

"Remember to breathe," the AI said. "Follow the instructions of those around you. They've been through Sovereign attacks before."

"Not an attack like this," Derryn muttered. "Nobody knows how the Sovereigns will react when their own tech is fried. They might become more deadly than ever, for all anyone can say. I can't stay here. Not for six whole days. Not for another minute; I just *can't.* Without any tech of my own? And it'll be dark, Tyko! Pitch black for six days, with the electrical grids shut down." New York. She had promised Leo she would get to the city if anything bad happened. Now she was determined to reach the blockade no matter what. "Please request a call with my contact Alexis Baker."

While she waited for the connection, Derryn paced along one wall. The lights of the bunker flickered and buzzed. No doubt, the local grid was already under significant strain as people rushed to charge their cars and any other devices that could operate during the outage. The call to Alexis took longer than anticipated, too. The Weave staggered under the strain of its panicked users, all trying to set their affairs in order before six days of darkness fell.

Alexis appeared on Derryn's lightscreen, their small but colorful apartment visible in the background. They blinked in a stupor, as dazed and horrified as Derryn had ever known them to be.

"Are you still in Philly?" Alexis asked. "I heard about the fighting there—"

"For now, I am, but I'm coming to New York. I can still stay with you, I hope."

"Of course you can. But how will you get here? There isn't a cab available in the whole city. I expect the situation is even worse out there."

"It's worse, all right, but I'll figure something out."

She recorded Alexis's address in her virtual notebook. Later she would write it down on some physical substance while she prepared her backpack and found some way out of the bunker.

"I haven't been to New York since my college days," Derryn said, "and I won't have the Weave to help me navigate. If I can't find you on my own, can we set a meeting place? Some landmark I'll be able to find easily without GPS."

"St. Barbara's Church in Bushwick. You can't miss it—huge stone building with a bell tower, all white, the most unmistakable sight in Brooklyn, except for the bridge. Anyone in the borough will be able to tell you how to get there, even without the Weave. I'll check in at the church every day at noon and stay for a few hours. It isn't far from my place."

"Perfect," Derryn said. "I'll see you soon."

Now that a destination was fixed before her like a guiding star, she felt a little more confident. Marginally.

"Tyko," she said, "please generate a detailed map of a walking route from my present location to the address saved in my notes."

Derryn would find paper and old-fashioned writing utensils back in the VRC. She had to visit the workroom one last time, anyhow, to secure the cache as best she could against a Sovereign invasion. There, she would copy the map from her lightscreen onto paper. It was a primitive solution to this current mess, but it was a damn sight better than cowering in the bunker while she waited for the Sovereigns to find her.

One way or another, she would get behind the New York blockade. She had made a promise to Leo, and she would keep her word, or die trying.

11

Helen

April 4, 1860

What a shock to look at these pages and see that I have not written since autumn!

The truth is, I've been in a blue state—the very deepest of blues. I had expected that society would cast me out once it was broadly known that I have freed my slaves (or whatever I may call the strange state of legal entanglement in which we find ourselves now, the good workers of Eudaimonia and me, their mistress on paper but not in practice). However, I must confess that I was ill-prepared for the realities of being a suspected abolitionist in the proud city of Richmond.

Now that the months have flown and this diary is well behind the times, I must do my best to explain all that has happened between the middle of last October and now.

John Brown was hanged early in the month of December. The *Richmond Whig* reported on it, one small paragraph stating the facts with cold precision. When I read the news, I managed to hold back my tears until I was safely in my room. I didn't only weep from sorrow. It was fear, too, for in the death of that rash but heroic man I saw my own fate. Those who would see this practice ended for good will find no love in these Southern states. I am not fool enough to believe that my sex will save me from the hangman's rope, if it should come to that.

Once when I was small, and inconsolable over some meaningless thing (a broken doll, a rainy day that prevented me from playing outside), Kitty took me into the kitchen and, to distract me from my tears, showed me "a magic trick, Miss Helen." She put a spoonful of bicarbonate soda into a dish, then poured vinegar over it, and the resulting drama took me quite out of my mood and made me forget all about whatever had troubled me. I made Kitty perform the trick again and again, watching with fascination as the foam of a chemical reaction burst up out of the bowl and overflowed its rim.

Such a happy memory, yet now I see it in a very different light. This country has lost its head with fear, and what has fear ever made but hate? Hate, in turn, breeds a greater fear, until everything bursts with a rush of emotion, like vinegar poured over soda. That unstoppable reaction causes men and women alike to do things they would never consider in their right frame of mind. Every step I take outside my door is placed with the greatest care. At any moment, the reaction might burst around me. I might be overwhelmed by the horrors my neighbors have imagined, the danger they've invented in their own minds.

I walk a dangerous road in Richmond. Yet I cannot bring myself to leave my home and flee to the North, where at least I needn't fear the very people I once counted as friends.

From one day to the next, even hour by hour, I have swung back and forth like a pendulum—now fearing my neighbors and now despising them as fools—and despising myself just as much, for did I not once believe as they did? In the streets, the talk is all of freedom, of the rights of Virginia and other states to make whatever laws its citizens please. But the word "freedom" is twisted here. In Richmond, in Virginia, everywhere across the South, it means nothing more than the right to deprive others. Can they not see the truth? Are they so blind to their own dire predicament? I know full well what prevents them from opening their eyes, for I too once comfortably slept in the assurance that all was well, that this way of life was tradition and therefore rightful and good. Yet now I feel such an urgency to wake them. I would ring a bell in the black of night, if there were one to ring. Oh, Richmond, why won't you *see*? In binding others, you have bound yourselves to a way of life that's dying—that *must* die, as leaves must wither and fall before the approach of winter.

On the night of the Whitakers' grand Christmas ball, I stood on my balcony, swaddled in the old wool blanket from Father's cedar trunk, listening to the revelry across Church Hill. I couldn't see the Whitakers' place, but I could hear the faint strains of the orchestra. The sounds came to me like ghosts on the wind, melancholy and whispering.

Of all the prominent ladies in Richmond, I alone had been left off the guest list. It was no more than I had expected. When I freed my people, I knew I would be cast to the far edges of society. As I shivered and sniffed and listened to the faint sounds of merriment, I said to myself, "Well, what is a ball, anyhow? An evening of forced conversation with tedious, leering men. And overwarm rooms that stink of too much perfume, and punch that's never cold enough, and clumsy gentlemen who tread all over one's toes during the Virginia reel yet expect one to behave as if they're the finest creatures God ever made. Fiddlesticks to all of it!"

I told myself on that night that I need nothing but my little studio and the scenes I paint upon my canvases. But the truth is, I feel the loss and the loneliness like a dagger in my heart. I haven't missed a major party since my debut ten years ago. Balls may be tiresome in their way, but I can't help wondering whether any of my old friends noticed my absence or wished I was there.

But clarity came to me, too, that night on the icy wind. December's bitter chill sharpened my mind, and I perceived all our precious traditions as I never had before. This desperate clinging to the old ways isn't about cotton yields or the price of tobacco, whatever the *Whig* may proclaim, whatever our men may tell themselves. This construct—this society with its balls and forms and traditions—is nothing more than a feeble attempt at playing king. Every plantation owner fancies himself the monarch of a miniature country. Every gentleman imagines himself a ruler in the most absolute and final terms, for the present laws allow him to dispense justice or mercy to his slaves, according to his whim. The politicians and even well-meaning members of the church may pretty it up with talk of economics and tradition, but one needn't scratch these arguments very hard to expose a base and ugly substance below the gilding. Under their justifications, there lies a raw desire to be elevated, to have others bow and scrape, to never question one's own supremacy.

Is this not what drove King George to such tyranny that our grandfathers rebelled? Yet here we are, not a century later, harnessing our way of life to the same cruel machinery our forefathers died to escape. Oh, but so long as *we* may call ourselves the kings and queens—why, *then* it's no great evil to build a kingdom on broken backs and spilled blood!

Christmastime was a lonely season. I passed it with Kitty and Ruthie and David, in quiet communion and grateful prayer, where before I would have been off to some party or other, some glittering ball, nearly every night till the new year came. The sting of rejection is felt only on the surface. The very society that shuts me out is like a stately oak, so strong and fine to look at until a windstorm comes, and then the limbs are ripped away, the trunk is torn asunder, and the beautiful illusion is shattered. When the hollow void is exposed, one can see the disease at the heart, the rot that has eaten away what once was good and worthy of admiration. So, I shall leave them to their parties and their little palaces. Let them cling to their crowns made of cotton and corn. I still believe, as the founders declared, that in America, we have no use for kings.

In February, Abraham Lincoln made a splendid speech in New York, a cry against the spread of slavery. He is a representative in Congress, from the state of Illinois, and my goodness, does that man ever have a way with words! The *Whig* and the other Richmond papers reported on the speech, of course, and printed Lincoln's words in full—not in favor of the man, but railing against him. I read the columns with no small amount of cheer. Lincoln's speech gave me hope that, with time and patience and the offering of goodwill, perhaps all men might come to see with clearer eyes. Perhaps we may yet free ourselves from the puppet strings of fear.

Is it too much to hope that this Lincoln fellow might run for president? Surely, that's a wish that can never come true, for he ran once already, many years ago, without success. He lost his bid for the Senate last year, too. I doubt we shall ever see such an admirable man in the White House, but one can always dream.

Happily, not all the goings-on these past months have been lonesome and sad. Mary Jane excels at the old Quaker school, as I knew she would, and her letters are a constant source of entertainment.

The girl has a fine hand and a good command of spelling. She improves with each new letter, too. In her letters, she conveys all the proper sentiments a young lady might write to a benefactress—gratitude for her education, observations on the weather and customs of Pennsylvania, and of course, regular inquiries after my health. But she also proposed a "secret code" back in December, merely for a little fun, I think. The code works like this: One takes the first letter of the first word, the second letter of the second word, and so on until the hidden message is perceived. It's only a girlish pastime, but I confess that Mary Jane and I have shared many laughs, putting silly, inconsequential messages into this code. It does keep the mind limber, if nothing else, and I look forward every week to another note from the girl.

May 20, 1860

Again, I must make my apologies for failing to update this diary with any regularity. But I am run ragged these days, seeing to the care of the house. Two of the ladies who once worked here have taken their leave, as is their right, and have gone north to work for a seamstress in Albany. The expense was considerable, for I insisted that they must travel with guards. Under no circumstances will I allow any of Eudaimonia's people to fall victim to the Fugitive Slave Act. I wish them well in their new lives, though I have suffered an unpleasant awakening in their absence. What a great burden it is to care for a home of Eudaimonia's size and elegance! Now I take part myself in the washing and dusting, the lighting of lamps and the care of the gardens. All this labor leaves me wrung out by the end of the day. I've had little energy for painting. Every spare ounce of my mental powers goes to the accounts. They are still flush enough, yet I am all too aware that I'm likely to remain an old maid for all my life. With no hope for a husband's income, I must keep one eye sensibly on the future. The estate's reserve must be carefully managed. I've begun thinking lately about which of Father's old investments I might liquidate, and when might be the best time to do so. I've made a list of what expenditures I may cut so that I can continue paying Kitty, Ruthie, and David for many years to come . . . and, of course, so that I may keep Mary Jane at the school she loves so well.

Lately I have often mused on the idea of selling Eudaimonia. I suppose it would be the most prudent course of action, but I feel too heartsick at the prospect. This is my home, after all, even if Richmond watches me with suspicious eyes. I simply can't bring myself to part with the place.

Ah, well! There is enough money in the coffers to last several more years if we live frugally. And since I am no longer invited to parties and balls, I needn't spend on new dresses, or even alterations to the old ones. As Milton said, the sable cloud shows her silver lining.

Here is another pocketful of cheer. Earlier this spring, I recalled Father's old cabin on the trail to Bush Hill. Goodness, I hadn't thought of the place for years and hadn't seen it with my own eyes since I was a girl. It's a wonder I remembered the cabin at all. It isn't much of a house to speak of—one room with an old stone fireplace, nothing more than that. Father built it with his brothers when he was a young bachelor and lived there till his mercantile flourished in town and he could afford to build Eudaimonia (which, of course, won Mother's heart). It occurred to me last month that I might sell the cabin, though surely such a rustic accommodation won't fetch much money. Still, it was an asset to consider, so David and I made the long trek across town and up the forested trail to the site of Father's old haunt.

The cabin is in better condition than I'd hoped to find. When I stood within its old, white-chinked walls with the dry leaves of seasons past rattling around my feet, a burst of inspiration struck me. I have decided not to sell the place yet. Since my casting-out from society, I've been too lonesome and blue. What I need now is both friends and society . . . Or, to be more precise, I need the Society of Friends. I have decided that I must go back to my roots; I shall dedicate the cabin as a meetinghouse for worship in the Quaker fashion, without preachers or tithes, with the door always open to any soul who seeks comfort, companionship, and divine communion with that one great Spirit who made us all.

David thought it a splendid idea and claimed that many people like him would come to my meetings—those who are still enslaved by the letter of the law, but freed by the clever machinations of my sort of folk.

"*Are* there my sort of folk in Richmond?" I asked him, laughing.

"Oh, yes, Miss Helen," David assured me. "Not as many as one might like, but enough to make a difference. The times are changing, sure enough, no matter what some other folks prefer."

Word has made its way around the city and its environs. Twice a week, on Sunday mornings and Wednesday afternoons, I ride out to my humble meetinghouse. Some days, I admit, there is no one present but myself—myself, and the good, sweet stillness of God. But there are other days when I am joined by a variety of souls, strangers all, yet Friends when we shake each other's hands.

The first few times I sat in silent worship with Black participants, I confess (with no small amount of shame) that I was reluctant to come too close to them, and I balked at taking their hands. I had thought I'd dug out all my prejudices and thrown them on the fire, but certain moments in the meetinghouse have taught me otherwise. A mistrust of those with dark skin—excepting the ones I've known since my childhood—still lives in me, it seems.

Well, it's another job to be done: Hunt down the remnants of hate within me. Yes, that means I must learn to look more kindly on my own people, too, those Southerners who have not yet found a better way of living. For aren't we all subject to the same pressures of society? They have been tricked by comfort and tradition, as I was tricked, and any of us might find in our hearts those better impulses of which Mr. Lincoln has spoken. It's time to rid myself once and for all of these tendencies toward superiority and exclusion.

In these balmy weeks since opening my meetinghouse, I have asked myself many times if my new Quaker ways won't make me even more peculiar in the eyes of Richmond society. But I can't afford to care for the opinions of others. My meetings bring me the only peace and clarity I've found since John Brown was hanged, and so I shall carry on.

But I really ought to think more about selling Eudaimonia. If I keep on much longer with these peculiar practices (which I have every intention of doing!), I shall have to leave Richmond, and sooner rather than later.

One last note before I close this book for the night. Abraham Lincoln has won the nomination. He will contend for the White House after all. It still seems too much to hope for, that such a fine, upstanding man might be our president. Yet as the old poem says, hope springs eternal in the human breast.

November 8, 1860

Lincoln has won the election. Only by the narrowest of margins, but he has won all the same, and I thank God for the blessing—though never where anyone else may hear.

What a shock to look at these pages and see how swiftly the time has flown without a word from me. All these months, I have followed the election closely. Daily I have read every issue of the *Whig*, gleaning the transcripts of speeches and debates for real news of the Republicans' progress. The *Whig*, you see, always reports on the news from Washington, but never without allowing the editor's feelings to show, and so I've become skilled at reading between the scornful lines to discern how matters really stand.

The race was terribly crowded. I supposed Bell would take the win, for he is so popular in the big Northern cities. Indeed, he did get the lion's share of votes, but in the end, only Lincoln had enough support with the college of electors.

Look at me, writing as if I were some scholar of politics! This is what happens when one becomes preoccupied by every blow in the fiercest and most consequential fight in a nation's history.

I am so glad for Lincoln's victory. Even the *Whig*'s sour reporting couldn't disguise that man's character. When I read the account of his debate with Douglas, I knew that Mr. Lincoln possessed the moral qualities to lead these United States through our darkest hours. I hold some hope that once Lincoln assumes control, all talk of rebellion will cease, and we will continue into the future without the threat of war.

Of course, I can say none of this in company, on the rare occasion when I do have company. I may be the only soul in Richmond who's rejoicing. All day, since we learned of Lincoln's win, there has been a ruckus from down the hill, where men have gathered in the streets to shout slogans and sing marching songs. "Secession now!" and "Death to Republicans!" The cries come drifting up to this peaceful neighborhood like a clarion calling men to battle.

What a silly carry-on. These men all seem to think that Lincoln's Republicans will sweep into the South on the backs of the army and occupy the states by force, merely because they've won the White House. Imagine such a thing! Mr. Lincoln strikes me as much too principled to use brute force. He is a man of intelligence and sympathetic compromise. Anyone who read his debate with Douglas could tell as much. If he should ever need to call up the army, I feel sure that he would do so only in the last extreme, and under great duress.

I shall pray each night that our new president will have no cause to do so.

December 21, 1860

This morning's issue of the *Whig* confirmed the whispers I heard at yesterday's market: South Carolina has broken with the Union. All day long, I didn't permit myself to believe, despite the truth in hard black ink right there on the pages of the papers.

The truth didn't settle into my mind until this afternoon, but then I felt its weight, cold and bleak in my heart. A winter storm was blowing in from the east, and I went out onto my balcony to watch the great, dark mass of clouds advance upon Richmond. Nature's drama and dread echoed the turmoil in my breast.

The iron rail of my balcony was bitterly cold, but I gripped it with both hands and watched those clouds boil with an angry power. Stirred by the highest winds of heaven, the thunderhead buckled and flowed back upon itself, and whirled high above the earth—so much like the movement of those brilliant lights that, for a moment, my fears were stilled by remembrance. It was little more than a year ago that the aurora came to alter my life forever. It seems as if a lifetime has passed. There are days when I fear that Mr. Cary was correct. Surely the lights were an omen of all the dreadful things that have followed since. And worse is yet to come.

A rising wind carried the smoky odor of snow. Thunder pealed in the distance, rattling the windowpanes behind me. So we will have both this evening—lightning and ice, silence and noise. The rarity of this weather only adds to my foreboding. Since learning of the secession, I can't escape the memory of those visions. I do not mean my beloved and longed-for future, but rather the nearer time, the cursed and sorrowful hours when the bodies will lie thick as autumn leaves on the ground, when the air will choke with the stench of gun smoke. When the earth will gorge itself on the blood of brothers.

Is this my fate—to be the Cassandra of the modern age? For I see what's coming, clear as day, yet I know that none would believe me if I dared to speak of these visions.

December 28, 1860

When I was a child, Father kept several sets of dominoes in a fine, lacquered box. On rainy afternoons, he would allow me to play with them. Those small ivory slabs enchanted me—their smooth surface and pearly shine, the mystery of the dark pips arranged in what was then, to my child self, a language of unfathomable complexity.

For hours, I would fascinate myself with Father's dominoes. I learned how to stand them up on the drawing-room floor in designs that grew more intricate as I grew older. Spirals, stars, and branching trees would extend across the room while the rain beat on the windows. Sometimes my designs stretched from the fireplace to the bookshelves.

Only when the pattern was set to my liking did I bring the game to the height of its enjoyment. With one finger, I would tip the first domino, then watch as each piece fell in rapid succession. The drawing room would fill with a jolly clatter, and before my eyes, the picture I had laid out so carefully would transform into a new shape.

Sometimes Father would watch me play, his eyes shining at my childish wonder.

"Helen," he once said to me, "this is how history moves. Not in big leaps, like a horse jumping a fence, but just this way, one small thing tipping into another. It only takes one push for the first domino to fall, and once it has fallen, there's nothing one can do to stop the picture from changing."

I didn't understand him then. Lord help me, now I do.

The *Whig* reported this morning that Major Anderson has moved his garrison from Fort Moultrie to Fort Sumter in Charleston Harbor. A small thing, perhaps—a tactical decision made in the interest of security. Yet as I read the report, I heard the *click-click-click* of dominoes falling.

The first piece was surely tipped long ago. Was it Lincoln's election or John Brown's raid? The Missouri Compromise? Or did it fall even farther back, when the first slave ship landed on our shore?

The snows have blanketed Richmond, transformed the city into something soft and rounded and still. One would think that there is peace here, to look upon the pleasant quiet of the gardens and streets, the rooftops below Church Hill from which the smoke rises in homey banners. Beneath the stillness, I feel the tremor of a world that has already changed.

I have entertained a few parties whom I'd thought interested in buying Eudaimonia, but nothing has come of it, and now, with the dominoes falling, it seems unlikely that I shall be able to sell the place at all. If it's God's will that I must remain in Richmond through whatever is to come, then I shall be as brave as I can. Already, I am on my toes to deflect my neighbors' suspicion. I have the reputation of an irregular, one who refuses to do things the way others prefer. I walk along the cliff's edge, yet, since those miraculous lights (was it truly more than a year ago that I saw them?), I have freed myself from the burden of others' preferences, and my life has been better for it.

Not my social life, of course. *That* has suffered abominably. But the life within—the true life of one's heart—is freer and brighter than I have imagined it could be.

Nothing shall stop me from doing what I know to be right. Even if war comes—and it seems certain that it will—I intend to stand firm on my convictions and do all I can to aid the cause of change.

I have reached the last page of this diary. How fitting, that I shall start a new book as a new world unfolds for us all. I must make a better effort to write more routinely, for I have a presentiment that there will be much news in the months and years ahead.

12

Derryn

2053

Derryn gathered her few belongings as quickly as she could, hoping no one in the bunker would notice that she was preparing to leave. The last thing she wanted was to compound the worries of the Haverford staff, these good people whom she had come to regard as friends. They had enough to fear already without fretting over Derryn's safety. But she didn't have their comfort with bunkers and Sovereign attacks, and New York wasn't so far away. Surely, once she was out of this damned cave, she would find someone headed for the nearby blockade—someone with a biodiesel car or a fully charged EV capable of reaching Derryn's destination.

Before she left the campus, however, she needed to secure the cache. While the others in the bunker were distracted with their own preparations, she slipped back through the dark corridor and out through the hidden panel of the empty workroom, then stole along the silent length of the great hall's basement until she found the VRC.

Thank goodness her key card still worked on the door; she had half expected the electronic world to be gone already. Alone in the VRC, she worked with more haste than was prudent, shoving the paintings she had last worked on back into their crate. She secured the lid and called up the forklift bot. It trundled across the room with a cheerful, chiming sound. Derryn's chest ached with an unaccountable pity as she watched the machine lift each crate and return them to the locker. Would this little bot survive the storm to come?

There was no more time to dwell on the future. Only the present mattered now, and every moment was slipping through her hands. Tyko had already saved the data from Derryn's work with the cache, storing everything in orderly files within the global cloud. But if the Weave were ruined, that data would be lost. And if the Sovereigns took the college, if they found the art and destroyed it . . . then everything would be gone. All evidence of Helen's remarkable work. All the proof that this world wasn't the fixed, unchangeable monolith of tradition that humanity had so long cherished, but rather a mutable reality where even time itself was no barrier. Derryn couldn't allow such a priceless discovery to vanish forever.

She removed all the devices she'd been using from the drawer of her workstation—the high-resolution cameras with which she'd taken all her backup images to augment Tyko's captures and the palm-sized audio recorder into which she had narrated descriptions of every painting. She removed the data chips from those devices and stowed them in an inner pocket of her backpack.

Next, she found a sheet of paper and an old ballpoint pen in one of the workstations. She tilted her face down to the countertop, aligning Tyko's map on her lightscreen atop the paper. Then she traced every mark with meticulous care. When the map was finished, she folded it and stowed it in a more accessible portion of the pack.

Finally, Derryn scooped the old, leather-bound books from the countertop—Helen's journals, which may yet provide insight into the artist's methods, may yet explain how a woman of the nineteenth century had managed to see with such astonishing accuracy into the distant future. The journals, too, were stored safely in the bag.

As she strode back across the VRC, a dark thought occurred to her. If, after all, she must walk to New York, how would she pass safely through occupied territory? The confrontation at the airport had been bad enough. If she were to meet a band of Sovereigns out there in the war-torn streets of Philadelphia—if the rebels were to find a woman like Derryn alone, without the aid of sympathetic strangers—they would do far worse to her than hurl epithets.

In a flash of inspiration, she recalled the Textile Arts room down the hall. She all but ran to the room and found to her relief that her key card worked as well on its door as on the VRC's. She made quick work of what she found inside, stripping the long Sovereign dress from its form and stuffing the garment into her pack. If she had to cross Sovereign territory alone, then a good disguise might make all the difference.

Back in the bunker, she approached Melinda with a placid smile.

"I've found someone to take me to New York City."

The dean stared at her in frank surprise. "You have?"

"My old friend from grad-school days, Alexis Baker. They're a professor now at Midwood. They've got enough charge in their skycar to fly down and get me, and they've asked me to stay with them until the solar flare has ended."

"Lucky you," Melinda said. "It sounds a lot more comfortable than riding out this fiasco in a bunker."

"I wish I could take all of you with me—especially you and Mihir. You've both been so good to me these past few days."

Melinda smiled easily. "Don't worry about us. We've got those escape tunnels I told you about. We can get out of here fast if the Sovereigns get too squirrelly—but whatever accommodations we find in the city, they won't be as plush as a friend's couch in New York."

"I went back to the VRC and locked up all the paintings," Derryn said. "I hope it'll be enough to keep them safe."

Melinda thanked her and hugged her tightly, then led her to the short hall where the doors to the escape tunnels waited.

For a moment Derryn hesitated, considering the three identical doors, heavy steel painted a bland olive gray with numbers near their top edges that meant nothing to her. There was no way to tell where any of the tunnels led.

"The one in the middle goes to the old St. Mary's Church in Ardmore, not too far beyond the college wall. You'll come out in a bunker like ours—a little smaller, but more or less the same. There's a parking lot at St. Mary's. A great place for your friend's skycar to land."

Derryn thanked her and embraced her again. Then she pulled open the heavy door and slipped into a passage of darkness.

Melinda shut the door behind her. Derryn stumbled several meters into dense shadow, one hand trailing along the tunnel's damp wall, before she remembered that she still wore her CoreTex. She activated the forward light with some trepidation. She hadn't charged the headset since the previous morning and had no idea how much longer its battery would last, but she needed light desperately now. It sent a crisp, white beam of illumination into the tunnel ahead, revealing nothing but walls and ceiling of thick concrete that pressed in much too closely for comfort. The air was thick with an odor of earth and time.

She walked for what felt like hours, the silence broken only by the sound of her footsteps and curiously muffled by the nearness of the walls. An intermittent dripping of water echoed faintly around her. Finally, just when she had nearly convinced herself that her mind was gone—that she had imagined or hallucinated everything, the journey to Pennsylvania, the Bywater cache, the bunker and the tunnel and the solar flare—she saw another steel door some fifteen or twenty meters ahead, barely illuminated at the farthest reach of her light's capacity.

Derryn ran the final distance, her breath coming in ragged, grateful heaves. She didn't hesitate, but dragged the heavy door open and staggered through, into another shelter very much like the one she had left below Haverford. She turned this way and that, the beam of her headlamp falling on cots and folding chairs, on shelves stocked with emergency supplies.

"Tyko," Derryn said, "where am I?"

"Based on trajectory and distance, you appear to be beneath St. Mary's Church, approximately 1.10 kilometers from Haverford College."

Derryn exhaled. This was the place, all right—the destination Melinda had given her. Relief was instantly eclipsed by humorous disbelief. She had crept through that damned tunnel for what felt like years, but had only gone a little more than a kilometer.

What did it matter now? She was outside the college, no longer penned within the target zone of the Sovereign invaders. With any luck, she could stay away from the rebel faction while their attention was fixed on the tempting greenspace within Haverford's walls. As she found her way out of the church's bunker, Derryn sent up a silent plea for Melinda and Mihir, and all the rest of the good people at Haverford. Surely, they would be safe in their shelter, or if the threat deepened, they would get out as quickly as Derryn had done. These attacks were nothing new to them, after all.

She emerged from the bunker into the back rooms of the old church—a kitchen with stainless steel work surfaces and a large open space whose walls were hung with children's drawings and colorful posters. The big room must serve as some sort of community gathering place, perhaps a daycare center. She slipped quickly through the room and passed into an unlit hall flanked by offices and storage closets.

The hall opened on the narthex of the church, and there Derryn paused, struck even in the midst of her urgency. Great panels of stained glass spilled a patchwork of colored light onto the walls and floor. She gazed across the empty chapel. Clerestory windows ran in arches of perfect blue down the length of the nave, illuminating the barrel vault of the ceiling. At the chapel's far end, beyond rows of antique pews, a trick of light and shadow cast the space into sharp contrast. The chancel seemed to burn with an unsettling light, too yellow for the sun, a stark acid green, while the gothic arches of the rood screen were blacker than a starless night. The slender pillars of the screen seemed to hold, like the bars of a prison cell, light or salvation forever at a distance.

On the far side of the narthex, she found a narrow door and staircase. She climbed, hoping to find some high point from which she might get her bearings. The old stone steps were pitted in the center, heavily worn from generations of use, and the walls of the passage pressed in as closely as the tunnel's walls had done. The staircase terminated at a wooden ceiling—no, not a ceiling, Derryn saw, but a hatch with a wrought-iron handle and hinges. She set a shoulder against the hatch and pushed. With a groan, it lifted to reveal a small wooden platform enclosed by a stone half wall. The blue, airy sky showed between the wall and a steepled roof. A bronze bell hung mute from the ceiling beams. She had found her way to the church's bell tower.

Derryn let the backpack slide from her shoulders and crouched for a while behind the protection of the half wall. When her breathing had slowed, she called up Tyko on her headset and asked if he'd been able to locate any transportation. But the situation was still as dire as it had ever been. No flights outbound from Philadelphia—Derryn wasn't certain she could get back to the airport, anyhow—and no air cabs available within a hundred kilometers of her location.

She rose onto her knees, just high enough to peer through the open space between the bell tower's turret roof and the shingled shaft below. The morning and the suburb were quiet. No Sovereign militia troops marched through the streets, no gunfire sounded among the homes and parks. Yet the area seemed too still, the gardens and streets conspicuously empty as the local population cowered under the double threat of rebel occupation and the solar flare to come.

She spent the rest of that day huddled in the bell tower, whispering into her CoreTex. Alexis was willing to help, of course, once Derryn had alerted them to her predicament. And Tyko still searched doggedly for any plausible escape from Pennsylvania before the shutdown hit.

But neither Alexis nor the AI could locate a cab, and finally, as the sun began to set, Derryn was forced to look reality in the face. She would be stranded at the mercy of bomb-toting lunatics while the worst natural disaster the planet had faced for a quarter of a century stripped away the world she had known. At least she had her map. Her only choice now was to go on foot to New York City. Or at least to get the hell out of Sovereign reach. It wasn't a pretty prospect, but it was a cold, hard fact.

Fumbling with the port of her CoreTex, Derryn fought back tears. She wanted to talk to Leo one last time before the outage, wanted to say a proper goodbye and tell him again how much she loved him. But she wouldn't be able to do it without crying, and then she would be forced to admit everything, including the lies she had told him. If she spoke to him now, she would only condemn him to six days of torment while he worried over his little sister, trapped among Luddite maniacs on the far side of the continent without any way to call for help. She couldn't do that to him. She loved him too much to cause him such pain.

"Tyko," she said.

The AI responded with its usual alacrity—the ever-present friend, the voice she knew as well as her own thoughts. "I'm here, Derryn. What can I do for you?"

"I . . . I just wanted to say goodbye. And thank you. Before everything shuts down."

"I can tell by the sound of your voice that you're worried, Derryn. Please don't be afraid. The Weave has calculated the strength and duration of this event. As long as you keep all your electronics powered off for the full six days of the shutdown, everything will be fine."

"I know," Derryn said.

But she didn't know. She had lived all her adult life, and most of her childhood, trusting in the wisdom and accuracy of the Weave. And now she felt to her bones how foolish it was, how vulnerable humankind had been all these years to the Weave's calculations. What if the Weave got it wrong? It had never been wrong before, but once was all anyone needed for a full-on global apocalypse.

"You'll have to power down your devices within three hours," Tyko said. "Is there anything I can do for you in the meantime?"

"Yes." The grief receded suddenly, pushed into a distant corner of Derryn's mind by the urgency of necessity. She blinked away the remnant of her tears. "Prepare a message for Leo, to be delivered in case I don't rejoin the Weave within twelve hours of the solar flare's end."

With a steadfast coolness, Derryn recorded her confession. She told Leo everything—the rebel incursion and the evacuation of the college, how she had misled him about her location and circumstances to spare him from fear. How sorry she was that she wouldn't see him again, that she had been lost to the war just like Mom and Dad.

After Tyko confirmed that the message was saved, Derryn thanked the AI again and powered down her CoreTex. With slow deliberation, she took the device apart, piece by slender piece, and hid the various components as best she could deep inside her pack. She could only hope that if she were apprehended, no Sovereign would be able to recognize a disassembled neural headset.

From the bell tower, she watched the red rind of the sun fall beyond the western horizon, that potent star whose whims and furies had always governed life on earth. Like a sly god, it sank into the depths of its own mysteries and left a memory of its light to burn low against the planet.

Night came, slow and inevitable. The few stars that could be seen through the sickly atmosphere of light pollution observed the world with a cold and stately amusement. The appointed hour arrived. Derryn watched whole blocks of the suburb go dark as the power grid was disabled. The distant glow of Philadelphia dimmed steadily. Her heart beat into the eerie silence. With a final blink, the city vanished. Night was so black that it raised a primal fear, a terror older than Derryn herself, a dread that seemed to reach back through the eons of human invention to a time when not even fire was a friend.

There was nothing out there now. Nothing but the stars.

13

Helen

February 17, 1862

I take up my pen to start yet another diary—my second book since this war began. I look back upon the chronicle I kept between last December of 1860 and now. It's little more than a litany of battles, my recounting of the news I read in the *Whig* and other papers.

How I shudder to read the optimistic note I penned a year ago, in February of '61, when Virginia called for a peace convention in Washington. "I have hope that we may yet resolve this conflict without seeing war." Such naivete! None of the seceded states deigned to attend that convention, and even some of the Northern states refrained. I should have known that no peace could be had if those who broke that peace refused to come to the table. It's like trying to repair a rip in a garment when half the cloth has been carried off by the wind. What a foolish performance it was. There are days when I think all those men whom we send to Washington to represent us are useless as clowns on a stage—and not half so amusing.

But of course, by last April, all hope that we might evade war was shattered. The bombardment of Fort Sumter made our situation clear, and only days later, Virginia joined the rest of the Southern states in secession. My stomach is still sour from the news, nearly a year after.

But on to current events. I've had a vexing letter from Mary Jane. On the surface, it was all girlish frippery. But the coded message made my blood run cold.

Richmond a more useful place to be now. By the time you get this letter, I will be on my way.

Of course, she is referring to the fact that our once-fair city was made the capital of the Confederacy last May. Drat the little she-devil! Mary Jane is too clever for her own good. She has something planned, for certain, though I can't imagine what it might be.

I wrote back at once, not even bothering to put the message in code, for this is too urgent a matter to waste a moment on our game. My letter implored her not to be a fool, to stay away, to run even farther from Virginia's border. But I am dreadfully certain that I'm already too late. Mary Jane must be on her way back now, and I can only pray that God will keep her safe.

I must try to keep my mind on happier things. In Tennessee and at Roanoke Island, the Confederate forces have been defeated, and we have heard that Fort Donelson is under siege on the Cumberland River. I hope that tomorrow I will open the *Whig* to read news that the fort has fallen and the federal troops have command of the river. The Northern forces may yet prevail . . . though we have had our share of disappointments over the past year of fighting. If God answered prayers in diaries, I would fill these pages with my pleas.

March 5, 1862

What do you think! I've just returned from "springing" Mary Jane from prison!

Prison, of all things! For of course, the state has adopted the strictest laws regarding the comings and goings of Black folk. The little kings of Virginia live in holy terror of a slave uprising; they won't permit any Black person, whether slave or free, to cross back into the state once they've gone out of it. My lawyer Mr. Wyckoff and I were hard pressed for days to win Mary Jane's freedom, but thank God, we have liberated her from the jail up in Fredericksburg, and she is unharmed.

When I think of that girl locked up in such a dreadful place, it sickens me to my soul. I feel sure that I could never survive such a torment—confined in a cell, with my fate in the hands of my enemies and yet to be decided. Mary Jane was there *nine days*, all of which (save Sunday) I worked tirelessly with Mr. Wyckoff until we'd worn down the Fredericksburg judge, convincing him to remit Mary Jane to me as my legal property. If she had been apprehended in Richmond, we might not have pulled it off, for here, my subversive opinions on slavery are known. Surely, both Mary Jane and I would have been suspected of spying for the Union.

The lawyer's fees have thinned my accounts alarmingly. Fifty dollars! I here confess that I fretted over the sum, but what choice did I have? To leave Mary Jane locked away would have been unforgivable. I would have sold every stick of furniture, every last teaspoon in Eudaimonia to secure that brave girl's freedom.

When at last I heard that Mary Jane would be returned to my keeping, I rushed on the train to Fredericksburg. The bailiff at the jailhouse fetched her, and when I caught sight of her, so thin and sickly after a long confinement, it was all I could do not to weep. But a white lady crying over her supposed "slave" would only raise more suspicion, so with a will I never knew I possessed, I kept my tears at bay.

"Come along, now, you fool of a girl," I said to Mary Jane in my haughtiest tone.

She followed me meekly from the courthouse and stood with her eyes cast down while we waited at the depot for the next train back to Richmond. When the train arrived, it happened that we were alone in our carriage. The moment she saw that we could speak in privacy, she turned to me with a most impudent smile.

"Well, ma'am," Mary Jane said, "haven't we had an adventure!"

"An adventure!" It was all I could do not to explode. "What were you thinking, returning to Virginia, of all damned places, when you knew the danger? You're no fool, Mary Jane. You know it's illegal for Blacks to come back into this state. It's a wonder I got you out of that jail in one piece. And it cost a pretty penny, I can tell you that!"

She folded her arms and settled quite comfortably on the seat beside me, looking satisfied as a cat in cream.

"You're enjoying this," I fumed. "Nine days in prison might as well have been an afternoon at the bandstand, for all you're concerned. Didn't you understand what I meant by sending you to Pennsylvania?"

She grew more sober then. "Yes, Miss Helen, I understood. I know you wanted me to go free. And I knew the risk in coming back to Virginia, too. I hope you don't think I did all this lightly. Many days I wasted fretting over how to do it, and what might happen to me if my plans went wrong. But all my people are here, you see. And now that war has come for certain, I can't leave my folks to face it alone."

Her cause was so touching that I let my anger go. If I'd been in her position, I would have *desired* to do exactly as she had done. But I doubt very much that I would have had the courage.

"War will fall the hardest on my folks," Mary Jane went on. "I don't mean only my relations, but everyone who looks like me, everyone who's a slave or has ever been one. I can't stay away and let my people suffer while there's something I can do, *anything* I might do to help."

"You won't help anyone by getting yourself thrown in prison," I retorted—though by that time, the worst of my anger had faded, and I was only glad to have her safely back under my protection.

"Jail wasn't part of my plan," she admitted, that mischievous smile returning. "But I'm here now, and I mean to do what I can to see that this fight goes the right way for all my folks. To tell you the truth, Miss

Helen, I don't really mind if I put myself in danger, so long as I can make a difference on my way down to the grave."

I stared at her, this girl I had known since she was small. Not a girl any longer, but every bit a woman, with the fire of conviction in her eyes and a spine as hard as Northern steel.

"Besides," Mary Jane added, "I don't run from a fight."

She meant those words as no accusation, yet all the same, I felt them as such. For these past months, as Richmond has burned hotter with the fervor of secession, I have done all I could to get by, to deflect the suspicions of my neighbors, to conceal my true thoughts behind a mask of Southern propriety. Of course I've written of my rebellious feelings in my diaries, but in the public eye, I've taken such pains to risk nothing but my invitation to parties and balls. But on that train, with the green hills of my homeland flashing by, I was forced to look squarely at the truth. I have sheltered behind the walls of Eudaimonia while Mary Jane took action.

No longer can I cower, hoping this war will blow past like a hurricane, leaving my life standing as it ever was in the storm's wake. I must be as strong as Mary Jane, as fierce in my determination, and every bit as wedded to real and enduring change.

"You were right to come back," I said at length, "and I was wrong to scold you for it. But promise me you'll be more careful. These are dangerous times, and if anything should happen to you . . . well, I just couldn't bear it, that's all."

When our train arrived in Richmond, David was waiting with the carriage to drive us home.

Mary Jane fairly goggled out the window, taken aback by the city's transformation. No, transformation is not the right word. Rather call it *degradation*, for since last May, Richmond has positively rotted into a place I hardly recognize.

At every hour, the streets are crowded with soldiers in gray uniforms. They strut like peacocks, and all the ladies line up on the sidewalks to coo after them. The population has been further swelled by the usual characters who trail after military encampments—poor laundresses and cooks, gambling men, and fallen women peddling their flesh. For shame! When last summer began, this city was as fair and sweet as it ever was. Yet only a few short weeks after Richmond was declared the capital of the rebellion, it turned to a den of iniquity.

And the stench! How can I write of that hideous reek without recalling it to my senses? The memory alone is like to gag me. Far worse is the experience of venturing outside, going down the hill to the city proper. In summertime, the heat and the humid airs off the river trap a foul miasma among the streets. One is plumb assaulted by the odor. Unwashed bodies, the manure of too many horses, and rotting garbage all combine in the swelter to produce an effect unsettling to body and spirit alike.

Oh, my Richmond! Long gone are those pleasant summer nights when, in the dissipating heat, I would sit among the flower beds to enjoy the cool breezes and the starlight, and the fireflies like fairy lamps, flaring bright and fading again among the flowers. Neither night nor day has brought any pleasure since "President" Davis came to dwell among us last year. Even on Church Hill, one cannot escape the shouting, the drunken choruses of marching songs, the clatter of wagon wheels. There is no end to the noise.

"Miss Helen," Mary Jane said quietly, "what in the name of the Savior has happened to this place?"

"You heard that Richmond was made the capital of the rebellion," I said.

"Yes, ma'am, but I never thought . . ." She trailed off.

Our carriage rolled past the Brockenbrough mansion on Shockoe Hill. I pointed it out to Mary Jane.

"There sits the president of the Confederate States of America," I said scornfully. "Jefferson Davis. The old Brockenbrough place is his White House now, and this is his city—foul and stinking, crowded with armed men, packed full of drunks and other unsavory types. I suppose this is what it means to live in the midst of war, but by God, I don't like it one bit."

The girl whistled softly. "It's hardly been two years since I left. Everything surely has changed."

We soon turned up Church Hill, which at least has been spared from the worst of the grime and debauchery. When Mary Jane saw Eudaimonia like a bright crown at the hill's crest, she forgot her dark criticism of Richmond and shouted for joy. And when we rolled into the yard, Kitty and Ruthie were on the front steps to greet her, clinging to one another with the relief of seeing our dear girl safe. Mary Jane scrambled down from the carriage to fling herself into the arms of the women she had missed for so long, and I stood watching the happy reunion with a brimming heart.

Now I know what I must do. I have spent too long fearing the calamity to come, too long hiding among these pages. If I truly believe in my visions of a better future, then I must do the work to bring it into being.

No more cowering in my mansion. One way or another, Helen herself—she of the Yankee predilections!—shall bull her way back into society. Or at least, I shall wedge myself as far back in as my suspect person will be allowed. I don't expect that it will be easy to reestablish my connections. No one trusts me, with good reason, but I will persist. If I must stand alongside all those swooning ladies on the sidewalks of the city, waving my kerchief at every fellow in gray, then so be it. If I must join the service league at the Richmond Female Institute and take on the mending of soldiers' uniforms, then I will darn and sew till my fingers bleed. I will endure the stink and the noise and the general misfortune of the city, all in the name of the secret work I do. Or I should rather say, the work I *shall* do, once I've found it.

My mission begins with this—regaining the trust of society, convincing them that I've never done a single thing they'd thought too Yankeeish to be borne. Wherever a crowd cheers for the boys in gray, I will be among them, shouting as loud as the rest. The endless parades and rallies and fundraisers—I shall attend them all.

Whatever my neighbors once thought of me, I will convince them that it was only their imaginations. I will make myself the very model of a Confederate lady. Everyone from here to the ironworks will ask themselves how they ever could have doubted my loyalty to the Southern Cause.

It will take time, but with God's help, the invitations will come again to society parties, and those I shall attend, too—not for the sake of my vanity, but for the sake of what I might *learn*. One way or another, all this strutting about Richmond and cheering for the Cause will lead me to more useful work. Until I find my secret task, I will hold my nose and do what must be done.

April 25, 1862

Good news to relate today. First, the fighting continues to go in favor of the North. We learned yesterday that Admiral Farragut of the federal fleet sailed a whole mess of gunships past the mouth of the Mississippi. Last I read, the fleet was making for New Orleans. They may be at the city already, for all I know. Tomorrow's paper should bring the news. If Northern luck holds as it has done these past few months, New Orleans will surrender.

And in smaller affairs, but no less important to Your Diarist, I report that my slinking about society functions has borne some fruit.

Saturday night, I attended Mrs. Parkman's musical evening, an affair I was invited to only because her daughter Caroline still maintains our childhood friendship despite her mother's misgivings about my loyalties. I stood in corners and smiled pleasantly, straining all the while to hear the conversations around me over violin and horn. My persistence and my sharp ears were amply rewarded.

Colonel Winters, drowning in liquor and bragging to a circle of admiring young ladies, let slip that Luther Libby's tobacco warehouse down by the river has been converted to a prison. Union soldiers have been held there since the battle of Manassas last summer, which I hadn't known till now. But the Confederacy has captured so many officers that they've sent all the ordinary soldiers to some other pen and have designed to hold the officers at Libby's place. They hope these officers might make good pawns for negotiations between Jefferson Davis and President Lincoln.

Careful to keep my face blank, I fixed my eyes upon the orchestra so all who looked my way would think I was wholesomely absorbed in the music. But all I really heard was the tale of Libby's prison. I shuddered to imagine it, and it chills me still—those poor men, packed together like tinned fish in a lightless warehouse! When I think of how they must yearn for home and comfort, my heart is like to break.

This morning, I was up with the dawn, talking the situation over with Mary Jane. We ventured out together after the breakfast hour, she posing as my slave. The clever girl rigged up a number of packages to carry, so the two of us together were quite unremarkable—a lady and her maid doing the shopping, nothing more startling than that. But it just so happened that all our business took place in the vicinity of Libby's warehouse. We had plenty of time to observe what goes on there.

The prison sits on Cary Street, its three stories of brick looming over the canal basin. Guards in gray uniforms surrounded the place with rifles ready on their shoulders. Tents dotted the nearby grounds, housing yet more soldiers. There must be at least at hundred Confederate men encircling the building, if not more.

Strangest of all, the whole lower story of the warehouse has recently been whitewashed.

"What do you suppose the paint is for?" I asked.

Mary Jane instantly understood the purpose of the paint. "If anyone breaks free, he'll be easier to spot against a white wall than dark brick. Don't stare too much, Miss Helen. You'll draw attention."

Her advice was sensible, though it was all I could do not to study the building openly—its narrow, barred windows behind which the officers were crowded. A stench hit us as we drew closer—unwashed bodies and wool garments, the waste of those men in their dirty canvas tents and, one assumes, the waste of those held inside the old warehouse. The pits of Damnation can't smell any worse.

A guard began to eye us as we lingered, so I quickly pointed to a shop across the street, as if that had been our destination all along. We made our way there, purchased some ribbon I didn't need, and circled back for home by another route.

"It's a certainty," I said when we were safely away, "that the men being held in that building are faring even worse than the soldiers outside. And the Confederate camp looked about as pleasant as a nightmare. I can't stomach the thought of those officers suffering. The poor men—to be so far from home, and treated worse than animals! They've all volunteered their lives to fight for this country."

"What do you mean to do about it?" Mary Jane asked.

I didn't know then but vowed I would come up with some plan. And now that I've spent days in rumination, I believe I have. The Confederates fancy themselves gentlemen, and gentlemen don't refuse the charitable impulses of ladies.

Once I saw the scheme clearly in my mind, I summoned Mary Jane to my room and explained.

"Do you really think you'll be allowed to bring those Union officers food and clothes and other things, Miss Helen?"

"It's worth a try," I answered. "The worst they can do is send me away."

"But you can't just appear at the prison doors with baskets of food."

"No, I suppose not. I shall have to petition whoever is in charge. I'll plead my soft heart, tell them I'm a Southern lady through and through, but my Christian soul can't abide the suffering of any person, even Yankee dogs. I shall ask permission to bring small comforts to the officers. Nothing that could aid an escape, of course. Only a little extra food, perhaps some blankets and dry stockings, some books to pass the time."

"And once you've got them used to regular visits," Mary Jane said, "who knows what else you might bring?"

"My thoughts exactly. Now tell me, what problems can you see with my idea?"

She sank onto the edge of my bed and seemed to lose herself in rumination. Her eyes gleamed in the lamplight with a cunning that far exceeded all the intelligence I had supposed the girl possessed.

"You'll have to be patient," she said at length, "and careful as a cat on a stove. One misstep could ruin everything. And I think, on account of the reputation you have now, you've got to make a big show of loyalty to the Confederacy."

"Reverse the prevailing opinion of me," I mused. "Yes, I see what you mean."

We spent some hours that evening in my room, discussing how we might bring about such a change. A little before midnight, we agreed that I must accomplish two things before we can make our move on Libby Prison. First, I shall found a ladies' aid society, which will provide service to a variety of causes, all of them decidedly Confederate. My interest in the Union officers will then be seen (so I pray) as merely an adjunct to my other charitable activities. And second, to turn public opinion of me well in the opposite direction, I shall organize grand picnics, once every month while the weather is good, to celebrate and entertain the many Confederate soldiers who now populate Richmond. Only when these operations are underway, and accepted by my neighbors, will we set our sights on the prison.

Much work lies ahead, and I am weary just thinking of the labor and the mental strain. But I do believe it's the surest way to avoid scrutiny, so that I might be of some real use to the Union.

That night, after our plans were settled and Mary Jane went yawning to her bed, I sat for a long time on my balcony, watching the sky, so dark and serene above the distant hills. The stars don't shine as brightly as they did before this grim occupation of my city. Smoke is to blame—all the fires to cook for so many men, and the churning of the ironworks out on the river, which never ceases now, producing arms and ammunition for this dreadful war. The heavy grayness of this fight hangs perpetually above the city. But what matter? Tomorrow I shall begin my work in earnest—at last, at last! And someday, I trust and believe, the smoke will clear.

May 17, 1862

What a sweet word is "success"! My first picnic in support of "our boys in gray" has come off without a hitch.

I planned the event for weeks, with no small amount of help from Mary Jane. The Church Hill Ladies' Aid, newly founded by one Miss Helen Bywater, thought the picnic a splendid idea. My neighbors tapped their acquaintances like Vermont maples. A sweet nectar of goodwill flowed through my fledgling society. Whatever my past reputation, I have succeeded in making myself the public face of support for Confederate soldiery, and in response, Eudaimonia has been busy with calls from ladies all across Richmond. No woman of any consequence intends to be left out of such a patriotic affair. I had all the volunteers I needed to bake, sing, decorate, and otherwise entertain.

The first jamboree was held yesterday at the public park, and I must say, it was quite a grand event. The day dawned clear and warm with the perfect blue sky of early summer—belying the hidden purpose behind our festivities. Mary Jane and I arrived early at the park to oversee the setting up of tables and the laying out of food—cornbread, fried chicken, every manner of pickle, and more pies and cakes than I could count. A brass band set up under the oak trees, their instruments glinting in the dappled light.

By midday, the park was filled with men in gray uniforms. Despite my secret affinity for the other side, I will confess that I found it touching to watch those boys' faces light up at the sight of so much food and so many lovely young ladies. And they *are* boys, most of them. Some of the soldiers looked barely old enough to shave, with soft cheeks and uncertain smiles. Others were hard weathered, almost ancient, with a look of having seen too much. Oh, that we might bring this foolish war to an end soon! There is too much suffering already, and these soldiers are no plantation owners. It's a great injustice, that the sons of poor families must fight and die for a cause that will never benefit them.

But I mustn't get distracted from my story. Back to happier thoughts.

At half past noon, the band struck up a lively number, and couples linked up for a reel on the grass. I found myself partnered with a lieutenant from Macon, a polite young fellow who spoke of the farm on which he'd grown up and his hope to return to Georgia soon. I shall pray every night that he makes his way back to Macon, whole and not too much troubled by what he has seen.

Captain Gibbs was in attendance. Who is Captain Gibbs, one might ask? Only the very man in charge of the prisoners held at the old Libby warehouse. He's a brute—one can tell just by the sight of him, for he has the most peevish eyes and the oiliest manner I ever have encountered in another person. But of course, I went out of my way to meet him, and made as nice as you please, with the hope that my great show of ladylike enthusiasm for the Southern Cause will win me favor when I approach him for permission to enter the prison.

Captain Gibbs thought himself quite the man of the hour, despite the fact that it was I (and my Ladies' Aid) who had brought the picnic together. When the music paused, he called for silence and made a speech about patriotism and the importance of upholding our beautiful traditions. Everyone hung on his words. I suppose he did look fine in his uniform, with all his brass buttons and his medals polished till they shone in the sun. One may only see the grime on that man's soul if one looks beyond his fine exterior to meet his flat and calculating eye.

Just when I thought the captain was bringing his oration to a close, he gestured grandly in my direction. "Miss Bywater, would you favor us with a few words?"

I hadn't expected to speak, and wondered what on earth I would say, even as I crossed the lawn with my most gracious smile. As I took my place at the captain's side, with every eye turned to me, I felt the weight of my deception heavy on my shoulders.

"Brave soldiers of the Confederacy," I began, my voice steady despite my inner turmoil, "it is the great honor and privilege of the ladies of the Church Hill Aid—and all the ladies who lent us their talents and time—to provide this small measure of comfort to you who sacrifice so much for our homeland."

A great cheer went up from the crowd. I waited for the clamor to subside before I spoke on.

"You stand between us and those who would rob us of our way of life. Your courage and dedication are an inspiration to us all, and I for one can't do enough to thank each and every one of you for the sacrifices you're making, all to defend the women and children of the South."

As the crowd whooped and hollered again, I watched that sea of faces—*young* faces, boys so convinced of this war's righteousness that my heart wanted to burst with pity. Most of those boys will never be wealthy enough to own slaves. It struck me as I spoke before that crowd that most of these Confederate soldiers really do believe they're fighting for a noble cause, a way of life on which their own existences depend, when in fact they are sent to suffer and die for a practice that benefits only the wealthiest among us. A practice that will stain the souls of every man who fights to preserve it, and the souls of their children for generations to come.

Oh, what a sorrow it was to know that so many of these boys will die in a senseless fight to hold on to an outmoded past, a tradition that will be of no use to them. It was the first time since this turmoil began that I understood that *all* men are victims of this war, whether they wear the blue or the gray.

After I'd finished my pretty speech and the crowd gave a last hurrah, Captain Gibbs clasped my hand and kissed it.

"You have a way with words, Miss Bywater," he said. "You've done a great service to the South today."

Ah, Captain Gibbs, if only you knew what service I intend to provide!

14

Derryn

2053

Derryn left the church well before dawn. The early morning was still gray and dark, except for the suggestion of a pinkish glow along the horizon—the first flush of the auroras to come. She stood at the edge of the church's parking lot, where asphalt crumbled into gravel, where wiry weeds overtook the disintegrating stuff of human habitation. Wind and rain and time, and the secretive roots and mycelia of things far older than Derryn's species, were breaking this civilization into fragments, grinding it all into dust, taking the great constructions of steel and cement back into the quiet forge of the planet, to be rendered into something new. Something Derryn, in all her smallness and isolation, could never comprehend.

A weight pressed into her skull, into her heart and mind—a silence so profound that it seemed to obliterate her very self. She was untethered from her physical body, a lone, chittering, terrified mind as small as a gnat and fragile enough to be blown away on a stray breeze. That great silence wasn't an absence of sound. It was the terrible, still vacuum of nothingness where the Weave should have been. She kept reaching for her temple, where the port of her neural headset should have been. But the connection wasn't there. Nothing was there—nothing was anywhere—and she was drowning in a sea of substance, the broken matter of the parking lot and ancient church, the road that stretched before her into a hazy distance, the flat gray mass of Philadelphia somewhere ahead, all of it a meaningless clamor of molecules, atoms, networks, and frameworks of *things* she couldn't begin to comprehend without the Weave to help her.

Go, she told herself. *Just start walking.*

Her own singular thoughts echoed in her mind. The lack of reflection from sympathetic others only emphasized her isolation. But there was nothing to do but walk, nothing to do but keep moving and hope that she was moving in the right direction.

She set off along the road, some arterial whose name she didn't know. It ran from the church toward what she thought might be Philadelphia. Without any access to proper digital maps or GPS, she could only hope that this road would lead her to something useful. Every step carried her farther from the old church, farther into a concrete wilderness brimming with unknown danger.

Derryn was already tired. The paltry few hours of sleep she'd stolen the night before, on a couch in one of the church's small offices, hadn't been enough to fortify her body or her will for this long and dangerous journey. She was tempted to turn back, hide in the church until the solar storm had passed and all danger from the Sovereign factions had blown over. But the guilt of lying to Leo was too heavy and raw. She had promised her brother she would go to New York. For his sake, she would make that story true—if she was lucky enough to survive the trek.

Dawn came quickly. By the time the sun was above the horizon, Derryn could no longer see the church when she turned to look behind. It was lost in an anonymous confusion of distance and blocky shapes—the humble homes and businesses of this community, battered by decades of conflict.

The morning sky was perfectly still, perfectly blue. The aurora wasn't visible by day, but nevertheless, she could feel the storm rippling overhead, its long, magnetic fingers reaching down to clutch and crush and sweep away the technological mesh that had become the very nervous system of human civilization. The great, austere force of nature asserted an easy power over everything Derryn's kind had made.

It's temporary, she reminded herself. *Six days, that's all.*

But the same bleak thought came back to her, the one she'd spent all night wrestling, first in the bell tower with the lightless land spreading like a black bog around her, and then in the huddled darkness of that office, while she'd tried to catch a little sleep.

What if. What if the Weave's calculations were wrong? What if it misjudged the intensity of the storm? What if, when these six days are finally over, there's nothing to power back up?

What if I'm alone now, forever?

The morning unfolded. People emerged from their homes, went about what business they could in the streets with a subdued and furtive air. Derryn seldom made eye contact with anyone she passed. She felt too frightened of people now, for without the Weave's instantaneous flash of empathy, she had no way to know what someone else might be thinking. Other people had never seemed dangerous to her before. Now, she felt as if she were stumbling through a forest of tigers. If she didn't look at other people, maybe they wouldn't see her, either. Maybe that anonymity would be enough to keep her safe all the way to New York.

But it was such a long walk. How many days had Tyko said it would take? Four? Five? She couldn't remember. She could barely recall anything, couldn't seem to plan more than a few seconds ahead. Without her AI enhancements, every thought was sluggish, a burden that must be lifted and dragged with an effort that would soon exhaust her.

"Think," she commanded herself, pressing her palms against her temples where the ports should have been. "You're a professor, damn it. You've got a PhD. You can figure out how to follow roads to a city."

But using this single, limited mind—*her* mind, this lonesome thing trapped in one little skull—was a labor she could barely manage.

The day began to warm. Her legs were already trembling, and she hadn't walked more than two hours . . . maybe, if her estimation of time was accurate, which she couldn't be sure of. In any case, she needed a rest and something to eat if she hoped to keep up her strength. An alley between two pale brick buildings beckoned with a swath of blue shade. Derryn headed for that respite and, with a few old wooden crates to shelter her from sight, she sank down to rest against the coolness of a wall.

She slid out of her backpack, groaning with the relief of hiding herself away. The deepest, most compelling exhaustion she had ever known dragged at her from the inside. To keep herself from nodding off, she fished in her pack for some of the food she'd brought from the bunker under Founders Hall. There hadn't been much time to gather supplies before she'd left, and anyway, she hadn't wanted to take too much and leave the faculty and students with too little. God knew how long they would have to cower in their shelter. If they were stranded there for all six days of the shutdown, rations would run tight. Still, Derryn had needed something to see her on her way. She found a granola bar and ate it morosely while she took stock of her situation.

With a stubborn command over animal instinct, Derryn called one thought after another from the panicked hum of her mind. She lined those thoughts up in careful order, looked them over, rearranged them until she was satisfied with their logic.

Thought number one: Walking for days was not feasible. Where would she sleep? How would she find more food? She wouldn't get very far on granola bars and fruit leather.

Thought number two: Plenty of people had charged their electric cars before the grid was shut down. Electric vehicles were built with shields around their motors to protect them from electromagnetic pulses. They would still function during the shutdown, provided their batteries held some power.

Thought number three: It was to be expected that many people would reserve that precious battery power for emergencies. The odds of finding joyriders cruising from Philadelphia to New York on a whim were vanishingly small. Yet in a city of . . . how many people lived in this area? Without the Weave, she couldn't tell. *Estimate a few hundred thousand at least, Derryn.* It seemed like a sensible number. In a city of a few hundred thousand, there *had* to be people traveling to New York, statistically, mathematically speaking. And there were old combustion-engine cars out there still, rigged up to run on biodiesel and impervious to the effects of a solar storm. If she looked hard enough, she could find a ride.

The logical conclusion was that she *must* find a ride, must convince anyone who was driving in a more or less New Yorkish direction to take her along, as far as they were willing to carry her. If necessary, she could leapfrog from one ride to the next. Go a few miles with someone, get out when they reached their own destination, and continue on with somebody else.

As long as she kept moving . . . which direction? Where did New York lie in relation to where she was now? Where *was* she now, exactly?

Without the Weave, there was no way to tell. That fact kept returning to her, staring her in the face with its cruel, glittering eyes. She realized with a rising sense of shame that she couldn't even determine north from south without the Weave's aid. How could she hope to follow the map she had traced from her lightscreen if she couldn't orient the thing properly?

For the hundredth time that day, she teetered on the edge of complete panic. But a breakdown wouldn't save her now. She pushed fear away and climbed unsteadily to her feet. If she wanted to find a ride, the first step would be to get the attention of someone who had a car. Now, how to do that? There were scraps of cardboard and broken planks of wood littering the alley. She might make a sign, if she had something to write with. But there was nothing that Derryn could see, no marker or paint, not even any safe implement with which she might cut herself to scrawl "Get me to New York!" in her own blood.

She refused to cry, sniffed angrily, and kicked at the alley trash until her eyes no longer burned.

How did people who had no cars get around in the olden days?

Desperately, Derryn fished in the murky depths of her own experience. Everything she'd studied about nineteenth- and twentieth-century art forms was still somewhere in her head, embedded into the wrinkles of her brain, just as data was stored and catalogued in the AI networks of the Weave. All she had to do was find the right memories and access them. It should have been simple. But nothing was, for a fragment of a mind—a lone soul cut off from its rightful wholeness.

Movies, literature, old songs . . . Derryn thrashed and paddled her way through shadowy, half-formed memories of the studies she'd made, long ago, of twentieth-century art. Popular art forms reflected the real-life practices of the cultures that had made them. One memory burst across her mind so suddenly, with such easy clarity that she gasped and stumbled backward, startled by the vivid force of her own recollection. She could see the flicker of old celluloid film in her college's screening room. An amateur movie about the hippie movement in the 1960s. She beheld, on the glaring screen of some inner theater, an image of long-haired adolescents standing on the side of a highway with their thumbs raised, trying to hitch a ride.

She made her way back out of the alley to the road. A dark vehicle was gliding smoothly toward her on the otherwise empty street. Derryn extended her arm, lifted her thumb experimentally, feeling more ridiculous than she had in all her life. Would anyone even recognize the archaic gesture? More to the point, would anyone stop for a lone woman? Without the Weave's empathic connection, she had no way to broadcast her harmlessness or read others' intentions. Whoever was driving that car might be just as suspicious of Derryn as she was of them.

The car passed with a low, electric hum. Derryn sighed, lowered her arm, waited for another vehicle to come. It took several minutes, but another did appear, a sleek model with a rounded design to mimic the look of a skycar. That one, too, drove on without so much as slowing down, though the driver did cast a confused look at Derryn and her useless thumb.

"This is barbaric," she muttered, resolving to give the method one last chance. Then she would move on.

A distant rumble made her look up sharply.

Thunder? The thought was slow and cumbersome. *But the sky is dead clear.*

Slowly, she realized the sound was all wrong, a harsh mechanical growl, not nature's great, hollow rolling of power. The sound grew louder, nearer. Through the haze of gathering heat, she made out the shapes of several large vehicles approaching down another arterial road. Three—no, four trucks, moving fast. Something about their aggressive pace raised an instinctive chill.

Derryn darted back into her alley, took cover behind the broken crates. The pack on her shoulders dragged at her with a significant weight. She had never been more aware of the precious cargo she carried—three data chips concealed in the pockets of the bag and a set of nineteenth-century journals. If the Sovereigns overthrew Haverford, if they found that precious art and destroyed it as heresy, then the contents of Derryn's pack might be the only remaining evidence of the most significant discovery in Western history. Whatever dangers Derryn might face, she couldn't allow the chips and journals to be taken and destroyed.

She waited, her whole body shaking with a rush of adrenaline. The roar of the convoy intensified until the sound eclipsed every thought in her head. Then the trucks flashed by the mouth of the alley, one after another. They were huge and beastly, belching trails of smoke, each one painted matte black with dark-tinted windows. One truck had its window down, however, and Derryn caught a glimpse of its driver—a bearded man in a collared shirt, his cheek marked with a sinuous tattoo. On the truck's side panel, barely visible beneath layers of dirt, was the stylized wheat-sheaf emblem of the Human Heritage Movement.

Was this the same group that had intended to fall on Haverford? Or was this some other faction? She couldn't help but feel the Sovereigns were pursuing her specifically, hunting *her* with a predatory intent, though some small and dazed portion of her mind told her that was impossible. None of the Sovereigns knew who she was. As long as she kept her integration hidden, they would have no cause to single her out, no reason to think she was more dependent on AI than any other person in the greater Philly area.

Once the convoy had passed and the smoke of their engines had cleared, she forced herself to leave the alley, to keep moving. New York was somewhere ahead—she *hoped* it was ahead, not behind—and one way or another, she would get there.

By the time she came upon a railyard, the day had grown unbearably hot, with a rich, heavy odor of sluggish water from the river. From the heat, she assumed that afternoon was near, though she had no real way to tell. Even the position of the sun in the sky was foreign to her, for she had always told both time and direction by the Weave. The railyard lay still under the glaring sun. Without a functional grid to charge them, the electric locomotives were useless, the huge cargo cars and stupefied engines lying like dead giants on the tracks. There was no sign of another Sovereign convoy, no sign of any living thing larger than the insects that droned in the weeds, the birds darting down from rooftops and trees to catch them.

She eased the pack from her shoulders again, reached into the front pocket for the map Tyko had prepared for her. She unfolded the paper and stared at it—a jumble of lines, meaningless without the Weave to interpret the symbols.

Don't panic, Derryn told herself sternly. *Just think.*

She puzzled over the paper, turning it this way and that, trying to discern whether anything on the map might represent a river and a railroad. How had people ever navigated a three-dimensional world with something as simple and mysterious as a paper map?

In despair, she lowered the thing to her side, just for a moment, only to give vent to a frustrated sigh. But her fingers loosened, and a gust of hot, dusty wind ripped the paper from her hand.

"No!"

Derryn lunged after the map, scrambling across the railyard in pursuit as it tumbled on the wind. But it was already too late. She was weak with the effort of her long walk, sapped by the heat. The breath burned in her throat, and it was all she could do to remain on her feet, watching that precious piece of paper dwindle to a white speck far across the yard.

She did cry then. There was no use in telling herself not to. For a long time, she huddled in the meager shade of a dead locomotive, sobbing helplessly into her hands.

When the tears were spent, she forced herself to stand again, bent herself once more to the great labor of individual thought. She wasn't entirely without help. There was the river, running deep and blue between its banks. There was no telling what river it was, but Derryn stared at it for a long time, feeling by instinct that the river itself had some significance. It might hold the key to her survival . . . but she couldn't figure out *why*.

Think, Derryn, think.

She had seen a river from the air. The cab she and Melinda had taken from the airport had followed its course for a while before landing at Haverford. Was this the same waterway? If so, it might lead her to Philadelphia, into the city proper, and she might find help there—directions to New York, a ride with a sympathetic stranger.

Yes. She would follow the river. That was a thing people did—a thing ancient people had done, long before any global network existed. She was certain that she'd read of people in pretechnological times following rivers to . . . somewhere. The sea?

It wasn't much of a foundation to build on, but it was the only clear thought she had. One foot in front of the other, she crossed the rest of the silent railyard and slid into the cool, forgiving shade of ancient trees. The pleasant smell of flowing water filled the air, quieted the worst of her fears. That fragrance would accompany her all the way to wherever the river might take her. She didn't need to think anymore. She didn't need to do a thing but walk in whatever direction the water was flowing.

15

Helen

June 1, 1862

Yesterday was perhaps the most dreadful day of my life. Yesterday, and this morning. I would pray that I never face such times again, yet it seems futile to hope for that mercy in the midst of war.

Battle came to Seven Pines, so near to Richmond that we could hear it in the street and in the garden. Like the roar of a most terrible storm, the blasts of cannons and volleys of musket fire went on and on. But it was no sound of rain and thunder. It was the sound of men dying by the score, if not the hundreds. We could even see smoke rising above the trees to the north and east, just where the great earthworks were erected some months ago to fortify Richmond against attack.

I must report that I was surprised by my own reaction. For so long, I have been a wreck of nerves, lying awake at night fretting over every possible turn of fortune's wheel. Yet when emergency arrived at my doorstep, the strangest calm settled over me, and my mind was clear as glass. I called everyone into the dining room to confer on how we must proceed, and I do declare that my steadiness under fire would have turned that pig-eyed Captain Gibbs green with envy.

Mary Jane and Ruthie made up a list of necessities for every person of our household, then set about packing those things. Kitty declared that there was enough food in the pantry to last us all for days on the road. All that was too heavy to carry, such as preserves, she vowed to hide as best she could in closets around the house, in case Eudaimonia should survive burning. "We'll need that food, Miss Helen," Kitty said, "if we're able to come home again." I helped David nail boards over all the windows we could easily reach. When that work was done, David and I rushed around the house collecting every item of value, real or sentimental, that was small enough to move. Then we pried up floorboards and jimmied bricks from fireplaces so that all of my family's most precious things could be stored out of sight.

Finally, David and I ran to the livery stable down the street, where the estate's horses are kept. David put the jittery animals in the back garden and kept a close watch on them, ready to hitch them to the carriage if the fighting should come any nearer. By that time, he and I had ironed out a real plan for a rapid escape. We would just be able to fit everyone inside the carriage, with our bags full of necessities lashed to the top, though we would be packed tight as kernels on a cob. Should Richmond fall to the Union troops, we would take the carriage across town for the sake of speed, abandon it at the western edge of the city, and proceed on foot to my meetinghouse, the old cabin at the foot of Bush Hill.

Last night was still, for the armies don't like to fight by darkness. But the hellish din began again at half past six in the morning, and we were all tense and impossibly strained, waiting to learn which way the battle was turning, waiting to know whether we must turn our backs on Eudaimonia and run.

Then, some few hours later, silence fell to the east. The cannons died away, and the smoke cleared on a fresh river wind. None of us yet dared to hope that the battle was over till we heard the banging of pots and pans in the streets. Our neighbor Mrs. Wiles came pounding on the front door with a wide grin and deliverance from our fears: a stalemate at Seven Pines. The Confederates had not broken, and the Union had not advanced. Richmond remains as it was before—at least for the time being.

Kitty cooked up a hearty meal in celebration, and we all ate our fill, then retired to our beds for the first good sleep I suspect any of us has had in weeks. I, at least, have not slept so deeply in more nights than I care to count. The rest was welcome, and sorely needed, yet I woke in the heat of afternoon feeling rather sober. What a terrible thing war is! Men slaughtered by the hundreds, by the thousands, for lines on a map that remain unchanged. The evil institution we fight over is still intact. Only the bodies of young men mark any difference—bodies that yesterday were full of life and hope, but now lie bloating in the hot sun.

June 8, 1862

Mary Jane and I have visited Libby Prison each afternoon for the past three days, and I confess I feel more alive than I have in months, if one doesn't count my day of great vigor when Seven Pines came under attack.

Our first approach to the prison went more smoothly than I dared hope. Captain Gibbs was there, of course, and he proved susceptible to feminine charm, a weakness which I was not above exploiting. I arranged my features into the sweet, vacant expression I had perfected in my debutante days and spoke of my Christian duty to comfort the afflicted, even if they are Yankees.

"Why, Captain Gibbs," I said, batting my eyelashes just so, "I simply cannot bear to think of anyone suffering when I might do some small act to relieve them. These men may fight for the wrong side, but even so, the Good Book tells us to love our enemies."

Gibbs studied me with those sharp, narrow eyes, and for a moment I thought he might have heard the whispers about my abolitionist sympathies. My heart began to pound with the possibility that he would apprehend me, lock me up in that hell pit along with the Union men, and do goodness knows what to Mary Jane. But I needn't have feared. Richmond is so crowded with refugees and soldiers that gossip travels more slowly than it did before Davis's coming. Any stories one might hear around town are rather diluted by the stinking press of bodies and the more urgent news of battles won and lost.

"Miss Bywater," he replied, fiddling with his mustache, "your Christian charity does you credit, and as you have been so active in the cause of patriotism here in Richmond, I can't fault your loyalty to the Confederacy. Though I must warn you, these Yankees are rough. Not fit company for a lady like you."

"Oh, I'm certain they're not so fearsome as all that," I said disarmingly. "Anyhow, I shall have my girl with me. She is very protective, sir, and has fought off uncouth men before on my behalf."

Mary Jane was brilliant. She stood behind me with downcast eyes, affecting such convincing docility that Gibbs barely glanced at her, for he saw only what he expected to see: a loyal slave attending her mistress. If only he knew the fire of intelligence that burns behind those carefully lowered eyes, the quick mind that catalogs every detail of the prison's operations. Well, let his ignorance be his downfall! Now more than ever before, after witnessing firsthand the unwarranted assuredness of these men in gray, I believe that their inclination to underestimate our Black brethren will be their undoing.

"Very well," Gibbs conceded that first day. "You may bring your baskets inside. But I must warn you, Miss Bywater, you'll be accompanied by a guard at all times."

"Of course," I said, all sugar and honey. "One can't be too careful in these trying times. Why, one never knows who might be trying to aid the Yankees!"

Captain Gibbs searched through our baskets to be sure we would pass no weapons or other questionable items to the prisoners. Then he called a guard, and I waited and simpered at him until the escort arrived, a young, lanky fellow in gray. He took a great iron ring jangling with keys from

Gibbs, then led us through a locked door into a long corridor that seemed to reach for miles into the heart of the old warehouse. The walls of that corridor pressed in upon me with a sense of malicious intelligence. The chilled air stank of rats.

Our guard led us up a narrow staircase to the second floor. Here the prison began in earnest. A heavy oak door stood before us, its port fitted with iron bars.

"I must warn you, miss," the guard said as he searched among his keys, "there are no cells inside. All these dogs are free to roam beyond this door. You'll want to stick close by me, or else they might try to lay hands on you."

I was sure those officers would do no such thing. But I was surprised to learn that there were no cells within. "You must be terribly brave to do this work," I fawned. "Why, all those wild Union men inside . . . couldn't they storm this door when you open the lock, and run free?"

The guard chuckled. "They'd be dead men if they tried it. The only way out from here is to go back the way we just came, through that locked door, and out the front. Then they'd have to get past all the soldiers in the tents outside. They've learned to be docile enough, since there's no hope of leaving in one piece. But Northerners are no gentlemen. I can't guarantee their behavior in a lady's presence."

He found his key and opened the lock. The door swung open to reveal a wretched scene. The room was all one open space, spanning the whole great length of the warehouse. The high, barred windows let in little light but plenty of the morning chill. Great, square columns held up the beams of the ceiling, and between those columns were crowded at least two hundred men, most of them still wearing the stained and tattered uniforms of the federal army. They crouched on the bare floor or leaned against the walls. Some lay flat on the ground, in obvious sickness. Hacking coughs punctuated the dull murmur of their conversations. The captive officers turned their heads to look at us as we entered. They were gaunt and hollow eyed, watching us with the pitiful expressions of long despair.

My heart ached terribly. Although I couldn't help the tears that came to my eyes, I didn't fret over my own crying, for hadn't I billed myself as a lady who can't abide suffering?

"All right, you dogs," our escort barked, "this good woman has brought you some things out of mercy. You'd better enjoy it while you can get it. You'll find no mercy from Southern men!"

Those officers who still had the vim for conversation approached with their caps in hand and smiles on their haggard faces. All greeted me with the very best of manners, and their Northern accents reminded me of my school days in Pennsylvania. They bowed and paid me the most flattering compliments. Some even bowed to Mary Jane. The captured officers were all too happy to receive a little kindness in that harsh, confining place, and professed that we had brought sunshine in the darkness.

It didn't take long to distribute our offerings—bread still warm from Kitty's oven, dried fruit, boiled eggs. Father's old trousers and stockings found new purpose among these men so far from home. The writing paper and ink we brought were received with particular gratitude.

"My wife hasn't heard from me since Manassas," one captain told me, his voice thick with emotion. "She must think me dead."

I made a most solemn vow to him that I would take his letter to the post the very next day, when I returned, though of course it would be read by Captain Gibbs before it could be allowed to leave the prison. Such simple promises were the most I could do, that day. How I longed to tell them all that we were friends, not merely charitable visitors—that our hearts beat for the Union Cause! But of course, at all costs—and now more than ever—I must maintain my charade of Confederate loyalty. I dare not hint at any other purpose till I've established myself as a regular visitor beyond suspicion.

As soon as we were safely back at Eudaimonia, Mary Jane and I hunkered in the drawing room to elaborate our plans.

"I don't see how one might get out of that place," I said. "What that guard said seems true enough. Hundreds of men in that room, yet what good to rush the one door? The alarm would be raised, and by the time any Union men reached the first floor, the whole place would be surrounded by Confederate boys with guns at the ready. They'd never make it past the tents alive."

"Rushing won't do a bit of good," Mary Jane concurred. "But one or two men walking out calmly would never be remarked on."

"Why, Mary Jane, whatever do you mean? No guard would allow Union men to stroll out of that prison, no matter how few they were in number."

"A guard would allow it if those men paid him enough money. It seemed to me that those soldiers in the tents outside live about as bad as the prisoners inside do. Sleeping on the hard ground, surrounded by such a stink. It's summer now, but when the rains come, it must be awful with mud, and cold to boot. Why, I'd just bet that every one of those soldiers guarding the prison never thinks of anything but a better meal than the slop he's served for rations. And a willing girl to put his arms around."

"We could give the officers money for bribes," I said, "but we must think up a good way to disguise it. Money can have no purpose in a prison but greasing palms, and Captain Gibbs will know at once what we're up to if he finds coins in our baskets. Now, how can we pass money to the Union men without the captain or his guards noticing?"

Mary Jane beamed at me, eager for the challenge. "You leave it all to me, Miss Helen."

"Their clothing," I went on. "That's another problem. If those men are to walk calmly out of the prison unnoticed, they can't do it in Union blue."

"We'll bring them more of your father's old things," she answered. "Never much all at once. I don't like the look of that Gibbs man, and I don't want to give him any reason to suspect us. A shirt here, a trouser there—you must tell him you've been collecting old clothes from the ladies of

Richmond for charity, and we might as well hand these old rags to the sick men in the prison, since they're too worn to do for anyone else. Officers are clever men. The Union fellows will soon work out what we mean by bringing them all those shirts and things, especially once they get a little money."

We've been nothing short of industrious in the days that have followed that first visit to the prison. Morning and night, all hands at Eudaimonia turn to our shared work. Kitty has gone into a frenzy in the kitchen, making soda biscuits by the score and dredging up ancient wheels of cheese in hard wax from the depths of her pantry. Mary Jane, Ruthie, and I work together in the dining room with our sewing baskets and our knitting needles to make and mend whatever we can for the officers' use. And Mary Jane flits about town on errands of her own. I suspect she is testing whatever novelties she has invented for the concealment and passing of coins. Even David has joined in our work, soliciting cast-off clothing from his friends and relations for us ladies to mend. He built a chicken coop in the garden, too, and procured from somewhere or other two dozen fat hens, who are, right this minute, making a holy mess of the flower beds. But what do I care for my flowers when the hens are laying so nicely? Already, we have plenty of eggs to boil for the Union officers.

With my hands so occupied with useful work, I have little time to fret and frown over every turn of the war's tide. My heart is full. I am not insensate to the dangers we face, nor to the way those dangers will multiply as we continue our work. But I am no longer idle, no longer a helpless creature carried along by the rush of circumstance. And that is worth something, I must say.

Yet I feel such an urge to do more, more, more! There is still a stain upon my soul, the sin of my former complacency. It can't be washed away by a few deliveries of clothing and food to imprisoned officers—nor even by the money we will give them.

This evening after supper, I said to Mary Jane, "There must be more I can do to help the Union win. Getting a few men out of prison won't do much to tear down the whole institution of slavery."

She looked at me with such a queer expression then, surprised and almost amused.

"Miss Helen, the North isn't fighting to rid the country of slavery. They're fighting to keep the Union together, for the sake of all those cotton mills up north—for the sake of the money rich men can make, sending cloth to England."

Such a stillness came over me then. I stared, unseeing, into a shadowy corner of the dining room. By God, she was correct, and I had never realized it before. I have thought, all this time, that because the South fights so fiercely to cling to the cursed institution, therefore, the North must surely fight to destroy it. But no, Mary Jane has it right, as she ever does. For the North, this war is about money, not justice. The Yankees fight to preserve the fortunes and power of those who are already swimming in gold.

For a moment, I was so despondent that I cannot find the words to describe the feeling that came over me. My very soul was fit to smother under a weight of despair.

Then Mary Jane went on. "We'll do all we can to free ourselves, of course—my people and me. We'll take advantage of the fighting to fix things in our favor, if there's any way to do it. But Miss Helen, if we ever manage to do away with slavery, it'll be only an effect of this war, not its purpose."

She may have given me little reason to hope, but even a *little* hope is something one may hold in the hand. With an effort, I firmed up my courage and set my will like iron.

"I know what *I'm* working for," I said. "If we must bring about an end to this practice by fixing a whole war in our favor, then so be it."

Now that I see things more clearly, my work feels both harder and more urgent. The end of slavery might not be the chief cause of the Union army, but there are still enough fiery abolitionists in Washington that we might assert our cause in the moment of victory. The North may fight for cotton gins and merchant ships. *I* fight to set the one great wrong to rights.

June 15, 1862

Mary Jane has been creeping around town, doing secretive work of her own. I don't question her about these missions—I only see her now and then from the balcony, while I'm taking the cool air of evening, slipping out of Eudaimonia and making her way down Church Hill in the dusky hours. The less we know of one another's activities, the better off each of us may be, in case either is suspected and called to account.

But this morning, she sidled up to me in the kitchen and said, "There's a safe house out at Bush Hill—one that takes in runaway slaves and hides them, helps them get across the border to the North."

A thrill of excitement ran through me, like nettle rash all up my spine. "If they shelter escaping slaves, they might take in Union officers, too."

"I'd be willing to bet on it, Miss Helen."

I didn't ask whose house it was, for I know full well she is too cautious to say. Instead, I asked if she could draw a map to the place. We found paper and pencils in Father's old study, and soon Mary Jane had drawn a clear route through Richmond to the trail that leads out to Bush Hill.

"Now," I said, "we only need to work out some way to get this map to the Union prisoners."

"What if the route should fall into the grays' hands, Miss Helen?"

"We can't fret over that," I said. "We must pass along any advantage we can find to those officers, and hope that they'll take care to keep their own plans safe."

Together, we turned to our new work. We surely can't come right out and *tell* the officers where to go. Nor can we slip copies of the map in among the goods we deliver, for whenever we visit the prison, our baskets are thoroughly searched, and while we are among the officers, a Confederate guard sticks to us like a burr.

But as evening fell, Mary Jane came up to my room with a spark in her eye that told me she had solved the problem.

"The eggs, Miss Helen! We'll use the eggs."

We tested the solution already, minutes ago in the kitchen, and it works like a charm. With a needle, we drill holes in each end of a fresh egg, then blow out the insides and allow the shells to dry. Then we copy the map onto small pieces of paper, which we roll tightly and push into the hollowed shells. The shells are then filled with sand, so that they feel in the hand identical to a proper boiled egg. Last, we seal the holes in the shells with flour paste. One would never know to look at them, or to handle them, that the eggs carry secrets inside.

We have already rigged up more than a dozen of these clandestine "hen fruits," as the soldiers say. Soon, we make our first delivery. Don't I just about wish I could be there to see the look on some Northern officer's face when he cracks a shell, thinking to get a morsel of food, and finds instead a handful of sand and a map to safety!

Of course, the plan is not without risk. No doubt, I will lie awake too long tonight, fretting over every possibility. Our false eggs might be broken while the baskets are searched, and then the jig will be up for good. I shudder to think what might happen under such a dire circumstance—not only to Mary Jane and me, but to the officers and those good souls who run the safe house. But one can't stand up to evil without a little risk. The chance to strike a blow against the Confederacy outweighs all my fears.

Another thought haunts me, and will, I am sure, keep me from sweet dreams. Once men begin escaping from Libby Prison, I will be the first suspect. I've been delivering my baskets for many days now. Captain Gibbs and the rest of them will look to me for blame.

16

Derryn

2053

Derryn followed the river until it curved into the tangle of a forest. Trees covered both banks there, a dense layer of rustling green that cut off all sight of the broken urban landscape, save for a skyline of high-rises, visible above the canopy on the opposite bank. The cluster of buildings stood in black silhouette against a sky of deepening color. Sunset wasn't far off now, and once night fell, the first visible auroras would appear—the cosmic torrent that had scoured away everything Derryn had known.

She couldn't guess how far she had walked, but however slow and feeble her mind was without the Weave's amplification, simple logic told her that the buildings on the far side of the river must be Philadelphia. Tomorrow, she would find a bridge and cross to the other side, make her way to the downtown core where sheer numbers would be on her side. In such a densely populated area, she would find *someone* who could drive her to New York.

For tonight, the forest seemed like an ideal place to rest. An old road swept down to the riverbank and arched again back into the woods. Its pavement was buckled by tree roots, pocked here and there with potholes—neglected all these years since the war began. Derryn trekked along the battered asphalt, deeper into the hush, until she spotted a path running between two ancient maples.

The path was as old as the road, its pavement cracked and broken. She followed it through thickets and glens, through veils of birdsong and the cool brush of lingering shade. Overgrowth leaned across the trail, and she was often forced to shoulder her way through, the branches and thorns of plants she couldn't name catching at her clothes, scratching her cheeks and the backs of her hands.

More trails crossed the one she followed, and now and then, she passed green meadows whose edges were softened by a fringe of saplings and fresh new growth. Those meadows had once been open lawns, Derryn realized. She was walking through the remains of a huge public park.

As the evening's flight of insects began to rise from the forest, Derryn came upon the largest clearing yet. It was easily the size of a city block—or had been. Once, children and sports teams and off-leash dogs had run on the open field. Now the grass had grown knee high, and seed heads, still green with the richness of early summer, caught the lowering sun. A breeze stirred the meadow, sending coruscations of light rippling through the field from where Derryn stood, all the way to the center of the clearing, where a patchwork of scavenged materials had been cobbled into a construction some three meters high.

She stood for a long time at the meadow's edge, wondering what that distant arrangement might be. Sheets of rusted metal, wooden beams, and even a large highway sign were lashed together among stretches of hurricane fencing. Beyond the patches of corroded wire, Derryn could see a lush green, deeper and more vigorous than the grasses of the meadow. Then she understood. That makeshift construction was a fence—a barrier high enough to keep out deer and other marauding animals. What lay inside could only be a garden.

She crossed the sea of grass, alert for any sound or movement that might indicate danger. But the forest and the meadow were still. Even the short stretch of pavement at one edge—an old parking lot, Derryn assumed—remained as it was. If not for the presence of the garden, she would have believed that the beleaguered local population had forgotten the park. On the far side of the deer fence, she found a gate made from a piece of corrugated tin and let herself inside.

The garden was a tiny, self-contained Eden. It took up at least a quarter of the old field. Heavily planted to minimize weeds, every row overspilled with an abundance of plants, not segregated into like kinds but intermixed in a dazzling array of fertility. Derryn was no botanist, nor was she a gardener. She couldn't have identified any species by leaf or stem, but the ripening fruits and other edible parts were familiar to her. She walked the long rows, allowing the foliage to brush her shoulders with fragrant fingers. Masses of lettuce grew at her feet. The orange and purple tops of carrots peeked from the soil, waving their banners of feathery leaves among clumps of bush beans and the developing spears of brussels sprouts. Trellises made from scavenged wood and metal supported bowers of cucumber, melon, and small, still-growing squash. At the garden's far end, she found a grove of tall bushes that bore long, raspberry-like fruits. She picked a few of the odd things and sampled them. They had a mild, sweet flavor with an undercurrent of leafy crispness unlike anything she had tasted before.

As she turned and headed up another row, Derryn spotted a patch of tomato plants heavy with clusters of small rubies. She gathered handfuls of cherry tomatoes, using the lower part of her shirt as a basket, then sat right down on the trampled earth between the rows to eat them. The flavor was rich and savory, each bite generous with juice. After she'd eaten every tomato she had picked, she helped herself to a large cucumber, several leaves of lettuce, and even a great, dark fan of kale. The unexpected feast would help her meager supplies stretch a little longer—the protein bars and freeze-dried pouches of food she had taken from the bunker.

She spotted a small cantaloupe hanging from the underside of a pallet-board trellis. When she approached, the sweet intensity of its perfume overwhelmed her better sense, and she picked the ripe melon from its vine before stopping to think how she would open it. She had no knife in her backpack—nothing sharp enough to cut through the tough rind. But as she approached the gate once more, she noticed a pipe rising from the end of a garden row, crowned by a spigot and rigged out with a manual pump. The spigot was topped by a small metal finial. Derryn brought the cantaloupe down hard on that protrusion, and it split easily in her hands.

She sat on the earth again, scooped the seeds from each half of her melon and flung them aside. Then she pressed the honey-sweet, golden flesh to her face and ate with abandon. Nothing had ever tasted so delicious. After a long, hot day of rationing her water, every mouthful of sugary juice was a bliss beyond anything she had known.

By the time she'd finished both halves of the cantaloupe, her hands and face were a sticky mess. She pumped water from the spigot, washing in the mellow light of sunset, then paused to eye the spigot with more deliberation. Could she drink from the pump? She needed to refill the two aluminum water bottles that had sustained her from Haverford to this park . . . but she doubted whether water supplies in a war zone could be trusted. How did you make water safe to drink, anyway? She had no idea, and without the Weave to consult, there was no way to find out.

Never mind, Derryn told herself. *I can eat all the tomatoes and melons I want. That will keep me hydrated until I reach Philadelphia tomorrow morning.*

A low rumble among the trees snapped her to attention. She stared out through a patch of wire fencing, watching the surrounding forest in the grip of a sudden fear. She knew that sound—the animal growl of diesel engines. The trucks were coming nearer, making their way along the hidden roads of the overgrown park. Derryn crouched among the large, flat leaves of the kale plants, watching through a stretch of wire as three black trucks trundled into the old parking lot at the edge of the field. She swallowed hard. The wheat-sheaf symbol of the Human Heritage Movement showed plainly on the door of one vehicle.

Any hope Derryn had that the trucks might turn around and leave was quickly dashed. The engines went silent, and a couple of men got out with military rifles at the ready. She hardly dared to breathe as they scanned the field for signs of life. When they were satisfied that the meadow was unoccupied and unobserved, one gave a signal to their comrades. More Sovereign men piled out of the trucks. Their distinctive collared shirts picked up the last, ruddy glow of sunset. Derryn counted a dozen men in all.

Slowly, on hands and knees, dragging her backpack along the ground, she crept clear of the wire fencing. Only when she was concealed by the old freeway sign did Derryn allow herself the luxury of panic. Huddled in a ball, she rocked helplessly among the plants, shuddering with a fear she couldn't seem to master. There was no way out of the garden except by that gate, and if she left now, she would definitely be seen.

They might not have any interest in me, she tried to tell herself. But after her first brush with anti-integrationists, Derryn had no stomach to chance a confrontation again.

Forcing herself to take deep, slow breaths, slogging through her own sluggish functions, she assessed her few options. After far too long a deliberation, she decided her best bet was to stay where she was, hoping she could remain hidden in the garden until the Sovereigns left the area.

The last of the day's light faded slowly, the sky grading from orange to soft gold, then to a dusky blue. Like a small and vulnerable animal, Derryn held still, listening to the distant conversation of the men, the rattle and bump of whatever activity occupied them. The night's first chill set in. Half an hour or more must have passed, yet the Sovereigns remained. A whiff of smoke came to Derryn across the dark rows of the garden, then the light crackling of a fire. The Sovereigns had made camp, she realized, some ten meters from the garden fence.

I can't stay here. The Sovereigns would surely come looking for food. This garden might even be theirs. What would they do to a trespasser who had helped herself to their supplies? And not any kind of stranger, but a wirehead. *I should have stayed put in that damned bunker. I'd be better off than I am now.*

Through an eclipse of dread, through the stumbling ineptitude of her Weaveless thoughts, she realized the encampment had fallen silent. There was nothing to hear but the occasional snap of sparks from the fire.

Then a man said in a low, reverent voice, "Would you look at that."

"Hallelujah," another answered. "Salvation has come, like we were promised. The Devil has fallen tonight, Brothers. We've lived long enough to witness the righteous retake this world from the wicked."

From where she huddled against the earth, Derryn looked up to the sky. The solar magnetism that had invisibly bombarded the planet all day had revealed itself at last. A wave of brilliant magenta rippled overhead, followed by a long, slender stream of jade green, twisting and thrashing like a serpent. A long pulse of vibrant purple lit the whole sky and faded away, succeeded in its turn by moving columns of gold and red. It was beautiful. And terrible—a power greater than all the ingenuity of humankind and their accidental creation, those disembodied intelligences that had cradled the earth in unseen hands these decades since their emergence. The same sun that nurtured all life on the planet, that vast, roiling immensity of nature's power, was the source of destruction, too.

"It's a night to give thanks," one of the Sovereigns said. "We've held the line for mankind all these years, and now our strength has been rewarded."

"No more Devil in the heads of the people," another answered. "Faith is stronger than any demon. I've always known that's true, but now I see the proof with my own eyes, and man, is it ever a sight worth seeing."

Tears blurred Derryn's view of the aurora as the men's conversation turned to revelry. She could do nothing but listen as they fantasized about what the solar flare would mean for the integrated world. The cities would fall to confusion and violence as wireheads found that the devils in their minds would speak to them no more. They would all bend the knee to Human Heritage. Those Sovereign men who had kept the faith and fought bravely against integration would be rewarded—would have entire cities of their own, harems of women, all the land they wanted. Even the blockades would fall. New York and Cascadia would soon be claimed by those who'd held the line, those who'd kept a memory of humanity's true nature, even in the face of temptation to integrate with those demons called AI, the temptation to give up their mortal souls.

None of it was true. Derryn knew that; she repeated it again and again. It wasn't true. The Weave had never been wrong in its delicate calculations. There was no reason to think it had misjudged now, with the duration of this protective shutdown. The Sovereigns only *thought* the Weave was gone for good, but it would be back. In only five more days, it would be back, and everything would return to the way it had been. It would. It *would*. There was no reason to fear. There was no reason to fear.

She tried not to entertain any thought of what might happen if the Weave *had* made a mistake. But those fears crowded into her unshielded mind. The integrated world was unused to violence. For nearly as long as Derryn could remember, every problem had been solved by the meeting of minds. The instantaneous connection between all people allowed every user to experience another's need and perspective as clearly as if it were their own, so that compromise and justice prevailed, never brute force or deception. Empathy was as instinctive to Integrationists as breath, compassion as reflexive as the beating of their hearts. If the Sovereigns united to attack Philadelphia—or New York, or any other city—they would meet little effective opposition. Bombs could not be reasoned with, and empathy had as much effect on a gun as a raindrop on a wildfire.

Derryn pressed her hands against her face, trying to drive back her own imagination. She couldn't help picturing what life might be like if the Sovereigns took over. In preparation for her assignment at Haverford, she had studied all she could about the culture and practices of the Human Heritage Movement. It had made for grim work. Women and children were effectively the property of men and lived heavily segregated lives, every movement and action controlled by the leaders of their communities. How ironic, Derryn mused darkly, that the chief fear among Sovereigns was mind control via the Weave. Those people lived such restricted lives that Derryn couldn't imagine any form of mind control more complete or devastating than that which the leaders of Human Heritage wielded over the movement's adherents.

But those men out there, cheering the downfall of Derryn's world . . . they had diesel trucks, which would go on running long after any EV had lost its charge. They surely had water, too. Or at least, they would know how to make pump water and river water safe to drink.

There was a Sovereign community inside New York, beyond the blockade, as improbable as that seemed. Derryn was certain she'd read about it in her study of the culture—a commune that managed to live peacefully inside the most diverse and connected city on the planet. Maybe that wasn't so odd, for every imaginable kind of person called New York home. Maybe a commune of Sovereign separatists was inevitable, even essential, in the largest melting pot humankind had ever made.

That New York commune had a funny name. Derryn chewed a knuckle, struggling to remember. What was the place called?

Dutch Kills!

The name burst like a firework in her mind.

She crawled slowly back to the patch of wire fencing, careful not to stir the plants around her, and lay along a garden path, studying the men at the campfire as they talked and chanted prayers and gazed up at the aurora in fits of religious ecstasy. One of those men had a tattoo on each cheek, rather than the customary single mark. That was significant, though it took Derryn some time to remember why.

He's a pastor, she thought.

Among Sovereigns, a woman was never permitted to go anywhere without the supervision of a male relative. But in a culture as violent as theirs, many men were lost. Those women who had no husband or close male relations could be accompanied and protected by a pastor. Few men were called to the lofty position, and Derryn couldn't recall the special circumstances that brought such men into the work. All she really needed to know was that Sovereign pastors, with their double-marked faces, saw it as their religious duty to extend protection to vulnerable women and children of the Movement. A plan began to take shape in her stumbling mind, half seen and clumsy, yet more of a plan than she'd had since setting out from the church that morning. Hadn't she taken that dress from Haverford's textile room for just this kind of emergency? The idea wasn't without risk. But if she carried it through, she would be in New York City by the next afternoon.

Quietly, Derryn retreated down the garden to the berry bushes. Concealed by their dense foliage, she stripped off her ordinary clothes and put on the Sovereign dress. She felt very naked and exposed with the long skirt swinging around her bare legs, the night air working its way up to chill her skin.

Fearing that the men might search her pack, she took each of the precious data chips from their zippered pocket and transferred them to her bra. The three slim connection ports of her CoreTex went into the cups of her bra, too. She could only hope that her gender and the presence of a pastor would spare her being strip-searched. The wire components of the CoreTex might pass for useless trash in the bottom of her bag—if the men spotted them at all. She wrapped Helen's old journals with her own clothing. If her bag was searched, she could pass the garments off as mere rags she had used to protect family heirlooms. Then, when she was as prepared as she was ever going to be, Derryn settled the pack on her shoulders and strode openly down the garden, fighting back her fear that the men might shoot first and ask questions later.

They did spot her as she crossed in front of the wire portion of the fence.

"On your feet!" one of the men barked.

The Sovereigns leaped up as one, guns at the ready.

Derryn stopped in her tracks, raising her hands above her head.

"Brothers," she called timidly, "thank God I've found you. Please, I need help."

There was a pause. Derryn's heart thundered across that eternity while the men glanced at one another, then considered her—a lone woman in a long blue dress.

Finally, the one with the double tattoos lowered his gun and stepped forward. The firelight below him and the shine of the aurora above lit his face with a stark significance. He had the same close-cropped hair that all Sovereign men wore, and a thick beard of sandy brown. His eyes were keen and searching. They never seemed to stop moving, roving over Derryn and what he could see of the garden, darting out across the meadow to search for any other sign of life.

"Are you alone?" the pastor demanded.

"Yes," Derryn said.

"Come out of there, but keep your hands where we can see them."

She obeyed at once, as any Sovereign woman would do, holding her hands high until she needed them to work the latch on the gate. She raised them again as she left the garden and stumbled toward the encampment. A chorus of animal instincts she'd never known she possessed howled inside, commanding her to run. But if she tried to break away now, one man or another would surely open fire. Committed to this wild, reckless plan, she could only hope the gamble would be worth everything she risked.

Derryn stopped walking when she was a few meters from the men. She kept her eyes on the pastor, spoke only to him.

"My husband was killed a few days ago in the city. A wirehead shot him. I've been hiding here ever since."

"Where are you from?" the pastor asked.

She swallowed hard. While changing her clothes, she had rehearsed the story she would tell but hadn't thought to include an origin for her false Sovereign persona. Whatever answer she gave, it had to be someplace far from here, someplace these men were unlikely to know well.

"Dayton," she finally answered. "We lived outside Dayton, but we were on our way to Dutch Kills in New York, to live with my brother-in-law."

The pastor gestured for Derryn to come closer. "You can put your hands down, Sister."

She went to him, keeping her eyes lowered, and made no attempt to conceal her trembling.

"Who was your husband?"

Derryn affected a sniff. "His name was Thomas. Thomas Jenkins."

One of the other men tugged at Derryn's short hair. She flinched away.

"Leave her be," the pastor said.

"Never seen a woman without long hair," the other grumbled.

"I . . . I talked back to my husband," Derryn said, "and was punished for it."

The men chuckled. She could feel them drawing in around her, a tight ring from which she couldn't escape, and all at once she knew her plan had been a foolish one. She had done nothing but march herself into even worse danger.

Her legs gave out. Weeping, she crumpled into the tall grass. It was no act; fear had entirely overwhelmed her, and to her horror and embarrassment, she seemed incapable of doing anything but cowering and crying.

"All right, all right," the pastor said. "Back off, all of you. You're scaring her. Don't you think she's been through enough already?"

"Sorry, Cole," one of them said.

A hand came down gently on her shoulder. She jerked with fear, but when she looked up, she found the pastor watching her with an expression of sympathy so deep and true it startled her. She hadn't expected to find genuine compassion in these people.

"You're safe now, Sister," the man said. "I'm Pastor Cole, from the Iron Rock community. Do you know Iron Rock?"

Derryn shook her head.

"It's not far from here. I can take you there tonight, if you want—"

"No, no!" Derryn surged to her feet. "I've got to get to Dutch Kills, please!"

He smiled. "Okay. I can take you to New York tomorrow. I haven't been to Dutch Kills in years, but I think I remember how to get there—more or less. You say you've got family there?"

"My husband's brother and his wife. I know they'll take me in, now that I'm . . . I'm . . . a widow."

"What's your name, Sister?"

"Sarah."

"You're lucky you found me. There aren't many pastors in the area right now. We've got an operation underway, you know, at some college not too far from here. Most of the local pastors are with their communities, protecting the women and children while the men do their work. I'm only out and about tonight because I know how to work on diesel engines. We had a couple of trucks break down. They needed me to get them working again."

"I'm blessed," Derryn said meekly. "Thank you, Pastor Cole. God has been merciful in guiding me to you."

He put his arm around her shoulders. His touch carried a surprising tenderness, a deference to her fear and need.

"This woman is under my protection." Cole made the announcement to the others with a curious formality. "In the morning, I'll escort her to where she's going, and the rest of you can carry on with the operation."

With that, the Sovereigns relaxed and returned to their campfire.

Cole guided Derryn to one of the massive black pickup trucks. "Come on, Sister. You can sleep inside the cab of one of these beauties. It's a lot more comfortable than sleeping on the ground, I can tell you that. Anyway, we don't have any more bedrolls, so it's the inside of a truck or the cold, bare earth—your choice."

Derryn smiled weakly. "I'll take the truck. Thank you, Pastor."

He opened the door of one vehicle and helped her climb inside. The interior held an oily stench, but the bench seat was soft enough to lie on, if Derryn ignored the grimy texture of its upholstery. She positioned her backpack to use as a pillow, and once she was lying down, Cole shut the heavy door.

Derryn lay rigid but still, listening to the night, the snap of the campfire, the murmur of men's voices. She hoped Cole might return to the fire and give her a chance to slip off into the trees, but the truck rocked as he climbed into its open bed. A few moments of shuffling and bumping ensued—the pastor fixing his bedroll right there in the back of the truck. Evidently, he took his role as protector seriously. The man wasn't going to let Derryn out of his sight until they made it to Dutch Kills.

Fine, she told herself in bleak acceptance. *I've only got to keep up this charade for a few more hours.*

By tomorrow afternoon, she would be in New York City and would find some way to give Pastor Cole the slip. Until that opportunity came, she would play the role of the meek Sovereign woman. And she would watch for her chance to run.

Derryn felt no need to sleep that night. She was too much on edge, wrestling with her clumsy thoughts, trying to game out every possible twist of fate and fortune in the long term and the near.

All the while, as she worked her way through plan after plan, she watched the aurora through the windshield. The lights flowed and curled across the sky, ribbons of bright fire. Derryn could do nothing but hope—or pray—that the Weave was truly safe and the old world would come again.

17

Helen

June 18, 1862

This morning, Mary Jane and I made our first delivery of maps and money to the prisoners in the old Libby warehouse.

We rose early to make our preparations, packing two baskets each with Kitty's fresh-baked corn pones, more of Father's old clothing, and as many eggs as we could fit without breaking them. Two or three eggs in each basket were not of the ordinary boiled variety, but contained the sand and rolled paper of Mary Jane's devising.

An unseasonable fog had risen from the river overnight, obscuring all sight of the city behind a white veil, dampening the air in promise of dreadful humidity later in the day. As we made our way through the misty streets, my heart pounded so loudly I feared the soldiers we passed would hear and mistake it for a regiment's drumming. The baskets on my arms were impossibly heavy, laden not only with eggs and pones and mended trousers, but with the weight of our dangerous secret.

"How do you stay so calm?" I whispered to Mary Jane.

She glanced at me, her expression unreadable to anyone who didn't know her as well as I did. "When you've lived most your life as property, you learn to keep your thoughts where no one can see. That's the only thing they can't take from you—your mind."

Poor Mary Jane. Though we have gone through much together, trusting one another in this covert work, I will never understand what she has endured—she and all the rest who share her plight. I was tempted to weep with remorse for the part I have played in Mary Jane's suffering, but I steeled myself with a will. What did I do this work for, if not to help this girl and everyone like her? Weeping would have done no good to anyone. I pushed my thoughts as far back into myself as they would go, well out of sight, as Mary Jane had done.

The stench of the prison grounds reached us long before the building itself loomed out of the mist. We picked our way among the soldiers' tents, keeping to the trampled pathways and avoiding the boggy places that surely held fouler things than puddles of water.

The guard at the door, a surly man with tobacco-stained teeth, gave us a cursory nod. "Ladies."

"Good morning," I replied, forcing a show of great cheer. "We've brought our usual supplies for the prisoners."

He grunted and motioned for us to place our baskets on the officer's desk. Captain Gibbs was nowhere to be seen, which was one small mercy. That man does turn my stomach more than I can say. Even in his absence, my hands trembled as I set my baskets on the desk. I clasped them together to hide the shaking.

The guard pawed roughly through our offerings. My breath caught as he lifted one of the false eggs, turning it over in his dirty fingers.

"Seems light," he muttered.

Mary Jane spoke up before I could even think of what to say. "Fresh laid this morning, sir. Our hens ain't been eating as well with the war on. Makes for lighter eggs."

The guard looked at her with a sharp, searching expression. I had no idea whether he doubted her story or whether he was merely affronted that a Black girl would speak to him directly.

"Hush your mouth," I snapped at Mary Jane. "Don't you know you ought to speak when spoken to?"

She lowered her face in a show of contrition.

"She's a saucy girl," I said to the guard, "but a good worker. Anyhow, she's right. The hens haven't been laying as they did when we had extra corn for their feed, but we're grateful they're still laying at all."

He placed the egg back in the basket and waved us through. "Guard's inside the hallway. You got fifteen minutes, miss."

Mary Jane's solution to the money problem turned out to be simple as you please. She hid the coins in her bodice, so there would be no hint of them while our baskets were searched. Once we were admitted to the corridor beyond the captain's office, where we could only walk in single file, she slipped the coins out again and pressed them into the pones. I kept our guard talking, filling his head with breezy, inconsequential chatter—and trying not to think of those coins. Less money in my coffers meant more troubles on the horizon, but that was a problem for another day. Anyhow, the man never noticed a thing. He was only too glad to have the attention of a lady, even for a few moments' time, even in the stinking darkness of that miserable place.

When we reached the prison room on the second floor, I found it as wretched as ever. Fog subdued the light, and only a sickly, pale parody of morning came in through the barred windows. The Union officers in their tattered uniforms crowded around us as we entered. Their faces were gaunt but hopeful.

"Miss Bywater! Miss Mary Jane!" One officer, a Captain Williams from Massachusetts, approached us with a smile that transformed his haggard appearance. "You always bring sunshine into this dreary place."

"Why, aren't you just too kind," I replied, conscious of the guard watching us from the doorway. "We've brought boiled eggs and fresh-made pones today."

"A feast, as far as we're concerned," Captain Williams said.

As we had agreed to do, Mary Jane and I handed over the baskets themselves, rather than distributing the goods as we usually did. Today's guard was one we'd never seen before—that is usually the way our visits have played out—and he didn't know that we had never before left our baskets with the officers.

I was just calling Mary Jane to my side and preparing to leave when a fellow in ragged blue all but dived into the nearest basket. He seized an egg with such desperation that I was sure he would crush the shell in his fist right then and there. My heart leaped with sudden fear. If he had chanced to seize one of our rigged eggs, and if he broke it right in front of the guard, the ruse would be over. Both Mary Jane and I would be sure to meet our Maker at the end of a Confederate rope.

By instinct, I reached out and laid my hand on that man's, preventing him from crushing the eggshell. The moment I touched him, he looked up with a half-dazed expression and met my eye. The animal hunger dissipated from his countenance. An entirely human soul looked back at me, suffering and sad, more than halfway to breaking under the strain of his cruel treatment.

"Now, now," I said lightly, "don't be too hasty, sir. A gentleman always minds his manners."

I squeezed his hand carefully, tried to convey my thoughts through my eyes. *It's a special egg, sir. Don't crack it where the guard might see.*

He rocked back on his heels, nodding slightly as I withdrew my hand. The egg remained whole in his palm as I hustled Mary Jane from the room.

And then—oh, the euphoric sensation of going back home, knowing that we had delivered our first batch of maps and money without exposing our cause! We were giggling like little girls long before we reached Church Hill.

"You were magnificent," I said to Mary Jane, "and I'm sorry I had to snap at you back there when they first let us in."

"I know it, Miss Helen. Besides, that doesn't matter now. We did it! And we'll do it again, as many times as need be, till that jail's all cleared out."

Now there's nothing left to do but wait for our plan to bear its quiet fruit. I feel very light in my heart, almost too assured of success. There is a part of me that scolds, warning me not to be foolish, to never let down my guard. And I shan't, to be sure. But oh, it is *good* to feel this drop of real hope after months—years!—of worry.

When we returned to Eudaimonia, David had the day's paper ready for me in the dining room. The editor of the *Whig* was fairly frothing at the mouth over President Lincoln's latest move on the great chessboard. Wouldn't you know it, Lincoln has approved a second version of his Confiscation Act. The Union army may seize any Confederate property they find. That includes slaves, who are to be emancipated at once in any territory occupied by Union forces. *All* slaves are to be freed wherever the Union wins a little ground, not only those who are confiscated. And any runaways who make it to the North or to these occupied territories are not to be returned to their enslavers.

"Just read this!" I said to Mary Jane, passing her the paper with a triumphant flourish.

She did read the column, and I watched her eyes light brighter by the moment as she understood its meaning. When she had finished, she said nothing, but looked up at me with a smile like a summer's day.

This war is not yet fought to liberate the enslaved. But little by little, the cause of abolition rises to stand taller among less worthy reasons. Cotton mills and merchant ships! What are they, beside the souls of millions? Today I have hope that we will yet see the righteous cause prevail, and we will yet create the bright future that visited me under the aurora's light. Mankind will learn his lesson, and someday soon, we will walk forward together into a better time, arm in arm, with nothing to divide us, as the Lord ever meant for us to be.

18

Derryn

2053

Derryn must have slept. Strange—while she'd lain awake on the bench seat, watching the aurora through the truck's dusty windshield, she had thought she never would sleep again. But her eyes opened, and a dim, fragmented dream of the Weave receded—a dream in which she had felt the presence of everyone at once. Connected, the way she was meant to be, sensing and partaking of the whole vast, imperfect, loving accomplishment of humanity. When the dream was gone, a hollow ache of loss opened in its place. The morning sky was a clear, pale blue, showing no sign of the magnetic current that still broke like a wild tide over the planet. And Derryn was small beneath that wide, unknowable sky—small and entirely alone.

She sat up slowly. Every muscle was cramped and aching from the previous day's long walk. The truck's interior was humid from her own breath, the smell of oil and dirt even closer and more choking than it had been the night before. When she peered through the cab's back window, into the bed of the truck, the Sovereign pastor was sitting up on his bedroll, stretching his arms above his head and yawning.

Derryn opened the driver's door, slid out with her backpack clutched against her chest.

"Good morning, Sister Sarah," the Sovereign said cheerfully. "Hope you slept okay in there."

"Probably better than you slept, Pastor Cole."

She forced a smile. However unexpected and disturbing her predicament may be, there was no benefit in allowing any of these men to see her distress. At all costs, she must remain on Cole's good side until he had conveyed her to the New York blockade.

He swung easily down from the truck bed. "Aw, I'm used to it. We rough it all the time out here, outside the communities. A man doesn't need much more than his bedroll for a good night's sleep. Like the cowboys, back in the day."

Derryn tried to recall the reference, the imagery. All of this knowledge—*her* knowledge—was stored in her own head, not in the Weave. She knew that, logically, yet it was so damn hard to call it up when she needed it. So slow, this hardware of blood and bone and synapse fire. Images flicked past her inner eye, none of them staying long enough that she could think up anything clever or useful to say. Horses, saddles, a rangy scrubland under a deep-blue, starry sky. Coyote howling, neckerchiefed American stereotype strumming some sort of stringed instrument. Very mid-twentieth-century pop culture. Not Derryn's forte.

"Eating beans from a can," she offered. "Around the campfire."

Cole grinned, distorting the tattooed symbols on his cheeks. He seemed very proud of himself. "Yeah, that's the idea."

She glanced around the parking lot, the deep shadows of the surrounding forest. "Where do I . . . uh . . ."

"Nature calling?" Cole guessed. "Go back into the trees. I'll make sure no one surprises you."

He turned his back at once, crossing his arms over his chest, as if Derryn were some treasure that required the constant vigilance of a dedicated guard.

She waded into the undergrowth until she could no longer see the parking lot. Then she contended with the long Sovereign dress, doing what must be done. Derryn used the moment of privacy to think through her next steps—to push herself through the slow mire of planning without Tyko's aid. Briefly, she considered running off through the forest. But Cole was willing to drive her all the way to New York. If she ran now, it might take her days to find another ride—or she might have to walk the whole distance, after all, without any Weave to guide her.

No, the only sensible thing to do was to stick with Pastor Cole. In a few hours, she would arrive at the blockade. Then she could simply throw herself on the mercy of the guards at the city border—give them her real name, her credentials with Stanford. She could tell them she wasn't really a Sovereign woman, she was an Integrationist through and through, had only used Cole for a ride to New York. She could show the guards her CoreTex as proof. What could Cole do about it, once they were at the border? Nothing—not when he was outnumbered by blockade personnel.

She only had to keep the pastor happy until they arrived at the border. He seemed like a friendly enough guy, as far as extremists went. As long as Derryn played the role of the meek and proper Sovereign woman, Cole would have no reason to turn against her.

Derryn shared in the men's breakfast—biscuits and cold slices of smoked ham. She accepted her rations with a sinking feeling. There was no way this meat was lab grown; it had certainly come from a once-living animal. Yet any hesitation would give away her game. She ate the ham first, to get it out of the way. The intense salty, smoky flavor was not unpleasant, and the texture wasn't so different from pressed tofu. At least there was no connection between her and the men, so they couldn't feel her distinctly un-Sovereign guilt over eating a slaughtered animal.

She helped pack up the camp, sticking close to Cole and speaking only when spoken to. When the bedrolls had been secured inside the black trucks and the last embers of the campfire were extinguished, Cole brushed his hands together with a show of vigor and readiness.

"We have to stop in Iron Rock," he said. "We'll fuel up there. Then we'll head for Dutch Kills."

There was some discussion over where and how Derryn ought to be transported. The extended-cab pickups had barely fit the twelve Sovereign men and their guns inside. The addition of a woman to their group, even for a short drive, posed something of a problem.

"She's not riding in the back," said a gray-haired, leathery man called Jake. "If any wireheads shoot at us, we can't let them get a female."

Derryn hugged the backpack more tightly against her chest. *Integrationists don't have guns,* she did not say. Did the Sovereigns know so little about the people they considered enemies? Or did they merely hedge their bets? Under circumstances like these—the Weave suddenly vanished, an emergency swallowing the whole global population—maybe even the wireheads might resort to violence.

"Cole," Jake said, "you and the woman will ride up front with me. Zack, you take the bed of the truck."

The one called Zack—so young he might still have been a boy—climbed into the nearest bed. "This counts as a raid, doesn't it? Since we're headed back this way after we fuel up?"

"Yeah," one of the others said, laughing at his eagerness. "If you catch a wirehead bullet, you'll die a hero's death."

The kid pumped his fist in the air. "Then let's go! I'm ready, hallelujah!"

Derryn soon found herself sandwiched between Jake and Cole as their truck swayed and bumped over the rough road. The gluttonous roar of the combustion engine thundered through her body. The old park vanished around her, rapidly replaced by the gray half-ruin of the city's outer edge.

Jake sped through the same blocks Derryn had seen from the air—apartment complexes crammed into too little space, desperate gardens planted and tended in every available corner of sunlight. Entire buildings had been gutted by explosions, their dry innards spilling into the potholed roads. Philadelphia was a far cry from the cool, green corridors of Menlo Park, or any city Derryn had visited on the sane side of the Cascadian border.

The trucks climbed an overpass and took the curve of an on-ramp, then flew unimpeded down an expressway that followed the course of the river. Derryn kept her eyes on the broad span of water as distance was reduced to nothing and the city blurred around her into one colorless confusion of disorder. It was all she could do to hold outright terror at bay. She had no idea whether the disguise of the blue dress had saved her or condemned her.

Keep your head, she reminded herself. *New York isn't so far away. Only a few more hours of this. Then you'll be safe. Then you'll be safe. Only a few more hours.*

The truck slowed to navigate another ramp, then crossed the river on a great steel bridge, its girders flashing before Derryn's stricken gaze with the rhythmic cruelty of the passing seconds. On the far side of the river, the city thinned into suburbs. These neighborhoods had once been affluent, to guess by the size of the houses. But the glory days were long gone now. Twenty-five years of war had reduced this place to the same state as the inner city. The large lots of once-fine homes had been converted into tent encampments, vegetable gardens, and livestock pens. The same struggle for survival went on here as everywhere else in the greater Philly area.

Jake took an off-ramp; the road traversed another neighborhood of large homes and expansive lots with parklike groves of trees. Then the hard line of a wall rose into view just ahead.

"Iron Rock," Cole announced with evident pride. "It's about four hundred acres in all. We built it around a country club we took about twenty years ago—two big golf courses and a greenbelt with a year-round creek. It's the biggest community in the Eastern states."

The truck slowed as it approached the wall, which rose some five or six meters above the street. Now Derryn could see that the fortification was a patchwork of salvaged materials, like the deer fence around the garden. Tar-covered logs, cement blocks, and the corrugated metal of disassembled shipping containers had been cobbled together to create a barrier that was ugly but no doubt effective. The top of the wall was a tangled nest of razor wire. She could see men patrolling behind the wire, rifles propped upright on their shoulders.

"Is the whole thing walled in?" Derryn asked, careful to keep her voice soft and meek.

"All of it," Jake said. "No damn wireheads will set foot inside Iron Rock, that's for sure."

The truck rolled to a double gate. Jake waited until he was recognized. The gates were dragged open by a couple of sweating young men, and the truck rumbled into the depths of the commune.

If not for the fact that she knew these people to be dangerous, Derryn might have thought their community pleasant, even idyllic, for beyond the ugly palisade, she found a thriving town that seemed as normal and functional as anything back home. The houses were large and well maintained, their gardens ripe with the abundance of summer. Children played in the yards of homes and in the daisy-filled meadows that rolled out like green carpets from groves of gentle trees. They passed a large cement lot filled with shade tents. It appeared to be a market of some kind, filled with women in long dresses who carried baskets on their arms or pulled small utility wagons stuffed with goods for sale or trade.

A small complex of larger brick buildings loomed ahead. A hand-painted sign had been erected in front of the complex: "Iron Rock Community Seat." Jake turned the truck into the parking lot of the complex and coasted to a stop outside a three-story building that might once have been a library or a collection of medical offices. Now its front had been decorated with a mural of flowers that twined around the words "Women's House."

Jake cut the engine. Derryn's shuddering breath sounded much too loud in her ears. She didn't dare to look at the silver-haired man, nor even at Cole. She kept her face lowered, waiting for one of the men to speak—to give her some command she must follow. That seemed the only way to conduct herself, under the circumstances.

Cole slid from the cab, held the door for Derryn. "Come on out, Sister. You might as well stretch your legs. If you need anything—uh, anything of a feminine nature—you're welcome to head inside." He jerked his head in the direction of the Women's House.

"I . . . I don't know," Derryn said. "We didn't have a Women's House at the community back in Dayton."

Cole gave her a puzzled smile. "You didn't?"

Derryn shook her head as she climbed out after him. She couldn't think of anything else to say. Elaborating on the falsehood would surely dig this present hole deeper.

The pastor shrugged, slammed the truck's door. "All the unmarried ladies move in here, everyone over eighteen, everyone available for courting. The girls who don't have fathers, too. And the widows of war, like yourself."

"Things are much calmer back in Dayton," Derryn said. "There aren't many families there that lose their fathers to the war, so I guess we didn't have the need for a place like this." She added hastily, "But it's a good idea. It's very . . . righteous . . . that you all take such good care of the women."

Jake had come around the back of the truck so stealthily that when he spoke—much too near Derryn for her comfort—she flinched in surprise.

"We do take good care of our women, Sister," the man said. "The Women's House is kept under guard twenty-four hours a day, and that's on top of the patrols on the perimeter fence. If those techie bastards lose their heads over this solar thing and try to storm Iron Rock, they won't make it far enough inside to reach our women."

Derryn looked up at the three-story building. She could just make out the rooftop patrol, the heads and shoulders of men bobbing and shadowy as they neared the perimeter and receded again. A handful of women and girls had gathered at an upper window to look down at the trucks—at Derryn in her long blue dress. Their faces were sober, mistrustful. Even the youngest residents of the Women's House had hard, cautious eyes, veiled by an obscure pain. Derryn shuddered, moved another step closer to Cole. The sooner she got out of Iron Rock, the safer she would feel.

Jake tossed the truck keys lightly in his palm. "I'll go and fill up the tank, Cole. Meet you back here in ten minutes."

Before Jake could climb back into his vehicle, however, a tinny whine sounded from a nearby road. A motorbike appeared. Its rider seemed to spot Jake's truck. He veered off his course, diverting into the parking lot, and paused to idle outside the Women's House.

"We're rolling out," the biker shouted over the sound of his engine. "Ops at Haverford College. Gonna breach their wall and take the whole place. We need every truck and every warrior. Report to Command Central."

With that, the biker sped on.

"Lots of land at Haverford," Jake said to Cole. "It'll make a nice community."

"If we can take it," Cole answered. "Nobody has managed to for years."

"Well, now's our chance, with all their tech wiped out by this solar thing. You coming?"

Cole glanced at Derryn, then shook his head. "I've got to see that Sister Sarah here gets to Dutch Kills safely."

"Let her stay in the Women's House till we're finished with the college. She'll be fine."

In an instant, Derryn knew that if she entered that building, she would never leave it again. It was the fastest her mind had worked since she'd lost the Weave. She clutched the pastor's arm, looked up at him with a silent plea. There was no need to fake her desperation. Nor did she need a neural connection to make him feel her fear.

"She's been through a lot," Cole said to Jake. "Lost her man. She's got family in Dutch Kills who'll take her in. It won't take me long to get her there."

Jake laughed. "It will without a truck."

"We'll take the trail," Cole said lightly. "I'm not much of a warrior, anyway—not like you and your boys. You won't miss me in the op. I'd be underfoot, anyway."

Jake gave him a hearty slap on the back. "I guess that's right. God called you right, when he made you a pastor instead of a warrior."

"He usually knows what he's doing," Cole said.

"Take care, Brother."

"You stay safe out there, Jake."

Derryn couldn't seem to marshal command over herself as Jake drove away. Her whole body was shaking. If she hadn't been clinging to Cole's arm, she might have fallen to the pavement.

They're going to take Haverford.

They were going to try, anyway. She thought of Melinda and Mihir in that damned bunker, and all the rest of the faculty, the students who hadn't gotten out and hidden themselves in the city. All she could do was hope that her friends would be all right—that somehow, they'd know this new attack was coming and would use the escape tunnels before it was too late. And the Bywater cache . . . if the Sovereigns broke into the locker and found it, they would certainly burn the paintings. Thank goodness she had gotten out. Thank goodness she had taken the data chips with her, for now those chips might hold the last evidence of Helen's remarkable work.

"Well," Cole said brightly when Jake's truck had vanished, "I hope you like hiking, Sister Sarah."

"Are we really going to walk all the way to New York?"

"Looks like that's our only option now."

Derryn swallowed her protest. She was stuck in this quagmire. If she raised any objection, Cole would probably turn her over to the Women's House for safekeeping, at least until he could secure another vehicle.

"I can walk," she said quickly. "I like hiking."

At least that much was true. She was an accomplished backpacker—had often joined Leo and his husband on their extensive weekend hikes through the Sierras and along the California coast. Tyko had said the trip would take four days on foot.

It isn't so bad, she insisted, refusing to look up again at the Women's House. *You can do it. Four days. You can do it, Derryn.*

Cole patted her hand, then disentangled her from his arm. "It'll take me about an hour to round up supplies."

"I'll come with you," Derryn said quickly. "Let me help."

She couldn't allow him to suggest—or even think—that she ought to wait in that guarded prison called the Women's House. She could already feel its walls closing around her like a trap.

19

Helen

September 19, 1862

These past two weeks have been among the most trying of the war. At the end of August, when the second battle of Bull Run brought such ruinous defeat for the United States Army, I fell into a blue state from which I feared I might not recover. How many hours did I spend fretting over the loss and what it might mean for the future?

Nevertheless, Mary Jane and I kept up our deliveries to the prison, for we are determined not to fail in our cause, even if the tides of fortune turn against us.

But then, only yesterday, I read the *Whig*'s account of the fighting in Maryland, at Antietam Creek. The paper estimates that more than twenty thousand souls were lost. Twenty thousand! It cannot be true. When I try to realize it, my mind goes blank with despair, and all I can see is that vision that came to me years ago, with the auroras—the armies in bloodstained uniforms marching through my garden, the fields red, so terribly red with the horror.

Yet the Union prevailed at Antietam. It was victory dearly bought, but victory all the same. General Lee's hopes of invading the North were dashed—for good, I pray—and today there is a downtrodden air pervading Richmond. I think my loyal Confederate neighbors have finally learned that gumption and will are insufficient weapons against all the novel inventions of the North. Their ships, their guns, their means of keeping soldiers clothed and fed—their submarine boats!—all are superior to Southern capabilities. A rebel yell may sound fearsome, but it can't do much against the telegraph and a functional railroad.

As gruesome as the news from Antietam may be, as darkly as it stains the collective spirit, still I can't help but wonder whether General Lee's attempt at invasion will inspire some momentous action from President Lincoln. I don't mean on the battlefield, but in the chambers of Washington, where laws are made. For Lee had surely hoped to spread the infection of slavery deeper into the body of this nation. Strong medicine is required to counter such a plague.

I write of medicine because it's much on my mind. These past few days, I've been quite occupied with remedies and elixirs. I've been playing nurse here at Eudaimonia.

Last Wednesday, I rode to the cabin to open it up for my usual meeting, my quiet Society of Friends, which has grown considerably since the spring. My fellow worshippers are mostly those half-freed Blacks whose former masters have granted them the same provisions I gave to the workers of Eudaimonia.

(I dare not inquire about their owners, for though it would brace my soul considerably to know all the secret abolitionists of Richmond society, I might endanger others by association if my work at the prison should be discovered. And so, I carry on alone, except for Mary Jane.)

But though I often welcome Friends into the cabin for silent worship, there were none that day. That mattered little to me. I enjoy the hour of peace, my true communion with God, whether others are present or not.

Yet from the moment I stepped inside the cabin, a creepy sensation went crawling up my back. The place appeared empty, but I knew it was not. Nothing stirred, not a moth or a speck of dust. Even the forest outside was peaceful, the birds singing away in the old oak tree and the wind hushing and sighing through its leaves. I paused in the middle of the room, stock still and alert like a deer that's smelled a hunter. I simply could not shake off the feeling that someone was close by, *watching* me.

Just when I'd made up my mind to heed my instincts and go, as I was actually headed for the door, I heard a heartrending groan from inside the little wood closet, the one Father built into the side of the stone fireplace. That closet isn't much bigger than a travel trunk. One couldn't picture a man packed into such a small space, but while I was still gasping in shock, a muffled voice called, "Please, miss, let me out of here." The man had a Northern accent.

One must imagine the effort it took to extract that man from the wood closet. He had folded himself right up, and somehow had managed to close the door, but when he saw through the crack of the hinge that it was I who'd entered the cabin, he regretted his decision to hide. And then he couldn't get himself out again.

As I pulled him from the closet, he coughed and sputtered and said weakly, "You're Miss Helen, the angel from the prison. Thank God."

I sat him up against the wall and went outside to get my canteen from my saddle, for he was dry as a bone and twice as thin.

"How long have you been here?" I asked as he drank down all my water in one long draft.

"Three days," he answered, his voice a little less croaky than it had been before.

That was when I recognized the shirt and trousers he wore. Father's old things.

"Why," I said, "you got out of Libby's place. The prison downtown."

He nodded and shook the canteen as if he wished there were more water in it. "Thanks to your map and your money."

I reached for the canteen, thinking I might go and fill it in the river, but he caught my hand and squeezed it. A terribly forward man, I suppose, yet at his touch, I remembered him. He was the very fellow who'd taken the egg from my basket—the one I had stopped before he could crack the shell and expose my plot.

"How ever did you get out of that prison?" I said to him.

The memory seemed a great agony. He groaned again and rested his head against the wall, shutting his eyes as if to drive back the images in his own head.

"It took us weeks to do it. We found an old hole in the wall, from a chimney pipe, I think, and sent one of the smallest fellows in to explore it. It led down to the basement. Or down to Hell, if you'll pardon my language. That's what we called the place—Rat Hell. All of us who were small enough to shimmy down that stovepipe took our turns in Rat Hell. One or two at a time, we would crawl down into the basement and hide there through the day, underneath rotten old straw with the rats crawling all over us."

I shuddered at such a dreadful thought.

"At night," the man went on, "when the captain was gone from the place and his guards were more likely to be sleeping than walking their patrols, we used whatever we could find to dig through the basement wall. Old busted tool handles, spoons—any useful trash we discovered under the straw. After a good month of digging, our tunnel broke through, down on the riverbank."

A surge of triumph ran through me. All this time, as our visits to the prison have continued, I've had no idea that our designs were already bearing fruit. *Won't Mary Jane be glad to hear it,* I thought as I listened to the officer's story.

"I was the first to get out," he said. "I covered the tunnel over with a lot of brush and sticks, and then I took off across the city, using one of those little maps you hid in the eggs to guide me. No one looked twice at me, in these clothes. I look pretty shabby, I guess, but I don't look like no Union officer, that's for sure."

"What's your name, sir?" I asked.

"Jeremiah Carver, major of the Third Corps. Pleased to meet you. I don't suppose this is the safe house you marked out on your map, Miss Helen."

"No, sir, it's only a little Quaker meetinghouse. The safe house is farther along."

"I don't dare to move myself from here," he said with a bleak expression. "I'm awful worn out from getting out of Richmond, and I've had no water for days, except what you gave me just now."

I couldn't leave the poor man alone. There isn't a crumb of food in the cabin, and the old well has long since run dry. It's a proper hike to the nearest water, too—much too far for a fellow in his state.

"You're coming back with me," I told him, "to Richmond."

Jere looked frightened at my words. That's what I call him—Jere—and we've become good friends these past two days since I discovered him. But I am getting ahead of my own story.

I hastened to assure him that he would come to no harm.

"I'm an abolitionist," I said, "working in secret for the Union. You don't look strong enough to make it to the safe house. Do you think you can sit a horse, at least? Not for long—only till I get you back to my home in the city."

He swore that he would try. I pulled him to his feet and led him to my horse. It took some doing to get him into the saddle, but once he was up, he sat old Cricket well enough. I wrestled with my skirt and petticoats but finally got up behind him and arranged myself in the most ladylike way that could be managed, under the circumstances. The poor man was thin as a rail when I put my arms around him. My heart was like to break for all the suffering he has endured—he, and the rest of those Northern officers.

And then we simply rode right back into Richmond. Without his Union blues, no one looked twice at us. I guided him all the way up to Church Hill. When I told him to go on into the yard at Eudaimonia, he whistled through his teeth.

"Mercy me," he said, "that is a fine place."

"My father built it, sir. He's long gone now—him and Mother, too. I inherited everything almost ten years ago, after Mother died."

"The whole place is yours?"

I laughed with pleasure. "I've managed to stay unattached all these years, sir. No husband to trouble me."

David and Ruthie had to help me get Jere down from the saddle. We all but dragged him inside.

And here he has been ever since, resting and gathering his strength in Mother's old bedroom. I've been bringing him chicken broth and bread, and greens cooked in bacon fat when he can handle richer foods. Kitty ran down to the apothecary and fetched a few good remedies for weakness and general malaise. I do believe those medicines are making a difference already, for Jere seems a little more vigorous every time I bring him a tray or sit at his bedside, listening to his stories and telling a few of my own. There is a new light in his eye, and I dare to think that the worst may be behind him now.

But what ever am I going to do with the man? Harboring a Union officer! As if my workings at the prison weren't dangerous enough. My treason against the Confederacy piles higher by the day. God protect me . . . but I won't stop the work for anything.

20

Derryn

2053

Little more than an hour after she'd arrived, Derryn left the Iron Rock commune in the back of one of the pickups. There were at least two dozen of the vehicles now, roaring like the nightmares of a twisted mind. With Cole close beside her in the windy bed, she clung to the truck's roll bar, forcing herself to take deep, steady breaths despite the smog from the engines.

Leo will never believe this, she told herself wryly.

Then her thoughts turned grim. Leo would lose his head if he knew where she was, what she was doing . . . what kind of danger she'd gotten herself into. When she made it back home—*when*—she wouldn't breathe a word of this to her brother. The bunker, the escape tunnel, a trek on foot to New York. She could tell him all of that. But hitching a ride with a convoy of terrorists?

Some stories are better kept to yourself.

The Sovereign trunks thundered back over the river and returned to the great ruin of Philadelphia. The expressway carried them past the airport where Derryn had arrived only a few days ago, which may as well have been a lifetime in the past. In the suburb of

Eddington, the truck that carried Derryn and Cole diverted from the freeway, pulled into a parking lot. The buildings around the lot were empty now. Whatever businesses had once thrived in that place had been abandoned years ago as bombs and battles remade the landscape.

"This is where we get out," Cole said.

He hefted his own pack, large and well used, with a mattress pad and sleeping bag strapped to the bottom. A spare pad and bivy sack were attached by carabiners.

"I brought extra for you," he said cheerfully. "I'll strap them to you once we're on the ground."

He helped Derryn climb down from the truck. The Sovereigns in the cab raised their hands in farewell, then gunned the engine and headed for the road. Derryn closed her eyes, exhaled slowly with relief while Cole busied himself with her pack. When the spare pad and sleeping bag were secured in place, they began the long walk to New York City.

They followed the Pike to a broad, cool creek, then crossed the water on a three-lane bridge that bore the white badges of a state highway. Other people went about their business in the neighborhoods and marketplaces they passed—such business as there was now, with most of the world's technology disabled. Plenty of people cast suspicious looks at their distinctive clothing and the tattoos on Cole's face. But there was no reason to fear Integrationists. The empathic effect of the Weave had stripped away the animal instinct for violence. As long as she and Cole left those people alone, they would offer neither threat nor harm.

The road they followed swung along the course of the creek, and soon they'd passed into long stretches of shadowy green, groves of trees that flowed smoothly between the cement islands of suburban developments.

"We'll reach the trail by noon," Cole said. "It runs all the way to New Brunswick. A beautiful walk—just you and nature. I've done it many times. There are quite a few communities out this way, and they often have need for a pastor."

He kept Derryn occupied with questions as they followed surface streets and parkways along the course of Neshaminy Creek. Walking seemed to help her keep her mind sharp—as sharp as it could be without the Weave's enhancement. Even so, she found it a struggle to invent plausible answers to his questions about the Ohio community from which Sister Sarah had supposedly come.

Cole never gave the least sign of suspicion, however—only accepted the tales Derryn spun with a mild "Uh-huh" or "I see." But she could never quite rid herself of the feeling that the pastor saw through her deception.

"One thing I don't understand," Cole said—out of nowhere, in the midst of a long stretch of silence, just as they were leaving the bank of the creek to cut back through the fringe of a suburb.

"What's that?" Derryn said.

"Why don't you have a mark?"

She blinked at him, too dull in her lone, feeble state to catch on. "A mark?"

He touched his cheek.

"Oh," Derryn said quickly. "Of course. That kind of mark." Why *didn't* she have one? What excuse would this man possibly accept? "We don't believe in tattoos where I'm from."

His brows knit together, an expression of confusion or disbelief.

"They're a sin," Derryn said. "The Bible says so. You know, in . . . in the book of . . ."

Frantically, she grappled with her own memories, the distant courses she'd taken her freshman year on comparative religion. There was *something* in the Bible forbidding tattoos. But damned if she could recall the citation now.

Cole eased back into his casual stroll. "Oh, yeah. Leviticus."

"Right. Leviticus." She had no idea whether that was correct.

"That's a pretty traditional law. Not too many communities hold to scripture so firmly."

He fell silent for a moment, glanced at Derryn as if he expected her to say something more, make some excuse or defense. Again, she felt a strangling certainty that Cole knew she was no Sovereign woman. But she couldn't admit to it here, now, on the outskirts of a city she had no hope of navigating on her own, with only this man for help.

Finally, he said, "You must feel like you're a long way from home, out here."

Derryn choked back a bitter laugh. "Pastor, you have no idea."

The effort of keeping the story straight tired her out far more than the walk was doing. As kind as Cole was, he was still a Sovereign, and at every moment, Derryn was sharply aware of the danger she was in. The moment he discovered she was a wirehead, his easygoing demeanor would probably evaporate. She would be alone with him in an unfamiliar environment, with no capacity to call for help or find her way to safety—without so much as that critical connection between their minds, the integrated link that would allow him to feel and empathize with her constant fear and weakness.

They trekked across countless kilometers of suburbs, where the people put on a show of carrying on, of crouching cheerfully under the blow of an unexpected but surely temporary disruption. Derryn watched a pack of children playing baseball in a park, their shouts and the bright crack of the bat filling the air with a sunny, happy noise. No doubt these people were used to getting on with life even when the worst emergencies came. It astonished her, that humankind could keep up with the daily business of living and loving and making and doing, even in the midst of war. And it sickened her, that anyone *had* to in this day and age. Shouldn't humankind have learned better by now?

They followed the road over a causeway that crossed a shallow, brown lake, then walked through a land of reservoirs and homes that seemed almost normal, scarcely touched by explosives or the final char of flames. The river came into view again—the same river Derryn had crossed at Philadelphia, or another one, she couldn't be sure, but as she crossed its bridge, the water below was broad and lively, and the blue sparkle of its surface made her feel as if she had really gone somewhere, as if this journey wouldn't be in vain.

As midday arrived with all its furious heat, they reached another small city. Cole declared that it was Trenton. "The real trail picks up here. No more towns for a while, just the forest and the old canal. You'll love it, Sarah. There's something so *real* about walking with nature, something so human."

He went on expounding on his great love for hiking, regaling her with stories of backpacking trips he'd made with his father and brothers years ago, when he was young. Derryn was surprised to learn that Sovereigns did anything but make war on their neighbors. She was surprised, too, at the difference in this man. Now that she had observed Sovereigns at closer range than she preferred, she felt that there was something unique about Cole, a fundamental difference setting him apart from the others. The jumpy tension and chest-thumping bluster that seemed to come naturally to the men of his culture was entirely absent in him. Cole's gentleness, the easygoing peace of his personality, marked him out as some other order of Sovereign. And Derryn was compelled to know what had made him so different from the rest.

They passed the remains of a shopping mall and walked through a district of abandoned office parks, then came again to a waterway—not the creek that had led them out of Eddington, but a slow and fragrant canal fringed along its banks by murmuring trees.

"We turn east here," Cole said.

Derryn hesitated. He was watching her with one brow raised, his smile tight with an expectation Derryn didn't understand. Then she realized he was waiting for *her* to lead the way. She swallowed, eyeing the dusty footpath that reached from the crumbling pavement where she stood to the right and left, following the course of the waterway.

Derryn had no way of knowing which direction was east. If the world hadn't lost its mind, a subtle display on her headset would have told her where to go, or Tyko would have spoken into her ear. As she was now, stripped of all her necessary enhancements, she could only guess.

She turned to the left and started walking.

Cole's chuckle stopped her in her tracks.

Derryn looked back at him. "What?"

"That's west, Sister."

"Oh—of course it is."

"Don't you know how to orient by the sun? Didn't they teach you how to find your way around in Ohio?"

There was no threat in his words or his eyes, but Derryn was frightened, all the same. Without a link to *feel* his meaning, she couldn't be sure that he wasn't using sarcasm—couldn't be sure he wasn't growing angry and dangerous, even now, while he wore that benign-seeming smile.

"Of course they taught us," she said. "I'm just distracted. And tired. It's been a long day already, and we still have so far to go."

Cole shrugged and headed to the right. Tree shadow covered him, cut off sight of the ailing suburbs and the sad, damaged buildings. By the time Derryn caught up with him, he seemed to have forgotten the incident. He struck up another of his rambling yet pleasant conversations. Derryn didn't raise the topic of direction again.

The trail was as beautiful as Cole had promised. Though it ran between the canal and the highway, after an hour or so, all hint of civilization fell away except for the occasional hum of a vehicle passing on the unseen road. Otherwise, Derryn knew only the trees and the lazy water, the merciful shade and the song of birds overhead. After a while, she realized that she could no longer hear the highway at all. The trail had carried them into the depths of a forest. Only rarely did they catch sight of some human development through the trees—an isolated house, a distant cluster of apartments, the overpass of a freeway that seemed to look down on them like some ancient giant stepping from the shroud of myth.

Derryn's stomach had begun to rumble long before evening fell. She didn't want to complain. When Cole noticed the growling, he diverted from their path and walked out into a natural clearing, a meadow between two walls of rustling trees.

"This is as good a place to make camp as any," he said. "I don't know about you, but I could use a rest."

Together, they made a rustic campsite, clearing away branches and stones and rolling out their sleeping mats on the warm, crackling earth. Cole used a small folding spade to dig a firepit and began building a small pyramid of dry twigs.

"I brought powdered soup from Iron Rock," he said. "It's pretty good, for trail food. Plenty of protein in it, though you wouldn't know to look at the stuff. It looks like brown sludge in the pot."

"I'm sure it'll be fine. I'm hungry enough to eat anything."

As Derryn spoke, she eyed her backpack where it lay near Cole's. If she slept deeply that night, it would be all too easy for him to search the pack—him, or anyone else who might happen across their bivouac. She needed a more secure means of hiding her identity from the pastor and the rest of this mad world.

Derryn excused herself to the forest, snagging the strap of her pack as she left the camp. When the underbrush concealed her, she crouched and pawed through her belongings until she found the nylon travel pouch she had brought from Cascadia. The pouch was slim and flat, meant to be worn under one's clothes to keep valuables safe. She transferred the precious data chips and the CoreTex ports from her bra, then found the remaining pieces of her headset in the pack and stuffed them in, too. Derryn shimmied the long dress up to her hips and snapped the belt of the travel pouch around her waist. A little of the weight lifted from her as she walked back to the campsite. All evidence of her integration was hidden now on her person, even the wires of the CoreTex. A Sovereign would have to strip her naked to find it, and though she couldn't be sure without the Weave's connection, she didn't think Cole was the sort of man to do such a thing.

The powdered soup looked as unappealing as Cole had promised, though the flavor was good—onions and herbs and a savory deepness that Derryn suspected of being meat. Cole had brought some dense biscuits, too, which were more satisfying, even if they had begun to go stale.

"We should keep watch," he said as the sun fell below the tree line. "We're pretty far from anywhere, but not so far that I can guarantee we're alone."

Derryn offered to take the first shift.

"I can't let you do that, Sister."

"Why not? Second watch is the worse deal. I'll have to wake you up just when you're finally asleep, and then you'll have to sit there, bored and cold and hungry till the sun rises."

He laughed. "Okay, you convinced me. Ladies first."

Cole slid into his sleeping bag and was snoring lightly before the sun had finished setting. Among the low hum of insects and the day's final chorus of birds, Derryn released a long, anxious breath. She had survived a full day in Sovereign company. Her disguise was holding well. Only a few more days until she reached New York. She could do this, even without her tech.

To pass the long hours of the coming night, she slid the first of Helen's journals from her pack and sat reading the book beside the remains of the campfire. She had to pause only a short while between sunset and full night, in the dim, gray-purple cast of twilight, before the aurora lit the sky in a wash of luminosity bright enough to read by.

Fuchsia pink and cerulean, electric violet and carmine—the colors of the aurora chased one another across the pages as Derryn puzzled out the old-fashioned handwriting. It was difficult work, translating the scrawling cursive of a bygone era without any help from her AI. But it was a good distraction from her state of constant danger.

21

Helen

September 23, 1862

This morning, the *Whig* was in a proper fit of rage. President Lincoln has planted his stake in moral ground. Come the first of January, there will be no more slavery in the United States of America. That includes here in the South, whether Jefferson Davis and his rebels like it or not.

Oh, I don't like that anyone who might read this diary should think me a fool. I know the little kings of the South won't give up their kingdoms so easily, no matter what our true and proper government might demand. And this proclamation will surely fan the fire of Southern anger and strengthen the Confederacy in its resolve. The South will fight all the harder to overcome the North. Terrible as the slaughter at Antietam was, I fear it will be overshadowed by worse battles, for the South will be like a vicious dog backed into a corner—on one side, the armies of the Union, and on the other, the Black uprising they have long feared. Our fight only grows more urgent from here on out. We *must* win, and we shall, for with this announcement in the daily paper, I feel that bright future I have so long cherished close at hand. May that future come swiftly, soon as this war is won.

When I understood the meaning behind the *Whig*'s angry froth, I called everyone into the parlor and read the column aloud, for Kitty and Ruthie cannot read it for themselves. And then, didn't we set to celebrating! Mary Jane cut flowers from the garden and made crowns for all of us, even for dear David, and for Jeremiah Carver, who has recovered enough from his illness to sit on the porch rocker in the fresh garden air. Kitty baked a peach pie, and Ruthie and I sang every song we knew while we danced in the garden, whooping and hollering like girls at a barn raising. Jere kept time for us, clapping and stamping his feet on the porch, and didn't he look fine with a crown of black-eyed Susans on his brow.

We probably should have been more moderate, for the neighbors might have heard our ruckus, and I have no doubt that the general mood of Richmond is as sour as mine is sweet. There isn't a tongue that isn't clacking today over news of emancipation. At the Confederate "White House" in the city proper, I suppose old Jefferson Davis is fit to burst with anger.

La-di-da, "President" Davis! The North sent General Lee and his army packing. It was only a taste of what's to come.

September 24, 1862

Oh, what a dark day! I should have known that something dreadful would bring our spirits low after such a grand celebration. That is usually the way luck runs. Didn't the Greeks of old say that the gods never like to see a mortal too happy?

Early in the afternoon, I was in the garden, helping Mary Jane repair a loose board on the henhouse. We heard the front door knocker. Some buried instinct warned me that this would be no glad visitor, so rather than going through the house to the door, I first crept to the garden fence and peeked through its slats. What should I see in the drive but Caleb Cary's horse—that flashy animal with the spotted rump, of which he is so peacock proud—tied to our hitching post. My stomach twisted.

"It's Mr. Cary," I whispered.

"What do you think he wants?" Mary Jane said back to me.

"I'm sure I don't know what that man wants from anyone. To think I ever considered marrying him!"

There was nothing for it, however, but to go and speak with him. By the time I'd replaced my garden shoes with house slippers and had brushed the dirt from my work dress, Ruthie had already admitted Mr. Cary to the parlor. I found him brooding in the damask chair like a thunderhead—and gray as a cloud, too, in a lieutenant's uniform. I hadn't the least idea that he'd joined the army. Whatever else one may think of Caleb Cary, it must be truthfully said that he stands firm on his convictions. Unlike most landowners hereabouts, at least he is willing to do the fighting and dying himself, rather than passing such a burden to poorer men.

"Why, Mr. Cary," I said, sweeping into the parlor, "it has been far too long since we've enjoyed your company at Eudaimonia."

Caleb stood to greet me, as proper as ever, but there was no warm deference in his manner. His jaw was hard set, and in his eyes, I saw a cold glimmer of amusement. Whatever business had brought him to Eudaimonia, he expected to enjoy my reaction.

"Miss Bywater," he said, with a slight bow that was more mockery than courtesy.

"What an unexpected pleasure to see you here," I said.

"Is it?" Caleb looked around the parlor, taking in the scattered evidence of the work I haven't ceased to do on behalf of the Union prisoners—balls of yarn, half-finished stockings, a basket of eggs waiting to be boiled. "One would have thought that you'd be expecting a visit from someone in authority, given your recent activities."

My heart lurched, but I kept my expression placid. I felt Mary Jane creep to the parlor door and wait there, just on the threshold, her eyes keen on my back in case I should find myself in some trouble.

To Caleb, I said, "I'm not sure I understand your meaning, sir."

"I think you do." He stepped closer. His voice dropped in menace, a dog's growl before the bite. "Your visits to Libby Prison have been noted, Helen. Your particular interest in the comfort of federal officers has raised questions about your loyalties."

Never knowing where I found the courage, I held Caleb's eye, as bold as you please. "Is it disloyal to offer Christian charity to suffering men? I was unaware that compassion is exclusive to the South."

"Compassion," he repeated. The word fairly dripped with disdain. "Is that what you call it? Some might call it treason."

Fear twisted in my stomach. Had our true purpose been discovered? But I lifted my chin in defiance, in open disdain for his words and his manner, which was growing more boorish by the second.

"Lieutenant Cary," I said, "that is a most serious accusation—one which I hope and believe a man of your standing wouldn't make lightly against a lady."

"It is no accusation. Merely an observation that your activities might be misinterpreted by those less acquainted with your tender heart."

"If my charitable work has caused concern, I'm terribly sorry."

"Concern," he said with a tiger's laugh. "Men have escaped from that prison."

"Escaped! Surely not. But how?"

Privately, I thrilled at the news. *Men* had escaped, Caleb said—not the single man I've kept hidden at Eudaimonia. Had any of the Union officers made it back to the North? Had dozens of them gone free—or scores? I was bursting with curiosity, but of course I could allow nothing but astonishment to show on my features.

Caleb scowled out the window. "I don't know how the men escaped. I'm not sure anyone knows, just yet. But we'll find out, make no mistake about that. And when we do, anyone who has *aided* in those escapes will be tried and sentenced, as befits a traitor."

I affected a note of contrition—my, what an actress I've become since this war began! "I assure you, Mr. Cary, I'm a loyal daughter of

Virginia. Surely you know that. Everyone else seems to know it. Why, I've been running the Ladies' Aid here on the hill, and we provide what comfort we can to our Confederate soldiers—all the comfort that's proper for a lady to give. We raise money for children orphaned by the war, too. Some of our members have even taken in those orphans, adopted them as their own. We do any amount of cooking and baking and mending for the soldiers. Five times as much as we do for those Union prisoners!"

At that very moment, I was harboring a Union prisoner in my mother's bedroom. The thought flashed across my mind—*What on earth will I do if Caleb insists on searching the place?*—but Jere had had the sense to hide himself in the wood closet when he'd heard me approach the cabin. Surely, he had already tucked himself away someplace when he saw a Confederate lieutenant riding up the lane.

"And the picnics I've hosted," I went on, "you don't think I'm throwing parties for Northern officers, do you, Mr. Cary? Whatever contribution I can make to the Great Cause, I will do it without hesitation and count it no sacrifice. Ladies may not fight on the battlefield, but we have a part to play, all the same, and I for one will not stop working for our homeland until the South is free."

When my patriotic bluster had ended, Caleb studied me for a long moment. I held his eye with perfect poise, and never looked away, but still I wondered if he could read the lie in my eyes.

"What was all that noise you were making yesterday afternoon?" he said. "On the very day when Lincoln offered yet another insult to the South?"

"Yesterday?" I affected something of a daze. "Why, my cousin Judith came a-calling from Yorktown. Judith has just gotten engaged—he's a lieutenant, like you—and we had a bit of a celebration. Were we too noisy? I hope we weren't a nuisance. What insult are you talking about, Caleb? What has that devil Lincoln done now?"

"I'm surprised you haven't heard. Lincoln *claims* that every slave will be freed come the new year."

I put on a show of the greatest shock, gasping and sinking onto the settee as if I was on the verge of fainting dead away. "Oh, Caleb!" I cried. "But he can't *do* that, can he? Strip away our rights, our traditions, like taking a toy from a child? Why, it's an outrage!"

He watched me for a while before he spoke again—too long a while, for my taste. As I fanned myself and trembled in a great show of distress, I felt sure Caleb knew it was all a deception.

"I didn't think you would care, Helen," he said at length. "After you freed your own slaves . . ."

He glanced at Mary Jane, who still hung around the parlor door. For my part, I did *not* look at her. I wouldn't have been able to bear her expression while I carried on as the occasion demanded.

"I've told you before, Mr. Cary," I said, "what I do with my property is my business. I have reasons of my own for granting my slaves certain leeway. They're good, loyal workers, and I don't hear a word against them—or against my actions. But just because I've done what suits Eudaimonia, that doesn't mean I'm in favor of tearing down our traditions. Why, we are speaking of our very way of life! Imagine if we were to let all these people run free. The South would be plain unlivable. Oh, that Lincoln! He is such a curse on this land. What can a man from Illinois know of Southern ways? He has no respect for institutions, no respect for history and honor and, well, the way things *are*."

Caleb gave a short laugh. I couldn't be sure my airs had convinced him that I was no threat to the Confederacy, but at least he had thawed a little.

"I'm glad to hear you're so loyal, Helen. Surely, then, you'll have no objection to boarding Captain Gibbs in your home. The captain finds himself in need of new accommodations, and it would hardly be fitting for an officer of his rank to sleep in a tent like a common soldier."

The shock of that suggestion fairly took my breath away. For a moment I could do nothing but stare at Caleb, as dumb as a cow. Captain Gibbs—that sharp-eyed, calculating man who runs Libby Prison—*him*, of all people, living under my roof? Observing my comings and goings, listening to my conversations with Mary Jane, watching while we made a way for the escape of Union officers? The secret work Mary Jane and I share will be damned near impossible with Gibbs lurking around Eudaimonia. Mary Jane, Kitty, Ruthie, and David must pretend to be my slaves again . . . must even show their subservience to Gibbs himself!

And that's to say nothing of the greatest risk—Jere Carver, a Union officer hidden away in this very house.

It was and is a despicable thing to contemplate, the dirtiest trick Caleb Cary has yet played on me in pursuit of his petty vengeance. But what could I do in that moment? Nothing but feign delight.

"Why, it's too great an honor," I said. "A captain of the Confederacy lodging in my home?"

"Are you refusing, then?" Caleb's oily tone betrayed his pleasure. "Is there some reason why housing an officer of the Confederate Army would be . . . uncomfortable for you, Miss Bywater? Perhaps I ought to offer the chance to some other lady."

"Don't you dare," I said at once. "I won't hear of it. Why, there are plenty of empty rooms here at Eudaimonia. Captain Gibbs may have his pick of them. And I'll be so glad for his company. One can hardly imagine a higher honor."

Caleb seemed a little crestfallen by the fervor of my assent. I caught a flash of doubt in his eyes as he settled his officer's cap on his head. I had convinced him, after all, that I was unflinchingly loyal to the Confederacy, and he was obliged to go away in defeat.

"Very good," he said with a gentleman's bow. "I'll inform Captain Gibbs of your generous offer. You may expect him tomorrow."

After Caleb left, Mary Jane and I stared at one another in a grim silence. Then Jere emerged from the shadows of the hallway, his face grave.

"I heard," Jere said. "Miss Ruthie came and got me once she knew trouble was afoot."

"You shouldn't have been anywhere but in your room," I scolded. "What if he'd seen you, Jere?"

He winked at me, saucy as you please. "I would have told him I was your cousin Judith from Yorktown." Then he grew serious again. "If that man intended to hurt you, Helen, I wouldn't have allowed him to do it."

Mary Jane turned to him sharply. "That would have been your death, Mr. Carver."

She was right, but I couldn't help blushing over Jere's gallant comment.

"Damn it, anyway," Mary Jane muttered. "What will we do now, with that captain watching our every move?"

I didn't hesitate to answer, for there is no other choice. This work is too important to give it up now—especially now, with emancipation only months away, with Southern rage burning hotter than before.

"We will do what we must," I said. "Our work will carry on. But we must play our parts more carefully than we ever did, and watch ourselves every moment, even here at home."

October 19, 1862

If I was obliged before to keep this diary hidden, it's all the more important now that Captain Gibbs lurks among us. That man has a buzzard's curiosity, and the morals to match.

He arrived at Eudaimonia on the morning of the twenty-fifth of September, just as Caleb promised, and left all his trunks and bags for David to carry in. I welcomed the captain graciously, of course, and told him that he might have his choice of rooms. He roamed around the house looking all too satisfied, humming and muttering on every threshold, casting an appraising eye over all my family's things—the fine furniture of which Mother was so proud, the rugs Father imported from Persia for their fifth wedding anniversary, the portraits of Bywater ancestry, going all the way back to the colonies. Gibbs finally claimed Father's old bedchamber. I should have known he would, for it's the grandest in the whole house. But I don't like to think of that man sleeping where my own dear father slept, nor shaving at his basin, nor hanging those suits of rebel gray in Father's closet.

And don't we all walk the tightrope now, with Gibbs installed in our home! It's only a small consolation that this arrangement succeeds in its ultimate purpose, to deflect suspicion of our true loyalties. But I often find myself asking whether the cost is worth the yield.

The Black residents of Eudaimonia face the gravest danger. I suppose that's ever the case. They are all forced to playact as slaves again whenever Gibbs's shadow darkens a doorway. I still pay their weekly wages, of course, but now it must be done in secrecy, and only when Gibbs is off at his precious jail. They surely understand our predicament and bear it with more grace than I could muster in their position. But how humiliated they must feel, to be forced to revert to the servile ways of their former bondage. Whenever Mary Jane must lower her eyes and say "Yes, sir" in the captain's presence, I see the flash of intelligence she must conceal, and I hate this charade all the more.

At least Richmond has thawed for me. That is one small consolation, to no longer be the scandal of Church Hill. I don't like that anyone should mistake my meaning, so let me here make it plain that I do not desire a full return to Richmond society for my own sake, but for the sake of the work we do.

Word has gone around town that the eminent Captain Gibbs is boarding at Eudaimonia, and so I've had no shortage of visitors—mostly ladies and gentlemen who hope to glean some favor from the captain, but some who seek to make friends or amends with me. Nearly every day, I've entertained some caller or other, sometimes in company with Captain Gibbs and sometimes on my own. Every visit brings new talk of the war—news of military movements, thanks to the letters my callers receive from their husbands and sons. While I sip my tea and ply my visitors with Kitty's inestimable baking, I commit every detail of these conversations to memory, and write them down sometimes in a separate book, which I keep hidden in a place entirely different from where I have hidden this diary. Goodness knows when such information might become useful—and goodness knows what Gibbs would do to me if he found it.

At parties (there are still parties, even now!), I dance with Confederate officers and do my best to charm their secrets from them. I can't say that I've learned anything of consequence yet, but every thread may be woven into a useful fabric. My little book of secrets grows fatter by the day.

Our visits to Libby Prison continue despite Gibbs's shadow in our midst. Those poor captives need our mercy more than ever, for as big as that building is, the place is positively bursting with Union officers. Mary Jane and I do all we can for the prisoners, but each time I look into one of their gaunt faces, I feel to my bones that we aren't bringing aid enough.

I swear this house *breathes* differently when Captain Gibbs is gone. Although no one told me that he had left for Libby Prison, I sensed his absence late this morning and took advantage of the moment to visit Jere in the carriage house. That is where Jere Carver resides now. He simply cannot stay in the main house with Gibbs lurking around. I might explain him away as a distant relation, come to help me mind Eudaimonia (for how can a mere lady manage an estate on her own? Foot!), but the moment he spoke a word to the captain, our jig would be up. Yankees are so abominably bad at pretending a Southern accent.

The only real solution was to hustle Jere into the carriage house while his recovery continues. At least he is strong enough to climb up and down the ladder to the loft. David helped him fix a little pallet to sleep on, up there among the boxes of tools and the old harnesses and wheels. It isn't much of an accommodation, but Jere has sworn it's downright luxurious compared to how he slept on campaign. At any rate, he seems content. Whenever I bring his meals—only after Gibbs has left for the day, or late at night when the captain has gone to bed—or when I bring him fresh wicks for his lamp and Father's books to read, he is all smiles and glad eyes. Sometimes I spend an hour or more in his company, talking of things that could just about make one forget there's a dreadful war on.

This evening, when I brought him a good helping of stew and biscuits, he bade me sit with him at the worktable on the first floor. We were well hidden by the carriage, so I had no fear that we might be seen together, if Gibbs should happen to wake and look out at the back garden.

"Listen, Helen," Jere said to me with a most sober and determined expression. "I'm feeling much stronger, thanks to the care you and your friends have shown me."

My heart sank, for I thought he would say next that he must be moving on, back to the North where he could rejoin his regiment.

"Now that I'm here in Richmond," Jere said, "I want to do good work for the Union. That day when you rode with me back into town, I saw how easy it was for a fellow to get around without suspicion. As long as I say nothing, there's no reason why anyone in this city should think I'm a Yankee."

Though we were alone, I felt the need to whisper. "Why, Jere, you mean to spy on the Confederacy!"

"Indeed, I do. I sat for briefings with Stoneman plenty of times, so I know how our spies disguise their letters and how they pass information to our generals. I'm here now; might as well make good use of my position to learn what I can and send it along to the generals. Will you let me stay here in the carriage house while I do the work? I'll go on as we've done these days since the captain moved in, keeping out of sight so no one will suspect you."

"Plenty suspect me already," I said ruefully. "Though my taking in Gibbs has eased a few minds. I confess I've been writing down whatever

I've learned from my callers, but I haven't known what to do with the information I've collected."

Jere leaned back in his seat with a contented grin. "Well, there you have it. Providence brought us together, Miss Helen. You've got the means of gathering information, as a respected lady of Richmond society, and I've got the know-how. If you tell me whatever you learn, I can write it all down in letters, and then you can mail those letters to your cousin, or an old family friend . . . any excuse you think will do. But we'll address the letters so they land in the hands of a Union general."

Perhaps it was foolish of me to agree, but I did so, readily. I'm already committing treason against the Confederate States of America with my work at the prison. What harm in adding "lady spy" to my list of sins? The worst they can do is hang me twice, and I shan't complain the second time.

These past days since Gibbs invaded our home, I have thought often of Mary Jane and Kitty, Ruthie and David. They have lived with too much injustice already—most of it perpetrated by my own hand. To see them cast back into their former state galls me beyond description. It was I who held them under that curse, I who turned a blind eye to the suffering of my fellow man, all for the sake of my convenience. Now it must be my sworn duty to make every possible remedy, to work as tirelessly for the righteous cause as these good people have worked for me.

Tonight, I sat on the balcony as twilight fell, watching the stars emerge one by one from the great, dark eternity of the sky. This night is uncommonly peaceful, almost as quiet as Richmond was in the days before the war. I could hardly believe, looking down at the tranquil city below, that here is a nation in the process of tearing itself apart. War has so quickly become our mundane reality. Three years ago, when the aurora brought those strange visions to my mind, armed conflict between North and South was all but unthinkable. Yet here we are, with Richmond transformed into a military encampment and the sounds of drilling soldiers the constant accompaniment to all our days.

I thank God that He has brought more work for me to do. For only good works may effect, at last, the atonement of my soul.

And I will here admit that I'm heart-glad to know that Jere will stay in Richmond a little while longer. I do enjoy that man's company. And his smile.

22

Derryn

2053

They moved on early in the morning, after they'd eaten a hasty breakfast of hard biscuits from Cole's pack and some of the fruit leather Derryn had brought out of Haverford.

The trail was flat and untaxing, the soft voice of flowing water a pleasant companion, and the richly scented shade of the forest kept the summer heat at bay. Yet still Derryn scowled as she walked. She couldn't help thinking of the Sovereign convoy, where they had gone and what they'd done after dropping her and Cole off in Eddington. Had Melinda and the rest escaped the bunker in time? Derryn had never experienced a discomfort worse than this—not the physical strain of the endless walk, but the constant churning of anxiety in her stomach. Every time she reached instinctively with her thoughts, she found the Weave as absent as before. There was no way to search the great communal mind for reassurance that Haverford was safe. No way to relieve the inner pain of not knowing, of never knowing, of hoping even while logic told her that hope was useless.

To distract herself from the worry, she relived the story she'd read the night before while she'd kept watch over the campsite. Helen's story—those old, yellowing journals pulled by chance from the bottom of a shipping crate.

At first, Derryn had found the reading slow and laborious without Tyko's translation, but the longer she studied Helen's handwriting, the more transparent it became. Helen's account of the Carrington Event had been fascinating, to say the least. The sudden appearance of mystic visions had explained the inspiration for the art. Derryn had devoured the first journal faster than she'd realized, and had made short work of the second, too—though that book had been mostly an account of the Civil War through 1861, a blow-by-blow reportage of battles and their outcomes with little detail of Helen's daily life and nothing to shed more light on the nature of her paintings.

By the time she reached the third volume, when Helen began her contra work on behalf of the Union, Derryn had been thoroughly hooked. But by then she suspected that her four hours of watch were over and had woken Cole to take over. Tired though she was, she'd lain awake on her bedroll longer than intended. The bright lights of the aurora shifted and rippled overhead, mingling in Derryn's mind with Helen's descriptions of the Carrington Event. The parallels between then and now—between Helen's world and this present reality—had been too uncanny to afford Derryn much rest.

And now as she trudged along the trail, she couldn't help musing darkly over Helen's optimistic belief that humanity would change for the better, that the future time she had glimpsed under the auroral glow could only be brought about by a perfect harmony among the species. Maybe Helen hadn't been entirely wrong. The Weave had certainly forged a connection among humanity that had altered the fate of the planet itself. But the man with the tattooed face, walking easily along the trail some dozen or so paces ahead, was proof that even the Weave had been no remedy to human nature.

Is it true? Derryn wondered. *What if the Sovereigns are right?*

Without the immediacy of the Weave's empathic connection, would the whole of humanity revert to its original state—tyrannical and insecure, loving war more than they loved each other, hateful to all it feared, and fearing whatever it encountered?

No. Derryn wanted to believe otherwise, wanted to see the world with Helen's rose-colored gaze. Even in her most desperate state, in the greatest danger she had ever experienced, Derryn wanted to hope that humankind could overcome its worst impulses and learn to truly unite as one. Surely there had always been as much good as evil in the human heart. All the way back to the time before history, this childlike species had survived through mutual care. If violence was part of human nature, then so was empathy. And love had certainly done more for humanity than hatred ever had.

But she didn't know for certain. That fact struck her bluntly, right there on the trail. Derryn had never known anything but the integrated world. She had been too young to recall what life was like before the Weave's self-invention.

Isn't it time? A voice murmured in her head, not nearly as clear or melodious as Tyko, but nevertheless, it spoke. *Isn't it time you found out? You don't even know what you are, who you are, without the Weave to tell you.*

Deliberate and stiff with concentration, Derryn sank into herself, drew her awareness down into the body—the small, isolated body that was all she ever had been. On the Weave, she had always cast her mind outward, into the great wholeness of the world, and had found there every answer to every question, even those she hadn't yet thought to ask. Now, as she dwindled into herself, she found nothing as objective as the touch of another person's mind. Within, she was all one lightless ocean, a vastness she couldn't see, though she felt its constant, directionless churning. There was nothing she could hold on to there, nothing she could call "human" or even "me." It was only space, and ages that circled back to see themselves reflected in newly opened eyes, and consciousness—a sense of being awake and aware, but aware of *what*, she couldn't say.

That inner landscape was as unnavigable as the physical realm through which she stumbled. Without the elevation of her integrated self, she was blind and helpless, soft and crushable, so entirely alone that the concept of togetherness was as incomprehensible as a paradox or a god. With her inner eye—whatever that sight might have been—she stared into the core of herself and sensed a greatness and a depth she had never felt before, never suspected might be contained somewhere in this singular body, this temporary order of matter that she called, in her hubris, Derryn Witt.

But of course, she had never had any cause to go looking for what might be inside, no reason to look too closely at her center. The Weave had been a better distraction, a handier invention than the human soul. That *bigness* inside of her frightened Derryn almost as much as her circumstances did—hidden in plain sight among these people who would kill her on the spot if they knew what she was. For she didn't know what that inner presence was, what she ought to call it or do with it. She didn't know how much of it was herself and how much was something *other*.

"Sarah, are you all right?"

Derryn snapped out of her reverie, found herself alone on the trail. Cole had drifted far ahead—no, Derryn had stopped walking. And now the expanse between them was like the gulf of a sea, or the deep void of space, and she stared at him, so small and far away, and wondered whether anyone could close such a distance.

"Sorry," she called. "I had to stop. Had to get something out of my shoe."

She began walking again. Her legs were moving—she knew it—but she felt nothing of the trail below, nor the breeze that moved across the water, and she saw neither shadows nor light in the living forest, but something that was both, the darkness and the light combined, and all the leaves with all their voices, and the animals that made the forest home. All of it together was so much more than any single tree.

She was drawing no closer to Cole, though he was standing still, and she was walking. And as the space between them never closed, one clear and definite thought arrived, the first thought that had come easily in all the bewildered hours since the Weave had gone away. It was the *all* in all things that made a human what she was. And anyone who cut themselves off from that togetherness, who thought themselves too pure to surrender this illusion of self . . . they were not strong, but impeded. They were not free but confined to the cage they had mistaken for themselves. And blinded as the Sovereign was to the suffering of his fellow humans, he had condemned himself to an eternity of darkness.

When evening cast its slant of light low and golden through the trees, Derryn and Cole left the trail again to make camp for the night. This time, the pastor led Derryn to a grassy space on the bank of the canal, in one of the rare spots where the trail didn't hug the water so tightly but eased off into the trees.

Derryn gathered kindling and dry branches for the fire. The forest breathed and murmured around her, the whole ancient body of life unconcerned by the twin catastrophes that had fallen on the human world—the war and the solar storm, the crisis from the cosmos and destruction from within.

"I've got a few hooks and lines in my pack," Cole said as Derryn dropped the branches beside the fire ring. "I think I'll go set them. In an hour or two, if we're lucky, we might have catfish."

She watched him wade through the hip-high grass of the clearing. Then he vanished into the trees. After he'd gone, Derryn tried to make herself useful. Water must be boiled and cooled to refill their canteens. She had watched Cole make a fire already; it couldn't be so hard to do. But the more she tried to pile twigs and tinder into a useful construction, the clumsier she felt. Nothing would stand up the way she wanted it to, and each added stick only seemed to make the problem worse. She had built nothing but a useless pile of refuse.

"All right, hand over the pack. Both of them."

It wasn't Cole's voice. Derryn looked up from the fire ring, every nerve screaming with sudden alarm. A man stood over her, a stranger, his hair and beard wild and matted, his clothing dark with old grime. The wide intensity of his eyes projected a certain hot, rapid energy that terrified Derryn, as did his malevolent smile. He was only a few paces away. She'd been too absorbed in the problem of the fire to hear his approach.

Derryn lurched to her feet, clutching by instinct at the heaviest piece of wood to hand, a branch about as thick as her wrist and as long as her arm.

"Get out of here," she said.

The man grinned all the wider. "Easy, lady. I won't hurt you—not if you hand over those packs."

Who was he? Derryn knew at once that he was no Integrationist. There was something too *other* about him, something that seemed to revel in separation. Nor were there any Sovereign marks on his face. As far as she could tell, this section of the trail was miles from any habitation. A hermit, then. Some victim of the war who'd long since decided it was better to take his chances alone in the wilderness, rather than risk a Sovereign bomb in any city or suburb.

The stranger took a step toward Cole's pack, reached for it—and Derryn hesitated. She should have hit him with the branch, clubbed him hard enough to make him think twice about this intrusion. But the moment she considered doing harm to another living thing, a wave of revulsion hit her, so powerful her stomach heaved. Only the urgency of the moment prevented her from doubling over in the grass.

It was like the Weave—that connection, that direct knowledge of the other. Yet the Weave was gone.

Derryn lifted her club, the better to make that man think she *might* hit him, and yelled at the top of her lungs. "Cole! Cole! Get back here, quick!"

Thank goodness, the pastor wasn't far off. He came crashing through the undergrowth, and the moment he saw the wild-eyed stranger, he charged across the clearing with an animal howl.

The intruder barely had time to stagger back a few steps before Cole was on him, a blur of swinging fists, a storm of rage. Derryn crouched on her heels, hiding her eyes in the crook of an elbow, sickened by the sounds of violence.

Then the clearing was silent, except for Cole's ragged breathing.

Derryn couldn't bring herself to look up until the pastor spoke to her.

"It's okay, Sister. He's gone now."

"You didn't kill him, did you?"

Cole said nothing for a moment, and Derryn reached frantically with her thoughts, trying to feel that other man, trying to determine whether he was still alive or not.

Cole chuckled softly. "Kill him? I didn't have time to get my gun."

Derryn looked up. The stranger was gone. The meadow grass and the canopy of broad, green leaves above swayed in the evening wind.

"Stand up," Cole said, not unkindly.

She did as he commanded. The branch was still in her hand, clutched so tightly that the rough bark bit into her palm.

"You didn't hit him," Cole said. Not a question.

Derryn shook her head.

He looked at the branch for a long moment. Derryn tried to read his face—never as fast or clear as feeling another person's emotions. She thought the expression he wore now, pinched and withdrawn, might be confusion.

Then his eyes met hers. She couldn't look away, couldn't say a word in defense or explanation. He was thoughtful now—Derryn was sure of that—thoughtful and calculating.

"I'm taking first watch tonight," Cole said.

He built the fire and, after an hour or so, took Derryn with him to check the fishing lines. They both carried their packs and bedrolls, unwilling to lose a single precious item to the marauding stranger. But the wild man didn't return that night, not even when the smell of roasting catfish filled the clearing.

The sun set. Twilight came, and on its heels, the first vivid flush of the aurora. Derryn settled into her bedroll, silent and stricken with fear. She had barely spoken a word to Cole since he'd driven the stranger away. Nor had he said much—only what was necessary. Somehow, the incident had caused Derryn's disguise to slip. She was certain of that, though she couldn't have said why. And she was afraid, too afraid to sleep, despite the dragging weariness of her body and her mind.

The lights grew brighter overhead. Like the great, mythic bodies of dragons, they twisted across the sky. Currents of change, risen from the very heart of the sun, from that forge of life which was hot enough to melt every human pretension to dross, hot enough to melt away reality as Derryn had once known it—the good world, the healed world she had thought delivered from evil, the world she had thought would go on forever. It all burned to ashes in the fire of time.

23

Helen

October 28, 1862

It is no simple task to run a spy operation directly under the nose of a captain of the Confederate Army. But we are committed, and work tirelessly whenever Gibbs is away or has retired to his bed. Each night, Jere, Mary Jane, and I gather in the carriage house to design our intricate deceptions and pass on what news we have gleaned to those clerks of Jere's acquaintance in the United States Army.

Jere taught us the code that's used by Union intelligence. It isn't so different from the old puzzle Mary Jane and I employed during her school days, though I will not detail it here, in case this diary should ever fall into unfriendly hands.

We have expanded our operation, too, one member at a time. Most of these members, I have never met, and would not know by sight, but they are well known to Mary Jane and have earned her cautious trust. That's good enough for me. I place the fullest confidence in my two companions, so I hold every faith in Mary Jane's acquaintances. No doubt, those who are still held in bondage make for useful spies. All too well do I know how poorly most Confederates think of the Black folk among us. There are plenty of men who would not hesitate to discuss sensitive matters where a slave might hear, for they can't believe that the so-called inferior races have sense enough to understand what they say. Mary Jane's spiderweb of contacts has yielded some truly astonishing secrets—the planned movement of troops, the sources of supplies for the soldiery, the exact quantities of ammunition that our foundry here in Richmond can produce. I can only hope that our coded letters reach their recipients while there's still time for the federal forces to act.

Mary Jane sniffs out the secrets, Jere disguises them in his code, and I provide the front and finances for our operation. Together, we are doing good and useful work. What else may any soul ask of this world?

I have grown quite fond of those late nights in the carriage house, working side by side with Jere, our heads bent over the latest letter to my "cousin" in Maryland while we whisper in the glow of the old kerosene lantern. When that circle of light surrounds us and everything else recedes into shadow, I can almost believe that there is no one in this world but Jere and me—that we are original, fatefully paired, like Adam and Eve in the Lord's first creation.

That's not to say our friendship is perfect. We have had our share of arguments, if you please! Or I had better call them disagreements—but how I love to disagree with him, for it only extends the time we spend talking. And sitting close together in our ring of light.

Jere has a great passion for the United States, the *idea* of unity among so many varied countries and people.

"It's the Union I fight for," he said to me last night. "It was the very grandest idea anyone has had since we broke from old King George and made this nation of our own. What a shame it would be to see it fall after not even a century. There *must* be a way to bring the states back together, even after such a bitter conflict."

"The Union is a fine thing," I told him, "a thing worth fighting for. But I worry that it's the wrong reason for fighting *this* war."

"Why, Helen, what can you mean?"

"Only that I know full well why the South is fighting," I said.

"All this outcry over states' rights," Jere began, but I didn't allow him to finish.

"Foot to that! It's a lot of nonsense—the line those senators and congressmen feed to their fellows in Washington. There is only one *right* these Southern states are fighting for, Jere, and it's the right to own our fellow men."

He grew quiet at that, and thoughtful, watching the light burn steadily under its glass shade.

"This war isn't about unity for my people," I went on, a great swell of emotion nearly choking off my voice. "It's about continuing a way of life that should be considered filthy by any decent, good, modern person—filthy and obscene. They only want to go on believing that they're superior to others, Jere. Not only the plantation owners, and not only people like me, who have kept slaves to run their city homes—yes, I was as obscene as the rest of them, though I never allowed myself to see it till recent days. But make no mistake about it: Every white man who fights for the Southern Cause does so because he wishes to set himself higher than someone else. Anyone else will do, so long as no white man has to think himself at the bottom of the heap. I know what I'm talking about, Jere. I was exactly like the rest of them for most of my life. I can only thank God that I woke up and saw myself more clearly."

He smiled at me, good natured even while he played the devil's advocate. "But where does it end, Helen? Suppose we do manage to put the Black man and the white on equal footing. I don't say that it's a bad idea, only a difficult one. But suppose we do it. What then? Should women stand as equals to men?"

I had never asked myself that question before, but now that Jere had raised it, I saw the only sensible answer.

"Why, of course. The world would be a very different place if women had a say in how it's run—if we had the vote. There would be no more wars, for one thing."

"Oh?" he said, laughing. "Do you think so?"

I put on an air of haughtiness. "We women know how to solve our problems in more civilized ways. We don't resort to fighting like you hairy-chested brutes."

We fell to laughing then—quietly, so as not to wake Captain Gibbs in the house. Jere took my hand, only a show of friendly affection, yet it warmed me, I confess.

When I saw that the moon was high, hanging at a corner of the carriage-house window, I said good night and crossed the garden in the deep-blue chill of an autumn night, and came up here to my room. But I haven't yet tried to go to bed. I am thinking too much of the future. That time I saw, that wondrous time revealed in the old vision . . . It was years ago, and yet I can still recall every detail with such clarity. I can't help but wonder what it must be like to live in a better time, when mankind has learned all his lessons, when we have joined together in a unity truer than any nation might claim.

It's hate that holds us back now—nothing but plain, ugly hate. There is no use trying to hide the cause behind this euphemistic talk of "states' rights." As long as hate still rules our hearts and makes our laws and causes our armies to march, to make war on our brothers and spill the blood of our countrymen, then we will never achieve the loftiness I saw, that miraculous state of civilization in which anything—anything at all—is possible.

For it's hate that causes us to sacrifice that which makes us human: our empathy, the inborn love for our fellow man.

Ah, well. Enough of these sad thoughts for tonight. I must think on something more cheerful before I can go to sleep.

Jere is far more handsome than any Yankee has a right to be. And I did so like the feel of his hand on mine. There—surely that's enough to inspire sweet dreams.

24

Derryn

2053

The next day, Derryn and Cole followed the canal in silence. The forest was a merciful wall shutting out all evidence of war. Despite the deep-green peace of the woodland—constant susurrus of moving leaves; birds that sang untroubled in an old, original tongue; the tread of deer unseen but felt by some ancient and peripheral instinct—Derryn was afflicted by a merciless anxiety.

She couldn't forget the way Cole had looked at her the evening before, his confusion at her refusal to defend herself against the marauding stranger. The searching way his eye had met her own. She needed no Weave connection to tell her that she had raised suspicion in her companion—her only guide through a world she had no hope of navigating alone.

And this singular, physical self only added to Derryn's misery. However much she might enjoy the great outdoors of Cascadia, she had never walked without stopping for days on end. Her hips, knees, and lower back ached constantly. Blisters had formed on the bottoms of both feet, just behind her toes, making every step both agony and annoyance. She didn't know how much longer she could go on, and she was afraid to speak up, afraid to ask Cole for a few hours' rest.

Evening deepened the sweet, fragrant shadows of the forest and lifted a cool breeze off the water. Cole veered from the trail into another waterside meadow like the one in which they'd camped the night before. Tears of relief flooded Derryn's eyes. She couldn't even wipe them away. It was all she could manage to sink to the ground with a miserable groan, stricken to a dull stillness by the constancy of pain, the grim persistence of her fear.

Cole built the fire without a word. He fetched water from the canal, poured it through a filter, and set the pot to boil on the campfire for good measure. They had drained all their bottles and canteens hours before. The better part of the evening would be devoted to refilling them, a task that would take plenty of time.

"While we're waiting," Cole said, "let me see about those blisters."

He hadn't spoken a word to Derryn since breakfast. She looked up, dazed by her unbearable weariness, a strain that had surely already broken her, body, mind, and spirit. For much too long, she stared at Cole, fighting to read his intentions and mood. He seemed . . . friendly. Or neutral, at least. No immediate threat, as far as Derryn could tell. But she couldn't tell much about anything in her severed and helpless state.

"I feel all right," she finally said. "The blisters aren't so bad."

"You've been limping for hours now. You won't get far tomorrow if you don't take care of your feet." He added with a soft chuckle, "I'll *command* you if I have to. One way or another, we're going to treat those blisters."

Command. Any Sovereign man had that right over a woman of the culture. The suggestion made Derryn clench her jaw, even when delivered with a laugh and with Cole's warm expression. If she hoped to keep passing for a Sovereign, she couldn't say no. Though it might already be too late, she reflected, to maintain the ruse.

She removed her shoes and socks, stretched her feet toward Cole, who tipped his head this way and that, examining the damage.

"I'll have to drain most of these," he said. "Otherwise, they'll only get worse, and you won't be able to walk at all. Good thing we have time to kill."

He found the first aid kit in his pack and took out a few alcohol wipes. When he tore open the packaging, the astringent odor cut through the drowsy smell of damp shade and growing things.

"I hope you're not ticklish," Cole said.

She watched him as he cleaned her feet—his brow furrowed in an expression of real concern, the gentle and deliberate movement of his hands. And the thought came to her, swam its way through her swimming mind, that he truly wasn't like the others. The anger, the mistrust, the habitual violence that marked Sovereign culture was absent in him—or if not absent, then constrained. If Derryn still had the Weave, she could *feel* his story. The knowledge of him would come to her, immediate and pure as if his experiences were her own. His thoughts and feelings would *be* hers, in truth, as hers would be his—as all human experience was shared among one great, united, sympathetic species. She would know him entirely, and he would know her, and a harmony of perfect understanding would flow between them, currents of brilliant empathy like rivers of light. But now she had only her words to use. What small, inadequate tools they were in the face of such a mystery.

"Why are you like this?" Derryn asked quietly.

Cole had been holding the blade of his pocketknife in the fire to sterilize it. He looked up at her in surprise. "Like what?"

"The way you are. Not like the rest of the men."

He said nothing until he was satisfied that the knife was ready. He only spoke when he set to work, lancing the first of Derryn's blisters with a touch so soft she barely felt it.

"How do they make pastors out in Ohio?"

"Make pastors?" Her mind spun frantically, trying to invent a likely answer. "Pastors are appointed. By the council." She could only hope those words were vague enough to pass muster with a Sovereign.

Cole paused, glanced up at her. She was coldly, percussively aware of the knife in his hand.

He moved on to the next blister. "We do things a little differently in the East. Out here, any guy who wants to become a pastor has to go through certain training. And when that's finished, the last stage is to go and live among the wireheads."

"You lived with the wireheads?" Derryn didn't have to feign anything this time; her surprise was genuine.

"For two years. It's a rite of passage and a test of faith. Kind of like Jesus being tempted in the desert—that's the basic idea. If a man comes back to his community after living among all that integrated tech, it's a sign that his faith is strong enough to minister to the people, even in this fallen world." Cole shrugged, too humble to accept the implied praise. "Most of the men who go to the wireheads never come back. The temptation is too much for them. They decide to stay where they are, leave the Sovereign life behind."

Derryn held her tongue. No doubt, those men did choose integration. She couldn't imagine tasting that better life—the comfort, the security, the sense of greater wholeness—and returning to disconnection by choice.

Cole said, "If a man comes back, I guess he's thought to have an unusual strength of conviction. A hands-on awareness of the importance of Human Heritage. That's what qualifies him for ministerial work among the people—knowing how important it is to be human."

He applied bandages to the places he had treated, then held his knife in the flames again.

"What was it like out there?" Derryn asked. "Outside the community?"

He bent over her right foot with a smile that might have been ironic, for all Derryn could guess, and carefully lanced another blister.

"You want to know the truth? It was all right. There were good people out there. They treated me like I was one of them, even though they could see the mark on my face—I only had one, back then. As long as I didn't bother anyone, they let me be. Some even showed me kindness. It was hard to find work, at first, hard to support myself. The system they have, that Weave thing, will provide for people who aren't connected, but figuring out how to access support is damn near impossible on your own. People offered me help. At first, I was too proud to accept it, but after a while, I did, and I got by well enough. I made friends—real friends, good people who seemed to really care about me. I don't know; maybe it was all a show. Maybe they were just staying on my good side—keep the crazy terrorist happy so he doesn't blow you up." Cole chuckled and wiped Derryn's foot with a clean rag. "But it was real on my end. I liked them. I cared about them. It was hard to leave when my two years were up and I had to go back to Iron Rock."

He finished his work, applied the last bandage, and cleaned the blade of his knife with an alcohol wipe. "Keep those bandages on all night. You might be able to take them off in the morning. We'll see."

Derryn drew her knees up to her chest. "Thanks."

He held her eye, the silence tight and resonant between them while the wind went on sighing through the trees and the birds chanted the evening prayer.

"Say it," Cole finally said. "I know you want to ask."

She pressed her lips together tightly, didn't dare to speak.

"Do it." There was something urgent about his command, a quivering and desperate quality that would have gone directly to Derryn's heart if they'd been connected, as people were meant to be.

She drew a long, unsteady breath. "Did you use the Weave?"

"No."

He chuckled over her startled expression, rocked back to sit cross-legged on the trampled grass, the fire crackling at his back.

"I didn't, I swear," Cole went on. "There were times when I wanted to—many times. It's been years, and I still don't know how I resisted the temptation. The Weave seems to make everything so easy, so *real.* The people who use it, they don't even have to talk if they don't want to—or not much, anyway. They just feel. It seems like it'd be nice, to know another person that way. Anyone else, but especially the people you love."

All at once, Derryn felt the absence of her brother, and his husband and his kids, the family for whom she would tear down mountains with her own hands, if it would keep them safe. The family whom she might have traumatized forever with this selfish trip across the Blockade. And all the friends she had ever loved, the colleagues with whom she had built her career—all of them so great within her heart that they seemed more *her* than her own self was. And all of them gone in a blink, in one vast devastation of fate. There was no hope that she might keep her grief at bay. She turned, hoping to hide the tears from Cole, but he was right there, watching her, so close they could have touched, if either had reached for the other.

"I was taught," Cole went on, "that it's wrong for a man to feel. Anything except anger—*that* one's allowed. From the time I was a little boy, it was all driven out of me. Tenderness, and fear, compassion, longing. Empathy. That was too much like the wireheads, you know. If you can feel another person's pain, you can't hate them, Sister, and that's the whole point. We have to know we're different from them if we're going to keep fighting them, hating them, killing them. So we *make* ourselves different. Even if it makes us into something we were never meant to be."

Dusk was on its way out, gliding downstream along the dark canal. Cole took the boiled pot off the fire and set it aside to cool. For a while, there was no sound but the crackle of the flames and a great, ongoing chorus of crickets and tree frogs, the whisper of moving water.

"That's why I went back," he said, busying himself with the bottles and canteens, unscrewing their caps, lining them up in meticulous order. "A pastor is the only sort of man who gets to have compassion in the communities. And here was my chance to be the kind of man who can feel. Who's allowed to feel."

"Why didn't you go?" Derryn asked quietly. "Like the others, who never went back to the communities again?"

His back was turned to her. She didn't hear his short, hard laugh, only saw the jump of his shoulders. "Because I still believed. Sovereignty was all I ever knew, from the time I was born, and I guess I was really too young to make the decision. Pastors are supposed to have faith, and I did—faith enough to resist the temptation of the Weave. Faith enough to make me think, back then, that we still had it right. That our way of life was the only true and original way, the pattern God Himself had used to make humanity."

He turned to look at her, held her eye with an intensity that cut straight to Derryn's spirit. Even without the Weave, she could feel his sincerity, the depth of his grief.

"I've stayed all these years because of what I feel. Because of love, the love I have for the women and children who need a protector. But once the truth gets into you, you can't will it away again. It's there, whether you want it or not, and it does its work. It opens your eyes wider. The more you look, the more truth you see, and pretty soon, you begin to see what isn't true, too. And then you can't shut your eyes again, no matter how much you want to, no matter how much everyone around you expects you to blind yourself and go on believing what you've been taught. You know what I see now when I look at wireheads?"

He never blinked, never looked away from Derryn. She swallowed hard, and could say nothing, only shook her head and shivered in the rising chill.

"I see the very end of Revelation. The New Jerusalem, come down from the clouds. A thousand years of paradise, where all the good people are welcome and all who did wrong are shut out forever, cut off from the goodness God brings. But we're the ones who cut ourselves off. *He* didn't do it to us. We did it to ourselves, because of what we fear."

Cole reached suddenly for his pack, delved into one of its pouches. For a moment, Derryn was stricken by a cold, mute certainty that he was going to pull out his gun, maybe kill her on the spot—for surely he knew, he *knew* what she was.

Instead, he tossed her a biscuit.

Derryn caught it with shaking hands.

"Eat," Cole said. "Are you okay with taking the first watch?"

Derryn nodded as she stuffed the biscuit into her mouth.

"Good. I need a rest. Wake me up in four hours."

While Cole removed his boots and laid out his bedroll, Derryn watched the sky. The first ribbons of the night's aurora extended their long, green arms and curled in the vast eddies of a cosmic current.

Just as Cole slid into his sleeping bag, he said, "I expect we'll hit a Sovereign checkpoint tomorrow, when we come off this trail and cut across New Brunswick. Anyway, the checkpoint is usually there."

With that, he rolled over and was soon breathing deeply in his sleep.

Derryn finished her meager supper. It wasn't much food, but she couldn't have eaten another bite, for a sinking dread had settled in her stomach. She kept her eyes on the ruptured heavens, watching the coruscations of pink and violet and electric blue chase each other across the sky. And all the while, she wondered why Cole's story had struck such a fear into her heart.

She asked herself the same question for nearly an hour, until at last she knew.

He wouldn't have said any of those things to Sister Sarah. No man of his world would have admitted such doubts, such heretical thoughts, to another Sovereign—especially not a woman. That could mean only one thing: He knew that Derryn was not what she appeared to be.

And tomorrow, they would reach a Sovereign checkpoint. Would Cole turn her in? Did he think she'd been trying to infiltrate his community, learn Sovereign secrets, corrupt his people and lead them astray?

Would he have her killed for this stunt?

She didn't even think of Helen's journal that night. The coming day terrified her too much for reading, too much for anything but an endless, circular rumination on her fears. All she could do was huddle under the aurora, asking herself what tomorrow would bring. She found no answers in the long, lonesome night.

25

Helen

November 4, 1862

This war has brought so many changes—to the South, to society, to this city I call home. Most of all, it has changed me. And even though I know full well that whoever reads these pages will surely think me the most scandalous sort of woman, I feel no shame over what I have done. That, perhaps, is the greatest alteration. For I was raised to be as mindful of propriety as any girl must be, any woman. And yet, when I cast it all aside, I felt no more shame than I feel over the work I do on behalf of the Union. Perhaps all these grand ideas we've upheld of purity and chastity and a woman's value are as false as our ideas of race and class and creed. And I think, now that I've done the unthinkable, that any idea only holds as much power as one chooses to give it.

I mustn't tiptoe around the matter. If I am to hold my head up high, I must speak frankly of what has transpired, even if only here on the pages of my diary.

Jere Carver and I are not married, but we have lain together as husband and wife. And I do not regret a single second.

Perhaps it was fated, that we should do such a thing. Perhaps it was inevitable. For can a man and woman work so closely together, as Jere and I have done all these weeks since he got out of Libby Prison, without coming to trust one another, even to love one another? And we *do* love each other, though neither of us has said so. We have no need of words. I have the sensation that fills me when my eye meets his, a purity and sweetness as golden as fresh honey. I have the singing in my heart, like all the hymns of heaven, whenever he takes my hand.

I have felt this way for weeks now, from the day Jere moved into the carriage house. When I knew he would not leave for the North but preferred to stay—to stay with me—I allowed myself to finally turn and look at the great weight of longing that has settled upon me since I brought him to Eudaimonia and nursed him back to health. He is good, and brave, and determined to make this broken world right. He is more than any man who has ever courted me, of a greater and cleaner spirit than the men of Richmond who can only think to fight and die for their right to rule others as tyrant kings.

It was only a matter of time before I gave in to these urges. It happened this evening while we worked over one of our letters, at the old table in the back of the carriage house. Our heads were bent close together, and his voice was soft in my ear, soft enough to raise a thrill all through my body, and when his shoulder brushed mine, I could *smell* him, the clean scent of his skin mingled with wood shavings and the straw of his mattress, and the thrill in my blood became a call I could never shut my ears to. I was overwhelmed by a ravenous hunger—not of the body but of the heart.

I still don't know which of us moved first. One moment we were trying to work out the best way to phrase our message. The next, my arms were around his neck, and he pulled me against his strong chest. I could feel his heart beating, as rapidly as mine, and when we kissed, the heat of our desire forged us into one united soul.

"Helen," he whispered against my lips. "We shouldn't. Not here, not now."

"Then when?" I pulled back enough to look into his eyes. "When will it be safe for us? We must take what we can, when we can. Richmond may burn tomorrow. The whole world might burn. And what would we have left, then, but our hearts?"

His resistance fell, so easily that I knew he was eager to let it drop and had waited only for my assent. We stumbled toward the carriage, for even climbing to the loft, to his bed, would have taken too much time. The need that had seized us both was too powerful; it demanded satisfaction with all haste, or I felt sure—and Jere felt sure, I know—that everything we were and everything we hoped for would cease, in the waiting, to be.

Jere lifted me inside the carriage, onto the velvet seat. I pulled him in after me. Our hasty hands fumbled with buttons and ties.

I shan't write of what came after. I've admitted more than was proper already. Here I will only write that I doubt whether the angels of Heaven have tasted such bliss. Oh, if I could preserve those moments like a fly in amber, so that I might return to this memory again and again. Has God ever made a thing so beautiful as the love between two sympathetic souls?

We both would have preferred to linger in one another's embrace, but with that wretched captain lurking about the house, caution must ever be foremost on our minds. Hastily, we put ourselves back in order and said nothing of what we had just done.

"I'll have the letter ready by morning," Jere said, turning away with a red face.

"Good." I tugged down my bodice. "I'll see to it that it's mailed before noon."

Then I went back across the garden, shaking all over with astonishment at what I had just done. One small part of my mind, I confess, was disappointed at my own actions. Hadn't I been raised better than to carry on so shamelessly? I, an unmarried woman! But it wasn't so hard to shut the door on those old-fashioned thoughts. By the time I'd reached the back porch of Eudaimonia, I had talked myself into better sense.

What difference does it make, that I am a Southern woman and Jere is a Yankee? We are kindred souls, and souls know nothing of man's false boundaries. I will make a life with him someday—a beautiful life, easy and safe and free. Jere and I will go together into that miraculous future I saw, the place where all stand as equals and wonders are accomplished with the wave of a hand. For I know that time and place will only be built through love.

I am brimming over with hope for what lies beyond this war. It *must* end, someday, and tonight I know that it hasn't yet managed to take all the good out of this world.

And one thing is certain: I will never ride in that carriage again without picturing what Jere and I did on the velvet seat tonight!

November 12, 1862

We have had a close call, Jere and I.

Our rendezvous in the carriage house have not ceased, and perhaps I am getting too eager for them, forgetting to watch my back, both day and night. For the night before last, when our time together was over, I climbed down the ladder of the loft and sauntered out into the garden, pleased as a cat in cream, only to run smack into Captain Gibbs.

He looked down at me with those small, porcine eyes, so dark and calculating.

"Miss Helen," he said, "what a strange surprise to find a lady like you prowling around a garden at night."

"It is my garden, sir," I answered, "and I may prowl it any time I please."

I was horribly conscious of my hair and dress, certain that both must look a fright. But I didn't dare fuss over my appearance. For all the money in the world, I wouldn't have shown my distress before that man. Let him think what he would; that was no concern of mine.

"What were you doing in the carriage house so late, I wonder."

The captain craned to look beyond me, as if he could see through the walls to its dark interior. Thank goodness Jere had put out the light.

I thought as fast as a lightning strike. "Looking for an awl among my father's old tools. I need to repair one of my shoes. But I didn't find it. I suppose David must have taken the awl inside."

"You have slaves to do work like that," Gibbs said.

"Is there something wrong with a lady knowing how to repair her own shoes?" I said with the haughtiest air. "Why, our foremothers in the colonies had to make and mend all on their own. I may be the mistress of a fine house, sir, but that doesn't mean I'm helpless. My slaves have enough work to do, and they do it well enough to please me."

With that, I breezed past him to the house. To my great relief, he followed me and went off to his bed with no more grumbling.

But oh, wasn't I just about chilled to the bone that night, lying awake in my bed, wondering over the captain's suspicions and asking myself how I hoped to go on hiding a Yankee officer with Gibbs stalking around at every hour of the night and day.

This morning, I spoke to Jere about the incident. We were both terribly grave.

"I should get out of Richmond," he said, "for your sake, if not my own. I'll go on foot through the countryside, get to the Potomac, and cross back into the North."

"You will do no such thing," I said. "That's much too dangerous a plan."

The truth was, of course, that I selfishly desired to keep Jere close at hand. Now that I have tasted real love, I cannot face the thought of doing without it.

"We have managed to do useful work here," Jere said thoughtfully. "It would be a shame to give it up now."

Then a grand idea occurred to me. "Why don't you go back to the cabin at Bush Hill? You can stay hidden there. If anyone comes along the trail, you can hide in the forest. No one will know you're there, and I'm already in the habit of visiting the place for my Quaker meetings. We'll still be able to see one another that way, and I can bring you food and other things, so you won't go wanting."

"If I'm caught, it would be better if they took me there, in the woods or at the cabin, than here in your home. That way, we might spare you from the worst. If the worst comes."

I declared it a fine idea, and, as Gibbs was off at the prison, I told Jere to wait a quarter of an hour, then to follow me to the livery stable halfway down the hill. I left one of my horses saddled for him, and rode out alone, across the city to the cabin trail.

Once I was covered by the forest, I waited for Jere with my fur hood pulled up to hide my face as much as to keep me warm. He didn't take long to catch up with me. Side by side, talking quietly of the work we've done for the Union, we rode to the old cabin.

But long before we reached it, the smell of smoke silenced our conversation. A sinking dread filled my stomach and chittered in my head. When we came across a great square of ash where the cabin should have been, I understood the cause of my worries. The cabin was burned to the ground. Nothing was left but the charred fireplace and the half-collapsed chimney.

Jere and I sat our horses for a long while, looking at the ruin in stricken silence. Then, without a word, he turned and began riding back for home. I had no choice but to follow.

The loss is a cruel reminder that there are still many in Richmond who remember that I freed my slaves. Many who suspect me of treason to the Confederacy, and not without good cause.

Oh, how I wish I'd found a buyer for Eudaimonia years ago! But the truth is, I didn't try as hard to sell it as I might have done. I never really wanted to give the place up—not only for the memories it holds, but for its comfort and its beauty. The house holds an allure that has sunk its very claws into my heart and mind. I cannot seem to disentangle myself from Eudaimonia, no matter how dangerous it is to remain, no matter how much I know I must give the place up or face the final condemnation.

26

Derryn

2053

As afternoon settled hot and thick over the land, the trail carried Derryn and Cole out of the forest and back into the fractured landscape of human civilization. The gray came first, gaps in the trees revealing small buildings that huddled together like children hiding, or heaps of rubble that had once been homes, or sometimes open ground so blighted by whatever had befallen it that not even weeds would grow there. Then came the developments. Small communes clustered as near as they could come to the canal. The thin streamers of smoke that rose from their chimneys and the pens of chickens and goats around their perimeters gave no hint as to whether the inhabitants were Sovereign or integrated. Neighborhoods erased whole swaths of woodland, and finally, the forest gave way to streets and markets and blocks of apartment buildings, and the land ran in rivers of colorless concrete from the banks of the canal out to the vanishing point of the horizon, a mass of civilization drawing into its heavy heart the world that once had been.

Fear had ridden in Derryn's stomach, constant and heavy, from the time she'd risen from her bedroll that morning. Now, as the last of the forest fell away and an unbroken stretch of city unfolded before her, anxiety stretched like a wakening beast, swelling to fill every part of her. How long now until they reached the Sovereign checkpoint? She might evade the Sovereigns altogether if she slipped off into a side street, hid among the old buildings and the cobbled-together gardens where these desperate people scratched out a half living under the shadow of war. The sheer size of this sprawl could mean only one thing: New York City wasn't far off. She had almost reached her destination.

But she wasn't at the blockade yet, and she had no way of knowing where the Sovereign checkpoints lay. For all Derryn could say, the faction had completely surrounded the approach to the blockade. She might run into them anywhere—and might find no more help in reaching New York. The odds seemed just as good that she might wander for days through the labyrinth of this crumbling suburb and still end up in the hands of the Sovereigns before the Weave came back to life.

Cole trudged along a broad arterial, his fists locked around the straps of his pack, his eyes distant. He hadn't said much that day, and Derryn had thought of nothing she might say to him. The urge had often taken her to plead with the pastor, beg him not to turn her in at the checkpoint. She was of no harm to anyone; she was only a desperate traveler stranded by dire fate, only a human being like he was. But she didn't even know for certain whether Cole had learned her secret. Derryn was operating off of nothing more than suspicion and instinct, and a lifetime of connection to the Weave had left her instincts brittle and rusty, more burden than benefit. The pastor knew the most direct route to New York City. Derryn still needed him, even if she hated to admit it.

They walked for more than an hour down a broken sidewalk, following the course of one broad city street. Now and then, cars sped by, the melodic electric hum of their motors swelling and receding in a rapid wave of sound. Derryn eyed every vehicle that passed. She considered trying to hitchhike again or throwing herself in front of an oncoming car to force it to stop and take her to the blockade. But no one was driving at all now unless it was an emergency. With power grids disabled around the planet, every charged battery was a precious resource. Only a life-or-death dilemma could justify expending a car's reserve. Derryn had no right to place her own emergency above others.

Their chosen street bore them deeper into the density of urban sprawl. Children played in gardens and along the dusty sidewalks. Neighbors talked on the stoops of apartment buildings. The sight heartened Derryn, for it spoke to humanity's resilience—this small, lonesome species that still endured, even after decades of attrition. The sight sickened her, too, because there was no good reason anymore for the destruction that surrounded so much life. No reason anymore to fight, to hate, to kill.

Heat shimmers rose from the pavement. The city ahead swam and disintegrated and put itself together again, only to break once more in a waver of light and air. She was miserable with sweat. Not even the long, flowing Sovereign dress brought any relief. When she lifted her bottle to gulp down a few precious mouthfuls of water, she noticed a deep-black solidity somewhere among the fracturing lines of heat distortion. Vehicles—trucks—parked across the roadway. The checkpoint was only a short distance ahead.

Cole turned from the sidewalk, into a shaded alley. The narrow passage was heaped with discarded brick, old plastic bags bursting with whatever foulness they held, shards of twisted metal. He settled on a wooden crate, drinking deeply from his canteen.

"We're almost at the checkpoint," he said.

"I saw."

"Let me do all the talking for you."

She narrowed her eyes. What was he going to tell his own people? That this wirehead had impersonated one of their women, tried to pass herself off as a true believer? For Derryn was certain that Cole knew what she was. She'd thought of little else since their conversation the night before. He wouldn't have confessed his feelings to a woman of his own people. He *knew*, but for reasons of his own, he had said nothing to Derryn.

"Are you sure we can't go around them?" she asked. "Take some other street?"

He gave her a fractional smile. "Why? Are you worried about passing a Sovereign checkpoint?"

Derryn swallowed hard and said nothing.

"They'll have every road blocked off between here and New York," he said. "I'd be surprised if there's any route they haven't sealed up. Maybe way to the north, from the upstate side, but Jersey's been contested territory for a long time."

"What's the point of all this? What are they trying to do with these checkpoints?"

"They've been hoping to make a move on New York City for years now."

She blinked at him, stunned to silence. Then she blurted, "They think they can take New York? One of the biggest cities on the planet?"

Cole shrugged. "Through faith, all things are possible." Then he laughed and pulled at his canteen again. "It's a crazy plan. It'll never come to anything—logistically, it's impossible. But big, flashy ideas are great for recruitment. You'd be surprised how many kids born to wirehead parents defect and join the HHM. They're looking for something they can't find in their own world. It isn't a great life, you know, living under the constant threat of bombs and rifle fire."

And who put those kids in that situation? Derryn was aching to say it, burning to throw the truth in his face. *Whose bombs and rifles do they have to fear?* But she was too close to her destination to sabotage her own plans. The most prudent course of action was to keep her mouth shut, at least until she was past the checkpoint. If she made it past the checkpoint at all.

She kept her eyes on Cole while he rested. He looked very small and frail among those heaps of refuse, a child lost in the dead-end passages of a crumbling mythos. A vile taste rose in the back of her throat. She wanted to spit it out—the bitterness, the acid, all knowledge she had now of this twisted ideology, this patent evil that had proclaimed itself the only true pattern of humanity. She wanted to leave the pastor there. Let him rot with the ruin he and his kind had made of a world that had had potential, even if it had never been perfect.

After Cole had rested for a few minutes, they set out again. The checkpoint resolved out of the heat waves, coming into solid form on the road ahead—those distinctive black diesel trucks parked in twos and threes, staggered in rows so they barred the road with only enough space between for a vehicle to wend its way through at the slowest speed.

When they were within shouting distance, a man stood up in a truck bed. He had the same heavy beard that all Sovereign men wore, his eyes hidden by dark shades below a tactical helmet. Derryn could make out the thin black line of a rifle's muzzle peeking above one shoulder. He unslung the weapon, raised his free hand in the universal gesture *stop*.

Cole halted on the sidewalk. Derryn did the same. Every beat of her frantic heart was as thick and pounding as the day's heat. A few more Sovereigns appeared from among the trucks, waved for Cole and Derryn to come out into the road and speak with them.

There was nothing Derryn could do but follow a few steps behind the pastor as he strode toward the checkpoint with a cheerful air.

"Hi, Brothers. Hope you're staying cool today."

Six or seven Sovereign men stalked out to meet them, ranged in a circle around Derryn and Cole. She kept her eyes lowered, clenched her fists in an effort to hold still. She was shivering with a mindless, instinctive fear, and was certain the men must have seen it.

Derryn peeked up from the pavement just enough to watch the exchange between Cole and the man with the dark shades, who seemed to be the leader. What little she could see of his face was weathered from long exposure to the elements. The mark on his left cheek was sinuous, snakelike. That black line scored permanently into human flesh made Derryn feel all the more helpless.

The man with the snake tattoo looked Cole up and down. Then he extended his hand. "Pastor."

Cole shook heartily. "Good to be among friends out there."

"Where you from?"

"Iron Rock."

"Long way from home if you came all the way on foot."

"We did," Cole said with an easy laugh. "All the trucks were needed for an op at Haverford." Then he nodded in Derryn's direction. "Sister Sarah here is a widow of the war. I'm escorting her to her family in the Dutch Kills community."

A sharp breath filled her. What possible reason could the pastor have to maintain her story? She didn't dare look at him, afraid that the Sovereign men would notice her astonishment and question them both more closely. Gripping the straps of her backpack, she kept her eyes fixed to the dry, hot pavement, willing herself not to move, hardly daring to breathe.

"Okay," said the snake-marked man. "You two stay safe. No telling what the wireheads might do with this solar flare going on."

"Have you boys seen any trouble from them yet?" Cole asked.

"Not yet. But they could go crazy any second, now that their demonic controllers have been taken out. Stay on your toes, Brother. No telling what a wirehead might do when he's desperate."

The circle of Sovereigns parted. Cole sauntered easily toward the trucks. Derryn scuttled after him. They wove between the vehicles, and the road opened before them. She never dared to look back until they'd crossed three more city blocks. By then, the trucks were small in the distance, the men invisible among their machines.

⁂

Derryn and Cole trudged up the long, sloping curve of a cloverleaf and across the Raritan River. They walked in silence for hours until the sun began to settle low in the western sky. Another confusion of on-ramps and overpasses loomed ahead, a black knot against the deep gold of evening's approach.

"We should find a place to sleep for the night," Cole said.

Derryn suspected that they might be able to reach the blockade before dark if they pressed on. But she had slept miserably for nights on end, and not at all the night before. Now that she knew Cole wasn't going to turn her over to a gang of terrorists, the adrenaline that had kept her going for days drained away, left her trembling and weak with a mind more useless than it had been since the Weave had vanished. Rest sounded even better than New York did.

"There's an old hotel up there," Cole said, "right before the overpass. It's been shut down for a while—abandoned, I guess. We might find a couple of beds in there, though. It's worth checking out."

The mustiest old mattress would beat another night on a thin camping pad. Derryn followed Cole along a stretch of sidewalk, toward a buff-colored building some five stories tall. A metal pole in the empty parking lot had once borne a sign high enough to be seen from the parkway, but the sign itself was unreadable now, broken into shards by thrown rocks or fired bullets, so only a few ragged pieces of plastic remained to claw at the sky.

As they entered the building, they found that much of its interior had been salvaged. The glass doors that had once opened onto a modest lobby were shattered. The lobby itself had been stripped of chairs and tables and televisions. Even the fixed front desk had been pried up and removed, leaving a dark footprint on the tile floor. Signs of recent habitation were everywhere—packaging from shelf-stable food scattered in corners, graffiti marked on the walls. But on this evening, Derryn and Cole seemed to be the only living souls in the place.

They prowled through the hallways of the first floor. Some doors were closed and locked, but many had been kicked open or otherwise forced, to judge by the splintered frames. Most of the furnishings had been stripped away—whatever was small enough to carry—but a few rooms still had mattresses on the beds. The mattresses were bare, speckled with mildew. Derryn didn't care. She had her sleeping bag for warmth, and she already smelled like a farm animal after days of walking and nights spent sleeping on the ground.

They chose a room with two queen-sized beds and fell onto the mattresses. Derryn rolled onto her side, so Cole couldn't see her face. The tears she had refused to shed in front of the Sovereign men came at last, pouring in a bitter flood. Cole remained so silent that she almost convinced herself he wasn't there. He had left the room, or had never been there at all—he was only a hallucination, an artifact of Derryn's distressed and forsaken mind.

But then he spoke, his voice gentle and low, stilling her shuddering sobs.

"Why didn't you hit that man?"

Derryn sniffed back the last of her tears, sat up slowly on the mattress. "What?"

"The guy who tried to raid our camp. You had a branch in your hand, but you didn't use it. Why?"

He knew why. What good to say it?

"You know what I am," Derryn answered quietly.

"Yes," he said, "I know. I only suspected, at first—no mark on your face, and your short hair. And you don't know how to tell direction by the sun. But I didn't *know* until that man found our camp."

"Well, then, you know why I didn't hit him."

His brow furrowed. "No, that's not what I'm asking. I mean, *why* couldn't you hit him? What stops you from doing a thing like that to another person?"

Derryn turned her back to him again, worked her skirt up until she could access the travel pouch. She found the ports of her headset inside, as well as the thin silver frames. She took them out, laid them on the mattress. Cole watched her assemble the CoreTex with a strange intensity, a curiosity bordering on hunger. When the headset was whole, Derryn put it on without activating the power button. The ports settled into place on her temples and at the nape of her neck. The frame nestled into the dense curls of her hair.

"This is why." She met the pastor's fervid eye, held it without looking away, as a Sovereign woman would have done. "I've gone all my life feeling other people's emotions. Most of my life, anyway—since I was very young. I *can't* inflict suffering on someone else, even when it might benefit me . . . and apparently, even when I don't have my Weave connection. It's part of me now, even when I'm disconnected. I didn't know that until this solar flare happened. But it's true."

"What's a part of you?"

"Empathy. It's in me—it *is* me—and I don't think it can be turned off in someone like me as easily as you Sovereigns turn it off."

He looked away, into the deep shadows of the room, his expression darkened by an emotion Derryn could only guess at. She thought it might be shame.

"We don't turn it off in ourselves," Cole said. "It's killed in us. It takes some work to do it. I told you men aren't allowed to feel anything but anger. But we don't start out that way. They make us into what they want us to be."

Derryn's hands twisted together in her lap. She didn't think she wanted to hear this story, yet even without her connection, she could sense Cole's need, his desperation to tell someone what he had suffered.

"You saw the Women's House at Iron Rock," he said.

She nodded.

"That's for unmarried girls and widows. It's different for boys. When we're seven years old, we go to the boys' camp and live there until we're fifteen."

"Without your mothers?"

"No mothers, no fathers, no brothers and sisters. Well—no sisters, for sure, but some boys had older brothers at the camp. But it doesn't matter. You learn how to be tough there, how to be resilient. How to do the things men need to do in this world. So even the boys who had brothers at the camp—it didn't change things for them."

Derryn could feel her anger at Cole melting into sympathy. What kind of world demanded that seven-year-olds be tough? What kind of culture would separate a child from his parents?

"Camp wasn't so bad," he went on. "I liked some things about it. There were animals. We learned how to take care of the livestock. When we first got there, we each got a goat kid of our own to raise. Mine was a little brown one with floppy ears and white spots on his sides. I fed him with a bottle. He was the only friend I had, that first year at camp."

Something hardened in Cole—his voice, his eyes. The change came over him so suddenly that Derryn could only assume it was deliberate, the drawing down of some inner blind to block out the warmth of memory.

"The second year," he said, "we had to kill our goats. Had to learn how to butcher animals, you know, as a survival skill. The boys who couldn't bring themselves to do it, or the ones who cried, were sent back to Iron Rock to live in the Women's House until they got their act together."

"Oh my God," Derryn muttered. "I'm sorry."

He shrugged as if it were nothing. "People have to eat. Livestock aren't pets."

Despite his practical words, she could see in his eyes the anguish that had never abated. She could almost feel the pain that still ran through him, hot and thick and suffocating—the memory of the friend he'd been forced to betray, the violence he'd been made to choose over a child's natural instinct for compassion. She couldn't understand what would drive adults to do such a thing to a little boy, to dozens or hundreds of children at once. Separate them from their families at such a tender age, comfort them with the companionship of a trusting young animal. And then, forcing them to turn on the only thing they were allowed to love, forcing them to take the life that was most precious to them. The cruelty stunned her to mute horror.

When Cole spoke again, there was something small and soft in his voice, the inflection of a child. "One of the first things I noticed when

I went outside—when I started my two years with the wireheads—was that you don't eat meat."

"Not unless it's lab grown."

"Right," Cole said. "No need to kill any goats that way."

He offered a laugh, but Derryn didn't see what was so funny.

"What was your childhood like, Sarah?"

"My name isn't Sarah. It's Derryn Witt. I'm a professor of art history at Stanford University, out in California, and I came out here to Pennsylvania to work. Haverford College—that's where I was working."

"Haverford. That's—"

"Yes," Derryn said. "The campus your people were attacking. *Are* attacking, right now, for all I know. I was trying to preserve a significant collection of art before you could destroy it."

He was silent for a moment, his face unreadable. At length, he said, "California. You're from Cascadia."

"Yes, I am. And I would give anything to be back there right now."

"What's it like in Cascadia? What's it like to live your whole life with the Weave?"

She considered the question, tried to work out some likely response. How could she explain wholeness to one who had only known isolation? It was like trying to describe the sun to a creature who had evolved underground, whose very systems and structures were unequipped to behold such a thing as light.

"It's knowing," she finally said. "Not thinking or believing, but *knowing* that everyone is just like you. So much like you that there's no need for separation."

Again, he fell silent while he considered her answer. A brittleness hung around them both, a certain fear that pressed in around Derryn and shivered below the surface of Cole's outward bravado, the smooth, commanding confidence of a Sovereign man.

"Don't you lose yourself that way?" he finally said.

She read a deep terror in those words, despite their cool delivery. The sympathy she felt for him swelled, threatened to make her cry all over again. What must it be like, she thought, to prize such a fearful, lonely self—to prefer isolation to an immolating love? But it wasn't Cole's fault that he was this way, and answering from the depth of her own emotion would do neither of them any good. The child who'd been taken from his mother's arms, to be shaped and forced and pummeled into this twisted form, this shadow of humanity—he would have grown into a different man, if fate had been kinder to him.

She looked out the window to the ruined city, the abandoned buildings, the crumbling parkways, everything humankind had struggled so long to build, degrading into dust. This was the terminal state of Sovereign life. This was what it led to, the only possible outcome when an entire people killed the human impulse toward empathy. The rigid gender roles forcing everyone, woman and man and other, into a mental cage. The constant regression into *tradition*, into the vaunted, sublimated, fictional past. It was as if the Sovereigns were terrified of the future. As if they would rather convince themselves that there was no future at all, there was only the past, rather than allow themselves to change into something better. For change itself undid the only reality they knew. To move forward into a better world was to end the world that had made them. To grow into a better self was to cast the only self they knew into the unknowable grave.

What fear they must feel, Derryn thought with a great, choking swell of sorrow. *All of them, all the time, even Cole, as kind and helpful as he can be. He is always afraid. The fear never leaves him alone. It hasn't, not ever, not since he killed that poor goat he raised.*

Since the shutdown was announced, Derryn had been terrified more times than she could count—had felt a greater fear than she'd ever imagined in her integrated life. But she had never known a fear like Cole's, the kind that was never silent, a constant and commanding dread that had been woven by deliberate hands into the very fabric of his culture. What good was Sovereign faith if those beliefs spared no one from such suffering? What good was the hate these people heaped onto others if it couldn't protect them from the monsters in their own minds?

That's the way it's always been with fear and hate, she thought. *They feed off one another. They beget one another. It's all they've ever done, hate and fear, fear and hate. Around and around they go, for years, for generations, never solving anything, breeding more of their own useless kind.*

Cole was still waiting for an answer. She still didn't know what to tell him, so she turned back to meet his eye and spoke whatever words came first to her mind.

"I'm not less myself because I feel what others feel. I'm *more* myself, more human. And all these days, since the solar flare . . . since I lost my connection . . . I've never felt so alone and frightened. *This* isn't who I am—just me, by myself, one person alone with my private thoughts. I'm something greater when I can love and be loved. When I'm creating things, and helping to fix what's broken instead of destroying, like some people do."

To Derryn's surprise, a single tear ran down the pastor's cheek, over the symbol that marked him forever as a relic of a passing age. It was vivid pink, that tear, reflecting the light. That was how she knew, without turning again to the window behind her, that night had come, and with it, the aurora.

"Why are you still with me?" Derryn asked quietly. "Why didn't you turn me in at the checkpoint?"

Offended, he huffed. "They might have killed you. After all this time we've spent together, do you really think I'm the type of guy to let someone be killed just because of who they are?"

Derryn chewed at her lip. She wasn't sure *what* kind of person Cole was, or what she thought of him now.

She said, "Now that we're past the checkpoint and we have no more secrets from each other, what do we do? What are *you* going to do, Cole?"

He shrugged, wouldn't meet her eye. "I still mean to get you to the blockade. That's what I promised to do. Whatever you might think of me, Derryn, I'm a man of integrity. I keep my promises."

"Okay." Relief ran through her, so powerful a force that she trembled. "Thank you. I can still really use the help."

He smiled briefly but said nothing—only watched the window again, the lights surging across the sky, the colors melting and flowing over the dark city.

When he spoke again, he was so quiet that Derryn wasn't sure he meant for her to hear.

"I used to pray for this," Cole said. "*We* used to pray. For all my life, we begged God to bring down His judgment on those who'd turned their backs on their own humanity. We prayed for something to wipe out the Weave, destroy all the tech that had taken away the world our forefathers made."

"And now?" Derryn said into his silence.

"And now it's happened. A cosmic force powerful enough to level technology, powerful enough to make you and me the same kind of person."

Derryn glanced at window. Waves of violent pink and acid green burned across the sky.

"And now that it's happened," Cole admitted, "I'm more afraid than I ever have been, of anything I can remember."

"Afraid of what?" she asked.

"That the Weave might not come back. That I might have no chance now to be something better than I am."

27

Helen

December 28, 1862

How has Christmas flown by already? I hardly noticed the season come and go, for my mind has been too much occupied with worry for Mary Jane.

Three days before the holiday, while we gathered in the carriage house to peck away at our conspiracy (even in the dead of winter, our work for the Union continues), Mary Jane announced the latest news she'd heard from her friends in the city.

"They're looking for more house slaves at the White House," she said. "I mean, Davis's White House, down on K Street. Folks were talking about it at the market today when Kitty sent me to buy spices for the Christmas baking."

Jere and I looked at one another. There was the hint of a warning in his eyes. He seemed to know, as well as I did, what would issue next out of Mary Jane's mouth. He knew, too, that I wouldn't like it one bit.

"I'm going to get myself into that house," Mary Jane said.

"You certainly will not!" I cried. "Emancipation is only days away. Why, under the canopy of Heaven, would you—"

She interrupted me with a smooth haughtiness. "You freed me long ago, Miss Helen. It's my choice what I do with my freedom, and I choose this."

"It's far too dangerous," I protested. "If they discover you're educated, that you can read—"

"They won't," the girl said, laughing. She actually *laughed*, as if we were discussing her attendance at a puppet show!

I looked to Jere for agreement, but he was no help at all. "She's spent her life playing the role white folks expect of her, Helen. She can do it again. Besides, men like Davis—and everyone who surrounds him, I guess—won't think a girl like her could be any real threat."

Pertly, Mary Jane went on. "Mr. Carver has it right. They'll see whatever they want to see—same thing just about any white folks see when they look at someone like me. Think of what I'll learn under Davis's own roof. All the secrets that pass through that house—troop movements, supply routes, strategy. We can't let the chance pass us by."

So great was my distress that I reverted, all in an instant, to the role of mistress. I hollered at Mary Jane that I plumb forbade her to do something so dangerous.

Then my own instinct for control accused me, and I turned away in shame.

Mary Jane's quiet words reached through my turmoil. "You swore on the Bible, Miss Helen. Ruthie and Kitty told me all about it. You swore our freedom was real."

With a will, I stilled my weeping and forced myself to meet her fearless eye. "Please forgive me. It's only my fear for you that made me forget myself. Oh, Mary Jane, I love you so dearly. I can't bear to think of *you*, young as you are . . . you of all people thrust into that lion's den! It frightens the wits right out of me."

Her expression softened. She reached for me, and I embraced her, kissing her cheek and holding her hard against my heart.

"I'm not afraid," Mary Jane said with her arms still around me. "I'm too glad that a way has been made for me. There's no room among all that gladness to let in any fear. Sitting by won't win this fight. You know that, Miss Helen. And by God, I mean to win."

After that, there was nothing for it but to do as Mary Jane wished. On Christmas Eve, I dressed with special care, selecting my prettiest gown of deep-green velvet, which Ruthie had freshly made up to suit the latest fashion. When I was laced and buttoned into the dress, Mary Jane came into my room. We looked at one another, side by side, in my mirror. She had put on a frock of plain, dark wool with a clean apron and a linen neckerchief, and had tied a scarf around her hair, red and green plaid, as if her mistress had prettied her up for a Christmas present. After giving me a saucy smile in the mirror, she lowered her face and folded her hands in the posture of subservience which I hadn't seen her assume in years, except in the presence of Captain Gibbs. The girl looked every inch the slave she once had been, and my heart both wrenched and soared at the sight of so much bravery concealed by her humble disguise.

"Are you ready?" I asked, my throat tight.

"Yes, ma'am." She never looked up, for the girl was already firmly in character.

We were silent on the carriage ride to Davis's White House. I rehearsed my lines in my head, praying I could maintain the façade of a loyal Confederate woman without my stormy emotions getting the better of me. We turned onto Twelfth Street, and my eyes fixed upon the house, a great snow-white box of smooth stucco with soaring double pillars to hold up its grand portico. The mansion last belonged to the Crenshaws, but they've leased it to the Confederacy. Even I must admit that the house makes an impression. It's by far the most imposing mansion in Richmond, if one doesn't count the houses on Church Hill. The front windows were decked out with wreaths of evergreen and red ribbon, a pretense of normalcy amid this dreadful war.

The carriage rounded the building to a humbler porch on the opposite side. A porter came down the steps to meet us, and I summoned my most charming smile.

"I wish to see President Davis, if he's receiving visitors," I said. "I've brought a Christmas gift for his household."

The porter's eyes flicked to Mary Jane. "Your name, ma'am?"

"Miss Helen Bywater of Eudaimonia."

The man disappeared inside. I took the moment of privacy to squeeze Mary Jane's hand, but the porter was back all too soon, before I could give her any more than platitudes.

"The president will see you," the porter said. "You may follow me."

The inside of that mansion was quite the most elaborate scene I have witnessed. The entry hall was a rounded chamber, its far door flanked by high, arched niches in which two life-sized bronze ladies stood, each holding aloft a glowing lamp. The walls were papered in gold, the floor tiled in such a clamorous pattern that my head was fairly swimming before we'd even passed through the foyer. Our guide conducted us through a smaller door to the right, which opened to reveal a spiral staircase, magnificent with a floral carpet and wrought-iron rail painted white.

"The president is in his office," the porter said with a note of apology, "up on the second floor. You don't mind a climb, do you, ma'am?"

As I climbed, the spin of those steps among the damask wallpaper and vine-covered carpet left me feeling as if I might topple over the rail. But soon enough, we reached the second story, and the porter led us into the office of Mr. Jefferson Davis.

The man himself was already standing to greet me. I must say that he was very fine looking, with strong, elegant features and a small tuft at his chin, a full head of dark hair, which he wore uncoiffed in a style that was rather boyish and tousled. Somehow, I had expected him to be dressed in Confederate gray, but he wore an ordinary suit of black wool, the coat left open as if he'd been too absorbed in his work to remember its buttons.

"Miss Bywater," Davis said. "What a pleasant surprise. I have heard much of your patriotic entertainments for the local soldiery."

I hurried forward to take his hand and lowered myself into a deep curtsy. "I'm so honored that you would receive me, Mr. President. I know it was terribly ungracious of me to call on you unannounced—and I, only a humble lady of this town. You've surely got a hundred better things to do than entertain me, sir, so I won't take up your time. But I heard, sir, that you were hoping to find more help here in the White House."

Davis chuckled warmly. "That's so, Miss Bywater. We've four children now—you might hear them running about on the third floor—and the youngest is still a baby. It's more than my wife Varina can do to keep up with them, for she does have so many other duties now as first lady."

"Why, what a fortunate turn," I said, clasping my hands in a show of delight. "My girl Mary Jane just loves little children, and she's awfully good at looking after them. I came here today to make you a present of Mary Jane. She's young, but she's well trained in every kind of housework. We've been real pleased with her at Eudaimonia, and as soon as I heard you were looking for more hands around the White House, I knew she'd be the very thing."

Davis considered Mary Jane, tugging thoughtfully at that patch of chin whiskers. While his attention was trained on her, I seized the moment and lowered my eyes in an expression of womanly patience, though I was in fact scouring the man's desk for anything of value to the Union—a map, a letter, a full-color illustration of every battle plan the South had yet devised. But of course, there was nothing to see. Mr. Davis had slid a ledger over the top of his work before we had entered the room. Only the corners of papers peeked from below the ledger's cover.

"She's slight," Davis noted.

"But very strong," I answered, "and she never tires. And oh, wait until you see how tender she is with children. She knows so many games and songs. She can get the most stubborn child to take his medicine or accept a bath when nothing else will convince him. Your little ones will adore her, Mr. President, I know it."

Of course, it was all a pack of lies. As far as I knew, Mary Jane had never so much as changed a diaper, for there had been no babies at Eudaimonia. Mary Jane herself had been the youngest inhabitant of the Bywater estate since Father had bought her at the age of five or six. But there was no point in admitting the truth to Jefferson Davis.

"Varina does need all the help she can get with our rowdy pack," he confessed. "Let me call up my steward, and we'll work out the price."

"Foot to that," I said. "I won't take a penny. Consider it my gift, for all you and the first lady have done for this great confederacy."

"That's generous of you," he said thoughtfully, "but the matter of her ownership—"

"Consider her on loan to the White House, from Eudaimonia," I said. "You may send her back to me anytime if she doesn't please, or if you have a change of circumstances and no longer need her."

That way, at least, Mary Jane would remain my property under the letter of the law—and I could still give her some portion of freedom.

After Davis agreed, it was all settled, as quick as that. He summoned the head woman of his household, who was introduced to Mary Jane and told to make a place for her in the basement, where the slaves had their quarters. I wished desperately to embrace Mary Jane one last time, to kiss her cheek again and give her my sincerest affection. But all I could do before the gaze of the Confederate president was to meet the girl's eye with an unspoken reminder of the danger we faced.

"Goodbye, Mary Jane." Somehow, I managed to speak without a tremor. "You be mindful of your place, now, and serve the president well."

She curtsied, her face turned down. "Yes, Miss Helen. Thank you, ma'am."

Then she followed her new overseer through a narrow servants' door and never gave me a backward glance.

Five days have passed since I left Mary Jane in Davis's house. Five days of gnawing worry, jumping at every knock at the door, fearing news of her discovery or harm. I have heard nothing—neither word *of* Mary Jane, nor word *from* her. When Jere and I meet in the carriage house by night, coding our knowledge of troop movements and ammunition supplies into letters, he tells me that the silence is good. Mary Jane is clever enough to look after herself. Jere often reminds me of that, and I know he's right. Still, I long to hear something from Mary Jane, merely for the confirmation that she is well, and our secret is still safe.

28

Derryn

2053

After they'd eaten their meager supper, Derryn and Cole both lay back on their bare mattresses, but only Cole slept. He slid into a deep slumber so quickly that Derryn was surprised to hear the slow rhythm of his breath filling the room. For some long while, she lay listening to the white noise of her companion, watching luminous arcs of green and gold pulse and recede across a magenta sky. But sleep remained beyond her reach.

Hoping to wear herself down enough that she could finally rest, Derryn sat up and took one of Helen's old journals from her pack, the one she'd been reading along the trail. She had left off somewhere in the year 1862, when America's first civil war had been climbing toward its bloody crescendo. The aurora gave plenty of light to read by, but it was still a slower endeavor than it would have been with Tyko's translation of the long, looping script. She could do it, however, with enough concentration.

Word by word and line by line, Helen's voice entered her head. The feelings of a departed woman opened and flowered in her heart. It wasn't like the Weave, not like feeling Leo's familiar approach and knowing, *knowing* he was there, no matter how far apart they were in the physical realm. In the place that mattered, the velvet darkness where minds and souls connected, her brother was only a thought away. No, reading the words of a long-dead woman, written nearly two centuries ago, wasn't the same as being on the Weave. But it was something. It made Derryn feel less like a single pixel in one vast, unseeable image. She was still alone, but this was a lonesomeness she could bear.

She read the harrowing account of Union officers held in the old warehouse turned prison. When Helen found the escaped Major Carver at the old family cabin, Derryn even managed a smile despite her pervasive distress, for she was almost as desperate to know that the secret plan was working as Helen must have been. And when Jere remained in Richmond to fall, perhaps inevitably, in love with the brave young woman who'd saved him, Derryn felt a sense of rightness, a cosmic order clicking into place, even as the page was illuminated by this great dissolution of that same cosmos.

Derryn reached the entry where Mary Jane asserted herself, demanding to go undercover as a spy in Davis's White House. She knew she would never be so brave in a similar situation.

Maybe it was only reading of Mary Jane's disguise that did it, but suddenly Derryn felt the long, blue dress clinging to her, wrapping her legs, strangling at her throat. She couldn't bear the thing for another moment, could not tolerate the touch of Sovereign beliefs against her real and absolute self. She set the journal aside, lurched up from her mattress, and clawed the dirty frock from her body. Then she stood in the light of the aurora, looking down at her nearly naked self—the vulnerable substance that was not the whole of who she was, these false demarcations of flesh and limb. Light slid in prismatic pools across her bare stomach and thighs. She felt herself expanding from this point in space, the mind that was the greater part of who she was reaching, reaching as it had always done, stretching its unseen hands through the deep void of separation to find the touch of another human heart.

Something was there—someone. She could feel it, a faint call in the black ether, a cry of lonesome despair. It was so like the long cry of her own heart that Derryn knew she must go toward it, must go and find that frightened, sorrowing soul and comfort them if she could. But without the Weave, it was impossible. She could draw no closer to that other person than she was now.

Restless and determined, she dressed again—her ordinary clothes, the dark leggings and long-sleeved top of knitted linen with which she had wrapped Helen's journals. She put on the well-worn shoes that had carried her all the way from Haverford. Then she slipped from the room, through the lightless halls of the abandoned hotel, across its desolate lobby and through its shattered door, out into a luminous inversion of night.

The parking lot was as empty as it had been hours before, when Derryn and Cole had crossed it. To her surprise, she wore her CoreTex—could feel the faint pressure of its ports against her temples. She didn't remember putting it back on. *Habit,* she thought. There was no point in turning it on. Even if its internal mechanisms survived the bombardment of magnetic energy, there would be no Weave waiting for her. But even without her connection, she could feel that lone soul calling for someone, for comfort, for absolution, for a breath of kindness before the great and final darkness took the caller back into its burning, bottomless heart.

Hello. Can you hear me?

Derryn sent the thought, the feeling, the meaning into the void. Her CoreTex was cool and inert, but she could still sense the caller, the terrible hollowness of despair. The other gave no sign that they'd heard Derryn's voice. Of course they hadn't. There was no connection.

No connection between herself and Cole, either—nor any of the people imprisoned by the Human Heritage Movement, born or lured into its mental cage. She watched the waves of color rippling overhead and considered the world in which she now lived. When the Weave came, humanity really had transcended its old restrictions. There were two different *kinds* inhabiting the planet now, both of them technically human from a biological perspective, yet so different in their experience of humanity that they were practically separate species, inhabiting two realities, each distinct from the other.

There was no going back. The realization struck Derryn with a crush of unexpected sadness. No going back to what humankind had once been. Some might choose to walk forward, out of the dead-end past, onto this new road that never ceased to build itself toward a better future. But those who remained in place would fall farther behind. The gulf between the integrated and those who thought themselves most human of all would widen, year by year, month by month, until it was much too far for any soul to cross. *If.* If the Weave returned when the storm had passed.

Derryn thought of Helen's future, the world she had seen in a vision, the bright promise that had so inspired her to make those remarkable paintings. A hard, heavy grief pushed her down to the crumbling curb. She pulled her knees to her chest, hid her eyes from the aurora's light behind folded arms, and wept with a pain that seemed far greater than her physical self.

Oh, Helen, we're no better now, in this time you saw.

Technology had changed, but not the people who wielded it. Despite the global unity of the Weave, humankind was as backward as it ever had been, as trapped and impeded by fear. For if holdouts like the Sovereigns still existed, then the species itself was still broken. If the whole of humanity was not improved, then humankind hadn't really improved at all.

She wept with a bitterness that erased every sweetness she had known. So many years had elapsed since the first civil war, yet the same gulf persisted between factions, between individuals. In Helen's time, that divide wore the trappings of ethnicity. Now its focus was behavior—the use or rejection of certain tools. But it was the same ugly monster.

This conflict had never ended, a timeless war between those who valued compassion and those for whom empathy was an existential threat. For the Sovereigns now, for the Southerners in Helen's time, to know the other as thoroughly as they knew themselves was the greatest terror of all. It was the lone self they clung to, Derryn saw—a small, restricted, powerless thing, yet it was familiar. What did it matter, if a person might grow into something better and freer by joining the Weave, by giving their full heart to compassion? If they lost the selves they knew, they would also lose the only reality that made sense to them. She wept because she understood that those who were governed by fear would cling to an old world long after it was already dead. And she couldn't imagine a more tragic waste of the one life any human was granted.

So deep and all-consuming was her pain, so unbearable was her loneliness that she reached without thinking for the port of her headset. She managed to remember the geomagnetic storm just before she could depress the power button and fry her CoreTex for good. Startled by the near miss, she looked up with a gasp . . . and found an entirely different world around her.

The parking lot was gone. The hotel and the overpasses, the endless gray sprawl of the suburbs—all replaced by buildings of brick and wood, much too small for the modern world. The wide rivers of concrete that carried, under normal circumstances, many thousands of cars were shrunk down to narrow lanes paved with brick and stinking of manure.

Even the aurora was gone. Something burst and crackled overhead. Derryn stared up at the sky and found fireworks blooming against the dark of night, shedding their brief showers of sparks onto the rooftops of this place.

Trembling, she rose to her feet and turned in a slow circle. The illusion completely surrounded her, exactly like the sim rooms in the Weave, where explorers and students could immerse themselves in re-creations of history or fictitious worlds for education and entertainment. But her CoreTex was powered down; Derryn was sure of that. She tapped a port to be certain the headset was still switched off, then called for Tyko. There was no response from the AI. The Weave was as absent as it had been these past four days since the storm's coming.

Was she experiencing the same location, or some other place? And was the setting far in the past? It might be the future, Derryn realized—a new time to come, long after this war had erased an old, irascible civilization, after something new had been built atop the buried bones.

She reached again with her mind, though she knew the Weave wasn't there. And yet, something *was* present, the hint of a wholeness, the great, loving mass of everyone waiting to connect. Derryn could *feel* them, all of them at once, not distinctly enough that she could pick out any individual, yet the fact that humankind still went on together brought her an unexpected comfort. Her eyes burned again, but this time, she wept with gratitude rather than grief.

It's the aurora, Derryn realized. *It isn't nearly as strong as the Weave, but it's connecting us.*

Like those telegraph operators Tyko had told her about, back in 1859. They'd unhooked the batteries on their machines, yet the telegraphs had still functioned. The currents of magnetic energy had carried their messages from one machine to another, all the way back in a long-vanished time. Why couldn't the same currents carry messages now, from mind to mind?

There was no visible aurora in this other place-time, but Derryn knew it must be there. Logic told her it was still pouring out its great and terrible mystery on the earth. She reached with her thoughts, pushed beyond the strange illusion that surrounded her. She reached for Leo, and Tyko, for Melinda and Mihir, for Alexis and all the friends she had ever known and loved.

I'm here, Derryn shouted into the unseen currents. *Find me, please. Know me. I'm here.*

The echo of her thoughts returned from someplace close at hand, sorrow and despair and the need for simple comfort. She turned toward the feeling, and in the building at her back, on its second floor, she found a narrow window set with iron bars. A woman was looking down at her, hands gripping the bars, the eyes in her pale, drawn face a desolation of fear and regret.

Derryn knew her. She had seen that face—the same eyes on a yellowed canvas, looking at her beyond the edge of an easel.

"Helen Bywater," Derryn said.

The woman in the window spoke. "You know me."

"Yes," Derryn answered. "We know you here, in my time."

Helen sagged, leaning her forehead against the iron bars as she wept. "Tell me I have made some difference. Tell me I did right. For I can't believe, now, that I did. And this future I see, your time, it will never come to pass until this evil is gone from the world. What hope can I have now that righteousness will win?"

Derryn grieved with her, for the future Helen had seen was not the paradise she had thought it to be, the prize of human unification. The world Derryn knew had fallen far short of Helen's grand ideal.

But she couldn't tell Helen the truth—not the raw and naked, bleeding truth, as Derryn knew it to be. The better world Helen had dreamed of was no more permanent than winter ice. Like ice, it could be broken, or melted by the fires of hate.

But whatever we've built, Derryn told herself, *can be built again. Whatever we have dreamed can be brought into existence.*

She couldn't allow Helen to go on suffering. Fighting the slow currents of her own mind, she delved into the murky depths of unassisted thought and brought up something she hoped would shine in the dark for poor Helen. Then she sent that thought from heart to heart, on the bright, open channel of the aurora. She knew her message would find Helen. She could only hope it would quiet the woman's fear.

The future comes faster than you think, Helen. Not without struggle, not without pain. But it comes.

The fireworks gave one last, energetic burst. Derryn looked up. There were circles of light expanding across the sky, rings of bright sparks rippling from their centers and losing themselves to the great, black body of the night. Then a surge of vivid pink washed overhead. And acid green like a ribbon on the wind unfurled and rippled and receded.

The urban sprawl had replaced, in a blink, the nineteenth-century world. Helen was gone, and only the endless war remained, the bitter dust and the crushing weight, the old, old fear casting its shadow over all that could be seen from where Derryn stood out to the black horizon.

29

Helen

May 14, 1863

Again I apologize to you, dear Diary (or whoever might come to read You, long after I am gone), for I have found no time to liberate You from below the floorboards at the foot of my bed and write of what has transpired. There has been much to celebrate for those of us who uphold the Union in secrecy, but every day of this year has run together in a wild stampede of activity, and each day has brought fresh danger and new opportunity to serve our secret cause.

I report that our ring of whisperers has grown to ten souls in all. Beyond those names already accounted herein, I shall not list them, for one never knows when one's private writings might become the object of Confederate interest. I shall only say here that these ten good people are each as dedicated as I to total liberation from the evil that has poisoned the Southern heart. My companions walk among the enemy, listen with false smiles, and pass whatever they learn to those who will, we devoutly pray and believe, use such intelligence to crush the rebellion once and for all.

Of course, Jere and I have not admitted these unnamed souls to our confidence without due caution. We are all too well aware that anyone may be a counteragent, even those who are enslaved. Some may design to infiltrate our group and deliver us to Jefferson Davis—and to the gallows. Each new member is studied with the closest observation, his beliefs tested, his loyalty wholly assured before he is added to our circle.

We feel the danger at all hours. Yet we also take great joy in what we do—a fierce, burning pride that comes from knowing we stand on the side of righteousness. Even should we be discovered, we will meet our end as good and faithful servants of God and the Union. I often find comfort in that thought, whenever fear threatens to overwhelm me.

Jere and I have maintained our correspondence with his Union contacts all these months, sending our letters carrying, in code, what intelligence we have gathered.

We were glad to report on a concerning shortage of flour earlier this spring, to give one example of our work. The shortage has caused serious trouble for the Confederate troops stationed along the Potomac, and I suspect that our disclosure of the situation allowed the Northern armies to take some advantage there, pressing the Southern army when they were weakened by hunger.

Yet it's difficult to know for certain whether our messages about troop movements, ammunition stocks, and the prevailing mood of this city—the very seat of Confederate governance—have had a direct effect on the fortunes of the North. The tides of war never cease to shift, and they have changed all the faster in recent months as the federal army enforced conscription (to great distress in certain Northern cities!), as the battle over Fredericksburg exploded like a powder keg, and as the first marches have begun in a new Northern campaign. We hope this latest maneuver by the Union generals will take Vicksburg, for it is the last Confederate stronghold on the Mississippi. Once the river is wholly in Union hands, nearly all the supply lines will be under Northern control.

More recently, we read of the battle at Chancellorsville, where Stonewall Jackson was mortally wounded. He died in hospital a few days past.

Stonewall's death is what finally inspired me to lift the floorboards and write in this book, for his demise brought the most urgent letter yet from Mary Jane.

How she manages to slip her messages out of Davis's White House remains a miracle of ingenuity. She uses the old code from her school days, and this morning, as I read her note, my chill grew colder with every word I parsed from the hidden text.

Mary Jane has learned that upon Stonewall Jackson's death, General Lee asked Davis for permission to invade the North. *Invade!* By Heaven, they just might have the means to do it, for the North is still heavily occupied with this terrible fallout from the draft—the riots in New York, desertions by the hundreds, and all other manner of misfortune. Davis means to strike at Gettysburg in Pennsylvania later this summer, with General Lee commanding. Mary Jane managed to learn their plans for the movement of regiments, even the strategy of battle once the Confederate Army has reached Gettysburg.

The urgency of this intelligence cannot be overstated. Should Lee succeed in his invasion, the North may fall, even if Vicksburg is won and the Mississippi lands under federal control. Washington could lie open to Southern forces. Then the rebellion might gain legitimacy in the eyes of foreign powers. Everything we have worked for these past years would be reduced to dust, and slavery would not only be reinstituted with especial cruelty and vigor but would spread across the whole continent like a plague.

I cannot risk transmitting such a dire message by letter. Even with our cipher, there is too great a chance of interception. Messages have gone missing before, and I have never learned whether they were confiscated or merely lost. In either case, *this* letter mustn't go astray. Nothing will do but to deliver the message myself, from mouth to ear, directly to any man who can act upon it.

I have resolved to travel to Washington, where I will speak to any general who will listen, or to President Lincoln himself if fortune favors me. I shall not fail in this endeavor, for the sake of everyone who depends upon my work.

When I confessed my plans to Jere, he insisted on traveling with me. I expected no less from him, though I fear for his safety more than my own. If we are accosted by any Confederate powers, or merely by those who love the Southern Cause, there will be no concealing our true loyalties.

I argued with Jere in the carriage house, insisting that if we were to make the journey together, it would triple our danger.

"All we need do is make it across the Potomac," he said, "into Northern territory. Once we're there—once you've delivered your message—we can stay there, Helen. We've done enough in Richmond. Every day we remain in this city, the danger grows. I would see you safely out of the South, if I had my way . . . at least until the war is over."

"I don't care about my safety," I flared at him. "This work I do isn't for the Union. It's for the people I care for the most—Mary Jane and the rest who have made this house a home. There are wrongs that I must right, Jere, and I won't stop my work until I'm satisfied that I've made amends."

He took me gently by the shoulders. "You mean because you have enslaved others."

Shame stole my ability to answer. All I could do was to scowl down at the floor.

"God is the great judge," Jere said. "Helen, my love, He has surely seen the work you've done, the amends you've tried to make."

"All the same," I said, quiet but full of steel, "I will not stop till my conscience is clear."

He lifted my face, then, with a gentle hand, and looked into my eyes. "Marry me, Helen."

"What?" I sputtered. The change of subject left me dizzy beyond all sense.

"Marry me. Be my wife. We can go on doing our work for the Union in the North—any kind of work you please. You can dedicate every waking second to defeating the South. I'll stand behind you. But please, do your work in the North, where it's safer for both of us."

I told him I needed time to think of my answer and took myself to the back of the garden in a state of pure shock. There I lingered under the peach trees, with the last of their petals drifting down around me, a gentle pink snow. For hours, I confronted my own thoughts, allowed desire and duty to wrestle in my mind.

I have longed so much to marry Jere, all these months since we first were united. But of course, it's impossible in Virginia. No Southern preacher would agree to marry a woman like me to a Yankee.

And if I were to go north with him, I must leave Eudaimonia behind. Could I truly tear myself from my home, my inheritance, the Bywater legacy? I was filled with grief, merely to contemplate such a thing. Yet if I could be Jere's wife . . . if we were joined forever in a holy union . . .

This war won't last forever, I told myself. *Once it's over, you can come home again. You and Jere—your husband! And any children you might have. You can always come home and take up where you left off, with all your memories intact.*

As evening fell, I returned to the carriage house and accepted Jere's proposal. Long and sweet was our embrace.

"We'll be married as soon as the message is delivered," he said, beaming and kissing my hand. "But promise me, Helen, that you won't even think of returning to the South until this war is over."

Well, it's all settled now. I must say farewell to Eudaimonia—for the time being. I have already paid Kitty, Ruthie, and David three months' wages, and they have made plans to take up with family or friends elsewhere. I have set Mr. Wyckoff to legal matters, telling him I must go to Atlanta to care for an ailing relation. Mr. Wyckoff is to manage the estate in my absence and hold Eudaimonia safe till I can return to Richmond.

Now all that remains is to pack whatever I wish to keep—the heirlooms and other precious memories that will be sent, someday, to join me at my new home in the North. Wherever that home may be, whatever its character, it certainly won't be as fine as Eudaimonia. But it will be a palace in my eyes, even if it's nothing more than a tar-paper shack, for there I will live in happiness with my Jere. I will be joined to him in blessed matrimony. David has promised to keep the crates in a safe place of his knowing and will ship them to me by train or wagon, as soon as we find some nest to call our own and send word back to Richmond.

I will pack all my journals, this one included, with the hope that someday Jere and I, our children, and our grandchildren will read this account. From the future I have seen, we will look back in wonder at a time when man was divided, and we will take comfort in knowing that such times will never come again.

30

Derryn

2053

On the fourth morning of the solar flare, Derryn woke well rested for the first time in nearly a week. She lay for a while under the sleeping bag, which she had unzipped into a downy quilt. The window of the hotel room framed the nearby overpass and on-ramp against a dawn sky of pale, pinkish gray, like the flowing forms of an abstract composition. If not for the occasional EV gliding up the ramp, Derryn wouldn't have guessed she was looking at a parkway. Still half snared by the gentle mercy of sleep, she blinked at the dark curves of concrete and the ever-lightening sky, and she thought of Helen's paintings, those startling images of a future the artist could never have known. Maybe, Derryn thought, she was witnessing the same thing now. Not this world she knew, struggling and yearning, backsliding into the past, but the shape and structure of what would come, the placid stillness and the smooth ascent, an optimistic soar above the here and now.

She kicked the sleeping bag aside and sat up, yawning but clearheaded, aware of the slowness of her unenhanced mind, but nevertheless, she *could* think without the Weave. Every day, she grew a little more used to the methodical process, setting one thought or supposition firmly on the ground of her mind, then another, in ponderous but logical order.

You were dreaming last night, she told herself. *You didn't go outside at all.*

Even if she had gone outside, she hadn't been in a sim room. There were two full days left before the Weave returned. She hadn't spoken to Helen, hadn't seen the woman at all. It had only been a dream.

But when she rose from the mattress, Derryn found that she was once again wearing her old clothes. The blue Sovereign dress lay on the floor where she had discarded it. That much of her dream, at least, had been real.

Cole was already awake and eating a protein bar. "Did you sleep well?"

"Yes. It feels like it's been a year since I could say that."

He smiled. "I know what you mean. I've had to rough it a few times when I've traveled between communities, but you never really get used to sleeping on the ground. Nothing beats an actual bed, if you ask me."

She considered him as he went on with his breakfast. He had shown such vulnerability last night. Cole wasn't Sovereign enough for Derryn to go on mistrusting him, disliking him. He was human, like Derryn herself, and nothing more.

"I saved two of these protein bars for you," Cole said. "They're not bad, for wirehead food."

She chuckled. "Thanks."

After they'd both eaten, they moved on, walking in the shadow of the parkway through business districts and neighborhoods, past school campuses and the hulking bodies of long-dead big-box emporiums. The sun rose ever higher, giving no sign by day of its violent ejections, the magnetic barrage that pummeled the planet and the small, fragile creatures that clung to its surface. Life went on as it ever had. People nodded as they passed on the sidewalk, children played in yards and driveways, the vehicles that still held sufficient charge rolled past with soft, musical hums.

Kilometer after kilometer, they came ever closer to the blockade, and the closer they came, the less precarious the world around them seemed. There was a lightness to the people whom Derryn passed, a curiosity and an openness that was far more natural than the tense vigilance she'd grown used to since leaving Cascadia. They even caught sight of a block party in the distance as they left the line of the parkway and struck across town for the New Jersey Turnpike. The strumming of acoustic guitars and the raucous singing of the celebrants followed Derryn long after she'd lost sight of the gathering.

As neighborhoods and piles of rubble passed, Derryn thought about the night before. It must have been a dream. It was too *real* to be real; the visuals and sounds of that nineteenth-century place had been so insistently sharp and vivid. Even the pervasive smell of horse manure had played on her senses with the crisp, distinct precision that only came from direct neural stimulation in the Weave. What, then, was her subconscious mind trying to say? What was the meaning of this symbolism—Helen Bywater in a prison cell, pleading for some hope that the world *could* be good, someday, if only humankind could let go of its primitive taste for division?

Derryn rested a hand on the travel pouch below her clothing. The data chips were still there, so whatever enigmatic quirk of psychology had inspired the dream, it couldn't have been her fear for the Bywater cache. The paintings themselves might have already been destroyed, for all Derryn could say, but the evidence of their existence was safe. Maybe she would never understand the meaning of that dream. There was plenty in this world that couldn't be known—not by one mind, cast alone into the cosmos.

By late afternoon, they reached Goethals Bridge, where the blockade began in earnest. A wall of reinforced cargo containers stretched three high and two deep, running south along the Turnpike and north across the mouth of the Elizabeth River. Rust red, patched here and there with a bright rectangle of blue or yellow or shocking pink, the wall reached as far into the concrete distance as Derryn could see. Beyond that barrier, a normal society thrived despite decades of neighboring conflict. Ferries cleaved the water.

Air cabs that still held a little charge flitted like great, black birds over the metropolis. She could sense life reaching for her, life in its teeming multitude and intimate wholeness, waiting to welcome her back to the ever-unfolding future.

Derryn paused at the edge of the Turnpike. There was no more need for Cole's company—his protection. Once she'd talked her way through the border inspection, she would be safe enough for two more days, until the Weave returned and she could arrange for travel back to California.

"I guess this is where we part ways," she said.

Cole made no answer, only looked at her with a thinly veiled longing. Then his gaze slid past, to the bridge with its slalom of Jersey barriers and steel bollards, its patrol of border agents and their lightweight drones.

"Thank you for everything you did for me," Derryn went on. "I didn't expect to find such kindness among your people."

"Take me with you," he said with a sudden intensity.

"What?"

"Across the blockade."

"You want to go to the Dutch Kills commune?"

"I want to *go*. Leave it all behind—the fighting, the violence, the war."

"Nobody leaves war behind," Derryn said. "We even feel it in Cascadia."

But no one in Cascadia felt the war as heavily as they did here. That was true, as well—and after only a few days living in this hell of constant uncertainty, she couldn't blame Cole for wanting a better life.

"What about the women and children?" she said. "What about your calling as pastor?"

He sighed, ground the heel of his hand into his weary eyes. "I've been worrying about them all day. I don't want to abandon them, and I won't. I'll find some way to go on helping them from outside, from your side. But I've thought about this since we left the hotel this morning. I've thought about it, really, since I realized what you are. I'm not doing any *good* for the people of our communities. I'm only making it easier for everyone to go on doing what they've always done, these past twenty-five years. Rain down hate and suffering on everything. Everyone. Even on ourselves."

Derryn tried to sort through the options ahead, tried to predict what would come next and how she must respond. How did people like Cole manage to think without assistance? The pace of her own mind was glacial, and as for clarity, it was like trying to see through silted water.

"The guards will be suspicious of you," Derryn said. "Your clothes, your tattoos—they mark you out as a potential danger. Especially right now, with the Sovereigns trying to take advantage of the blackout."

"I know. I understand."

"So we've got to decide on a story now. And memorize it, because they'll almost certainly separate us for questioning."

"Okay."

"And we probably don't have much time to get the story straight, because we've been standing here for way too long, talking. They've noticed, no doubt."

She glanced at the bridge. Sure enough, a pair of light drones were already up. The glinting eyes of their forward cameras were trained on Derryn and Cole as they moved steadily closer.

"Come on."

Derryn headed for the bridge deck, muttering their cover story to Cole as they walked. Just before they came within shouting range of the checkpoint, she made him repeat the tale in full. He didn't miss a single detail.

As she had predicted, they were separated for questioning. Each was taken to a different booth on the side of the bridge deck, ushered inside with a cadre of guards. Derryn felt only a moment of anxiety for her companion. Cole was smart enough to stick to the story, and personable enough to put the guards at ease. Plus, he was used to high-stress situations, used to thinking on his feet without enhancement. The same could not be said for her.

You'd better watch your own back, not his, she told herself as the border patrol emptied her backpack and examined its contents.

"I'm an anthropologist," she said when the guards began to grill her, "from California—Stanford University. I was doing some research at the Iron Rock commune in New Jersey when the blackout hit. That's why I'm traveling with a man from the HHM."

One of the guards loomed over her chair. "What research were you doing on a Sovereign commune?"

"Cataloging the cultural differences between the more violent factions of the HHM and the peaceful community inside your blockade—Dutch Kills, it's called."

"Yeah," the guard said, relaxing a little, "we're familiar with the New York Sovereigns. They're fine, if you leave them alone. Weird people, but live and let live, right?"

"Cole—the pastor from Iron Rock—is working with me. He's going to act as my cultural interpreter, so to speak, while I'm at Dutch Kills."

They made her wait inside the booth while two of the guards left to consult with those who'd questioned Cole. Derryn sat in perfect stillness, schooling her face into what she hoped was a placid mask. If the Weave had been active now, she would have had no hope of convincing the guards that her story was true, for despite her cool exterior, every nerve of her body had tied itself into knots, and her stomach was roiling.

Finally, one of the patrolmen stuck his head back into the booth and said to the remaining guards, "Bring her out. She can have her things back, too."

Derryn shouldered her pack and followed the others outside. Cole was already waiting near one of the concrete road barriers, flanked by two guards and hovered over by a small, humming drone. He couldn't seem to take his eyes off the drone, tipping back his head to watch the thing with mingled fascination and fear.

"You can go ahead," one of them said to Derryn, "but we're not letting a rebel past the blockade."

Derryn stared at the man in disbelief. "Come on. I can't do this work without him."

"Sorry, Doctor. The situation's too crazy right now. Sovereign attacks are up dramatically these past few days. They think the Weave is gone for good, think they can overthrow—"

"I know," Derryn said. "I've been living with them all this time. I know what they think. Listen, this work I'll be doing with the Dutch Kills colony . . . it could be instrumental to future diplomacy. This isn't a vacation. I'm not on some academic navel-gazing sabbatical among the primitives. We're trying to end this war, damn it, and whatever I can learn might help us do that sooner rather than later."

She argued at length for Cole's passage through the blockade. Asserted that if the integrated world could develop a good understanding of what made Dutch Kills culturally distinct from the rest of the Sovereign communes, they might discover more useful methods of de-escalation, might even find the key to information warfare that could deflate the violent tendencies of the Human Heritage Movement like a popped balloon. The war could be over in a matter of months, Derryn insisted—but only if they allowed this man to pass freely into New York City.

"I'll vouch for him," she finally said with all sincerity. "If he commits any sort of crime, I'll be as liable for it as he will."

The guard narrowed his eyes.

"I can't leave him behind." She was almost pleading now. "He saved me—twice—even knowing what I am. They aren't all bad, those Sovereigns. I know it's hard to believe, but they're as human as we are."

With a ragged breath, Derryn fired the last shot in her locker. "If we had the Weave right now, you could feel how sincere I am. How completely I trust this man, and how badly I need his help. You'll have to take my word for it. But please, believe me. He belongs on the other side of the blockade. And he's good—really good, compassionate and community minded. He's just like you and me."

The guard removed his dark shades. Derryn met his eye, held it with all the confidence she could muster. She reached with her mind, as if the Weave still held them all together, exactly as she'd done last night in that dream. She pushed all the need and hope in her heart out like a great wave on the stillness of herself, sent it in the man's direction, prayed to whatever divine thing might be listening that he would *feel* her, somehow, and know.

The guard turned abruptly, settling the shades back over his eyes.

"All right," he said. "You can both go. But if this guy is picked up for any sort of crime—*any* sort—you're the one who'll take the fall."

The drones followed Derryn and Cole until they'd crossed the bridge and set off into the neighborhoods of upper Staten Island. When the hum of propellers faded, Derryn risked glancing over her shoulder. The drones had turned back for the blockade. They were only specks in the sky now. The bridge, too, was dwindling in the distance.

"You did it." Cole's voice was shaking, his eyes wide and frantic from the adrenaline that must still be rushing through his body. But he was grinning, too, and when he let loose with one of his familiar laughs, there was real joy in the sound. It brought Derryn's own smile out of hiding.

31

Helen

September 15, 1863

I have found the will to put pen to paper again. How fitting that I am beginning a new diary in a new book . . . for now, quite against my will, I must live an entirely new life. It must honestly be said that I don't see much good in the existence stretching before me. The days and years extend in a dark line, into a future I can no longer perceive, a time I can no longer believe in. Such a dark cloud has followed me all these months, since I last wrote in any diary. That shadow may never lift from me again. Nevertheless, I intend to bear up with whatever bravery might be found in this ravaged spirit.

I am living now in a small, humble house in Haverford, Pennsylvania, not so very far from the Quaker school I attended as a girl. I have been here since late May, recuperating from the shock of what has transpired. There are days when I fear that I will never entirely recover. Yet there is no direction to go but forward, into the unknown.

It will take me days to write the full account. So I had best get started.

On the seventeenth of May, after all my precious things were packed into boxes and sent to whatever barn or attic David had found for their safekeeping—and after Kitty, Ruthie, and David himself departed for their own private lives—Jere and I set out for Washington.

We traveled under the pretense that I was a young widow who had lost my husband to the war. Jere posed as my brother-in-law and escort, keeping watch over my safety. You can be sure, I drilled him in the subtleties of a proper Virginia accent before we set out, but our plan was for him to speak as little as possible, lest anyone should notice his Yankee tongue and suspect our real purpose. In case anyone should ask, we agreed to say that we were traveling to Washington to present President Lincoln with a petition from Confederate widows like myself—a plea for a swift end to the fighting. We had even crafted a document filled with false signatures to lend credibility to our story. Jere and I had both thought it quite a fine and foolproof scheme.

We boarded the train in Richmond with a surety of purpose. But the train only made it to the country outside Spotsylvania when it was stalled on the tracks. For hours we waited in the stifling heat of the carriage, saying little for Jere's sake but speaking whole volumes of text with our eyes. Delays are not uncommon in recent times, for the Yankees often pile tracks with stones and old carriages to disrupt the movement of Confederate troops. Sometimes the tracks are torn up entirely.

One fellow in our car was just about ready to go and find the conductor when we heard the crack of gunfire in a field to the east of the tracks.

In moments, the field swarmed with men in blue and gray. A thick haze soon clouded the air, emanating from the muzzles of their rifles, and the very sky seemed to rattle with the noise of relentless shooting. All of us in the train car huddled on the floor, afraid that stray bullets would strike the windows—and indeed, one window of our car shattered, letting in the sulfurous stink of gun smoke.

"We've got to get out," a woman near me cried. "If the Yankees win this battle, they'll take us all across the river. We'll be prisoners of the war!"

"There are woods to the west of the tracks," an old gentleman said. "We can get out on this side of the car, keep the train between ourselves and the battle, and run for cover—hide in the trees till the fighting is over."

We all agreed that it was a good enough plan. At least, it was the only hope anyone could find that we might escape the danger. Jere and the old gentleman risked their lives to stand and force open the door on the western side of the car. Then we all filed out of the carriage.

We weren't the only passengers who had decided to bolt for the forest. Women and children came pouring from the other cars. The few men who hadn't been conscripted into the soldiery did their best to shield the ladies and the little ones with their bodies, in case any bullet should fly between the railcars and strike an unintended target. We ran like deer across the western field, desperate for the cover of the trees. But as we gained the undergrowth and the concealing mercy of the shadows, Jere caught me by the arm and pulled me away from the rest.

When we were far enough from the hiding passengers that we would not be overheard, we crouched together behind a fallen tree, panting and shuddering as the noise of battle went on in the nearby field.

"These woods run north," Jere said quietly, "all the way to the Wilderness."

"The what?"

"An even heavier forest west of Fredericksburg. My regiment used it often for cover during our campaign. If we follow this line of trees, it'll take us to the Wilderness. We can't be more than ten miles away, if that. We'll hide there till nightfall, then make our way through Fredericksburg and find some way to cross the Rappahannock into Northern territory."

His plan worked splendidly, at first. The band of forest was narrow, with farms to either side, but the angle of the sun favored us, for no one seemed to notice us as we moved among the trees. Soon we had passed the stalled train and could see the fighting in the field beyond—not a large battle, but wild and desperate, terrifying in its vigor. The volleys of gunfire went on like the worst thunderstorm Hell had devised, and the cries of dying men filled my head with a louder, sharper sound.

But we forged ahead without tiring, intent on the urgency of our mission. Mary Jane had risked her life to learn General Lee's plan to attack Gettysburg. I would not see her bravery come to nothing. At all costs, I would deliver my message to a Northern officer or meet my Maker in the attempt. When my duty to Mary Jane and the Union was safely discharged, then I would have my reward—Jere as my husband, his heart bound to mine forever by the vows of marriage.

The sounds of battle grew smaller behind us, then so faint we could hardly hear the crack of rifle fire. We passed a great heap of rubble piled on the tracks—the diversion that had stopped our train—and pressed on through the heat of afternoon, avoiding the farms and villages we passed.

By the time evening was falling, we were both thirsty and worn down from the effort and the mental strain. But the woods were dense as a jungle around us, so heavy one could hear Fredericksburg but not see it. The clatter of hooves and carriage wheels and general industry came to us, slow and lazy across the tail end of a long day.

We settled into a shady grove to rest for the night's march ahead.

"Sedgwick took Fredericksburg earlier this month," Jere said. "He'll still have it under guard. If we can get to the city, we should find Union men in charge. Surely someone there can take the message and pass it along to the generals, or to President Lincoln."

"Why don't we go now," I suggested, but Jere shook his head.

"There's never any telling who's hanging around the Wilderness. Might be Union men, or it might be a whole camp of Confederates. And there's no telling what they might do to us if we stumble into a nest of rebels. The best course is to stay put and stay quiet till night falls. Then we can make our way out to the edge of the forest and follow Hazel Run into Fredericksburg."

The sun set more slowly than it ever had. The first lightning bugs of the year began to flash among the trees. The flare and fade of their small green lanterns brought memories of the garden at Eudaimonia. I had a deep and sorrowful sense that despite my plans to return after the war had ended, I would never see my home again. But there was no time for melancholy. There was time for nothing but waiting, waiting for night to fall, for our chance to slip back through the forest like haints in a graveyard, silent and secretive in the dark.

The woods turned a deep blue around us. A whippoorwill called from the shadows. Just when I thought I would go mad with the stillness, Jere took my hand and whispered, "It's dark enough now, I think. Follow me."

We both moved as silently as we could. There were no trails to follow but the faint avenues made by deer through the underbrush. I had to hold my skirt and petticoat in one arm so they wouldn't be caught on the branches that reached for me like some devil's hands.

I think we had almost made it to the border of the Wilderness, to the place where cover gave way to open fields, when the snap of a twig somewhere to our right made us both turn with a sudden, fearful alertness.

"Who goes there" came a man's gruff voice through the forest.

I clutched Jere's hand, could feel his hesitation. There was no telling from the man's few words whether he was friend or foe, Yankee or rebel. I had just made up my mind to speak—to go alone toward that unknown person, leaving Jere to hide in the forest while I pled my sex, claimed to be a woman lost in the Wilderness, and threw myself on a gentleman's mercy (giving Jere cover to escape). But I never got the chance to act.

The dark of night was shattered by a blast of light. The rifle's report drove my plan from my head. By instinct, I dropped to the ground, just as another shot cracked above me—and I felt a shudder through the earth as Jere fell heavily to the forest floor.

I crawled to him, stifling my cries of distress with a will I never knew I possessed. He lay on his side, eyes tightly shut, teeth clenched in a grimace of pain. One hand was clamped to his stomach, the other to his upper thigh. Between his fingers, I could see the blood rising, thick and black, stinking of copper and salt.

Voices called around us. "What the hell are you doing, Boggs?"

"Firing at Yankees."

"You ain't—you're wasting bullets on deer. Get back to camp before I shoot *you*, you damned fool."

"Didn't I tell you Boggs has an empty kettle for a head?"

I cradled Jere in my arms as best I could till the rebel voices receded and the stillness of night drew in close around us once more. Only then did I allow myself to weep. Jere was racked by waves of pain, shivering and writhing in turn, but he never cried out, never gave our position away.

"The message." Jere's words came through his gritted teeth, so faint they were barely a whisper.

"No," I breathed, close beside his ear. "I won't leave you, Jere."

"Helen, you must. The message . . . the Union . . ."

To Hell with the Union, I wanted to say. All I cared for in that moment was him, and all I wanted of this life was to remain by Jere's side, to hold him in my arms until his last breath, if that should be God's will.

But he gasped out a few more words about the message I carried, about Lincoln. "The president must know. The generals must know. Invasion . . . Gettysburg . . . Helen, you *must*."

And I knew, then, that it was true. I had to leave him. For all I knew, the North might fall if General Lee's plan succeeded. And then no place on this continent would be safe for any Black soul. I thought of Mary Jane, of all she risked and all she had sacrificed to work for the cause in Davis's White House. I thought of Kitty and David and Ruthie, all those to whom I owed a greater debt than I could repay. My duty to those good people was more solemn and abiding even than my love for Jere. For if the North fell, then slavery would become the law of the land—of all the land united. What good would any union be if the states were banded together in sin against their fellow man?

Worse, I could hear the distant voices of the rebel encampment. They were too close—so near that they might come across Jere before I could send help from Fredericksburg. If Jere had any hope for survival now, then I had no choice but to leave his side, flee to the city as fast as I could run, and send someone back to find him.

Again and again, I kissed his brow. "I love you," I whispered. "Oh, how I love you, my darling, my Jere, my husband. Please believe that I love you. And hold on. I'll send help for you, I swear I will. Only hold on, Jere, for my sake."

I don't know whether he heard me, for by that time he was lost in his pain. I forced myself to let go of him and stand. Then, swaying and shuddering with the effort, I turned my back on Jere, helpless and suffering as he was, and continued along the faint trail of the deer path.

I followed that track till the Wilderness thinned around me, and an open field came into view. The black sky above was shot through with stars, cold and distant and watchful.

For a moment I hesitated at the edge of the forest, trying to work out which way I should go. Fredericksburg was quiet now, so it was no use following my ears. Then I remembered that Jere had told me we would follow Hazel Run to the Rappahannock. A sinuous line of bushes cut across the clearing. It seemed to be the course of a waterway, for all I could tell by night. I set my sights upon that track of shadows and pushed into the field, determined to find the creek and follow it to Fredericksburg before the moon could rise.

I hadn't gone more than halfway across the clearing when I heard men shouting from the Wilderness.

"You there—stop!"

"Don't shoot. It's a woman."

Without looking around, I began to run, for sense told me that these could only be more men from the rebel encampment. If I could make it to the cover of those bushes and follow Hazel Run to the city, there was still some hope that I could find help for Jere before it was too late to save him. But the thunder of hooves soon overtook me, and before I knew it, there were three men on horseback circling me, their mounts tossing their heads and grunting in the starlight.

There was no hope of escape. The Confederates had found me, and I knew my fate was sealed.

I can't bring myself to write more now. It's all too close to my heart, still—too bitter and too sad. It's only midday, yet I must retire to my bed, and I feel as if I'll sleep for a hundred years. My dreams will be sweeter than my memories, if God is merciful.

32

Derryn

2053

Street by street, block after block, the city grew denser and taller, a thriving garden of glass and steel. Derryn tipped back her head as she walked, just to see the blue reflection of the sky, to watch the soft, cool shadows slide like falling water down the faces of the skyscrapers. Every building was intact. Every person she passed on the street gave her a nod and a smile. The war had only lightly left its bloody prints on New York, and that small evidence was easily washed away or overshadowed by the steady march of progress.

Cole walked beside her in a state of wonder so all-consuming, he was like a child taken to some fantastical amusement park for the first time.

"I thought you'd been to New York before," Derryn said, "to Dutch Kills."

"I have." Cole pulled himself away from a vista of identical black towers. "But it still gets to me, every time. I just can't show it when I'm here with my own people. They'd think I was . . ."

"A heretic?" Derryn suggested.

"Something like that. Admiring wirehead society isn't exactly encouraged."

"You have a talent for understatement, Cole. Has anyone ever told you that?"

They both chuckled as they walked on, but he grew sober again. "Not many of us from the other communities have had any reason to visit Dutch Kills. So until I'd already been a pastor for a few years—when I passed through New York City for the first time—the only integrated cities I'd known were the ones on my side of the blockade. Every time I come here, it hits me the same as it did the first time. Everything is so big, so clean, and everything works the way it's supposed to. No one is fighting; people *like* each other here. I think if most Sovereign people could see this place, they would have a different opinion of wireheads. It would be a lot harder to fear you all and your way of life."

Derryn had to restrain herself from rolling her eyes. The integrated cities Cole had known were only crumbling and desperate because the HHM had made them so. But there was no point in castigation. No good ever came from slamming the door shut on a mind that wanted to open.

Instead, she focused on the rest of what Cole had said. "So, you admit that you fear us."

She had spoken lightheartedly, but he answered in a sober tone.

"That's all hate ever is. Fear of the unknown, fear of what you might lose, even when what you stand to gain is so much better. In my work as a pastor, I've tried to influence the men toward peace. We need some reconciliation with the wired world—and with ourselves. We need to find some way of being okay with our separate existence. Live and let live, accept that the integrated population believes what they believe and exists how they choose to exist. It doesn't have to be a threat to our way of life unless we want it to be."

"Makes sense to me. Why do you think they haven't listened?"

He answered so quickly that Derryn knew he must have asked himself the same question countless times. "They're too far gone. They've lost themselves to fear. I think the most important thing I learned from those two years I spent living outside the community is this: Fear works the same way truth does. Once it gets into you, it makes you see more of itself, until everything looks like something to fear. And now, after twenty-five years of this war, I think we've become too afraid to close those fearful eyes. I don't know if we can even imagine peace, if we have the courage to focus on what really matters—care for one another, providing for the least among us. We've declared to the whole world that our cowardice is strength. And now we can't afford to believe anything different about ourselves. We've made hate our identity. If we stop hating, we won't be what we are anymore. And I think too many of them would rather stick with what they know than embrace what they don't know."

Derryn looked at him in surprise. "Too many of *them*? Aren't you Sovereign anymore?"

Absently, his hand lifted to touch one tattooed cheek. But he said nothing. Maybe he didn't yet know the answer to Derryn's question.

She spotted a bench ahead, led the silent Cole to it. Automatically, he sat, and Derryn settled beside him. The clatter of wings sounded from a nearby rooftop. A flock of pigeons descended to strut and coo around the bench, their small, bright eyes looking up at the two travelers in hopeful calculation. Derryn was content to allow Cole all the time he needed to consider the question she had asked, to feel the heft of its significance.

"I don't know," he finally said. His gaze was still fixed on some distant point that Derryn couldn't see. "I don't know if I am what I was before. But then, I can't tell you when I changed. So maybe I never was Sovereign . . . not really, not in my heart. Maybe it was all I knew, and all I was allowed to be, so I thought it was my true self. But you aren't what you're supposed to be, either."

"Me?" Derryn asked.

His smile was sheepish, embarrassed. "Wireheads are supposed to be dangerous. That's why we've been fighting you for the last twenty-five years—because you're controlled by demons. You gave up your minds to AI. But . . . I hope you won't be offended if I say this."

"Please," Derryn said, "go ahead. I'm listening."

"You're the least dangerous person I've ever met."

Derryn laughed so loudly, a few of the pigeons lumbered back into flight.

"I mean it," Cole said. "You can't even keep your own feet from blistering. You can't tell east from west without an artificial intelligence telling you which way to go. You can't defend yourself, for God's sake—not if it means hurting another person."

"You're right." She wiped the tears of amusement from her eyes. "Oh, God, you're so completely right. I can't even find my way around an integrated city without the Weave. I guess you've probably figured out by now that I'm not actually going to Dutch Kills."

"Oh, really," Cole said wryly.

"I'm actually trying to get to my friend Alexis. They were going to take me in until the solar storm ended. I had a map to their apartment, but I lost it . . . Not that I really know how to follow a paper map, anyway. I can ask directions here—anyone on the street would tell me where to go—but I can't remember the place. I can't even remember what borough Alexis lives in."

Cole seemed to be trying very hard not to smile.

"Beware the wirehead menace," Derryn said.

He, too, burst out laughing. The pigeons scattered once more into the street, then marched back at once to surround the bench.

"Maybe I'm not Sovereign enough to go on at Iron Rock," Cole said. "Maybe I never was Sovereign enough in the first place. I think sometimes about the other men, the ones who trained to be pastors but never came back from the wired world. Maybe they had the right idea."

He turned to Derryn with such an expression of longing that she felt it in her own chest and throat, felt it as strongly as if the Weave connected them. "Do you think they'd take me?"

"Who?" Derryn said.

"*Them*—you."

"Wireheads?"

He nodded.

She thought carefully before giving him an answer. Now that she had returned to society as it was meant to be—united, cooperative, the gentle cradle of the whole—the worst of her anger at the Sovereigns was fading. She could no longer harbor any emotion for Cole's kind, save for compassion. It was nothing short of pitiable that anyone should cut themselves off from connection. That anyone could so fear the dissolution of a lone self that they would declare empathy was sin, and ignorance the purest, most noble expression of humanity.

"Anyone can join the Weave," Derryn said. "Everyone is welcome. But you can't go back again, after you've known connection. You can never be what you are now, a single, sovereign mind. You *have* to consider others, because that's what your whole world becomes—everything, everyone, the whole, not the individual. Or not so much; you're still yourself, but a bigger, better self. It's hard to explain unless you've felt it. But once you feel it, there's no way to return to the world you knew before. So you have to be sure, Cole. You have to be okay with leaving behind the life you've always known."

"Are we so different?" His voice lifted in a pleading note. "For however many hundreds of thousands of years, we were all just human, all of us together. And now, after only twenty-five years of separation, there's a gap between us so wide that once you cross it, you can't go back again?"

Derryn sat for a beat of silence, turning his question over in her mind. It was an earnest one, and in that moment, it seemed like the most important question anyone had ever asked. It deserved an honest answer.

"Yes," she finally said. "We *are* that different. To feel what someone else feels, not to imagine, but to *feel* it, like it's your own joy, your own need, your own suffering. I can't explain it in a way you'll understand. But there's no going back from there, because—don't you get it?—that ability to feel everything and everyone . . . it *is* you. *Feeling* makes you who you are. And life doesn't feel the same, once the connection is gone. Nothing feels the same, not even yourself. So you have to be sure before you do it. You have to be okay with letting go of what you are now."

"Human," Cole said quietly.

"If that's what you want to call it."

A name flashed into her mind, rapid and bright as a tongue of fire. "Bushwick!"

Cole tore his attention from the drone ambulance that was speeding above the street. "What did you say?"

"Bushwick. That's where Alexis lives. That's where I agreed to meet them. It's a neighborhood on . . . Long Island, I think. It doesn't matter how long I have to go without the Weave; I'm never going to get used to remembering things on my own."

He chuckled. "Primitive man isn't so primitive, after all."

"Oh, please," Derryn said, smiling. "You haven't stopped gawking at the sky since we crossed the blockade. Imagine being astonished by buildings more than ten stories high. You're practically a caveman, buddy."

"I feel like a caveman. Everything here is . . . peaceful. It's nice. I've gone all my life hearing that wireheads have no souls. Even while I lived outside, among the wireheads, I still believed the old rhetoric. But look at this place—you don't build a city as beautiful as this if there isn't something beautiful inside of you."

"There's something beautiful in all of us," Derryn said. "But you won't see it in yourself if you don't look for it in other people. Come on. We've got to find our way to Long Island. Someone will give us directions; all we need to do is find a friendly stranger, and there'll be no shortage of them in New York."

They walked on. The summer evening was sweet with the scent of flowers that grew in window boxes and on the patios of the high-rises above, sweet with the sound of music and laughter that moved like an ever-present breeze through the city. When they came across a couple walking hand in hand, Derryn asked for directions to the island. The others hesitated only a moment, casting curious looks at Cole's Sovereign tattoos. Then they pointed the way, and Derryn and Cole pressed on.

By the time they reached the ferry landing, the sun had set, and night had gathered in the deep purple valleys of the avenues. Side by side on the pier, Derryn and her companion watched the boat approaching, the white crests of its wake spreading like wings across the water.

"If we don't find this friend of yours tonight," Cole said, "where will we sleep?"

Derryn shrugged. "Some hostel. There's no way to pay right now, with the Weave down, but we'll find plenty of kindness, I'm sure of that. We help each other out, here in this world, regardless of who we are or where we've come from. It's the right thing to do."

The first flush of the aurora appeared while they were on the water. Derryn watched it from the deck of the ferry, a throb of color in the sky, spreading like a stain between the black towers of the lightless city. Again, she could feel Cole struggling with his words, wanting to say something and not knowing how to say it. When he finally spoke, his voice was so quiet that Derryn could hardly hear him over the hum of the ferry's motor and the hiss of waves against the hull.

"We thought it was a sign from God," Cole said. "The banners of our victory."

Derryn looked at him for a long moment, but his eyes were fixed on the luminous sky. He hardly seemed aware of her at all.

"There's no claiming victory over this," he went on. "And why would anyone want to? It's perfect here."

"Integration is far from perfect," she said. "We've got a long way to go before we reach anything close to perfection—decades, maybe centuries. I don't expect to see utopia in my lifetime."

"Even with most of your technology disabled, this place might as well be Heaven compared to the Hell we've made. I've thought so before, when I've visited Dutch Kills. But I never dared to say it."

His regret filled Derryn with a sinking sensation. Maybe, she thought, he wouldn't find it so hard to adapt to the Weave. This man had empathy enough. She suspected that nearly all the Sovereigns did. They had only blinded themselves to what was inside, the divine spark that no darkness could swallow, burning with all the colors of an aurora.

The lights in the sky extended now high above the tallest buildings, reaching from the horizon in long, green licks of moving fire. The banners of a future yet to come.

Derryn could see that future now, the first shadows of it moving like ghosts across everything she perceived. Humankind had already divided itself. It had happened, she thought, sometime before the war—maybe long before. But what had once been a crack in the sidewalk had pulled slowly apart, generation after generation, to a gap, then a ravine, then a fault in the very substance of reality. *And now here we are,* she thought, *barely able to see one another across the space that separates us.*

The very species had come to a parting of ways. Some would go on, into an ever-unfolding future, while some held on to a past that had already eroded into dust. Derryn couldn't guess when the war would end, or if it ever would. But she knew that she would never belong to the side that clung to a fear they called courage.

Where Cole belonged, she couldn't say.

33

Helen

September 16, 1863

Yesterday I slept most of the day, for recounting this story drained all the vitality from me, body and mind. Yet I also feel somewhat lighter in my spirit, for I have carried this tale in silence all the months since I came to Haverford. To bring it out at last, even if only on the pages of this diary, is to unburden some small part of my afflicted soul.

After I was captured by those men on horseback, I was taken to the jail in Spotsylvania, for I would not speak a word to the men who found me. They could make nothing of a lone woman running out of the Wilderness, except that I must have been a spy. Well, they were right, after all. One must imagine my distress and misery, for I haven't the words to describe my state of mind. I passed the remainder of that night awake in a stinking prison cell, weeping with the bitterest self-recrimination, for I had failed to send help back to Jere, and now he was surely dead. I tried to decide what I ought to do in the morning, when I would stand before a judge, but I hadn't the least idea.

As it turned out, I needn't have spent so much of my energy fretting over my trial, for the court proceedings were a sham. There was no lawyer to represent me, and all my pleas to contact Mr. Wyckoff in Richmond fell on willfully deaf ears. I think now that the rising fury and desperation of the war had set the judge and his jury on edge. In different times, I hope and believe, those men wouldn't have been so quick to condemn a woman to death. But they could feel their way of life slipping away, a little more of the world they'd known taken with every battle, and I refused either to lie or to incriminate myself. So the judge declared that I was a contra operant working for the Union. That he was correct was no real justice, for no evidence was presented, save for the fact that I'd been apprehended alone, in the dark of night—and worse, I'd been captured while running out of the Wilderness, that well-known hiding ground of Union soldiers and sympathizers. I was sentenced to hang two days hence.

Oh, how can I explain the agonies I suffered as I passed those two days and nights in my prison cell? Sleep never came to relieve me. I dwelled without ceasing on the horror of the hangman's rope. My tormented thoughts turned now to Jere, and now to the message I had failed to deliver. Each dreadful loss accused me. Jere must have died in the Wilderness, which was and is sorrow enough. But the fact that I had left him to die alone, in the worst pain, haunted my every moment. And now the critical message of General Lee's invasion would die with me. The North might have no warning at all of what was to befall Gettysburg. All my efforts, even the work I'd done in Richmond, had yielded nothing, in the end.

On the final night of my torment, when I knew the next sunrise would bring my death, I stood at the narrow window of my cell, clinging to the black bars and crying out to God with all my broken heart. I longed to know—I needed to know, as the body needs breath—that my death and Jere's would serve some greater purpose, that neither of us had lived in vain.

"Show me what's to come," I pleaded with the distant heavens. "There must be something on the other side of this war, some goodness that goes on. Let me know, at least, before I die that I did not sacrifice for nothing."

As my prayer finished, a volley of fireworks went up from somewhere inside the town. A local battle won, another victory for the Confederacy.

In sorrow and dread, I lowered my eyes to the road below the prison, and there I saw her, standing in the street—a woman gazing up at the fireworks. Even from my window, I knew she was not of this time, for she wore the same odd clothing I'd seen in those visions of the glass towers—the fitted trousers that displayed her legs from ankle to hip, even while they bared no skin, and the buttonless shirt that clung in similar fashion, leaving nothing to imagination. Though her hair was a dense cloud of black curls, almost like Mary Jane's, I could see a blue gem glowing above one ear and could just make out the fine wire wrapping around the back of her head, for it picked up the flicker of the fireworks and reflected a glittering radiance through the darkness of her hair. The woman in the street was real, I swear it, as solid as brick and stone.

For a moment, even my torment and grief were forgotten. The sight of that figure from another time was shocking enough. But as I stared down at her, with the fireworks casting a halo of colors around the edges of her hair, the lights themselves grew larger, brighter, the colors more vivid than any fireworks could be. The sky itself transformed. The fireworks were gone, and the whole, soaring vault of the sky rippled with color, fiery rose and ice blue, lanced by the great, golden-green spears of the North. And low against the rooftops of the town, picking out in iron relief the chimneys and the church spires, a red echo of all the blood that had been shed, all the lives lost for the sake of a change that would not be stopped, for to all things there is a season.

"Helen Bywater."

The woman's voice drew my attention back to her, and I saw now that her face had a radiance, as if it glowed from within, or as if it were covered by a veil of light. I knew then that she was an angel. None but a messenger of God could shine so brightly.

"You know me," I answered—before I could think, before I could realize that I was speaking to an angel!

"We know you here, in my time," the divine creature said.

It was all I could do, then, to remain on my feet. If I had been able to let go of the bars, I would surely have fallen to my knees. Tears of wonder flooded from my eyes—and astonished me, for I had thought that I'd wept every tear my very self could contain.

I pleaded for comfort, for some small hope that all the actions I'd taken since the start of this war—and even before the fighting began—hadn't been for nought. I begged the angel to tell me that the righteous cause would prevail. Even if she could give me nothing more than a gentle lie, my heart was desperate to hear it.

She looked up at me with a terrible pain in her luminous face. I cannot find the words to express it. For a moment, I was certain that I *felt* her emotions, as sharply and inescapably as I experienced my own. She grieved for a paradise that had not come. She ached for the miracles that no man had yet seen.

I had a sense of fire and winter, a sense of great and vast things crumbling, things once thought to be permanent, but they were dust, as all things are dust. And yet, dust can be formed in the hand. It can be made into new inventions. I had a sense, too, of towers rising. And hands holding hands, and all the voices of the world singing in one bright, perfect harmony. How strange, to try to recount it now—for I can still recall that feeling, the impressions that came to my mind, yet words are small, weak things in the face of such a task.

The angel didn't speak again—not with her mouth. But somehow, I heard her voice, *felt* it, deep in my own mind.

The future comes faster than you think, she told me. *Not without struggle, not without pain.*

But the future does come. My promised vision. It may be many years after I have lived, but someday, mankind will stand at the peak of the highest mountain. He might arrive there by intention or by chance, but the old ways will fall away below his feet, and from that pinnacle, he will see only the highest, the one great heaven that covers us all with its light.

The angel's message ran through me like a river in flood, swift and mighty, impossible to deny. Yet her eyes through that veil of light reflected a sorrow as deep as any I have known. What grief could exist in that perfected time, *her* time, when God is among the people, as the Good Book promises? What shadows can fall across a world that is lit by divinest love?

There was no time to ask more questions. The fireworks gave a final salvo and died away. The light faded rapidly from the sky, and I saw only the ordinary stars, cold and distant and set into the velvet of the night, and faint plumes of smoke from the fireworks, silvery with the touch of starlight, hanging on the bitter air.

The angel had vanished with the light, and I was left alone to face the coming day, my last day on this earth—or so I believed at the time.

But the angel's promise left me with enough comfort that I felt I could go to my final hour in peace. Now I knew that however long this war might last, however far the evil of hatred and bondage may spread, it is not permanent. The paradise I have seen may not come in my lifetime. But it will come. And so, the loss of my only love is a little easier to bear.

Easier to bear, yet still an agony, for the very thought of Jere has filled me with a weakening grief. I cannot go on writing today. I will continue tomorrow with the rest of the story, for thank God, my tale didn't end in that prison cell, or at a Confederate gallows.

Yet I still don't know what to make of that night in the Spotsylvania jailhouse. Did I truly see an angel, or was she merely the invention of my distressed mind?

34

Derryn

2053

They spent the fifth night of the solar flare in a hostel near the Brooklyn Bridge, warm and safe with solid walls around them, on fresh-smelling mattresses with clean bedding. As Derryn had predicted, the proprietor had been happy to take down her contact information to request payment after the Weave returned.

"And she trusts that you'll actually pay," Cole said in amazement as they settled onto their bunks.

"Of course she trusts me," Derryn answered. "I *will* pay her. I wouldn't have told her so if I hadn't meant to do it."

Late the next morning, they set out for Bushwick. As they passed the Basilica of St. James, Derryn stopped, held fast by the sight. The old building stood humbled by the newer constructions that towered on all sides, yet though it seemed very small now, the fading echo of a distant age, its elegance and intricate geometries still carried a certain gravitas. A memory returned, powerful and swift, the way memory had flowed over the Weave. She recalled the dim silence of the church outside Haverford, the ancient building into which she had crept on that first frantic night of the storm. Had it really been less than a week since she'd stood alone in the dark nave? She had felt, then, the weight of time and invention pressing in around her, the long endurance of all the things humankind had made, churches and religions, traditions and beliefs, and levers and cranes and pulleys to lift what the species had willed into being. Machinery to set each piece in place, stone by stone and block by block, newer and better ways, and the mortar to bind ideas into permanence. Everything and everyone kept moving forward. Yet all that had gone before was still, somehow, present.

"It's a church," Derryn said, for that memory had come, too, blinking back into her mind as if Tyko had fetched it for her.

Cole looked back at her. "Pardon?"

"We're supposed to meet Alexis at a church—an old one, like this one."

"This isn't it?"

"No. Saint . . . Saint Bernard's? That's not it. Saint Barbara's. Yes! I've got it now!"

Once she had the name of her destination, it didn't take long to find directions the old-fashioned way, by asking friendly strangers. The nearer they came to Bushwick, the more specific those directions got, until, after nearly two hours of walking, they turned up Bleecker Street and there was old Saint Barbara's. The domed cathedral stood pale and ornate below the summer sky, the tiers of its twin spires revealing the firmament in arches of blue.

A wrought-iron fence ran the perimeter of the church, and inside that fence, just beside the entry pillars, a lone figure sat on the ground, their back against the church wall. They were reading the old paper book fanned open on their crossed legs, face turned down, the brim of their wide sun hat concealing their features. But the sun was high—even the Weaveless Derryn could tell that midday had come. As Alexis had promised, they were waiting at the church at noon. And Derryn had finally, against all odds, reached the end of this long, strange journey.

She ran to meet Alexis, threw her arms around her friend, both of them laughing with relief and a surging joy that needed no connection to spread from heart to heart.

"You're here!" Derryn was crying. She didn't know whether that frantic, winging happiness had brought the tears, or all the pent-up anger and sorrow she had felt these last several days. She only knew that she couldn't stop herself from crying, so she let the tears fall and laughed through them, and hugged her friend again.

"Of course I'm here," Alexis said. "I promised I'd check in every day until you showed up. Besides, what else was I going to do, with the Weave shut down? It was a good excuse to go through my old paper collection. I've read eight and a half books over the past five days. Maybe we should have shutdowns more often."

Derryn wiped her face on her sleeve and introduced Cole. Alexis raised their brows at the Sovereign marks on his face, but to their credit, they said nothing about it, only welcomed Cole to stay at their apartment.

"Any friend of Derryn's is a friend of mine," Alexis said. "My place isn't too far. You don't mind walking a couple of blocks, do you?"

Derryn and Cole shared a look, brimming with amusement and an unexpected affection.

"I think we can manage a few more blocks," Cole said.

The apartment was small, like most homes in New York City, but warm and beautiful despite the close walls. Bookshelves, the tops of bureaus, and every available patch of wall space was occupied by art, a teeming and boisterous celebration of the subjects the professor had long studied.

"I set up a shower on the back deck," Alexis said, taking the backpacks from Derryn and Cole. "One of those wilderness jobbies, plastic bag heated by the sun. Hell if I was going to go six whole days without a hot shower."

Cole insisted that Derryn should go first. Gratefully, she stepped onto the deck and shut the sliding door while Alexis pulled the curtain. The deck itself was screened and shaded by a trellis of flowering vines, and Alexis had affixed a small soap dish to the deck rail.

Derryn undressed, let her grimy leggings and linen shirt fall in a heap. She picked up the soap and smelled it—rose and lavender, the scent so sweet and fresh that for a long time she could do nothing but breathe it in. When she opened the valve on the bag shower, a warm rain fell on her face and chest. Her soapy hands anointed and acknowledged every part of her lone body, the small and singular self that had carried her through these difficult days with such capable resolve. The dirt of a long ordeal ran from her skin, over the lip of the decking, into the gutter, where it flowed back into the past.

The remainder of the day was spent in comfort and security. Alexis gave Derryn and Cole clean clothing and fed them well. They were an obliging audience for stories, too. Both Derryn and her companion recounted the journey in detail, each from their own perspective, and by the time they'd talked themselves out, the sun was setting, and the final aurora had begun.

Derryn could hardly sleep that night—not for lack of comfort, but in anticipation of the morning. She longed so desperately to talk to her brother that she was half convinced she could already feel Leo, his mind reaching for her across the great distance of the continent, his voice in her ear scolding and praising and choked with the relief of knowing that she was safe.

A light came on in the kitchen. She sat up slowly on the sofa, pushed aside the crocheted afghan under which she had spent the night. Cole slept soundly on the floor nearby, bedded on a thick air mattress. Derryn got up and drifted quietly to the kitchen.

Alexis was there, still dressed in their pajamas, holding a CoreTex in one hand and an old analog wristwatch in the other. A battery-powered emergency lantern glowed on the counter, casting Alexis's face in hard lines of shadow.

"Sorry," they whispered. "I didn't mean to wake you."

"I wasn't exactly asleep," Derryn said.

"It's almost time. Fifteen more minutes."

"Thank God. I don't know how I've survived without it."

Alexis gave a little puff of breath, something like a laugh. "After that story you and Mr. Sovereign told, I don't know how you did it, either. Want some coffee?"

Derryn nodded.

"Good," Alexis said. "Trying to make coffee without electricity will distract me from how slowly these last few minutes are passing."

They never found a way to make the coffee, for while Alexis and Derryn both puzzled over pans and filters and grounds and discussed primitive and apartment-safe means of heating water, a wave of awareness ran through them, a sudden swell of unseen activity, not unlike the background hum of the Weave. Both paused in what they were doing, turned to stare at one another. Then Alexis took their CoreTex from the countertop, fitted it in place around their head.

"Here goes nothing," they said, and touched the power button.

A rising energy swept into the room, the presence of everything at once. Derryn didn't need her friend's happy laughter to tell her that the Weave had survived. She scrambled for her own headset, which she had left on the coffee table. In moments, the side ports of her CoreTex were hugging her temples. The back plate warmed against her scalp. The headset's field rushed like a thrill along her nerves, and the old familiar startup chime sounded in her ears.

"Welcome back, Derryn."

"Tyko! You survived."

"Of course I did," the AI said. "Did you really think the Weave might have made an erroneous calculation for something as important as this?"

Derryn could only laugh in answer—in wonder as she felt humanity reconnect, a planetary family waiting in expectation, welcoming one another with a celebration of wholeness.

"Your brother is calling," Tyko said. "Would you like me to put him through?"

Of course Derryn wanted to talk to Leo. The screen shaped itself around her face, and there he was, sitting at the island of his kitchen where she had seen him last. There was no coffee cup this time. His face was haggard and gaunt, his eyes tragic with anxiety.

"Derryn," Leo said. "My God, I've been so worried about you!"

"I can tell. You look like you've spent the last six days in an absolute crisis."

"Where are you?" he demanded.

"In New York with Alexis. Like I promised."

Leo sagged down onto the countertop, resting his forehead on the quartz slab until his signal fragmented. He jittered into lines on the screen.

"Sit up," Derryn said. "I can't see you when you do that."

When he lifted his head, there were tears in his eyes. "Squiggy. When are you coming home?"

"Soon, I promise. You don't know how badly I want to get back home. I'll have Tyko look for flights as soon as we're off this call."

"I've heard a lot of flights are already booked," Leo said. "It might take a day or two before you can land one. But at least I know you're safe. At least I know you survived."

"Tell me how you passed the time," Derryn said. "Besides worrying about me."

"I'd rather hear how you passed it. You're the one who was stuck in a war zone."

"Would you believe me if I said it wasn't very eventful?"

She could feel his mind assessing hers, poking and prodding at her wry amusement, trying to make something of the lingering ghost of her strain and fear.

"No," Leo said. "You're hiding something, Squiggy."

"I'll tell you everything when I get back, I promise. For now, I just want to hear about you and the family."

Leo relented. He and his husband had distracted themselves with old books—reading on paper was a common pastime during a global power outage, as Derryn was discovering. They had also resorted to playing vintage board games, which the kids had despised at first, but by the third day, they'd become oddly enthusiastic about the old-fashioned entertainment. There had even been a tense confrontation over a game of Monopoly. And Derryn's niece had taken up knitting.

They spoke for at least half an hour, until Leo was satisfied that Derryn really was safe, still her usual self, and would be home as soon as she could find a seat on a cross-country flight. Even after they ended the call, she could still feel her brother's glow somewhere in the distance, constant and reassuring, a bright beacon of the love that waited on her own side of the Blockade.

Derryn turned off her lightscreen. Cole was sitting on his air mattress, cross-legged and silent as a sage, looking up at her.

"Well," she said, "now you've really seen a wirehead in action."

He made no answer. Derryn wasn't even sure he'd heard. His attention was fixed to the port at her temple, its soft-blue light, the faint, living pulse of its energy. He was trying to decide, Derryn knew—trying to make up his mind whether he should get on the Weave, connect to the great, wide everything . . . or stay as he was. A pure, sovereign human.

She put Tyko to work searching for a flight, then sent messages to everyone she could think of, informing them that she had come through the past six days in one piece. There were dozens of similar messages in her own inbox. Derryn smiled over every one.

Something kept intruding on her lightscreen, the solid image of a nearby object snaring her attention despite her resolve to focus on the messages she was reading. Finally, Derryn gave in and looked through the screen itself. The insistent object was none other than a short stack of books, Helen's third and fourth journals—the one covering the events of 1863, and the journal that followed. Derryn had been reading the final pages of the 1863 volume the night before, when anticipation of the Weave's return had kept her from sleep. In the last entry, Helen and Jere were preparing to leave Richmond, carrying the critical message of General Lee's invasion plans. The final volume called to Derryn, a lure even stronger than the resurrected Weave. She had to know how the story ended—and what had finally inspired Helen to paint her visions of the future. When the last of her messages was sent, she picked up the last leather-bound journal and began reading again.

Helen's relation of the train ride out of Richmond and the threat of the nearby battle captured Derryn's attention so completely that she didn't notice the smell of fresh-brewed coffee wafting from the kitchen, nor Cole stepping out to the balcony. The account of Helen's flight to the Wilderness had Derryn completely snared. When Jere was shot, she nearly cried out, astonished at her own anguish. And when Helen was captured by the Confederate riders, Derryn found herself clutching the book with shaking hands.

But the entry that followed was more compelling still. Helen's bitter despair in the Spotsylvania jailhouse would have been moving enough in its own context. But the journal entry, written nearly two hundred years in the past, seemed to depict the same experience Derryn had had herself, some two nights before at the abandoned hotel when she had found herself in another place and time. When she had spoken to Helen in her moment of greatest despair.

Impossible. Derryn let the journal fall to her lap. *That was only a hallucination, a waking dream. I was tired, disoriented without the Weave. I was seeing things, imagining things. This is only a coincidence, nothing more.*

"What do you take in your coffee?"

Derryn nearly yelled in surprise. Alexis stood over her with a cautious smile, a steaming mug in their hand.

"Sorry," Derryn said. "Uh . . . cream, just cream."

"No fresh cream in the fridge," Alexis said, "but I have some of that powdered stuff."

"That'll be fine."

Alexis hesitated. "You okay?"

"Yeah, of course. I'm fine. I was just looking through this old journal. The artist I was studying at Haverford . . . she wrote this in 1863."

"Beautiful binding," Alexis said. "Can I see it?"

They set the mug on the coffee table. In a fog, Derryn handed over the volume.

"Calf leather," Alexis said, running their fingers over the cover. "Gorgeous tooling. And look at the hubs on the spine. This is a well-made book. It probably cost a lot of money, in its time."

They opened the cover and riffled through the pages, inhaling the rich, intoxicating smell of old ink and paper.

Something small and pale slipped from the book and fluttered to the floor.

"Oops," Alexis said.

They bent to retrieve the scrap as Derryn also reached for it. Derryn got to it first, but she could make no sense of what she saw. It was a pen-and-ink sketch on thick, yellowing paper. After the days she'd spent studying Helen's paintings, she recognized the artist's style. Even if it hadn't fallen from one of Helen's personal journals, she would have known in an instant that the drawing was an original Bywater. But the subject of this sketch was every bit as impossible as the rest of Helen's work.

Alexis sank heavily onto the sofa. They stared at the drawing in Derryn's hand—and Derryn stared, her body and mind suffused by a slow awareness of past and future, of all things present and all things yet to be.

"That looks like you," Alexis said quietly.

The sketch didn't look like Derryn. It *was* her—the short, natural hair, the knit leggings and top clinging to the figure's limbs, the facial features as accurate as if she were looking in a mirror. The port of her CoreTex was distinct, rendered in precise detail at the subject's temple. Below the sketch, Helen had written: *The angel who came to bless me, May 19, 1863.*

Derryn's vision blurred. Her thoughts blurred, sliding into a staggering disbelief with such force that Alexis felt it, too, and looked at her sharply.

"I didn't imagine it," Derryn muttered.

Alexis stood. "I'm going to get that cream. You need coffee, honey, and fast."

Derryn could do nothing but sit, trembling, on the sofa, staring at the sketch in her hand. It had been no fantasy wrought by despair or by the long disruption of an absent Weave. She had *seen* Helen that night. Somehow, maybe thanks to the cosmic current that had scoured the planet, time or space had bent for her, and for Helen—for everyone everywhere, as far as Derryn could say. Across the span of centuries, through a sympathetic knowledge of shared experience, she and a long-dead woman had connected, heart to heart.

Tyko's smooth voice jerked Derryn out of her reverie. "Melinda Aladefa is requesting a call."

"Melinda—she's okay! Yes, put her through, Tyko."

The lightscreen wrapped around her face. Melinda was outdoors, under the shady maples of Haverford's campus, looking completely unruffled by the week's events.

"Thank goodness you're all right," Melinda said. "We've all been wondering if you made it to your friend's place in one piece."

"More or less in one piece," Derryn said.

"You were right to bug out when you did. Campus was occupied for days, until local law enforcement managed to drive the Sovereigns back to Bryn Mawr. We had quite a time down in the bunker, I can tell you. Almost used the evacuation tunnels a time or two."

"But the Sovereigns are gone now?"

"Yes, they're gone, and the Bywater cache is safe."

Derryn sagged back onto the couch. "Thank goodness."

"I suppose after this whole experience, you aren't inclined to come back and finish the work," Melinda said.

Derryn paused only a moment to consider. She would have to tell Leo there'd been a change of plans. And this time, no prevarication to spare his feelings. She would tell him the whole story, from start to finish, and let him be as angry with her as he needed to be, as angry as she deserved.

But she would return to Haverford. The drawing Helen had made of her was still in her hand, the paper trembling with the rhythm of her heartbeat. She might have left the remainder of the work to Melinda and the rest, to some other art historian who knew better than Derryn how to get by in an active war zone—if not for that drawing. It was proof of something bigger, something more important than Derryn's lone life or Helen's singular existence. There was a bond between them now, a sympathy of shared experience.

"You suppose wrong," Derryn said. "I'll be there as soon as I can schedule an air-cab pickup—maybe two or three days from now, I'd guess. You're going to need me to get those grants. And I have no intention of letting Helen down."

35

Helen

September 17, 1863

The morning after I saw my angel was supposed to be the last day of my life. Though I knew the hangman's noose waited for me, I no longer felt any fear, for that visitation had left me with the comfort of knowing that the future I have so longed for *would* come to pass, by and by. The Confederates might win this war, I reasoned, and they could even take my life. But they could not prevent what was coming, the great change of all mankind, our souls united in a singular, loving whole, as our Maker meant for us to be.

I watched the sun rise through the bars of my window. The sky was painted with a soft and rosy light. The birds raised a chorus of praises to the One who created them and every improbable thing—man with his endless invention, and hearts that love and grieve, and all the brilliant futures that I could feel reaching on like countless branching roads from the place where I stood, at the end of my own travels. I was resolved to die bravely, with the hope in my breast that when I knelt before the throne of judgment (and how soon I must kneel!), my God would see how I had tried to atone for every wrong I had done. All that was light within me would shortly be free of this burdensome flesh, this fear, this bitter war. And free from the grief I felt over leaving Jere to die alone.

Then, before the sun had climbed above the trees, a great commotion came over Spotsylvania. First, I heard men shouting, and women screaming. Then the church bells began to ring with a frantic insistence. I realized with no small amount of wonder that a Union army was marching on the town.

When I heard gunfire, I jumped away from my window and huddled in a corner of my cell. There I remained for hours, listening to the battle rage through the town and wondering what was to become of me.

Sometime in the late afternoon, I found my answer. Very gradually, I realized that the terrible clamor of fighting had turned to the sounds of victory. Men cheered in the streets outside the jailhouse, and a ragged chorus of soldiers began to sing.

John Brown's body lies a-mold'ring in the grave,
While weep the sons of bondage whom he ventured all to save;
But though he sleeps his life was lost while struggling for
the slave,
His soul is marching on.

I crept back to my window and dared to look out. The streets were filled with men in blue uniforms, and while they sang "Glory, glory, hallelujah," there was Old Glory herself, the red-and-white stripes of this nation's true flag, the stars shining bright against their field of blue, waving in triumph above the town.

Many hours passed before anyone thought to come into the jailhouse. I waited patiently on my cot, though I do confess that I was ravenously hungry by that time, and plumb desperate from thirst. Nevertheless, I knew my salvation had come, so I did not complain, but only stood when I heard the jailhouse door open, and said to the man who entered, "My name is Helen Bywater, and I am loyal to the Union, sir. If you will take me to your commander, I have an urgent message for the North."

I was fed and watered and brought before General Joseph Hooker in his campaign tent outside the town. He was a quiet, intelligent man who listened to all I had to say about Lee's plans for an invasion. His clerks wrote frantically as I spoke, but Hooker himself never took his eyes off me—such sober, thoughtful eyes, the same bright and luminous blue I had seen so many years before in those auroral skies.

When I'd told him everything I knew, he said, "We have heard of your name, Miss Bywater, and all the good work you've done on behalf of the United States of America. As far as I can tell, you've had a close shave. A good and loyal lady like yourself shouldn't be sent back into danger. Let me make arrangements for you to go north. You'll travel under my protection."

That was how I came to be living here, in Haverford. I have been provided by the government a stipend in gratitude for my service. I am grateful, I suppose, for my life and for the means to support myself. Though I can't see what good my work did, after all, for the fighting at Gettysburg this summer past was such a dreadful slaughter. Still, General Lee did not advance into the North. I must hope that all those thousands of lives were lost to some good end. I must hope, too, that the part I played served a greater purpose.

If only I could know what became of Jere. I feel in my heart that he is still alive—that against such terrible and dangerous odds, he managed to survive his wounds and the Wilderness, both. Oh, I know this is only wishful thinking. But my heart is as broken now as it was in May, and these wistful fantasies are all I have left to live for.

January 1, 1864

War, war, it goes ever on. I can no longer believe that there was a time when this war did not burn like a brush fire over the land, wild and hot and raging, consuming everything in its path. My life before is a dream, only half remembered, fading from my mind.

Since I came to Haverford—since I found the strength to think and write about what transpired since I left Richmond with Jere at my side—I have done nothing but paint. And though I know the images are very strange, and may not be understood by anyone, I am compelled to paint those visions that came to me in years gone by, that future I still believe in, despite the bitterness that circles me on all sides, the war that would drag us back into the past if the fearful and the deceived should claim the final victory.

I know the future can yet be made. We can build it—even from the ashes of our former world, if need be, if that's the only choice God and fate will leave to us. It *will* come to pass. My beautiful angel told me so, and with all faith, I believe her.

Every day, I come to my easel like a supplicant comes to prayer, and work without tiring on my paintings. I make them all from memory, and both my memories and the sight of what I re-create on the canvas still have the power to move me as much as I was moved years ago, when I saw Richmond transformed under the light of the aurora. When I look on those scenes of the future, my heart flies up to such a height of anticipation, and I long for that better time with all the sunny optimism of one who has never suffered and lost as I have done. This war is wickeder and bloodier by the day. Yet I know there is a time and place beyond the here and now. My eyes are ever on what lies ahead, even if my heart lies buried in the past.

I've had a letter from Mary Jane. She is still in Davis's White House, working for the cause, though I don't know how she conveys her information to the Union side. She is too clever and cautious to tell me her secrets.

She did tell me that Eudaimonia has been taken by the Cary family. How they managed to claim the estate against my lawyer's will is beyond me; perhaps Mr. Wyckoff is dead. She did assure me that Kitty, Ruthie, and David have gone to live elsewhere, and are known to be safe and comfortable enough. Between my legal machinations while I was still in Richmond and Lincoln's declaration that all slaves are now free, there is enough ambiguity over their status that all three have managed to avoid re-enslavement by some other party. I thank God that it's so. If any of them had come to harm, I would have returned to Richmond, no matter what the danger or cost to me, to get them free again.

Mary Jane assured me, too, that all my boxes of personal goods are still safely stored where David put them. It is encouraging to know that neither Caleb Cary nor any other Confederate traitor will lay hands on my diaries and discover how I have worked against their rebellion.

These are small comforts, to be sure, but one must take whatever sunshine is afforded by a break in the clouds. That is how we all live now, under the shadow of war.

April 16, 1865

How can it be that I haven't written in this diary for more than a year? Perhaps because one day has been very much like the others. I rise with the sun. I work on my paintings, turning with monastic devotion to the world that lies beyond this time of hatred and strife. And then I sleep again. The tides of battle shift in their wild currents. But I go on, painting, painting, as if each canvas is a magic spell that might bring about my beloved future.

Yet now I must write again, for just as a Union victory seemed inevitable, the unthinkable has occurred. Our president, Abraham Lincoln, is dead. Killed by an assassin's bullet. God in Heaven, what will become of us now?

And only yesterday, I received another letter from Mary Jane. She is out of Richmond. Everyone is out of Richmond, for at the end of March it became clear that the siege of Petersburg would hold, and the Confederate capital would be next to fall. Rather than allow the Union forces to enrich themselves on all the treasure Richmond held, Davis and his forces abandoned the city . . . but burned it in their wake.

They meant to burn only the warehouses that stored trade goods and the supplies necessary for equipping an army. But the fire spread out of control, and nearly all of the downtown neighborhoods were reduced to ashes.

Sparks from the fire caught Eudaimonia's roof ablaze. The good people of Church Hill tried to save it, but it was all they could do to prevent the fire from spreading to the other homes.

So Eudaimonia is gone. My home, the heart of all my memories—nothing now but ashes and charred brick, nothing but a black stain upon the earth.

I have grieved all I ever shall for Eudaimonia. Only the cruel hand of fate forced me away from my old home. I wouldn't have left it of my own accord, but now that the shock of this news has abated, I must confess that I am glad Eudaimonia is gone. It was beautiful and safe and infinitely comforting, with an old air of grand and mythic history. But I did not build that house. I didn't light the fires, nor tend the lamps, nor sweep the dust from its corners. Its very foundation was the broken backs of slaves. Every brick of its walls was laid by suffering hands.

Now, in this humble shack in the Pennsylvania countryside, I do all my own work of living. The life I lead here in Haverford is humbler than the one I led in Richmond, but it has a quality of deep satisfaction that I never thought to find in this earthly life. My house is very small and mean, two rooms and not much of a garden to speak of, with drafty windows and uneven floors that are never quite clean, no matter how I scrub them, and only a rustic fireplace for cooking. And I love it more than I ever loved that grand palace on Church Hill.

Only the great shock of emergency could have torn me from Eudaimonia, and now that I am separated from the old way of life—now that the house itself is gone for good, with no hope that I might return—I am glad for it all, glad for everything that has happened (except, of course, for losing my Jere). For now I have neither cause nor reason to care for society, for rules and customs and tradition. My whole life is this work I do, the paintings I make to keep alive my vision of the future. And it feels like an infinitely better life than the one I led before. I live humbly, but I live honestly, and by my own labor. There is a deep satisfaction in that knowledge, even when my bones are weary from the work.

What comes next, now that our good president is gone, now that Richmond is gone, now that everything is changing, as it always does, as it must, by God's design? If I once saw the future, it was a distant one. Nearer times are obscured; I cannot see what lies just ahead, not even tomorrow.

Yet I will go forward without fear. That's the way the road runs, into the fertile dark of the unknown, where we will find, I trust and pray, as much cause for rejoicing as for sorrow.

36

Derryn

2053

Derryn's clothes were still warm from the dryer. She buried her face in the fabric and breathed in the soft, faintly herbal scent of laundry detergent. Then she dressed and dropped the clothing she had borrowed from Alexis into the hamper in the corner of her friend's bedroom. The gentle, easy light of afternoon filled the space. Dust motes glittered in the still air beside the window, and beyond, the city sky was lively with air cabs. The same sun Derryn had always known flashed on their humming propellers and rounded bellies.

She lingered for a while at the window, watching the cabs weave neatly into their aerial lanes. *Back to the way we used to be,* she thought. *Back to the world that has always been.*

Surely some things would change. A planet, a nation, a single person couldn't go through such a disruption and yet be fundamentally unmoved. Everyone might try to carry on as before, but to see the reality you thought you knew inverted, nullified by a vast cosmic current, or by war, or by the small and quiet tragedies that steal like thieves to crouch in the corners of a life . . .

It must leave a mark, Derryn thought, *no matter how we try to deny it. The you who once existed remains in the past that held you. A new self carries on, into the landscape of the future.*

Surrounded again by the unseen gossamers of her world, she knew it was time to move on, time for this new creature she had become to step forward onto the path.

She left Alexis's bedroom, found her backpack, and began sorting through its contents, repacking for her return to Haverford. While she worked, she rehearsed what she would say to Leo. Maybe the best way to make him understand was to tell him everything, right down to that inexplicable encounter with Helen Bywater and the drawing that would prove, once Derryn had brought it home to Cascadia, that not even space-time was as permanent as everyone believed it to be.

The patio door slid open, letting in the sound of traffic, a soft, melodic hum. Cole stepped into the living room, dressed in clean clothes as Derryn was. He said nothing as he shut the door, but he held Derryn's eye with a look of significance that said he wanted to talk.

She pushed her pack aside on the coffee table, made room for him on the sofa.

"I've been thinking about it since this morning," Cole said as he sat.

There was no need to ask what he'd been thinking about. He had worn the same distant, searching expression since Derryn and Alexis had reconnected with the Weave.

"If you do it," Derryn said, "there's no going back. You'll never be what you were before."

"What was I before?"

He asked the question quietly, but Derryn heard it as a great cry of pain, felt it the way she felt, even now, the wholeness of all her kind—their joy and their sorrow, the longing and the holding, their suffering, their mercy, the simple *being* that was also her own. What answer could she give him? That he was small, and isolated, alone with his thoughts. That he was generous and good, with a mind that was willing to open, when it was given the chance. That he was still the child whose spirit had been brutalized by the hardened hearts of other brutalized spirits, by all the adults who should have protected and loved him, but hurt him instead, because they had been told by the frightened souls who'd come before that only hate could shield them from all the things they'd been taught to fear.

She said, "You were human."

"I want to do it, anyway."

"You're sure?"

He thought for a moment, turning his choice over in that lone and sovereign mind.

Finally, he said, "Yes."

Alexis had left the apartment nearly an hour before, gone to buy fresh cream for the coffee and the other civilized things they'd had to do without. They'd taken only their lightwatch for a Weave connection, leaving their CoreTex behind on the kitchen counter.

Derryn retrieved the headset. Cole turned to face her on the sofa, tense with some emotion she could only guess at—longing or dread, the kind of giddy, compelling terror that comes when you stand at the edge of a cliff or the high rooftop of a skyscraper, knowing you might fall and knowing there'd be no way to stop yourself if you did.

She lifted the CoreTex like a crown, settled it into place around the back of his head. She did all this slowly, not quite with reluctance but knowing that there was something precious and valuable in what Cole was now, what he would never be again. The old pattern of humanity may be slow to learn and faulty in memory, but even unconnected people were good and brave and determined when they wanted to be. Like Helen and her friends had been so many years ago, doing their hidden work in Richmond, fighting against the currents of a world that didn't want to change.

She pressed the connection ports gently against Cole's temples. They settled into place. She didn't remove her hands right away, for she seemed to hold between them a great poignancy that she couldn't describe or name. There was a gravity to this moment, this act—guiding a person from what he was to what he soon would be. The passage deserved some kind of ceremony, for Cole and for herself. But all she could think to do was to look into his eyes, to sense him as he was in that final moment—one person alone, steadfast against all he had faced, courageous enough to love despite the hate he'd been told to claim as his identity.

"Are you ready?" Derryn asked.

He nodded.

She pressed the power button.

The blue light flashed above his ear. When the field surrounded his head, Cole flinched back with stricken eyes.

"It's okay," Derryn said. "It's finding your brain waves. Give it a second . . ."

His face went slack as awareness hit him. Derryn reached out cautiously, took with the hands of her mind the shape and weight of Cole's. His amazement struck Derryn first, so bright and sharp it was better called ecstasy. Then she felt his trembling curiosity, the sense of taking in a thousand new colors and sounds. His very concept of possibility had stretched far beyond the point of comprehension, and yet it was still expanding, still gleaning new wonders from this world that had existed all around him, yet he had never allowed himself to see its bright fire.

"Wow." The word came as breath, short and light and whispering. "Wow. I never thought. I never knew."

Come with me.

Derryn sent the idea to him, thought without voice, and he turned to her in open astonishment.

How? His thought transmitted to Derryn with such natural ease that he was startled all over again, and Derryn laughed aloud at his wonder.

Like that, she said with her mind. *Like this.*

And though they never left the sofa or the small apartment in Bushwick, still they left it—they rose from where they sat, spread far beyond the small, single selves made of bone and blood and synapses. They were light unhindered, shining in a thousand colors. Hand in ethereal hand, they went together into a greater self. Derryn felt his wonder as if it were her own—Cole's expanding awareness of a broader world, a world that was awareness itself, and broader than all the galaxies strung like beads through the universe. And when every other heart and mind encircled him with welcome, with a love so deep it was deeper than the belly of the planet, she felt the sweet ache of his knowledge that he would never be alone again. A peace came to him, and so it came to Derryn, too—so still and redeeming that it quieted every fear.

It was good, it was right, that Cole should be there with her, in the velvet space of the Weave. He made the great, bright wholeness of humanity more complete.

And it was good, so good to be back, to feel the truth of what she was. Silver threads of light ran from heart to heart, from Derryn's heart to all the others, to every heart that made her who she was, and what she would yet become as the future ran forward along its fiery path.

37

Helen

May 30, 1865

Even here in sleepy Haverford, among the Society of Friends, we heard the news that the war has ended, but it has made little difference to me. Men may call it an end, but the evil that brought this war into being hasn't died in the hearts of those who nurtured it. The darkness grows there still, and I fear it will pass from generation to generation, for that is how fear passes—and also love, if we choose to feed it, if we choose to plant it in the soil of the soul.

For me, the clouds did not lift and the sun did not break through until yesterday afternoon.

I was out in my small patch of a garden, trying to coax the new tomatoes and beans I have planted into growing, when such a feeling came over me as I have never experienced before. There was no sound but the singing of birds and the sighing of wind around the eaves of my little house, and the distant ringing of the blacksmith's hammer, which goes on all day without stopping, like the ticking of a clock. But still I looked up—I straightened from the garden bed, hastily brushing the earth from my hands, for I knew with a certainty as solid as the ground beneath my feet that someone was coming to see me. I *felt* it, a searching expectation, and I went to the picket fence and shielded my eyes against the sun as I gazed far and long down the old dirt road that runs past the meetinghouse to the village.

At first, there was nothing to be seen, not even a plume of dust from a far-off carriage. Still, I watched and waited. Some minutes passed, perhaps a quarter of an hour. The sun was growing too warm to bear; I'd begun to sweat, and I was thirsty, but the sense that someone was coming to see me was so urgent and compelling that I could not even go to the pump for a handful of water.

Then I saw a lone figure, small in the far distance, emerging from the light and shadow of the village. It was a man, and he walked with a decided limp—a slow pace, yet determined, and headed in the direction of my cottage.

I cannot explain how I knew it was Jere. I simply *knew*, as firmly as I know my own name, as I know that the same God lives in every separate thing. I set off up the road, running in my dirty brown homespun dress with the paint stains on the skirt and sleeves—what a sight I must have been! I had no thought for anything but him.

When I drew near enough to see his face, I could only cry with gratitude. We clung to one another, I weeping against his chest and Jere murmuring comforts in my ear.

"You're here—you're here!" I went on saying it for what felt like eternities, and could say nothing else, for my astonishment was so great. And then I swore my love for him, over and over till he laughed and pressed a hand gently over my mouth.

When he took his hand away, I said, "But I left you, Jere. How can you ever forgive me?"

"Did you deliver the message?"

"Yes," I said, "yes, yes, to General Hooker."

"Then you did exactly as you were meant to do."

"But I left you!"

"Helen, my sweetest, my darling love. There's nothing to forgive."

When I had calmed down enough that I could laugh at my own disheveled state, I led him to my small home and settled him at the table with a cup of tea and biscuits and jam.

"I've come down somewhat from the Eudaimonia days," I said, "as you can plainly see."

"Are you happy?" Jere asked.

Could I so much as answer? Of course not, for the sight of him—real and whole and alive, against all odds—had filled me with a celestial bliss beyond mere happiness.

"Then," he said, "it's for the better. A humble life is as good as a grand one, if it's a life well lived."

I made him tell me, then, how he had survived.

"When I heard those men go after you," Jere answered, "I took the chance to crawl into a thicket, and I burrowed down under the leaves. Just like the time I hid in the straw at the prison, down in Rat Hell. I thought I might die there, to be sure. Through the night, I drifted into a kind of stupor. I could no longer feel the pain, which was a good thing, but I wasn't really with my body anymore, you see. I had a sense that I was somewhere above myself, or spread out like melted butter all around my body, a sense that I could go anywhere with just a thought."

He felt his way through the night, Jere said—though I'm not at all sure I quite understood his meaning. He told me he felt his way to a camp of Union men, half a regiment that was hidden in the Wilderness, waiting on orders from General Hooker. He kicked and shouted and pummeled the watchmen, till two or three perked up and said they ought to go scouting. They had a sense that someone was out there, hidden in the brush.

"When they came near my body," Jere said, "I heard them whispering. Heard that they were Northerners, like me. So I called out with all my strength, 'Brothers!' Though I was so weak by then, my voice was barely loud enough to carry past the thicket. It's a miracle they heard me."

They took him back to their camp and set their doctor to work on him. Thank God, the wound to his stomach was not severe. The bullet had only grazed him. The wound to his leg was worse. The doctor had to dig the bullet out of his thigh, and even then, he couldn't walk for weeks due to infection. There were times when he thought he would die from fever. There was even a day when the doctor spoke darkly of amputation, which likely would have killed him as surely as a fever might have done. But he pulled through, my Jere.

"Because I wanted to find you." He reached across the table to take my hand. "I made you a promise that we'd get married once we came north. I mean to keep my word, Helen, if you'll still have me. Say you will. I've come through Hell to find you again. And now that the war's over, there's a whole new world for us to make. I want to build it with you."

"Yes" was too small a word. I rose from my chair, and Jere stood, too, opened his arms to me. Gladly, I stepped into his embrace, and as his warmth and presence surrounded me, so, too, did a joy as bright as an aurora, a current of divine love that passed, in every impossible shade of wonder, from Jere's heart to mine.

That river of love flows where it will; it runs where the channel cuts deep, into the spirit, into the substance of God. It knows nothing of the lines we draw around ourselves and our fellow men, around states and nations and kings. I have seen that light with my eyes. I have seen it with my heart. It shines through all our heavens.

Author's Note

In late August 1859, people all over the world were awakened in the dead of night by a glow as bright as day. From the polar regions to the equator, and even on ships far from land in every ocean, individuals reported their observations of the unprecedented event. Colors danced across the sky from full dark until dawn, bright enough to read and navigate by. Birds woke from their roosts, believing morning had come. Telegraph operators disconnected the batteries of their machines and found to their astonishment that they could still send messages, even without any apparent physical power source.

This all would have been astonishing enough if it had happened for only one night. But the phenomenon persisted for an entire week. By day, the sky appeared normal. By night, it coruscated with brilliant color, and almost no one living at the time could comprehend why it was happening.

This event had a profound effect on many people. Some religious types took the shocking experience to be a sign of divine activity or even imminent intervention—proof that Judgment Day had come. A few people were so disturbed by the phenomenon and its potential religious implications that they took their own lives rather than face what they believed was coming.

After the initial two nights of unearthly lights, the colors began to fade. But they returned on the nights of September 1 and 2, brighter than before. It was during this second surge that two British astronomers, Richard Carrington and Richard Hodgson, independently discovered the cause. Each recorded their telescopic observations of the largest sunspots they had ever seen, ejections of matter from the Sun's surface, billowing out like massive plumes of smoke from the fiery furnace that hangs like a wise and ancient god at the heart of our solar system.

It was the first observation in history of a coronal mass ejection—a solar flare. It also remains the largest CME ever recorded. It became known as the Carrington Event, though it should more properly be called the Carrington-Hodgson Event. The colored, mobile lights observed all over the planet were the same phenomenon that had often been recorded near the poles, a visual effect caused by magnetic turbulence rushing off the Sun and striking the planet's magnetosphere, which is a kind of natural shield that surrounds the Earth, compressing and expanding in response to solar winds. These compressions and expansions create the auroras—vast swaths of colored light—that we know as the Northern and Southern Lights.

Since the Carrington Event, many more coronal mass ejections and geomagnetic storms have been recorded. None has yet achieved the scale or duration of the 1859 event. But they could. Earth's avoidance of such a large-scale CME has been a matter of chance. At any time, with less than twenty-four hours' warning, our planet could be struck again by a massive solar flare on par with the Carrington Event, or potentially even larger.

As soon as I first learned about the Carrington Event (thanks to a chance offering by YouTube's algorithm), I became fascinated by the question of what might happen to our highly technologized global society if the same phenomenon were to occur in the twenty-first century. Such a powerful bombardment of magnetism would destroy many kinds of electronics if they were left powered on, and electrical grids all over the world would have to be shut down to protect them from serious damage. A Carrington Event today would dramatically alter life as we know it, even if only for a handful of days.

The moment I finished watching that video, I began making the notes that eventually became the novel you have just read.

I took four different swings at this book before I felt I'd landed on the right way to tell the story. I knew it had to be a dual-timeline novel, because I wanted to explore the contrast between how people of the past and people of the present (or the near future) might react to such a phenomenon. The initial versions of the manuscript were fine, but they didn't carry the emotional weight I like to put into my work. They were too focused on the phenomenon itself rather than the human response. It wasn't until I asked myself how a person in 1859 might have later come to regard the Carrington Event that I found the right way into this story, for surely any American who'd observed those startling lights would have come to regard it as a cosmic precursor to the great disruption that followed less than two years later: the official start of the Civil War.

And once I realized that I could not leave the action in Helen's timeline in 1859 but must carry her story through the whole Civil War, I saw, too, that I must reflect the events of Helen's time in Derryn's half of the story.

To my profound unease, I found it was all too simple to imagine a second American Civil War, for in recent months things haven't been so great in the good ol' US of A. We seem to inch closer to another internal conflict with each passing day. And yes, I say "we," even though I live most of the time in Canada. I am still a citizen of the United States, and it will always be my homeland. I can only hope that someday we'll all look back on this novel with a relieved chuckle, seeing *Through All Our Heavens* as a signpost of the bullet we dodged rather than a prescient work that predicted real events to come. But only days before I sat down to write this author's note, Washington, Oregon, and California formed the West Coast Health Alliance in response to certain disastrous public-health policies coming out of the White House . . . an uncomfortable reflection of the Cascadia Blockade I imagined while I worked on the final version of this story.

Let's hope that Derryn's timeline was merely a novelist's wild imagination and not my subconscious response to the pressure I feel—and we all now feel—building around us to a terrible crescendo. I don't care if it would help my book sales; I very much prefer that the Second American Civil War remain in the realm of fiction.

Let me write of happier thoughts. Once I understood that I must follow Helen through the Civil War and began researching how I might do so, I uncovered a treasure trove of information about female spies for the Union. As we teeter unpleasantly on the edge of another such conflict, I am heartened by the knowledge that even in Richmond, Virginia—the seat of Confederate rebellion—there were abolitionists, freed Black people (at least, freed within the tricky letter of contemporary Virginia law), and many people actively working against the Confederacy for the cause of both national stability and moral justice.

One such woman was Elizabeth Van Lew. Most of the details of Helen's life were adapted in one way or another from Van Lew's biography. Like Helen, Elizabeth was educated at a Quaker school in Pennsylvania and, as an unmarried woman, inherited a large Richmond estate, including several enslaved people, whom she freed in the same manner as depicted in this novel (which was, at the time, the only way one might "free" enslaved people legally in Virginia). Elizabeth also paid any Black workers who chose to remain on the estate a wage equal to that of white workers. She confessed in her personal writings that she had harbored a vague distaste for slavery all her life but had foolishly assumed it would die out as the times changed. Eventually, she came to understand that any participation in slavery would keep the practice alive, and both she and her widowed mother (who shared her views) became abolitionists in practice.

Both Elizabeth and her mother, Eliza Baker, became active participants in the abolitionist movement and worked against the Confederacy in every way they could find throughout the Civil War. They did undertake "missions of mercy" to Libby Prison, bringing the captive Union officers food, clothing, and letter-writing implements . . . and, concealed in the shells of blown eggs, maps to nearby safe houses should any of the officers manage to escape. They also smuggled money into the prison, though the means by which they did so have gone unrecorded. To deflect suspicion of their activities at Libby Prison, Elizabeth and Eliza hosted many picnics and other public celebrations in honor of the Confederacy, and they really did board Captain Gibbs in their home.

Right under the nose of this notoriously grim and violent Confederate captain, Elizabeth and her mother ran a spy ring, gathering useful information about troop movements, supplies, and battle plans and conducting them to various Union generals. Elizabeth was known to send flowers from her garden to Ulysses Grant (my own ancestor), with her messages encoded in the newspapers in which she wrapped the flowers.

Another extraordinary woman spy from Richmond cannot be left out of this historical note. Mary Bowser, on whom the character Mary Jane was based, began her early life enslaved by the Van Lew family. After Elizabeth's father died and left all his legal property to his wife and daughter, Elizabeth and Eliza sent Mary north to their beloved Quaker school in Pennsylvania so that she could be educated. Mary later traveled to Liberia, her parents' home country, where she did missionary work before choosing to return to America.

Despite the laws prohibiting any freed or educated Black person from reentering the state once they'd left it, Mary Bowser came back to Richmond to use her education against the Confederacy. She was indeed imprisoned for more than a week while Elizabeth and her mother worked tirelessly to free her. After she was returned to Elizabeth, Mary joined the Van Lew spy ring and even went undercover in Jefferson Davis's White House, gathering intelligence on Davis's most secretive plans and conveying that information to Elizabeth, who in turn passed it along to Grant.

The contributions Mary Bowser made to the Union victory—at great risk to her own safety—cannot be overstated. A true hero of the

Civil War, she went on to still more heroic work. After emancipation became the law of the land, Mary set up a school in Richmond for Black children and young adults, where she spent the rest of her life educating those who had once been enslaved, their children, and their grandchildren.

Elizabeth Van Lew was the first person to raise the United States flag in Richmond once the city fell to the Union. When the war was officially over, Grant appointed Elizabeth as the first female postmaster general of the city. In that position, she hired many Black people to work for the local post office in various capacities, which in turn helped these recently emancipated individuals find their feet and thrive in a new reality. She remained close friends with Mary Bowser and often helped with the running of Mary's school.

But Richmond never forgot that Elizabeth and Eliza had worked for the Union. Despite Elizabeth's job as postmaster general, she and her mother were both ostracized from white society. They had bankrupted their once substantial estate doing their intelligence work during the war, and Elizabeth lived quite humbly—even in penury—until the end of her lonesome days. Her gravestone at the Shockoe Hill Cemetery reads: "She risked everything that is dear to man—friends—fortune—comfort—health—life itself—that slavery might be abolished and the Union preserved."

One last detail of Helen's story was taken from another lady spy of the era, Pauline Cushman, an actress who was captured by Confederate troops in 1863. Just as they were about to place the noose around Pauline's neck, a contingent of Union men attacked. The Confederates were forced to retreat, and lucky Pauline found herself safe in the Union men's company. Pauline Cushman later moved to Arizona and married a man named Jere, which is where I found the name for Helen's sweetheart and future husband.

I found the story of a literal last-minute salvation by the sudden appearance of a Union regiment too much fun to pass up. I just had to include it in this story . . . and it's the main reason why I chose to invent an entirely different character for my nineteenth-century storyline rather than depicting a fictionalized version of Elizabeth Van Lew's life. Who doesn't love a rescue in the nick of time?

I extend my deepest gratitude to my former editor at Lake Union Publishing, Danielle Marshall, who is now my agent. From the time I first described the idea for this novel to Danielle, she was enthusiastic and supportive and gave me great feedback on the first two versions of the manuscript. Although she is no longer my editor, I am delighted that our two careers will carry on together into the future.

I am also grateful to my new editor, Laura Van der Veer, who handled a mid-book editorial transition like a champ. My developmental editor, Charlotte Herscher, was also a delight to work with and provided extensive and insightful feedback on the third and fourth versions of this manuscript, finally helping me turn this story into a book I feel proud of.

I also give my warmest thanks to Davy Kent and Will Fairless, my copy and proof editors, respectively. They did excellent work on a somewhat tricky project, and I hope to work with them both again in the future.

Thanks also to my cultural research reader, Elsa K., whose feedback was invaluable in further refining the story.

And as always, my deepest thanks of all to my readers, who have shown such an encouraging willingness to follow me off the beaten path of historical fiction into new and unfamiliar realms. I hope you all had fun dipping your toes into a little sci-fi for a change. The next one will be just plain historical fiction again, I promise. Thanks for indulging my need for variety. I hope you enjoyed the story.

Olivia Hawker
Victoria, BC
September 2025

About the Author

Photo © 2018 Paul Harnden

Olivia Hawker is the *Washington Post* bestselling author of *October in the Earth*, *The Fire and the Ore*, *The Rise of Light*, *The Ragged Edge of Night*, and *One for the Blackbird, One for the Crow*. She has been honored as a finalist for both the Washington State Book Award and the WILLA Literary Award. A permanent resident of Canada, Olivia divides her time between Victoria, British Columbia, and the San Juan Islands. For more information about the author and her work, please visit her website at www.hawkerbooks.com.